A PRIMITIVE HEART

ALSO BY DAVID RABE

Plays

A PRIMITIVE HEART

Stories
DAVID RABE

Grove Press
New York

Two of these stories have previously appeared in slightly different versions: "A Primitive Heart" in the May/June 1995 issue of *The North American Review* and "Some Loose Change" in the 1998 collection *Shorts: New Writing from Granta Books*.

Published simultaneously in Canada
Printed in the United States of America

FIRST EDITION

Library of Congress Cataloging-in-Publication Data

Rabe, David.
A primitive heart : stories / David Rabe—1st ed.
p. cm.
ISBN 0-8021-1807-0
1. United States—Social life and customs—Fiction.   I. Title.
PS3568.A23P75 2005
813'.54—dc22   2005050206

Grove Press
an imprint of Grove/Atlantic, Inc.
841 Broadway
New York, NY 10003

05 06 07 08 09   10 9 8 7 6 5 4 3 2 1

For

Raymond Roseliep

CONTENTS

A PRIMITIVE HEART

HIS WIFE PHONED him from California to tell him she was spotting. She was at a girlfriend's house in the hills north of Malibu. She had just flown back from Hawaii where she had been vacationing with her friend. Staying at inns in the backcountry, they had hiked through jungle trails and climbed barren volcanic slopes.

It was a strange phrase, "spotting." Pushing one foot and then the other against the floor, he started pivoting his swivel chair back and forth. Her words had provided him with an image of her panties darkly mottled like pavement with the first few flecks of rain. She was a little over four months pregnant.

"What does it mean?" he asked.

"They don't know. I mean, exactly. Or they won't say."

"But it's not good."

"No, it's not good. How could it be good?"

"What started it?"

"It started on the plane."

"Is that what caused it? The trip, somehow. The plane— the altitude or something."

"No."

"Did the doctor say 'no'? Did you ask him that?"

"He said that he didn't know. He said a number of things could have caused it. We might never know."

"But could it have been the trip? Could one of those things have been the trip, or did he say that wasn't possible?"

"Are you trying to blame me? Is that what you want?"

"No."

"It sounds like it. It sounds like that's what you're trying to do. You can if you want. I don't care what caused it."

"What are you supposed to do?"

"It's here, that's all I know. It's here. It's happening. It's terrible and it's happening. That's all I know."

"What are you supposed to do?"

"I don't care what caused it. He said I should rest here a couple of days and then if it's stopped, which it probably will, he said, then I can fly back to New York."

Daniel sat for a moment silently leaning forward on his desk. His elbows adjusted to support his chin with one hand, while the other held the phone to his ear.

"It might have been the amniocentesis," she said.

"What do you mean?"

"It might have been the amniocentesis."

"What?" he said. Her words had thumped into his brain, leaving him startled as if someone had just shouted at him.

"They might have nicked the sack, the placenta, when they went in and that could have caused this. Somehow."

"How?"

"I don't know exactly. But it's a foreign body. The needle. If it nicked the placenta, then there could be a flaw in the sack that might get better or it might get worse or it might be infected."

"Oh," he said.

"I could miscarry."

He noticed now that he had started doodling on his phone message pad: a series of interlocking triangles, one of which was adorned with a sort of bowler hat. He had never liked the prospect of these men going in there with their foot-long goddamn needle. He started blocking out the open spaces in the triangles, obliterating every speck of open space.

"Sarah and Biff are fighting," she said. Sarah was the girl she had traveled to Hawaii with and Biff was Sarah's husband.

"What about?"

"Well, when he was helping her unpack, he found that she had taken her diaphragm with her and that really pissed him off. He'd been under the illusion that she didn't take it with her. So there's a lot of diaphragm rancor around here at the moment."

"Oh," he said. He could see it. Biff was robust and macho. He kept a lot of guns in the house. "Why was he helping her unpack?"

"Nobody knows."

"He probably just figures a person wouldn't take her diaphragm with her unless she was planning to get laid. I can see his point."

"Yeh, but he's hysterical on the subject. You know. Very righteous."

"Oh, well, we wouldn't want that."

"Is that sarcasm? I hope not—I don't have the energy. You should save it for the office, Daniel."

The silence that followed grew increasingly uneasy until he ended it by asking her if she was scared that they might lose the baby. That brought on another pause. He imagined her pacing out from the kitchen of Biff and Sarah's house onto the deck that overlooked foothills descending to the Pacific Coast Highway and the ocean itself. He imagined her carrying the phone as she crossed the planking that Biff had cut and planed and nailed in place, her dark hair fuzzily unkempt at this early California hour, a mug of coffee in her hand, her lithe body camouflaged by one or another of the gigantic men's T-shirts she liked to wear to bed. Leaning on the railing, she looked out of her clear dark eyes toward the ocean that appeared a restless haze beneath the faint mist. He imagined her listening to the wind snaking though the gullies in the hillside, bouncing off the rocky slopes. She didn't have to answer his question. "Try not to worry," he said.

"Yeh," she said. "Sure."

When he hung up, Daniel busied himself with a quick perusal of several briefs, then told his secretary to hold all his calls. The file he chose contained a week's worth of financial pages along with his notes and analysis. Reviewing the data quickly, he punched his broker's code on the speed dial. When Arthur Simmons answered, Daniel announced that he wanted to make the move they had been debating, and he wanted to do it before the bell closed the day down. "I don't care if the gap is ominous, Arthur," he said. "It's a mirage and it'll be gone by tomorrow. I want to get in at today's closing price and I want options."

"I think this is folly, Daniel. We're both looking at the same charts."

"The fluctuations are over. It's going to break out and I want to be in it as big as I can manage."

"I don't quite understand what's going on here," said Arthur in a concerned tone that suggested Daniel was on the verge of making an error.

"You understand what I want, though, don't you," Daniel said, treating Arthur's implied perils as a dare to be met with defiance.

"Is that how we're going to operate, you and me? What's going on here?"

"It's how we're going to operate today."

Looking out the window afterward, he watched the sun lowering beyond the wall of buildings that in their irregular heights appeared brutish, inhospitable spires. He saw Melissa and Sarah walking through these craggy, volcanic shapes, talking about him. Then he saw and heard the hours of his own conflict with Melissa that had filled the days just before her departure to Hawaii. He'd opposed the whole thing, laying out his reasons lucidly, in measured, neutral terms. Guided by his belief that a systematic presentation would be most effective, he knew better than to challenge her, or to give her a chance to accuse him of bullying her. Even after she'd climbed into the cab that would speed her to the airport, his faith in the power of his arguments lingered, and he waited for the points he knew he'd made to win her over before she boarded the plane, envisioning her at the airport canceling the trip in a last-minute reversal. She could be so careless, he thought, so willful. So unaware of consequences.

* * *

He arrived for his tennis match early and changed hurriedly into his shorts and shirt before pacing and brooding over a Diet Coke. He felt restless and edgy and ready to play. More often than not work-related stress or personal aggravation fueled his game, enabling him to play at a very high level. But once he was on the court it didn't take long for him to see that things weren't going to be that way for him today. His opponent Otto Weber believed that talk was a legitimate weapon to be used along with a sharp volley or a spin serve, and so he peppered his matches with a array of distracting curses, idle conversation, an occasional compliment, along with whatever else came into his mind. Today, he was brazenly subversive, reporting on the nature of every error Daniel made, and there were many of them. Daniel struggled for a while, trying to ignore Otto and find a way into the game, but he couldn't concentrate. He seemed unable to mount even a mild curiosity regarding the course of the ball. With a forehand stroke half completed, his shoulder inexplicably locked, launching the ball in a high floating arc out of bounds. Every time he pressed the ball skyward to serve, it seemed to sail into a great vat of liquid, where a fishy figure with human arms and eyes squirmed.

Before going home, he stopped at a bar and ordered a double Jack Daniel's on the rocks. The after-work hubbub and dimness was filled with men, predominantly. He studied the few women, especially a blonde in a suit rooting through her briefcase. He contemplated her, wondering what kind of life she would give him, considering his options. For an hour, he nibbled peanuts, nursed drinks, and asked himself what the hell was going on, while the local news and then the network news flashed across the television elevated in a corner above the tiers of bottles. The blonde, joined by two other fashionably attired career types, moved to a table and ordered dinner.

At a bookstore near the West End apartment he shared with his wife, he went in expecting to pick up some detective fiction and came out with a sack full of books on pregnancy, birth, babies, prenatal life. Data. Research. Evidence. Logic was useless without preparation. He hated feeling ignorant. At a Chinese restaurant down the street from the bookstore, he purchased a container of egg drop soup and some Szechuan chicken.

Their apartment was on the twelfth floor. Certain angles in the spacious living room offered a view of the flat gray Hudson River. As he strode through the empty rooms to set his parcels down on the dining room table, he caught sight of the running lights of a tugboat in a wedge of fading sun unblocked by the intervening buildings. Then their dog, a female yellow Lab, Gracie, came running up. He patted her, and went to the kitchen, filling her red plastic bowl with food. She wanted his attention but he wasn't interested as he hurried to establish himself with his books, a yellow legal pad, some seltzer and a glass of ice, along with the Chinese food on the dining room table near the window.

Sniffing the chicken, he picked a piece and took a bite, and sat there chewing as he read that in the third week the embryo altered from a ball to a sort of hook-shaped pear, that it developed a head and tail, a neural groove, a primitive heart. By the fifth week, the head, brain, and mouth had begun to form. Nutrients, hormones, oxygen, antibodies were passed from the mother's bloodstream to the infant in exchange for waste products that the mother's bowels and kidneys eliminated. By the eighth or ninth week, budlike protrusions on the sides and base of the torso would be identifiable as arms and legs. The eyes, ears, nose, and sex organs also would be established by this time. In the third month, there would be fingernails, toenails, bones, and facial characteristics.

Suddenly, he felt a pang, a grumbling in his bowels, and he had to go to the bathroom so violently that he leaped to his feet and ran for the toilet, fearing that he might actually go in his pants. Flinging his trousers down, he erupted with hissing, splashing, and stink. He was fretting as he sat there that the food might have been tainted, or that he was coming down with the flu.

When he felt better, he wanted some fresh air, so he hooked the dog to her leash and set out to walk her in the park. Once on the street, he detoured to Broadway and a little liquor store that he frequented near Eighty-third Street. He bought a pint of Jack Daniel's. His path to Riverside took him past the outstretched hands of several street-corner beggars. With a bottle in his own back pocket he felt a faint, indirect kinship that inclined him to drop some change into the paper cup of a black man with empty eyes and a white crud on his lips.

At the edge of the park, Daniel scouted the shadows and opened the bottle. As he let the dog off the leash, he glanced up at the sky and took his first drink. He settled onto a bench close to the entrance. He sat there, feeling outside the norm, like the panhandlers behind him.

Returning from her amniocentesis a month ago, his wife had been shaken. She had phoned him at work to tell him what had happened. The doctor who had administered the test at Manhattan Hospital had been recommended highly, described as someone both experienced and specialized. But with his officious nurse, he had struck Melissa as far more intent on instructing the murmuring students bunched around her belly than on the actual task he was performing on her. When he missed on his first try, he snorted in amazed disbelief and went in again. She felt, she said, like an example of something that wasn't working out. She nearly fainted getting out of the cab at home. On the phone with Daniel, her voice was disoriented and feeble. Immediately, he called the hospital to speak to the doctor. But he never got beyond a smug nurse, who said that she hadn't been at the procedure but she could assure him that working before students only made professional people more professional, and that if something should go wrong it would be due to "indeterminable elements" and not "the procedure." He told her he was a lawyer and he was going to sue them if there was any problem. He would become, he said, an "indeterminable element." Sounding genuinely confused, she said she didn't know what he was talking about, but that he couldn't sue them under any circumstances because he and his wife had signed a release. Had he forgotten? He screamed at her that he was a lawyer and he had ways.

He opened his eyes, surprised that he had closed them in the park, and startled, also, to catch himself thinking that maybe if the baby died he would leave Melissa. It could be the right thing and he knew it. If it was, then maybe losing the baby would be the best thing. The marriage was not exactly a rock. More like something made of glass, something glittering and flawed and dangerous if broken. What the hell was she doing traipsing around Hawaiian jungles and volcanoes anyway when she was pregnant? He'd warned her. Maybe too tactfully. But when he came on too strong she just got more stubborn no matter what the issue. Maybe if the baby died she would at least start listening to him.

Back at the apartment, he watched a sitcom for a while, but it irritated him more than it amused him. He tapped the OFF button on the remote and decided to look over the charts that he and Arthur had disagreed about that morning. But then, made just a tinge insolent by the bourbon, he picked up the phone and called the Midwest to speak to his father. With the charts spread out on his lap, he leafed through them idly while he and his father indulged in some fragmented chitchat about various sports and teams. He took a hit of bourbon and, feeling like he was making a joke, found himself grinning as he managed to ask, "Did you have any ambivalence—I mean, do you remember having any ambivalence when I was born?"

"What?"

"I'm just wondering if you had any ambivalence about being a father."

"Whata you mean?"

"Well, I'm having ambivalence—you know, wondering if I really want—"

"No," he said. His voice had something extraneous in it, like he was suppressing a cough or laugh. "We didn't have that in those days."

"Oh," Daniel said, looking out the nearby window at a filthy pigeon strutting along a ledge. "That's right. You didn't. I forgot."

"It wasn't allowed."

"I forgot that. Too bad."

"What's that supposed to mean?"

"It has its uses, I think."

"What kind of smart-assed answer is that? I'm drunk, you know. I just want you to know who you're talking to."

"What're you drinking?"

"None of your business."

"I'm drinking, too. Jack Daniel's."

"Good stuff. I gotta go. Gotta take a leak. You wanna hang on?"

"No."

"All right then. Bottoms up."

Daniel took several rapid gulps of whiskey. Gracie was lying nearby and he turned to stare at her. She stirred, first raising her eyes to peek at him, then cocking her head as the force of his attention made her uneasy. He dropped to his knees and growled. With a worried start, the dog stood up. Daniel mocked her again, and Gracie lowered her head and shoulders until her chest touched the floor. From her fluttering lips came a whine of protest that evolved into a kind of grumble and ended in a sneeze. He snarled at her and moved in, nudging her with his shoulder. To escape her confusion she barked at him, and then she collapsed onto her side, rolling onto her back and lifting her legs in submission, her eyes pleading that he resume his proper role. He said, "Gimme a kiss. " Her eyes darted left and then right as she panted and raised her paws higher as if she thought perhaps he hadn't seen them and didn't know she was giving up. "You have to gimme a kiss," he said.

Her confusion was giving way to sadness. He placed his hands on either side of her head and massaged the velvety raggedness of her ears. He flopped back on the floor, staring at the white ceiling where leaks from the apartment above had made a cluster of blisters, his arm extended so that his hand could flex in her fur.

It was a year since he had found out about his wife's affair. They had been fighting regularly at the time that it happened, each retreating into a personal sanctuary from which they issued attacks and claims of righteousness. After a while, the air between them turned into a cold, disputed territory, and then business took him out of town. She said it hadn't meant anything, and though he didn't believe her, he knew that in a sense what she said was true. In the sense that the affair hadn't been a matter of love, but a matter of bitterness between them, a matter of sex, a matter of consolation, a matter of keeping the upper hand, a matter of asserting a first-strike capability. If the only meaning permitted to qualify as meaning was love, then one could say that the affair had no meaning. On the other hand, it had a lot of meanings. It had left him miserable and wary of her. She, in her turn, declared that having the affair had convinced her that she wanted things to work out between them and that she wanted to get pregnant, if he was willing.

They had been apart when it happened—she in New York, he on a case in Texas for a six-week period that both knew was a sort of informal trial separation. He might have handled a confession of one encounter gracefully, but more than that meant she had liked it enough to go back for more. The thing she confessed to—they argued about whether to call it a "relationship" and never really settled the matter—had gone on for more than three weeks. He felt that made it a "relationship," but she didn't. He demanded details, received them, then broke several pieces of furniture.

Now he picked up the whiskey bottle; there was only a little left. He sipped it, saving some, then padded to the bedroom, where he took off his clothes and flopped down on the empty white bed. Though he could not see the moon out the window, the glow washing the sill and dresser told him the moon was over the river. Phrases and jargon from the reading he'd done kept bobbing up amid his other thoughts: *hormones, antibodies, neu-*

ral groove. The baby was a boy, but it wasn't a baby yet, medically. What was it then and how was he to feel about the peril it was in? He wondered what was happening at the shifting markets all around the globe. Had he outsmarted them? He saw them starting up and stopping with the turning globe and blazing sun, Tokyo, Bonn, London. As he teetered at the edge of sleep, the term *a primitive heart* arose in a glare. He reached for the bottle, finished it. He turned to the window and it seemed his gaze was traversing the continent all the way to California, where his wife's belly was flowering. The literal meaning of the phrase was a clinical description of a rudimentary pump, a basic functioning, but he kept seeing a wild creature, a little jungle figure; he felt scared for it, scared that it was inside her like it was. He thought about calling her. When he realized he was waking up, he saw he must have dozed off. It was still early in California. He turned on the light. But when he got the phone to his ear, he dialed Arthur's number instead. A machine answered, and Daniel told it, "I hope you did what I said, Arthur, because this shit is going to happen and it's going to happen big. I want my share. I'll talk to you tomorrow."

Twenty minutes after the opening bell sent "the wheels of commerce into motion" the next morning, Daniel's pick, a pharmaceutical stock, started to climb. Throughout the next week, it rose a little each day. Daniel watched its gradual but steady ascent and called Melissa several times a day. At the end of a week, the stock leveled off, and late that Friday, Melissa called him to say she would be arriving at Kennedy Airport Sunday evening.

He drove out early, parked, and sat in the lounge sipping a bourbon as he watched planes lumber into the sky, while others settled down. At the gate, he embraced her, trying to read the slim body pressed against him. He took her head between his hands and kissed her. Her belly was a little swollen. "You okay?" he said.

"So far so good."

"Any trouble on the flight?"

"I'm fine."

When they had walked to the exit of the terminal, he told her to wait where the skycap was piling her luggage, while he hastened off to get the car. The sun was making her squint as he drove back up. The wind was stirring her hair, pressing her rose-colored blouse and flounced skirt tightly around her, the hem flapping out on either side like fins. She was very tan. He smiled, relieved and a little surprised at how happy he was to see her. He pulled the trunk release and ran around to load her bags. Carefully placing each suitcase, he hoped to make the task a demonstration of his concern for her. When she reached for a small carry-on, he said, "No, no," and snatched it up. Her response was hard to read, because she turned away, climbing into the car, but he thought she was pleased.

By the time he joined her, she had a k. d. lang tape playing. Smiling at him then, she said, "I'm really glad to be home. God, am I glad."

"We'll be okay," he said. "You'll just have to take it easy."

"I'm up for that."

They talked about politics. Melissa was optimistic, while Daniel felt there was always too much that was unknown. Catching sight of the tollgates on the Triborough Bridge ahead, he reached to the slot under the ashtray where he kept some tokens. An accident along the shoulder had left a bright red Jeep Cherokee nosed up against a dilapidated old Ford, the drivers gesticulating and contemplating their fender bender, and he was about to make a joke about it when she grunted, and he whirled to look at her.

"Oh," she said. "Oh, shit."

"What?" His heart leaped, leaving a socket of emptiness.

"I'm bleeding."

"Oh, no."

"Just go home. They said this might happen."

"Maybe we should go to the doctor."

"No. Just go home."

He double-parked, alerted the doorman to watch the car, and helped her up to the apartment. She said she would call the doctor while he went back down to find a temporary parking place. He argued that they should place the call before he put the car in the garage, in case the doctor wanted them to come in right away. She insisted. It was twenty minutes before he returned and found her lying down in the bedroom. She had a fashion magazine open as if she had been reading, but her eyes were red, her cheeks streaked where she had angrily wiped away tears.

"He wants me to come in first thing in the morning."

"What did he say?"

"He said I should come in."

"I know, but what does he think?"

"I'm supposed to stay in bed until the morning and then come in."

"And then what?"

"What do you mean?"

"Has he any idea what's going to happen? I mean how are we supposed to handle this—what can we expect?"

"He didn't say. I'm going to try to go to sleep."

"Do you think you can sleep?"

"I hope so. I'm tired."

"Can I bring you anything? Do you want me to bring you anything? I'm a little hungry. I'm going to eat something in the kitchen."

"Just come to bed, too, okay? Can you? Bring whatever you're going to eat in here."

When they woke up, it was seven-thirty and the bleeding had stopped. He phoned work to tell them he would not be in and then he accompanied her to the doctor's office. In the waiting room, he tried to read *Newsweek* but found himself peeking at the pregnant women surrounding him on the leather chairs beneath the tiers of potted plants and antique wallpaper. They seemed to attest to something prosaic, even luxuriant in pregnancy that he and Melissa were being denied. At last he was called in to join her.

Dr. Hefflin's office was elegant, yet formal, with a big mahogany desk backed by bookcases. As Daniel entered, Dr. Hefflin, a lean whippet of a man with black intense eyes, stood up and reached out to shake hands. He wore a chalkstripe suit, a gray, burgundy-striped silk tie. Behind him hung pictures of his three children, ranging from an infant to a handsome sandy-haired boy of at least fifteen.

"I have to stay in bed," said Melissa.

"That's the way it looks," Dr. Hefflin added in a tone that suggested a possible alternative.

"For how long?" asked Daniel.

"The whole pregnancy," said Dr. Hefflin, removing whatever hope he had seemed to offer.

"So that's what I'll do," she said, smiling bravely. "If it's what I have to do, then I'll do it."

"Mind you," said the doctor, "there's no guarantee that even that will safeguard the pregnancy. She could spontaneously abort at any moment."

"It was the amniocentesis that caused it, wasn't it?" said Daniel.

"I don't know. I mean, that's a possibility, but I can't say for sure. I only wish I'd administered it, then this would not have happened—if that is the cause, which I can't really say it is."

"Did she tell you how they went in twice?"

"That's normal procedure if the first attempt is unsuccessful."

"What would have caused this, though—this trouble, I mean. What else—if it wasn't them nicking the placenta?"

"It's a perfected technique. If that's what happened, it's most unusual. With ultrasound the baby's position is so accurately defined that the chances of harm are very low. It's something less than a two percent chance that the baby could be caused to abort."

"And if you go in twice, what are the odds? Do they double?"

"This could be the result of something else entirely."

"But there's nothing wrong with him, is there? I mean, in all the sonograms and everything, there's nothing really wrong with him."

"Not as far as we can tell. But sometimes there's just no way to know what makes these things happen. If she rests, if she's careful and lucky, and the contractions don't start, then we could make it. But if the placental tissue has been harmed or if there's any other difficulty that we might not know about, then contractions could begin, and there'll be a spontaneous abortion. Harm to the placenta will create a flawed aura about the pregnancy making it seem incapable of getting to term— just as if there were something wrong with the baby, or something naturally or inherently wrong with the placenta—so it's nature's way of getting rid of imperfect babies. Once contractions start and continue with any regularity, there'll be no turning back. The baby will just be delivered."

"But too young to survive."

"Well, yes. Presently. But if we get through the next couple of months and we are in a later term, well, we might make it then."

When they got back to their building, Daniel double-parked again, then helped her to the elevator and into their apartment and down the hallway to the bedroom. She moved very slowly, her attention directed within, as if she had heard a faint and frightening noise and she was waiting for it to come again.

"I hope I can do it," she said, lying down on the bed. "I just don't know if I can stay in bed for five months. It's such a long time. How can I? I want to. I want this little baby to be born. I'll try. I just don't know if I can."

"I know," he said. "It's going to be hard."

"I feel like my body will just fall apart. What will my body be like after month after stupid month of just lying in this bed? I won't have the strength to give birth. I won't have had any exercise, I'll just lie here."

"We'll have to figure out things for you to do."

"Right," she said. "But what? I mean, five months in bed. Five months. Think of it!" She lunged sideways as if to throw herself onto her stomach, but she froze. "I'm afraid to move."

"If only we hadn't had that goddamn amniocentesis," he said.

"You're going to have to shut up about that," she told him. "We had to have it. I'm too old not to have had it."

"I didn't want it."

"I know you didn't. But I had to have it."

"We could have taken our chances just like everybody used to."

"And ended up with a Down syndrome baby who—"

"Well, now we've got a perfectly healthy baby who's in jeopardy because . . ." He stopped and shook his head as if his thoughts were annoying insects he could escape by startling them away.

"Because of *what*?" she said.

"I didn't want it, that's all."

"I'm not so sure you even wanted to get pregnant, is the truth."

He stared at her, feeling cold, and he thought, I'm divorcing her if this baby's dead. I'm divorcing her. But he said, "I'm going shopping. We shouldn't fight."

"I don't want to. I need you."

"I know."

"I need your help, Danny. On this thing. I really do."

"I have to put the car away," he said. "And get some groceries. I'll walk the dog."

It was more than an hour before he was back unloading the food in the kitchen. He plunked two slices of bread into the toaster, and when they popped he slapped on some butter, then added and mashed down gobs of peanut butter and jelly. He filled a blue plastic tumbler with milk. He paced to the living room table by the window. The Hudson was coated with a restless shimmer. He dropped a hunk of sandwich onto the floor for the dog to eat and stuffed the remainder into his own mouth. He finished the milk and undressed so he could climb into bed with a minimal disturbance of Melissa, whom he hoped to find sleeping.

She was lying flat on her back, motionless and breathing smoothly, as he peered in. Sneaking onto the empty space beside her, he hoped he would doze off quickly and sleep long and deep, but with his eyes closed he found he was worried about the infant. Misperceived as tainted, it might be expunged at any moment.

The scratching at the door was the dog. After a moment she nosed her way in. Studying him, she set her chin on the edge of the mattress. He looked into her eyes, and the rage he felt startled him. He saw himself chasing her from the room and following her into the kitchen where he slapped her and slapped her, knocking her down, kicking her. He felt fragile as he rose from bed, his bones artificial, his breath cold. "No," he whispered, the force of his tone sending the dog away, as he pressed the door shut behind her.

The next day Daniel started on Melissa's accommodations. He was haunted by a need to atone for a misdeed he couldn't specify. It seemed connected to her, and he wanted to ask her what she thought it was, but he knew that she had enough to take care of without him yammering at her. Instead, he would pour himself into tending her, ignoring his suspicion that his solicitude had antagonistic roots. His feelings were irrelevant. What was needed was consideration. He bought a new TV and had it installed in the bedroom where they already had a cable outlet. Calling from his office, he made arrangements to subscribe to every possible cable hookup. At 47th Street Photo, he bought the best VCR on the market. The one they already had in the living room was basic. Besides, he wanted to keep it where it was, so he could watch it without bothering her if she was sleeping, or had visitors, or wanted to watch something that didn't interest him. Making a quick stop at a Broadway video store he purchased a number of tapes and grabbed several copies of the catalog teeming with films to rent and to buy. By the time he sat down on the bed beside her with the new VCR installed and the catalogues spread around them, he felt changed. The bustle and the nature of his actions seemed to have eliminated his complaints, converting them into a cheery sense of duty. As he explained to her how she could use the catalogues to have almost any movie she wanted delivered, he felt they were a team, their interests identical, their loyalty firm.

"This won't be so bad," she said.

"No, no, no."

"But what if I can't do it? What if I just can't lie here for five months?" Tears brimmed from her eyes; they gleamed in little bubbles that collapsed down her cheeks. She shook her head, her lips shaping words that her silent glance declared foolish. She turned away; he stroked her temple and then her ear with his knuckle. "It's okay," he said. But it wasn't. Her inability to renounce her own needs made her seem unreliable and selfish, someone he wasn't sure he liked. He worried she lacked the necessary discipline and self-restraint. She was a woman after all, her emotions easily overwhelming her, making her erratic, so it was difficult for her to follow a steady course. How could she fail to understand her responsibility here, that it was something she didn't have the right to shirk just because it was hard?

With his arm around her, he soothed her brow, hoping to deliver affection and sympathy, while fearing that he was communicating little more than civility.

Most days, several of her girlfriends showed up to visit. They sat around the bed making jokes, telling her about their adventures at work or the developments in their love lives. Melissa's spirits seemed high most of the time, and as a consequence Daniel was also in a less troubled state. There was no denying the tedium, the aggravation, of what she was trying to do. As he watched her searching for the resources that would enable her to cope, he saw more clearly the depths of her courage. Yet there were moments when she was preoccupied and he lost track of himself, and then he would catch himself studying her intently, almost bitterly, wondering what she was really thinking.

In the middle of the first week, she excitedly informed him that she had received permission from Dr. Hefflin to exercise while lying in bed. "And that's not a sex joke," she told Daniel as he opened his mouth to speak. She had devised a series of leg lifts and arm lifts, which she proceeded to show him. The qualms he felt as he watched her gamely trying to enjoy herself were related to the baby's welfare. He could imagine her pestering Dr. Hefflin about how she couldn't stand just lying there until he gave in and prescribed a routine. His impulse to tell her that maybe she shouldn't exercise, that maybe it would be dangerous appeared to highlight some petty grudging factor in his own nature whose demands he did not want to obey. Instead of speaking, he looked down approvingly at her ingenuity and industry. When she laughed he found himself joining her.

Toward the end of the second week, four girlfriends appeared on the same evening. Daniel had to haul extra chairs into the bedroom. Two of the girls had brought Indian food from a new restaurant on Columbus Avenue. When Daniel, at about ten o'clock, returned from walking the dog, the pungent odor of curry and other exotic flavors was in the air. The mood was festive. Melissa was laughing and telling the story of Sarah and her husband and the diaphragm. A chain reaction of knowing looks traveled the room. Holding up her plate in order to be served by Carrie, an investment banker and friend since college, Melissa said, "More please. More."

"Yes, Your Royalness," said Carrie, dumping curried lamb over scoops of rice.

"That's right," said Melissa. "I feel like a queen."

"Yeh," said Ruth, an independent movie producer who had met Melissa when they were both working on a Democratic fund-raiser a few years ago. "I'm starting to envy this con of yours. This is not such a bad lifestyle you have devised for yourself."

When they were gone and Daniel had climbed into bed, Melissa gave him a pat, then curled into him as he lay on his side, facing away. "I had fun," she said. " How many days has it been?"

"Almost two weeks."

"I think I'm getting the hang of it."

The next morning, with dawn still hours away, Daniel awoke to pee. As he pulled himself into a sitting position, something in the twilight nature of the moment gripped him with an over-whelming sense of nearby authority and presence. A kind of voice was addressing him. It seemed to belong to an animal with big ears and dark hairy eyebrows. The glowing nimbus back-ing the event somehow identified the speaker as a messenger and the message was that today was the day to sell the stocks that Daniel had ordered Arthur to buy less than a month ago. He was on his feet by now, staggering into the bathroom to stand wavering at the toilet.

From the second his shrill alarm clock battered him back to consciousness in the morning, he was haunted by the sensation that he'd thought of something important in the night, or maybe been told it yesterday at work, and its significance had been obvious at the time but now he could recall nothing. He hated the feeling, and as he shaved and made some eggs and coffee, as he sat on the subway jerking and flashing to his stop, as he hastened the few blocks to work and rode the elevator, he kept trying to salvage the lost idea or fact. But then his first meeting demanded that he cope amiably with Richard Trefil, a surgeon who insisted on devising tax strategies of his own that managed to be both convoluted and doltish. Daniel emerged from the hour with his annoyance barely suppressed. He walked Dr. Trefil to the elevator and returned to his desk only to find that his next appointment had been canceled.

He allowed himself to go out to the front desk, where a new secretary was floundering with her tasks. In her dark-eyed, svelte presence he quickly found himself beginning to flirt. When he caught a wave of availability starting up in the girl, he saw what he was doing. With a sly, double-edged remark to oil his departure, he fled to his office. He wanted a sympathetic, compatible, male mind, which led him to Arthur. Soon Daniel was leaning back in his chair, his feet on the windowsill where he kept nudging the toe of his shoe into a vase, perversely tipping it to point where its balance could be lost. Then he would save it. With Arthur on the speakerphone, Daniel was rambling away, trying to be amusing. Every now and then he heard the click of a golf ball followed by a wisecrack from Arthur's new talking putting mat. "Bet you can't do that again," said the weird little voice. "Way to go, big guy. Hey, you must be ready for the tour."

"Wait a minute," he said to Arthur.

"What?"

He sat up in his chair, his feet slamming to the floor as if to set himself physically for the opposition a part of him knew he was about to meet. "Sell," he said. For a second, he didn't even know what he was talking about.

"Sell what? Oh, no. Not the pharmaceuticals."

"How much am I up?"

"I don't know exactly—eight or ten thousand. But the indicators are all good. This thing has legs. It's not even close to peaking."

"It's over, Arthur. Sell."

"Oh, for God's sake, you're not going to do this to me again."

"And if you put anything of your own in, get it out now."

"This is nuts! It's idiotic. It's totally, categorically unprofessional."

"Just do it!"

"Why?"

"I don't know. But it's my money!"

Two days later, the stock started to plummet and Arthur sounded shrill and slightly enfeebled, like he was coming down with the flu, when he called to declare that Daniel had saved their mutual ass, and did he want to switch jobs with him. "You have to tell me how you did it. Not now. I couldn't take it now. But some day. When I'm feeling a little more indestructible than I am just at this instant."

Daniel was laughing as the door to his office appeared to vanish and a towheaded boy, a toddler in a blue T-shirt and shorts, glided into the room with Melissa behind him and then disappeared in a gleam of light, the residue leaping back into Daniel's eye. He felt anointed, touched with clairvoyance, as he filled with potency so vast he knew that everything in his life was going to change for the best. When he called Melissa to tell her about the money, he didn't mention what he'd seen, but it made him feel petty and selfish to exclude her, and so he ended the conversation with the words, "Listen. It's going to be all right. It is." They both knew the point he was making.

"Do you think so?" she said.

"Yes," he said. "Yes."

His mood was extreme, the aftereffects of the transaction leaving him so juiced he couldn't work and he went rattling around his office, teasing secretaries and making risky, inappropriate remarks to clients on the phone. It was clear that he was going to do himself more harm than good if he stayed at work, but he didn't really know where to aim himself. He headed out for an early lunch, hoping to convert his mood into something a little less audacious, a little more utilitarian. As he stood before the elevator, asking himself in a half-facetious voice who or what he should conquer next, up popped Otto Weber, his face like a goldfish against the glass of its bowl. Daniel directed his secretary to call Otto and to keep calling every fifteen minutes until she had him on the phone. Using another line, he ordered some takeout from the corner deli, and by the time he was finished she had reached Otto. Daniel felt like a dog salivating over fresh meat as Otto eagerly agreed to meet at the tennis club for a rematch. Though Daniel's tone was amiable, the fact that his invitation was a challenge was not lost on either of them. As Otto rose to the bait, Daniel could feel each individual pump of his heart.

Otto started strongly, the initial points developing into complex struggles. But by the end of the second game, a subtle shift was evident. The force of Daniel's ground strokes started to take command. His topspin was heavy, the bounce high, his approach shots exact. The third and fourth games went by at an increasing speed, unforced errors and a desperate uncertainty infecting and eroding Otto's style. Suddenly, the set was over with a 6–1 score. Otto drank some water and plucked his racket's strings. He put his ear against them and made a discovery about their tension. Scrutinizing Daniel, he threw out several radical observations on the current real estate market. Then he jumped to the subject of Melissa, inquiring somberly. Daniel grinned and strode back onto the court, leaving Otto with no option except to follow.

When Daniel opened the second set, playing serve and volley, Otto was startled and confused. Daniel's first serve was a laser into the Har-Tru. The ball erupted from a gray puff of dust with overwhelming height and spin. Every volley was delivered with a geometric precision that landed well out of Otto's reach and left him gaping and offended as if Daniel were cheating. At match point, Otto was serving. After making a brisk return that put Otto at an immediate disadvantage, Daniel started moving Otto from one corner to the other. Daniel felt he could do anything he wanted and keep it up forever. Otto was gasping and stabbing at the ball, sending up weak defensive lobs. With almost any shot, Daniel could have delivered a game-ending blow but, instead, he stroked the ball to a point that was just within Otto's reach. Otto was like a trained animal, his maximum effort delivering him to the ball just in time to pop it high across the net. Daniel chased Otto around, goading him until he was nothing but mangled ego and fading legs, his breath a miserable bleating. From Daniel's vantage, the ball was slow and huge as it floated to the point where it must meet his rising racket, and he wished the baby were there to see him. A little boy to witness Daniel's firm wrist, his low-to-high stroke riding a fluid transfer of weight. To admire his prowess. The ball knifed into the corner, and Otto staggered and toppled onto his belly with a grunt like a baby about to cry. Bearing witness to his own dominance, Daniel filled with the adulation of a child.

In the shower stall, with hot water rushing over him, he felt great. Just beyond the wall, Otto was babbling to another club member, and his assortment of alibis and rationalizations seemed a lullaby to Daniel. When there was a rapping on the wall, he plucked back the curtain, expecting to find Otto demanding a rematch. But it was Charlie, the desk attendant, telling him that his wife was on the phone.

"I wasn't doing anything," she shouted when he grabbed up the phone. "I wasn't doing anything. I was just lying here."

"What?" He was standing in the clubhouse wrapped in a towel, water dappling the rug around his feet.

"It's contractions. They've started."

By the time he got home, forty minutes more had passed. The contractions were still coming regularly. He wanted to call Dr. Hefflin but she forbade him. At the two-hour mark, he defied her, and the doctor told them to time both the lengths of the contractions and the intervals between them. After half an hour of this there was no doubt that the pace had accelerated, the duration lengthened. When they relayed this information to Dr. Hefflin, his voice blasted over the speakerphone. "They're not going to stop!"

"But could they?" Melissa asked.

"They're not going to. Meet me at the hospital."

"No."

"We have to meet him at the hospital," Daniel told Melissa.

"Shit," she said. "Shit. Goddamnit. Let me just lie real still."

Arriving at the hospital, they nearly collided with a UPS deliveryman who, absorbed in a clipboard of receipts, strode out the door without looking. Seeing them, and registering her stricken, distracted expression, he jumped out of the way and sped on. "Sorry," he said. Daniel glared after the man, who shrugged.

Melissa was taken off by wheelchair, clutching her overnight case. The nurse who pressed her forward was a rotund, unsmiling black woman. Daniel hastened toward the street to transfer his car from the front of the building down to the parking lot in the basement. As he reached the door, he paused to look back at her. She was seated rather properly before the bank of elevators. She was studying the blinking numbers, her hands on her lap, her manner docile, her complexion pale. Then she winced, took a breath, and doubled over, her knees lifting with the crushing force of a contraction. The elevator door opened and the black woman pushed Melissa out of sight.

For a while he was kept waiting in the hall as they prepped Melissa. He fidgeted and paced about, wondering what to do, picking up magazines he couldn't manage to read. Then a dark-haired nurse raced out to tell him that Dr. Hefflin had arrived. Briskly, she started giving Daniel orders, telling him where to go, what to do, what to wear.

Clad in a hospital gown of green cotton tied at the back of the neck and waist, he felt altered in some strange and irrevocable way. The nurse marched him into the delivery room. At the sight of Melissa stretched upon a stainless steel bed, her legs immodestly gapped and pinioned by the wide stirrups, he looked away. His gaze fell upon a window framing the tops of the taller trees in Central Park, which lay just across the street. Nurses scurried in and out of the room. Stepping close, he took Melissa's hand. A contraction had just subsided. She was breathing rapidly through her mouth, sweat dripping off her nose.

"That was a big one," she said.

"No," the doctor told her.

She seemed to take his denial as a personal criticism. "It was," she insisted.

"I think we should induce—intervene to accelerate the labor."

"Why? Aren't I doing it right?"

"You're doing fine."

"If you see I'm doing it wrong, Daniel, you tell me."

"You're not doing it wrong," Daniel said. He looked to the doctor for confirmation and saw a narrow, exasperated thought leaving its traces. Dr. Hefflin blinked rapidly, then glanced down at the floor. He seemed annoyed with Daniel. He probably resented having to contend with husbands, with their emotions and interference. As if to assert the legitimacy of his participation, Daniel sank into a crouch beside Melissa. "You're doing great," he said. "You're doing the very best you can, or that anybody could."

"Good," she said. "Can I have some ice, please?"

Daniel thrust the cup of chipped ice up to her mouth. Birdlike she picked up pieces with her teeth, then sucked them into her mouth.

"This is what I think we have to do, all right?" Dr. Hefflin said.

"Is he still alive?" Daniel asked.

Doctor Hefflin gave Daniel a look whose reasonable veneer failed to conceal the exasperation and scorn at its core. "There's a fetal heartbeat. Yes."

Melissa had closed her eyes.

"I want to accelerate the labor. I think we have to intervene and move things along. There's no hope that the process will reverse itself. That's not an option. The contractions will proceed to delivery, but at the present rate I feel certain it would be prolonged—another fifteen to twenty hours or even more. There's no point in putting you through that, Melissa, not in our circumstances. Pitocin can move us to transition in a matter of minutes. So it's my recommendation that we administer an epidural, which will remove sensation from the waist down. You're capacity to push will be reduced—I think even a little Demerol might be appropriate—but that's an acceptable loss in these circumstances. You'll have relief from the full stress of the labor, and I'll probably have to do a forceps delivery. But some Pitocin in the IV will launch us and we can get this over with."

The drastic cloud of feeling in which Daniel was caught had swayed him to believe that everyone in that room shared his dismay. But Dr. Hefflin met his panicked look with an impersonal firmness that seemed a betrayal.

"It's really what has to be done," said Dr. Hefflin. "You have to understand that."

"All right," Melissa said, looking toward the wall.

Daniel was watching the solution traveling from the bag atop the stainless steel pole and falling down the tube to the catheter piercing her vein and taped to her arm. He was trying to determine which drop, which bubble was the glucose, which revolving thread was the Pitocin whose effect would detonate the contractions. Quickly, Melissa got woozy. She was smiling up at him and retreating wistfully into the drug. From a new and slightly inaccessible place she sought him out with a lopsided smile and asked him if he knew the weather forecast for tomorrow. Would it be cloudy, would it be sunny?

"I'll check," he said.

"You're humoring me, aren't you."

"No."

"I think you are, you little snotnose," she said, winking.

He was searching for a playful comeback, but before he could find one, the outer wall of her stomach rose up and then shook and she grunted, as if she had just remembered something that had hurt badly a long time ago.

"Push," said Dr. Hefflin, and she tried, but what she produced was reminiscent of a drunk trying to stuff his feet into his shoes while standing.

"Oh, this is weird," she said.

"You're stoned," Daniel told her.

Tears blurred her eyes and she looked directly at him.

"Again," said Dr. Hefflin. "Again." She fumbled around, wondering aloud where her feet were at times. But it didn't matter. The drug had taken over and it was irresistible, rhythmically blowing spasms through her. "Push," he said. "Push." And then he said, "One more. One more!"

Melissa groaned and seemed to be involved in the elevation of a gigantic weight. It's happening, thought Daniel.

"He's coming," the doctor said.

And with this report, Daniel felt that he was falling, help-lessly, a dizzying, hopeless vertigo. Melissa's face was one of dreamy drug-induced effort, and he was convinced that her cooperation in this matter was unthinking, and that she was callous and selfish and impervious to little things. He felt that she should not be doing this, that he should not allow it. And then she thrashed in the expression of a wild, unloving wrath.

"Good," said Dr. Hefflin.

Daniel was following the cord from Melissa's crotch to the dripping cloth sack in the nurse's hands. A strip of mucus-coated belly was visible just where the cord entered and the clamp and scissors were sweeping into view, the clamp shutting down with a moist chomping sound just before the scissors gnawed the bloody linkage. He was looking into an aftermath of gore, the copious cord pulsing with life as it swayed and seemed some-how to plunge back into the sheeted void between Melissa's legs. Then the end of the amputated cord bounded out of Dr. Hef-flin's hand. He had to grab it again, as if it were struggling to snake away. Daniel felt a rising icy fear. He wasn't a hundred percent certain that he had actually seen the baby, or fetus, or whatever it was, come out.

"I'm sorry," said Melissa. She was sweating, her face a pale slack oval turning toward him, and when their eyes met, hers gleamed with a kind of sovereign sorrow. "I'm sorry, honey."

He nodded. "I know." He nodded again and kept nodding. He gave her some ice. He reached for her hand.

The nurse was at the door, trying to slip from the room with a thief's veneer of nonchalance, the bag blocked by her body from their view.

"Is that—?" said Daniel. "What's she got?"

"What?"

"I want to see him. Is that him?"

Dr. Hefflin's first impulse was absolute opposition, but then he must have found something in Daniel's stance that made him reconsider. "Certainly," he said, his tone suggesting that this was the course of action he had intended all along. "Let me take care of Melissa first. You don't want to see it, do you, Melissa?"

Slowly, dreamily, she said, "No."

"I'll have to stitch her up," he said and stepped away.

Though he went only a few steps, Melissa seemed puzzled watching him. "Daniel?" she said. "Why'd they hit the baby with a hammer?"

"What?"

"I don't know why they hit the baby with that big hammer."

"No, no," he said. "Who?" he asked, and looking closely he saw how far adrift she was in the funhouse distortions of drugs and exhaustion.

"You know," she said. "These people." Her eyes searched for a nurse or Dr. Hefflin.

"They didn't do that, Melissa."

"Are you sure?"

"I was here all the while. That didn't happen. No, no."

"Oh." She seemed to grow instantly sleepy. "Good."

"No."

"I thought it did, but I'm glad it didn't. I'm drunk, I guess." She thought for a second or two and then said, "It's true. I'm drunk."

Dr. Hefflin had returned and was waiting patiently. Daniel nodded and walked to the door.

A few minutes later Daniel was in a small room full of stainless steel instruments and stainless steel drawers and contraptions, watching Dr. Hefflin lift a stainless steel basin containing the little corpse from inside a drawer. It was far more developed than Daniel had expected and the color was disturbingly ruddy. The thighs were thick, the calves quite sturdy. He was a tiny robust figure, barrel-chested and hard-bellied with a little plug of a head, his fingers clutched, his eyes closed.

When Daniel's own body seemed to split open, he was caught completely off guard by the vertical seam parting his torso from his crotch to his brow in order for these big hoots of grief to start coming out of him. The startled doctor pivoted, as if concealment of the little corpse might rectify the situation. "Maybe you shouldn't have seen him."

"No," Daniel said. "It's okay. I'm done," he said. "It's okay." It was like somebody very large had leaped out of nowhere and hit him hard.

"I don't know what your thinking on this issue is but, most commonly with a fetus at this stage, what most people opt for, and the most efficient procedure now, I think, would be cremation. They have the capability in the basement."

"All right," he said, and turned and walked away into the hall. He took off the gown and wandered about looking for someone he might return it to. Finally an orderly told him to put it in a laundry basket, and he pointed out a large canvas sack in the corner.

On the way to her room, Melissa slept on a gurney that Daniel shepherded warily through corridors that he found unsafe in some indefinable way. The small room was wedged into a corner of the building, a solid stone wall visible through the window, its surface grimy and punitive. Standing there, looking out, he felt they had been sealed away in an underground chamber. When he turned from the dismal view of smog-encrusted stone to look down at her, he was surprised to find she was awake. "Did you see him?" she said.

"Yes."

"Did you really?"

"Yes."

For a while they were quiet, each settled into a musing pause. She lay in her bed, while he stood beside her shifting his weight back and forth.

"You must be tired," she said.

"You're the one who's tired."

"Yes," she said. "I am."

"I need a drink," he smiled.

"What was he like?"

"Well . . . robust. Barrel-chested. He looked like he would have been real strong."

"He was that developed?"

"Yes," he said, turning to look out the window.

They were high enough that the dirt and pollution layering the city in the gathering evening turned Central Park into a surreal grid of gleaming nocturnal fragments, hunks of pavement, strips of grass, a park bench here, another one there, clots of trees and illuminated pathways radiating off into the dark where they turned into patterns of light.

He had to walk three blocks before he found a liquor store. He entered, browsed for several minutes as if his purpose was unclear, then bought two half pints of bourbon. With one deposited in a jacket pocket, he opened the second before he'd walked a block. At a pay phone, he used his credit card to call his father. When the old man answered, he told him, "Pop, the baby's dead."

"Oh, no, oh, no," the old man bellowed.

"She just couldn't . . . I don't know. Melissa miscarried."

"Oh God no. What happened? The poor little baby. Oh, God, how could it happen? Oh, God, oh God. NO. NOOOOO!"

"Pop, what're—"

"The baby. The poor little baby! He's dead!"

"Dad!"

"Oh, God, oh, God. Nothing ever works out for me. I never get anything. Nothing that I want. Never. Never. He's dead, he's dead. The poor little baby."

"Dad, will you—" The clatter in Daniel's ear informed him that the phone had slammed into the floor. The loud and elongated banging that followed was less immediately understood. "Dad," he said. "Dad, are you all right?' In the seconds that passed he heard breathing, a kind of squeal.

"Who is this?" said his father.

"What?"

"What time is it? Who is this?"

"Dad are you all right?"

"Danny? Danny, that you?"

"Yeh."

"What's up?"

"Whata you mean?"

"Whata you want? You never call me unless you want something. Whata you want?"

For a second, Daniel stood there wondering what was going on and then he made the obvious conclusion: his dad was in a drunken blackout. "I just called to say hello," he said. "But I gotta go now. Bye."

They were holding hands and dozing side by side, Melissa in her hospital bed, Daniel in the tattered, cloth-covered recliner that he'd dragged from across the room, nudging it obsessively until the edges of the bed and chair were snug. He was content, he thought, and she was asleep and they were both adrift. He was floating and she was floating, and they were together in some ways and separate in other ways. While he had certain questions about her and what she might be thinking, he knew that, as far as he was concerned, the baby, or whatever it was, with its hooked pearlike length, its fishy head and tail, lay nestled somewhere in the lush hillsides of California. It was burrowed deep in the layered earth like a seed waiting to bloom; it was curled amid the roots of bushes and small trees, the four little buds along the sides straining to become limbs, the neural groove like a dust of diamonds poised upon a string, the knob of the brain caught in a bulb of meat, the eyes and ears on the verge of sprouting amid the amniotic fluid surging and receding with a sound like thunder in a seashell punctuated by the regular beat of a hushed and reclusive heart huddled like a fugitive in a cave hoping to go undiscovered by the darkness approaching.

He sat up with a gasp, his eyes blinking and pulses racing as he saw that he was in a chair beside Melissa who lay in her hospital bed. She felt far away, somewhere in a realm of druggy sleep, while he was frightened for the baby. He hadn't really been asleep, he didn't think—just lying there remembering, and then he'd grown afraid. But how could he still be worried when it was over, when it was gone from inside her, when there was nothing in there anymore?

Through the door came the solitary footsteps of the night nurse patrolling the hall. The room was dark except for the artificial swell of the night-light. From another room came a miserable cry, a mix of breath and groaning. And then, though his question had not really required an answer, one came. It was himself he was worried about. It had always been himself he was frightened for. He wanted to turn away from this strange and shameful thought. It was lit by the light of that little body burning in an oven he knew to lie stoked and roaring in the bowels of this building. As if he was inside her himself, and his life, if he loved her, was hers to grant or withhold, and she was selfish and willful and impulsive.

"What are you thinking?" she said.

She was looking up at him, her eyelids fluttering.

"What?" he said.

"You looked so worried."

"No, no." He was startled, his sense of being intruded upon jarring him out of the place into which he had been settling.

"What was it?"

And then he realized that his momentary experience was receding. Trying to retrieve it seemed to push it further away. "What?" he said.

"Daniel? Tell me."

He looked at her. There was just this pang now, like a strange unrecognizable sound marking the way that something had approached and passed, and now it was gone.

"Tell me."

"I don't know," he said, and it was true; he didn't. He had no idea.

EARLY
MADONNA

1

THOUGH SHE WAS JUST STANDING in front of her bedroom mirror fitting the tiny clasp of a pearl earring to her ear, she might as well have been on a bridge getting ready to jump. The edgy unpleasantness she was coping with was enough to mess up a week, but something worse was on its way, a jolt of the purely maniacal so that even forewarned she'd end up wanting to throw things or cry or just feel bad. It was so very delightful the way her moods were like muggers jumping out of the dark. Shouldn't she at least have a clue?

The last hour at work had kept her tidying up the greeting cards by category and subcategory, replacing them in their labeled slots: Birthday, Anniversary, Mother's Day, Father's Day, Mother, Uncle, Nephew. It was enough to make you puke. While she made her way to the minimall parking lot, the winter sky darkened, hinting at a crushing outcome.

Now she sat at her dressing table in the hazy output of a floor lamp. When she turned on her makeup mirror, reflections jumped about. She swept outward with her hand as if to somehow organize the light. At the same time an angry little action figure threw a glass and turned a chair over in a room in her mind where she stomped and challenged the source of her annoyance, which, if she had to put a name on it, was her stupid self. What is it? What do you want? Is there something you want?

For the third or fourth time, she rebuckled the black plastic belt no wider than her thumb. It was too damn hard to look like Madonna. Madonna made it look easy, but it wasn't. But then Madonna was Madonna, and she kept changing it, anyway, bitch that she was. Though as far as Kathy was concerned the only chill version was the one at the start, that vision of lace and virginal frenzy on the bow of that boat. It had been out of nowhere, the way it happened. Kathy'd been racing through every damn thing the satellite had to offer, tapping the remote, tapping, tapping, desperate for who knew what and there was this blonde on that boat, dancing in front of a lion as if daring the beast to take her in some raunchy hump on the steps of that city with all that water. She knew the name but couldn't think of it. It was in Italy. But chancing upon the video that very first time she'd felt that as soon as the cameras stopped, Madonna and the lion had hooked up, and that she had dealt. She had coped. Maybe Mr. Lion was the one who got more than he bargained for. (Bestiality. Right. They should try Rick Boltzunger.) That was the Madonna who counted. Even if she wasn't really Madonna and Madonna was what was left after she lopped off everything she was bored of carrying around. Louise Veronica Ciccone out the window and every-thing left was her own personal invention. It was like she waved a magic wand and said, Let there be . . . and I will be . . . Madonna.

Having tossed the first earring, Kathy was working the clasp of a replacement with a large scarlet hoop, and damnit, she hated this itchy feeling. Because she had to get ready. She had to get everything right and out of the way because Janet was coming home. Her younger sister who seemed older. Her baby sister who was so damn mature. So damn organized and purposeful, while Kathy was the mistress of mess. Somehow the common sense gene, the logic gene had skipped her. Like now, she was changing the earring again, this time on the basis of the color of the dangling hoop. She was almost sure she wanted a hoop, but what the hell was the right color. Finding the right color seemed the only way to dissolve her misgivings. She could re-member leaving work in a mood vague enough to imagine her-self cheerful, and so she hadn't expected to end up like this. With a growing worry that she'd never get it right. She thought she might fix things by changing her belt. She'd like to go to that city on the water sometime, ride one of those boats. The black water. She'd read somewhere how the lion was a statue. Or was based on a statue and so the statue might still be there. She saw herself riding one of the boats, prowling for that lion and standing on the front part. The water would spray up over her. She could dance and sing. That was the only real Madonna, the early one, the true one. She saw her in her dreams even sometimes, intense and blonde, a kind of flame, enigmatic and maybe disapproving. Over what? But that was something else. The dreams and whatever that was all about. Mainly, Kathy saw early Madonna as this kind of ideal that needed to be kept alive like the Olympic flame. This truth of something. But those were reasons for people who needed reasons, when she really didn't know if there was a reason for the magic that she felt, this sense of irresistible secret connection so that she took the image as her personal guide, her personal adviser on everything but starting with first of all the simplest most basic stuff like her clothes and makeup. The additional and satisfying fact that Madonna gave her blessing to outlaw aims, well, sure, that was important, too, and could be a kind of reason, because that was how Kathy saw her mistakes. Not that she wanted to forget how she was to some degree a look-alike for early Madonna, either, the soft abundance, the slightly fleshy sprawl, indulgent and appetizing. That's what Kathy was seeking, dressing in layers, replacing the belt with a wider vinyl cinch. She'd thought it was a game at first and it was, but it had become something else, this desire to see how close she could get. One day she realized she'd only pretended it was a game to sort of fool herself for some reason that didn't matter. And then people took notice and that made it even more enticing. The push-up bra, the black, sloppy T-shirt cut off unevenly at the sleeves and waist so her belly showed as she moved, a tease, and the upper part of her breasts, their parting like an invitation to come on in especially if she raised her arms. Once she put her spandex imitation denim jacket on, she could be demure (sort of) or provocative, depending on how far she unzipped. Like she was this trampy time traveler with an outlaw heart. Or she could snap the hem of her stockings to her garter belt and then when she got to the club just unhook one of the snaps, so it dangled, the fallen stocking showing skin. She knew her power; it wasn't exactly beauty, but eyes seeing her let her know. They kind of groaned, these eyes stuck in some guy's head and they said, Oh, baby, all the while watching her through waves of stupidity swamping their little brains. She was blinking and, stupid or not, she wished he was with her now, whoever he was (anybody but Rick, of course), drugged and whispering that he didn't want to go out and party now, because he had to have her naked because she was so irresistibly hot in those clothes, in his bed, or her bed. Or on the floor. Against a wall. (Where was he anyway, that jerkoff Rick.) That was all she wanted—some hot guy mad for her. But then it swept over her, the way she had lost so much, just the way it used to sweep over Madonna when she and Sean Penn were first divorced. She talked about how sad it was in all those interviews, how the hurt went on and just wouldn't let up over losing the love of her life. Kathy felt sad, like Madonna felt sad. What were they to do?

When the cigarette she'd forgotten burned her knuckle, she said, "Shit," and stabbed it into the silver ashtray and left it there, blunted, issuing a fitful string of smoke while her other hand went sideways to seize her eyeliner from off the vanity.

In all the homes along the narrow, snow-rutted streets surrounding her, families were getting ready for dinner. Televisions yammered and flickered, broadcasting news for adults or cartoons for kids. All the homes had kids, hers included. Any minute now they would call her, she was the kid here. The runaway who had run away and then run back. A daredevil at eighteen she was a refugee seeking refuge. Five years and she'd come staggering back, seeking rescue, but not too much.

Outside her window a streetlight clicked on, forming a yellowish cone filled with snow. She felt the dim sky lower over her mood and for the moment she turned into a character in a horror movie with dread on its way to find her. Something black and sinister was climbing the stairs. Something merciless and deadly. Something very cunning. Through the window she could see dusk disappearing into night, the transition skipped, the dark just there, and she felt suspended with nothing stirring except her own fingers. And then she heard a flock of crows cawing above her. She didn't have to think to picture them, black flecks in this unreal sky beyond the rooftop angling off into the frozen farmland, their cries signaling doom and dread and disaster coming up the stairs as they fled.

Hurriedly, she started removing her clothes, having settled on what she'd wear once she got out the door and into her car headed for some fun. So now she had to pack it all up and disguise her real aims by putting on jeans and a sweater. She'd change back later in her car, or in the bathroom at the club. Like superwoman going in the door ordinary and coming back out as this time-warped superslut, hot and ready, a little evil. She loathed where she stood tugging up the zipper of her jeans because the room confined her and kept her from a raucous unknown event commencing somewhere she wasn't at this exact second.

She flopped back onto her bed. Her sister was airborne in the night, winging home for Christmas vacation (what if the plane crashed) after her first few months away at a college in Pennsylvania (imagine that). Janet was slender and dark and (what if the plane crashed) her hair was straight, and (planes did crash) a dirty straw yellow, but her eyes were large and warm and (if the plane crashed the house would incinerate and flame up, her parents exploding like firebombs). Janet's eyes were in fact too large so they exaggerated something about her, giving her ordinary features an underlying sense of insistence and know-how. When she'd been younger the size of her eyes had thrown out any expectation of beauty. But now something else was developing and their impression of secret depths and maybe even secret powers left you wondering about her. Kathy felt stalked and edgy, as if

Janet was in the room, radiating virtue and peering into Kathy. What did Janet know? What did she know about you that you had decided no one should know? Janet claimed she liked to observe and think, that's all; she wasn't judging; she liked to consider and comment, make a joke, or tease, offer a suggestion, but it wasn't judgment.

Popping her iPod earphones on, Kathy plugged herself into "Material Girl," the icy cynicism of the simple dim-witted greed of the music rousing her. She didn't care about Madonna's evolution into this and that. She liked this old stuff, the stuff where Madonna came out of nowhere, and then it had all sort of ended with "Like a Prayer." In fact the rest of it all sickened her and felt like this betrayal because it was betrayal. That blonde on that boat rushing over the black water in that old city was the captivating, spellbound, spell-inducing thing Kathy wanted to keep alive. Unlike this current bullshit, which felt like the phony conniving of some imposter. First she had to have the one kid with that dancer guy, and okay, he was hot, and anybody could make a mistake, but then she married this English guy and went totally nuts with another kid. So all of a sudden she's got two kids and she's writing these stupid books for kids and blabbing about religion. She'd be better off dead. It was utterly ridiculous. (And, well, if the plane crashed there would be no more family. Not this one anyway. Not the one in this household.) Growing up, Kathy had barely registered Madonna other than pre-Britney something or other, and what did register hadn't had the slightest pop to it until that accident with the TV and she just happened to land on that channel and it just happened to be the perfect instant so that something amazing, something maybe even psychic and life changing could occur. At first she hadn't even recognized who it was. MTV had been running this stuff from the past and there was the boat, the blonde, the lion. Madonna? Really? Madonna! MADONNA! They ran it and reran it any number of times that day. Kathy recorded it to have it like it was a drug she wanted to take over and over and then she went out and found the video at Blockbuster for the better quality. She ended up buying it then, the video and then the DVD. It was like she was falling in love only it was more than that. It was something else.

In the humming bright illumination of an airplane boring down a corridor in her mind, her sister's cheek rested against the window as she dozed and dreamed and— No, no, Janet wasn't sleeping. That wasn't it. Janet was awake and quiet and thinking about clouds bounding past while a small boy rocked in the seat next to her and leaned against her shoulder. And he was asleep. That's who was sleeping. The little boy in the seat next to Janet. Janet was serene; she had talked to him and calmed his fears about airplane rides until he couldn't stay awake. (And if the plane crashed and there was in fact no longer a family at this particular address, it wouldn't really be all that bad. She imagined arriving in a cab even though she didn't know where she was coming from but she was getting out and walking up to the front door of this very house, coming home again, only when she paused to ring the bell and peered inside she saw strangers. Her parents weren't inside. Nor was she. Who were these people? Where were her parents? Where was she?) Meanwhile Janet in her airplane listened to the soothing confidences whispered behind her by two elderly women reminiscing about the times they shared when they were young. Beyond the window, clouds filled the night sky with layered—

Why was her mother standing in front of her waving wildly? Kathy ripped the earphones from her head. "What?"

"Will you hurry?" Her mother's voice was like a snarl. "Will you hurry, Kathy?"

"Will I what?"

"It's Janet on the phone. She's on the phone long distance and she wants to say hi."

Kathy gaped. She felt as if Janet had arrived and was impatiently pacing downstairs, while her mother shouted: "What are you doing?"

She couldn't say, I'm remembering something, I'm feeling something. Because it was all happening too fast and, anyway, she was on her feet and jumping to the stairs (even as she flew back in time, and the baby sister who could hardly walk and who she was about to instruct on the decor of her dollhouse, on the placement of the furniture and the clothes her dolls must wear, studied her with disinterest before waddling away).

When she reached the bottom of the stairs, her father was clutching the cordless phone and striding off into the living room where he wheeled and marched back, his face wrinkled and flushed as if he were tasting something unbearably sweet. At the sight of this aroused expression, or maybe just finding something in his tone, or some actual word picked up before she actually saw him, or maybe nothing she could identify, she halted at the foot of the stairs, feeling left out. (Of what? I don't think so because I know the deal. So where's the surprise?) But the plane hadn't crashed; Janet was flying high and Dad was thrilled just to hear the altogether satisfying music he found Janet's voice. His eyes had vaporized as if he'd been overtaken by that stupefied sensation that overtook the boys when they looked at Kathy and thought what they'd like to do to her. A strange little feeling followed but didn't last and left in its place unease as if she were hearing the ominous music that the doomed character in a horror movie never got to hear and so she was feeling the fear they never got to feel until it was too late, although they would have been filled with terror had they glimpsed their real situation. The creature walking the street. Searching for their door. Finding the open window. Climbing in. As her father caught sight of her he winked in a way that had nothing to do with welcome (God, he hates me), and she smiled back in a way that had nothing to do with recognition, and said, "I don't need to talk to her."

She turned to leave, and he screamed: "Kathy!"

When she looked back, he was smiling and holding his hand up as if the living room wall were about to fall but they'd all survive as long as he was there forcing ruin back.

"Yeh, yeh, fine, okay," he said into the phone. "But are you taking anything for it, because it doesn't sound good. Get some Theraflu or something. Have you been getting enough rest? Theraflu is pretty good we think." His tone was managing to turn worry into adoration and then he paused and listened. When he next went to speak, he floundered, and she wondered what he'd heard. Because something had sent him off to some remote site and held him there and he had to fight somehow to get to say into the phone, "Hey, Heartthrob, wanna talk to Kathy a second? She's right here waiting. Yeh, she's managed it." He spun and Kathy thought he was going to throw the phone at her. But he handed it off with a coy look and then struck the Heisman trophy pose, one leg up as if to stride off forever from all tacklers, arm out to push away the most deter-mined adversary, head elevated and eyes scanning a distant horizon beyond which greatness awaited him.

But what Kathy felt coming off him was like the panic of the driver of an out-of-control car. What had happened? What had gone wrong? The heat of his hand lingered on the plastic phone. His presence crowded her and she turned away. The way his eyes were bright with so many questions reminded her of an animal, and not just any animal but a particular rat that Rick Boltzunger had shot with his pistol. She'd been arguing with Rick, the two of them drunk and fighting all day about whether he loved her enough, because if he did, he would not have spilled bleach on her special blouse. And what was enough in the world of love, anyway, and how would they ever know? And she'd screamed, "I'm not going to do that! I'm not doing it!" and pounded her fist on the table as she told him she wanted to put aside the question of whether she loved him enough or not. Because only the bleach on her blouse had to be dealt with and somehow explained. How could he not know that? But he was sick of trying to live with Madonna, he said. Sick of it, and he was crying and drinking and crying and drink-ing and crying and getting "helplessly" (his word) pissed off, and "heartbrokenly" (another of his words) beyond control, so he felt the only way to prove he loved her was to shoot her and then shoot himself, or maybe just shoot himself, but he could see the relative pointlessness of both those options so he said he was going kill something else every time she made him feel that she did not know him at all, not even a little. Every time she made him feel that she had in fact never ever fucking known anything about him. Okay, she said, whatever. She had her feelings and they were goddamn important to her, and she wasn't going to goddamn stifle them just because of his goddamn threats. That was fine. Fine with him. He didn't want to stifle her. And he knew it wasn't enough that he was sorry about the bleach. Knew it couldn't ever be enough. So that meant that before the day was over there were dead animals—three rats at least, the first being the one she remembered, and a squirrel, a rabbit, a neighborhood cat, even a dog that wandered into their bargaining mayhem.

Her father's shirt was dark with sweat along the top of his belt. The lowest button might pop (maybe she could sew it). He was Mr. Desperation, having jumped in front of her and taken up the pose of a discus thrower, which he'd been in high school. Good God, Dad, she thought, could you send yourself a message. But she smiled (his bitterness was in the room, storm clouds overhead). Still, she turned her back to him as a way into a kind of privacy. She had been talking to Janet, neither saying much, just saying things like, "Yeh, yeh," and "Hi," and "Of course, I'm here," and "What . . . ?" and "Kath . . . ?" and "Where are you?" and "O'Hare!" and "Still?" and "I've been ambushed by democracy or something."

Kathy guessed it was time to focus when her father touched her arm. When she turned, he said, "I know what's happening there, I can tell you."

To Janet she said, "What are you talking about, Janet?"

"I'm trapped here. The airline attendants are threatening a strike. It's a splinter group or something, but—"

"A what?"

"A splinter group. Not the main group, but somebody wants more money. Who doesn't, right?"

"I know all about it," her father said. "Let me talk to her."

"Are you all right?" she said to Janet.

"Sure. Fine, though I'd like to get out of here."

"Kathy. She told me all about it!" His voice shook with his effort to keep from shouting.

Though she might have thought he was simply annoyed, and so what, there was more to it. The way his hands wavered signaled something. What? She didn't know. But they prompted sadness that made no sense and she thought of Rick's word "heartbrokenly" (oh, Rick).

"She told me everything," he said again. "Everything."

"He knows all about all that," said her mother.

Kathy looked from one to the other.

"Pickets and signs all over the place," said Janet. "Anyway, do you have your cell phone, Kathy?"

"What?"

"Where are you? What room?"

"Living room. Why?"

"I want to call you on your cell phone. I want to talk, okay?"

"I don't have one."

"Let me call you, okay? What's your number?"

"I don't have a cell phone. I just said that."

"You don't have a cell phone?"

"No."

"How do you live?"

"I'm suffering certain budgetary constraints."

"I wanted to show you a picture. What about a computer? I could e-mail from a café; there's got to be a café in this—"

"Janet. This is me."

"I know, I know, but everybody—"

"Not everybody."

"I had this picture I was hoping to show you. I have this new Verizon LG. I can browse the Web, take pictures, send e-mail, send pictures. It's incredible. Games. You should think about it when you get ready to buy."

"Okay. I'm starting right now. Thinking about it."

"I really wanted you to see this picture."

"Listen, I know somebody who has a picture phone and I might see her later. I guess I'll go out, since you're going to be late—"

"Where are you going?"

Before she could answer, her mother was after her: "What do you mean you're going out? You're not going out. Where are you going?"

"Please," said her father, and he swooped in, encompassing both her hand and much of the phone in his sizable grasp.

"Dad wants the phone," she said. "Janet!" She felt like she was warning her sister.

"So you call me if you hook up with that friend, okay?" yelled Janet.

Even though it was obvious she intended to give him the phone and was just trying to avoid dropping it or hitting the wrong button, he snatched it as if she were resisting. The flash of his eyes declared he was sick of her trying to frustrate him. He wanted to leave no doubt regarding the ongoing trouble between them.

Through the window she could see moonlight moving in a mist above the snow. She saw crevices and stains, the lid of a tin can rusting in the yard. She turned, intending to meet her father's anger, her mother's worry, but he was busy with the phone, while her mother appeared vacant, just totally glazed over. She laughed, because the three of them disappeared this way one after the other, each in their own way. Her mother might have just inhaled some weed, for she seemed both befuddled and tolerant of the perplexing world around her.

"I didn't like the sound of that cough she had, Mom. Did you?"

"Hmmmmmmmmmm?"

"The way she was coughing."

"Oh I know. It was hard to hear half of what she said."

"I said something to her about it, but she didn't answer."

"What'd you say?"

"I asked her if she had a cold."

"And she didn't answer?"

"No. She just kept talking about something else. The plane business, I think. And that's when Dad started yelling about wanting the phone and so I don't really—"

"I didn't yell." His tone was more fed up than pissed off, letting them know that as far as he was concerned he was making his one thousandth unnecessary correction of the day. He was off the phone, having hung up while she wasn't watching.

"You know what I mean," she said and shrugged.

"Actually, I don't. Unless you mean you were exaggerating."

"I was just talking."

"No you weren't."

"I was too."

"Well, I don't think so. It's a common practice for people when they're in fact talking in order to describe something that happened that they in fact want to get across their idea of what happened. That's what they're trying to do. To be sharp, be clear. To communicate. And so it's a common practice in these circumstances to at least attempt to be accurate."

"I think you're right."

"And so if I wasn't yelling and we both know it, why say it?"

"You know, I guess I don't know why."

"I'll tell you, okay? Because I think I have a pretty good idea. One that I'm going to guarantee has very little exaggeration in it. In fact I think I'm going to look it over and make sure to remove every bit of exaggeration before I say it. I think you were hoping to push my buttons. One of my buttons. Because somehow that amuses you."

Kathy smiled in a mirthless way, feeling full of mockery and surrender in a clumsy mix. With a suddenness that asked for confrontation, she headed up the stairs. Her mother, seeing the darkening clouds, called out, "Supper will be ready in just a few more minutes." It was her version of household sorcery, an incantation of normality and habit, so that the three of them could sink into the cloudy comforts of pretending and avoiding.

"Okay, Mom," Kathy called back, happy to appear spellbound while running for her life, even though there was really nowhere to go. Still the stairs appeared to lead somewhere. But then the second floor arrived with her still in the house. The roof hemmed her in, and marching past the family bookcase at the top of the stairs, something grabbed at her so she stopped and said, "What?"

A series of lace doilies decorated the top. Two sets of bronzed baby shoes balanced the glow on either side of a miniature hurricane lamp. The shelves were filled with books. The majority were her father's, but many were Janet's. A hundred at most, but to her they felt like thousands. Many were slender and longish; others had a squat, belligerent quality, like fat little bullies. She'd dropped out of high school and hadn't gone back or gotten her GED. Hooked up to and totally deranged by Rick Boltzunger and his harebrained ideas she'd wandered off imagining she'd arrive at something she could not even remember having a name for. Probably just him. More of him, after the first taste she had when his fingers closed on her legs under the river as she waded a short distance from shore with the sun like lightning the gleam so bright and blinding and she heard this splash and looked and saw the spray and ripples as his fingers grabbed her right up on her thighs. (Bestiality, for real this time.) Lifted and hurled, she sailed sideways into the deeper water, where he followed, his hands all over her.

All she knew of the college her sister was going to was that it was in the East and fancy. The opportunity had come for a scholarship because of a meddlesome high school teacher, Mrs. Macabee, who'd had no time for Kathy but had hatched a dream for Janet, yammering at her and her parents with phone calls and visits, seeing to the whole application process, because for bullshit reasons it had become her mission in life to see that

Janet had a chance to "maximize her potential." In the brochures her parents left lying around, Kathy found photographs of the place and there were actual ivy-covered stone walls around the campus. Something in these pictures made her think of mists and black umbrellas and calm, boring moods and she didn't know why until she remembered the school in that Robin Williams movie where he was this weird, gloppy teacher trying to help everybody. It was an old movie and Kathy'd seen it late one night sitting up alone while Rick was out somewhere and when she saw the photographs of Janet's school it came right back. She'd had a terrible fight with Rick that night. But when hadn't they been fighting? So they were screaming at each other probably all the while Mrs. Macabee was tutoring Janet in SATs and ACTs, and gathering her grades and "stellar" (her father's word) papers, and writing "exultant" (her father's word) letters of recommendation. The struggle to figure out the major points of what was going on in her marriage had lasted a long time. Like whether she was right or Rick was right? Which of them was nuts, because she felt nuts? One of them had to be the fucking victim didn't they? By the time she woke up to the idea of bullshit everywhere and the alarm bell so loud she couldn't stand it, by the time she asked for a divorce and started divorce proceedings and then arrived to knock on her parents' door, scared shitless that Rick would screech up at any instant, and scared just as shitless that Mom and Dad weren't home or that seeing her they would bar the door, Janet was in her dorm out east. Kathy tried to catch up on what there was to know, but the phone calls she and Janet managed were short and awkward. She filled in the gaps by daydreaming over the brochures and picturing Robin Williams giving Janet advice the way he had those kids in *The Dead Poets Society*. That was it. A weird name that Kathy liked because it sounded spooky and creepy and scary, and she liked to think of Janet in the company of such a weird character determined to help her, to teach her, to offer her escape. Pacing over slight plateaus of grass, while thinking over complicated matters, while conversing with himself inside his own thoughts, or aloud with a companion, this Robin-Williams-man seemed to make everything peaceful, just as Robin Williams himself had been made peaceful by the movie. They strolled around the grass lawns and athletic fields and library aisles, a horde of just such Robin-Williams-men, their heads tilted in thoughtful examination of their pipe smoke as they advised Kathy. In spite of cell phones ringing and TVs blaring and computers flashing, they appeared to have a certain satisfying music piped into their heads (in the same way that there were scores in movies so you couldn't help but feel certain feelings), which, though faint, was uplifting.

She smiled and lit a cigarette and lay down upon the bed with her wrists crossed over her brow. Madonna kept changing her hair, her clothes, and her body even. She kept acting like she could change what it was to be Madonna. Like even she didn't really understand the true value in it all, and so she threw it away. Like she didn't care if she was losing what mattered; she was just doing it in order to keep going as whatever it was that kept going. But Kathy felt she knew what mattered, what had to be preserved and she would do it for Madonna, now that Madonna seemed to have lost track. In that *Vanity Fair* interview Madonna explained that all her changing around had something to do with daring and challenging everybody all the time. Or was that the television interview? She'd said that she liked to provoke people because it was good for people to be provoked, and if things got dangerous, well, then that was just what happened and she just didn't think about the consequences. If she wanted to change she did. Whatever. That was her attitude and you had to admire it even though it made it hard for Kathy to persevere in what she believed in. She remembered reading that Madonna had had trouble with her father, and she wondered if maybe that was really why she kept changing. When he got close, she'd just change. Poof. Gone. Where'd she go? Certainly, there'd been a degree of mystery gained with her own father. She'd been experimenting with dressing up like Madonna, just following a whim, a carefree impulse for maybe the second time, when he walked in on her, and the way he froze for several unforgettable, bewildered seconds jolted her with satisfaction. He apologized and wheeled away as if she were a blazing light. The next time she tried it they argued. He mocked her, told her she looked ridiculous, but she hung on to that first image, the one in which he looked helpless, his confounded assumptions bared. That was the discomfort he was trying to avoid, that sense of dismayed irrelevance. It was something new, and the taste was addictive and she could not help but try to see how far she could push it. In the *Vanity Fair* article Madonna said her relationship with her father was difficult. He liked her when she was vulnerable. When she needed help. Men, Kathy thought, planning on filing through all she knew about Madonna's father, but instead she bounced past him, expecting her own father until she slammed into Rick, looking like he always did, surly and hot. The feeling of wanting another chance raced through her, leaving her flushed. Just to go back. Find the innocent good Rick. The loving, sexy Rick, who still had to be somewhere wanting only her. When they'd first married, she put Madonna away, but toward the end the masquerade resurfaced with a dizzying claim. Rick, she thought. And then it was not her own life unfolding but the life of Madonna, and it was Madonna who had married Rick. Blonde and fanatical and tough, Madonna looked backward into her life that long ago exploded, leaving wreckage all over the place the way dumped trash spills blood and torn clothes and underwear and used tampons and bottles, some of them broken, all of them empty, beer, whiskey, broken glass flying and twirling, even sprinkling the table and dishes, all shimmering in the air. All Madonna, all pieces of Madonna. She started laughing mostly in her mind and almost without a sound just thinking about Madonna in her life, in her town, in Belger, Iowa, in a tavern here or there, the one on Elm, Parkers on Elm, and wouldn't that pathetic bunch be surprised when she walked in. Or out by the river past the lumberyard, that turnaround where cars parked at night under the big trees and the sound of the river could be heard, and the tits emerging from the bra Rick unsnapped were Madonna's tits, and Rick was amazed and ravenous and grateful to have Madonna's tits in his hands, so deranged to have Madonna's nipples in his mouth that all the coming screaming and yearning and bitter grief, all the coming strife never happened. No dingy kitchen with dirty windows and a splintered door and Rick turned into this thug with his gym bag and NFL Troy Aikman (whom he didn't resemble at all, though he did look a little like Sean Penn) jersey, cursing her and walking out the door.

Her mother was calling and she rose and went to the stairs in a daze half expecting to find Rick at their kitchen table, and Madonna, too, waiting to step into his arms.

The table was overly prepared, like who the hell did her mother think was coming. Viewed in profile, her father appeared relaxed with his chin resting on the top edge of the door as he peered into the white interior. At one end of the table lay a crystal plate of radishes, chunks of celery, several scallions. The effort all this detail and order must have taken was fucking insane. Diced carrots had their own bowl. Pepper speckled the mashed potatoes, a curl of butter melting at the center. Good God. Beef was carved in four steaming hunks. Her mother hovered, coffeepot in hand. "Anybody want coffee now, or everybody for it later?" She smiled with the charm of another homey incantation and Kathy felt that the hex her mother had been put under long ago was immutable and contagious so that perhaps Kathy was only imagining she could escape from its grasp.

"Later," her father said. He hauled a portion of beef onto his plate and passed the platter to Kathy, who smiled. Then for no reason she knew she sat staring at him. She discovered herself in the midst of doing it, and for an instant he was just as fixed on her, and neither could pull away from the weirdness jumping back and forth between them. It was like she had come upon him naked or sobbing until he said, "God," and "Molly," to his wife who, unaware that another of her spells was needed, was spooning potatoes and carrots to her plate.

"What?" she said.

"Never you mind," he told her, his shoulders and neck straining with the force it took for him to break free and refuse further acknowledgment of Kathy, no matter how slight. The instant was very confusing and yet as she turned to her food something previously unclear stood revealed. Out of this bizarre little exchange flew the secret behind the mood that had harassed her all evening. She'd known she wanted out of the house, but she had not understood the importance of fleeing before Janet arrived. In fact that was the whole idea. That was the alarm, and the humming demand. She wanted no part in this phony, bullshit homecoming. Waiting around as if no end could be found for any of them to all the sacrifices they would make just to participate in some fawning reception. All these months she'd been imagining herself relieved that Janet's life was going well. She'd felt grateful that at least there was that for her parents. She'd been aware of nothing jealous or envious or even remotely like the animosity rising now against this "little sister." Brilliant Janet, eager Janet, confident Janet, successful Janet, arrogant Janet, brainy Janet. She would just have to make her return without Kathy to kiss her ass.

"It was one of the damnedest things I ever saw," her father said.

"What was?" her mother said.

"A thing that happened at work today."

"What?"

"This man, this stranger who stood at the counter watching me work."

Blah, blah, blah, thought Kathy. Blah, blah, blah, fucking blah.

2

BARELY AWARE OF WHERE SHE WAS, she fiddled with the radio and sent the car over the ice and rutted dirty snow. The heater was acting half-assed so she was shivering even though her racing thoughts had her boiling: What in the name of sweet Christ did people think they were doing, standing there like that, the three of them, stupid, mindless, beating each other into boredom about whether she could or should leave when right through it all they all knew the deal and could have said it? She was going out the door. Where? Why? How? For a ride? In the snow? Was she crazy? And no boots. Look at her. Her bare damn feet almost. What was wrong with her? And Janet might get there at any second, or at least might call again. Didn't she care? Oh, stay, oh, stay.

Ahead the skyline was splattered with a haze of colored light, as if burning rags had been tossed up and they floated somehow. The glow was a quivering bowl upside down in the night above the shingled roof of her destination, the Golden Squire, a dance club at the edge of town. On Friday and Saturday nights the place shook with a thousand or more jumping dancing shouting sweating bodies. Boys and girls looking for the moment. Friday nights it was teenagers, at least that was the purpose, although some who wanted to get their hands on something younger were always working the floor, even though no liquor was served. Still, liquor was there. Saturday was a mob of legal drinkers and the teenagers with false ID. Bouncers were on patrol because whatever the night there were fights. Some stood around the floor, their big arms folded, while others roamed the hubbub of dancers. Their fists loved faces breaking under force. It was there in their eyes, this thick-lipped pleasure coming off them in the mix of their cologne and sweat as they swaggered back from the parking lot where some poor drunk had just been slammed into the grille of a car.

Kathy veered off the highway onto the uneven gravel, the dips of mud and snow. She parked hurriedly. She was already far gone in the fantasy of the dance floor where the melee of body parts and noise would swallow her. Shutting off the ignition and struggling to change clothes, she was already floating from table to table, bodies everywhere. Excitement held her as she clambered from the car and hurried to pay her entrance fee. Inside the booth sat a hard glare of a man, his sneer suggesting pool halls, all-night poker games. His hair was black, his shirt and jacket white, his tie black. The muscles of his mouth smiled at her, and he pressed the two fives she had given him flat on the counter with the edge of his hand while his eyes moved over her. "It ain't Halloween, you know," he said.

"I don't know, maybe it is," she said. "You look pretty creepy."

"That's a costume, right? Whatshername?"

"Right again," she said and turned away.

"We have those singer-impersonator nights," he called after her. "You should come back."

"Fuck you."

"I get off at midnight!"

"You should check yourself into a mental ward."

"I done that. They got fed up with me."

"Well, try again."

"You know what, bitch," he said, almost snarling suddenly, and he stood up and took a step like he might pursue her. "I ain't your bitch. Check your downloads, bitch."

She was having fun already. The figure she cut in her Madonna outfit worked like a spotlight. People would have to wake up to the mystery. This big bright light singling her out, and then they thought what they thought.

EARLY MADONNA   **59**

The evening's events were posted on the wall in cartoonlike splashes of color. Three boxing matches first and then the Whatevers, a live rock 'n' roll band. Through the doorway ahead figures were visible moving in swells of light and color. She went in, her hand angled at the floor like a coded sign, as if she were entering a cult. A gnomic old man in a green shirt and weird bow tie and dark gothic makeup grinned in a way that left him looking unhappy and lopsided as he popped an ink insignia on her hand. "Hey," he said. "I remember you."

She nodded, shrugged, smiled, went on.

"Where was it?"

With her back to him now, she exaggerated the slide of her hips and waded into the pressure and smell of people, smoke, and beer. Through massed heads and shoulders in front of her, she caught glimpses of two boxers flashing about in the ring. Beyond it four teenagers in red pegged pants, identical red, spangled jackets, and bow ties wandered about the elevated bandstand. Their instruments, twin guitars, an elaborate set of drums, and a keyboard, spangled.

As a bell rang ending the round, she turned and dove down a lane of tables. She hopped an outstretched trousered leg and headed to the bar for a beer and then on to the stairway. Reaching the second floor, which was a kind of track ringing the building, she wiggled her way through elbows and hips to the rail. The dance floor was a stew of people and clothing moving around the glare of the canvas floor of the boxing ring ablaze with floodlights. A stocky redheaded boy shifted and changed directions in front of a large black man in golden trunks who prowled, stalking and firing right-hand punches so fast they seemed invisible. His fists dropped from his height like clubs that grazed and frightened but never solidly struck. He was sinewy and lithe (and could beat the crap out of Rick any day of the week [Oh, poor Rick], leaving him a bloody mess in need of help just as he needed a beating, and she might come upon him, she might find him). The agility of the black fighter's movement drew her along, parting her lips, her hands, loose on the rail. The red-haired boxer kept sticking his left hand out like a pole to strike the black in the face or chest just often and hard enough to stall the murderous violence he was working to deliver. She had a sense of him fighting for his life on these bad-assed streets with hip-hop blasting out of ghetto blasters so he learned to fight without rules and to the death. But the red-haired boxer kept disturbing his plans, messing up his rhythm so that he could not turn his idea into the bloodshed he hungered for. And then the bell rang, the fight was over, and a balding bulb-shaped man shouted a name and the red-haired boxer pranced about while the black man's chest sagged. He shook his head. As she booed, she swore he laughed, bitterly. She stomped her feet and, turning her back on all of them, was surprised to find Annie Boyle standing there speaking to her over the noise: "The things you see when you don't have a gun."

"Did you see that bullshit?" She slapped out at something in the air. The momentum forced her sideways until she was gazing at the bandstand again. She gulped her beer, head rearing back so that the girders of the ceiling filled her view. "I need some music. I need to move."

"You liked that black bastard, huh?"

"I think I did." She wanted to sound defiant yet casual.

"He was hot."

"Is that what you think?"

"I guess I must since it sounded to me like I just said so."

"Graceful, too."

"In a way."

"Dangerous. Scary."

"Big."

"Yeh. Tall."

"Yeh." Annie nodded, pondering their exchange as if to savor its significance, but then she stepped forward and dumped an ashtray over the rail. They looked down at the debris floating through the artificial light onto the heads and shoulders of people who failed to notice.

In seconds, they were going down the stairs. The swollen heaving crowd that lay ahead broke into pieces of color and anatomy bobbing like apples in water enclosing her with Annie Boyle at her side, the perfect buddy, twice married, twice divorced.

"Ten minutes," Kathy said. "If I'm down there without somebody grabbing me I'll get out on that floor and attack some poor doofus."

With an expression of fake worry, Annie took care of the problem by seizing Kathy's hand and leading her onto the dance floor where they whirled and spun and shook and embraced until both were panting, their limbs slick with sweat. Together they came to rest at the bar where they'd gone for a beer and to catch their breath. Annie was working some guy who'd made a remark as they walked up, while Kathy studied the way Annie's makeup intensified the harsh, startling lines of her eyes. Her purple skirt was short, and she wore a fishnet tank top over a T-shirt so tight her nipples were like little lightbulbs and the guy kept squinting at them like they might just blink on and off at any second. She shifted as she talked, leaning into the guy in this idle way, then leaning out, taking her weight from hip to hip and maintaining the same skating, predatory grace that styled her walk. Somehow she offered up these little hints of nasty pleasure, skin clawed open, a ready appetite for whatever. Her gaze could play and replay this promo of a carnival ride dangerous and not exactly fun, maybe even nuts but worth a try.

Kathy turned away. How long was she supposed to stand there waiting? It looked like her power to amuse Annie was short-term and the channel had been changed now that Annie had hopped on to this boy, and so Kathy was forgotten (it wasn't the first time and wouldn't be the last). Shouldering her way through the crowd she eyed the bartender as if he might be her new best friend and said, "Gimme a Rolling Rock."

The bar stood in the midst of a small settlement of tables beneath a lower section of the balcony with bodies crammed like heavy underbrush. She narrowed her gaze to the beer sliding across the counter. There was her face caught and crooked in a kind of cartoon of her future in the sheen on the surface and she was no longer Madonna but simply some faded Annie Boyle living out another kind of Annie Boyle dingy life: bad marriage, then some hate, little bitterness, second marriage (why not?), a try at crazy, maybe even suicide (maybe real, maybe not). Then what? Who cared? (What a recipe!) When she turned and found Annie leaning close to her, creating intimacy between them with some of the same devices at play she'd used on the guy who had now totally disappeared, Kathy grinned and said, "You are so full of shit."

"Is that right?"

"It's just a notion."

"I got to end this inner argument, okay, and just air the question, okay. Now pay some goddamn attention, because your fashion sense has gone demented, Kathy. What maybe should have been a whim has traveled beyond interesting or retro or whatever. I thought you were headed for way cool, okay, and yet look at you."

"Could you take a breath?"

"And then what? Let you go on like this?"

"Could people maybe relax about my choices?"

"These are choices made freely, of your own free will?"

"They're my clothes. Okay?"

"But they're not your clothes. They're someone else's."

"People do not need to get into such a shit storm about it. I'm just doing what I believe in. I'm not asking anybody else to do it. Could they maybe just ignore it. You know, just think about themselves."

"But people take notice. They have to take notice. Even that guy back there who thought he might lock things up with me given time. He said it. You look like old Madonna."

"It's a statement."

"What do you mean?"

"It's my statement."

"About what?"

"Look. Something that was incredible when I first saw it, and has been forgotten. Well not by me. I have not forgotten."

"Yeh, but for the rest of us, you should forget it. There are some of us who care for you, and from where we're standing it's like you've fallen under some mind-control cult thing."

"I'm making a point about my personal beliefs. Why can't I have personal beliefs?"

"Nobody's talking about your personal beliefs!"

"Where is that guy?"

"Who?"

"The one who said it about me."

Annie shrugged in a way that conveyed in rapid succession disinterest in the guy followed by authentic and then mock dismay at Kathy's stance and aims. "He's just this idiot."

Kathy wrinkled her nose and stuck her tongue out as a form of goofy retort before searching for the guy, trying to remember what he looked like, rising up on her toes and scanning. "Where is he? Where'd he go?"

"I don't think he meant what he said as a plus."

"Where'd he go? I don't see him."

"Listen. I don't know where he went. Could you stop? He gave me an idea that guy. I mean, having to endure him."

"I guess he's gone." Kathy drank the last of her beer. "Do you know what they got lined up for me?"

"Who?"

"My parents."

"Why are we talking about them?"

"I don't know."

"Spare me, okay." Annie's smirk turned Kathy's parents into idiots who could do no better than chatter in some completely irrelevant way on any subject and Kathy laughed, pleased to see them in this light (at last).

Annie turned and began to walk. Kathy followed along. A pair of plaid shirts parted to let them pass.

"It's counseling," she said. "They got meetings set for me with Father Roosevelt. And I'm not talking about confession, I'm talking about counseling."

"You know what I was thinking. I'd like to punk some guy. You know like on that Ashton Kutcher show. Really embarrass some jerk."

"Sure."

"You ever watch it?"

"Sure."

"It's gotta be nasty, though. We gotta come up with something deep and nasty. Or like Girls Behaving Badly. Really make a fool out of some guy."

"Okay. How do we do it?"

"And another thing, I'm bored. Let's do something. We got to make things happen. That's who we want to be. Those kind of people."

"Okay."

"Right. Except don't say okay."

"Why?"

"Just listen to me. You know I saw this thing on TV about the sixties and if something was really a good idea and one person said it and another person heard it, the person who heard it would say, 'Right on. Right on.'"

"Okay. Sure."

"You didn't know that? Or did you?"

"When was this?"

"Blacks in particular. It was this movie. It was cool. So what I'm thinking is I'd like to come up with something along those lines but better. So we would say, 'Wild on,' instead. Same deal except not 'Right on,' but 'Wild on.' Not to try to bring back the old and boring but give it new life."

"Wild on."

"Right. That's what we'd say."

"No, no, I'm doing it. I'm saying it. I like your idea so I'm doing it. I'm saying, 'Wild on.'"

"Right. We could start a trend."

"Wild on."

"Wild on."

They had snagged a table and were sitting and a man, his bald head blistered with sweat, was dragging himself on his hands and knees past them, barking like a dog, growling, and occasionally snapping at a woman's leg. His butt was so skinny he looked like nothing but bones under his trousers. "Anyway, my parents are stressing to the max that Father Roosevelt might lay some heavy shit on me, that I'm this scandal to the church and so Father—"

"Oh who cares what they do. They can say what they want, sure, make their threats, who can stop them. But the question is, can they do anything? In reality, I mean. Tell you that you can't go to Communion or whatever? Just go to some other parish. How are they going to know? Tell me that. Whatever. Just watch out for the priests, though." Annie was frowning into the eyes of absent but well-known enemies. "Tell him to do some penance. Tell him to light some candles for his own sad self."

"I'm supposed to sit with him and explain what happened and how I'm sorry."

The air seemed filled with flying things, squares of color, people shouting, a thousand pieces of noise and vibration. Annie, though near, felt far away in the fluctuating light as she said, "I saw Rick the other day. He was in Marcia Tomkins' car and he was driving."

"No, no. My Rick?"

"Yeh. At the mall. Or coming out of the parking lot anyway, but I had the sense they'd been to the Cineplex."

"It couldn't have been. He's gone. He's gone to Denver."

"Denver? You mean, like *Denver*?"

"Yeh. He's gone. Colorado." (If only he wasn't.) The thought that he might be near ignited an elemental desire to see him, a perfect optimism untroubled by the past in every way. If only he walked in now, she would go to him and they would start over. She could see it, feel it all, an invitation, and she trailed off into it. Soon she caught herself emerging from a deep and coded realm, the subject, context, tone, everything receding as if, briefly, she had been implanted with this futuristic alternative person and they were stealing away now, this other someone she'd just been, and all she had to go by in the aftermath was Dad, Dad. You say it but that's not it. But I just . . . wish you could . . . why can't you? It was like wind taking her thoughts off, leaving her to watch them lose their shape. Huh? she thought. "What was that?"

"What?" Annie looked at her and eyes narrowing, turned away. "What was what?"

Kathy shrugged, remembering how she had believed for a time that her mother's moods with their startling onsets and stark content were a matter of ghosts.

"My mom sometimes lays in bed and doesn't move for hours and hours."

"What?"

They were in the bathroom now, fussing with makeup on faces floating around smudges in the mirror.

"I mean not so much now, but she used to and I remember once I thought she was dead."

"But she wasn't."

"No, silly. I came in and started talking to her and she didn't respond in any way, so I went over and touched her and she was cold. She looked gray and I picked her hand up and it fell down."

"Was she trashed?"

"No. I don't think so. I started talking to her and everything I said seemed stupid to me, though she didn't seem to mind, but I did, and there was this story. One from school. So I started saying it to her just to keep talking, you know—one of those fairy tales from way back. So I finished that up and she still didn't say anything. I was like dazed and went down to the kitchen and opened a can of tomato soup and heated it up and ate it and went back up and she still hadn't moved. I called my dad at work and he said she was fine. He said not to worry and go watch television. I didn't believe him. But I had no idea what was wrong or what to do to fix it and so I was glad to be told to just go away. I remember I watched this rerun of a *Cheers* episode in which Frasier was pompous and got dissed and I don't think he even knew it, and then some MTV."

"Sounds like she was trashed."

"Another time I came home from school and she wasn't there, but her footprints were. And they went out the back door and off into that little patch of trees behind Kamber's house, the ones catty-corner from us, you know. I followed them in the snow and she was there sitting in the snow."

The guitars at their beginning had been shrill and violent, but now they soothed. Not quite certain how or when she had moved and not really caring, she was at the bar with the effects of beer after beer changing things around inside her. She imagined the music and drumming as physical shapes like distinct actual forms of things or animals. The guy on her left was leaning on the bar and he slid toward her until he pressed against her, as if they were old conspirators. "Hey, man," he whispered, "you still want to go outside to my car?"

She tried to remember if she'd said anything to him about anything at all and found no convincing evidence either way and so she said, "Go to the big city. You're way urban, man."

He laughed and edged his mouth toward her cheek, but she evaded, feeling like that red-haired boxer as she came up drinking until he snatched the bottle from her hand.

He was dark and tall as they danced. His body had a solid confidence against her that made her think of the way that black guy boxed. "Did you see that fight?" she asked.

"What a load of bullshit."

"What?"

"That black guy."

"What was wrong with—?"

"Walk, walk, walk, then swing. Like some goddamn Munster Frankenstein machine. Walk, walk. Swing. He was bullshit. I could make him my bitch."

She gazed up, trying to evaluate what he'd said, because she really didn't know anything about boxing.

"Where you from?" He floated his palm up her arm, working his fingers under her sleeve to her shoulder. "I'd rather make you my bitch."

"What?" She wished she wasn't so small. His foot poked between her ankles. "Could you try to be a little less boring?" she said.

He laughed and tightened against her, tilting. She exaggerated her loss of balance, pulling at him, and then, as if trying to stay upright, slammed her heel against his instep until his face winced out of shape. He sort of threw her. Falling toward a thicket of legs, she expected to be scolded or maybe slapped. But his hands around her waist saved her. His voice clowned; he was happy, though she spied a puzzled notion speeding amid his thoughts.

"Man, one of us is drunk," he said.

"I think maybe I did that on purpose."

"Me, too. So where is it you're from? If I'm too urban."

"Didn't we do this part?"

"I don't think so, man. Not completely."

"But we started. I didn't say too urban, anyway."

"I gotta tell you. Your outfit is like from another time zone, man. You must know it. You do know it, right. I don't know much, but I do know that much, man."

"Wake up to the mystery."

"Okay. But did you do it on purpose? You had to do it on purpose. It's somebody, right. Who the hell are you dressed up like?"

"If only I knew what you were getting at."

It wasn't long before she felt unreal. Somehow they danced to the bar, grabbed beers, and danced back. Then the globe receding above her was his face in a haze that seemed a side effect of the music. "Where the hell are you from anyway?" she hissed, mysteriously angry. "A farm. You a farmer?"

Indignation rippled from his chest to hers. "A farm? Is that what you said?"

"Because—excuse me, but there's an odor."

Now he wasn't so much smiling as trying to smile. "It's like satellite TV," he said. "Everything's there, man. Old movies. All the actors are dead. New movies. Seventies, eighties, man. Baseball games from fifty years back. Boxing from a week ago and ten years ago. Movies. Football games. Cartoons. You name it. There's no set time on satellite TV. And you—you're like that. The way you're dressed. Too much satellite TV, man."

She flicked her eyes sideways but saw only his ear and then a boy she wanted to dance with passing so close her reaching fingers touched his elbow. A cell phone rang with a stupid tune and several people reached to respond, but it belonged to the boy she'd yearned for seconds ago, and when he started speaking this icy almost reptilian look came into his eyes as his lips wrestled with his words like they were vile.

"Just by dancing with a guy, I can tell where he's from and I'm never wrong," she said to the one holding her. She was getting ready, feeling everything getting very, very of the moment. I'm going to punk you good, she thought, and to puzzle him she spurted laughter and said, "Wild on."

"What?"

"No matter where he's from. Sometimes . . ." She faltered, advising herself to prepare the ground. "Oh, hey, I like you. I didn't at first and so I was whatever, but I do now."

"It had to happen, man."

"Happens all the time, I bet."

"Sure." His hands locked and squeezed in the small of her back.

"Like this once I was dancing with a guy. And I kept thinking, Greenland, this guy's from Greenland. So I finally said it.

You're from Greenland. And he wasn't, of course, but he said he'd love to go there."

He was mildly confused but not at all concerned.

"I'm a divorcée," she said. "What about you?"

"I'm from Greenland."

"You been punked."

"Whatayou mean?"

"You been punked. Big time."

"By you. Oh, I don't think so," he said.

"Well, you have. Oh, yeh. Oh, yeh."

"I don't think so."

"Think back."

"About what? How?"

"Like on this show where Ashton Kutcher and his friends go around and they—"

"I know the show. But I ain't been punked. Tell me how!"

"By this whole thing, you idiot."

"What whole thing? This Greenland—"

"Not just that. All of it, by all of—"

"I ain't been punked. At least not by you."

"I'm telling you, you have."

"I don't care what you tell me!"

"Oh, you're not worth the bother."

"Maybe, maybe not!"

The snow-silver hills appeared to emit the moonlight. Shadow sharpened the crests and blackened the wedges between. She was leaning and remembering how hard that guy ended up laughing and the way he made no effort to keep her from stomping away. She was not drunk, but she was out of control. She'd left the building to seek a remedy in the icy outdoor air. Now she stood with her elbows on the rail, wondering about her parents and how she could hide the fact that she was trashed when she got home (how could it be that one little girl with the same Mommy and the same Daddy was one way and the other so different, that the older and bigger was the baby, that the one who arrived first got ignored, that the one with the head start was left behind) and what would happen when they found out?

Kathy shuddered in the cold (it was never enough, whatever she did, whatever she was). She needed to find her coat wherever she had left it, and then to come back out to find her car and drive carefully to the nearest diner for some breakfast and black black black black coffee.

Above the rounded hills and below the muddy clouds sailed the trembling red specks of an airplane. She couldn't help but think that Janet was inside (so there was still time for it to crash, still time for Janet to plummet and set even the snow on fire). She heard the reverberation of the engine and watched it gliding above the city lights, feeling bile at the back of her throat (because she was a shit, a dirty little shit), and though she did not want to vomit, she couldn't keep from it, slamming her fists at the wood of the rail, hearing the splatter, as some door opened, and the music came out in notes that seemed as hard and exact as the water splashing against her cheek from icicles in the eaves. The night was cold enough to keep her shivering even though sweat bubbled from her brow. She licked the water from her lips.

"Hi, Rick," she said into the phone having discovered it in her hand, so she could talk to her guy in Colorado (because that's what he was: he was her guy). "How you doin'? It's me, hon. Your ex. Listen, I didn't interrupt you at anything, did I? How are tricks out there in Denver by the way? Can you say? Lotsa cowgirls? I bet you roll your own and wear a ten-gallon rubber."

"Shut up," he said. And then away from the phone, it sounded like he muttered, "It's beer, or bear . . ."

He had to come back; he had to return and talk to her, just talk on and on the way they could. She felt irresistible and really capable, and if he came home late it would be okay, or if he got drunk and mean she'd know to see through it to the mess behind it, the way he'd been kicked around by his asshole father and run out on by everybody—everybody—and she would be strong, she felt suddenly, made strong by love and its capacity to take what he did and return it transformed, so that he could not help but reach out to her because she had not run out. "Rick," she said.

"What? What do you want? Do you want something?"

"Listen, honestly. Mom and Dad send their love, and everybody here asks about you. Annie. You remember Annie. She thought she saw you. But mainly me. I'm talking about me, mainly." And then she took a breath, and he did the same, but the way he dragged his in was almost this growl, like he'd interrupted her. It was too loud and felt rude and the rudeness was a warning, and she surprised herself when she said, "And you been punked. You been punked!"

"What?"

"You heard me. Now lemme say hello to her, okay. Your little bunkmate, I mean, whoever she may be out there in—"

"You're buried," he said. "Don't you know that? There's a marker on the grave and all the flowers are dead."

"Wake up to the mystery," she told him.

Then a woman was somehow on the phone saying, "Hi, y'all," followed by a dry electrical humming of a hangup.

To be suddenly jolted as though down from cushions to gravel and find herself face-to-face with the silver grille of an automobile startled her. She felt fractured and vowed to get some goddamn order into her life. But the present was completely a mess, especially with her sagging toward what looked like a fender while he came prancing through the haze toward her. No, no, she warned him and, seeking to escape, tried getting her unbelievably heavy body up, but couldn't. Hey, help me, will you? she called to anyone who might be around and while waiting thought she heard someone far off scream. Then he came swaggering back and near enough to ask her what was the matter. So she told him her feet were cold and she'd lost her jacket and she was so damn heavy she couldn't stand up; but he disagreed, not thinking she was heavy at all because he could lift her with his finger if he fit it in her just right and lifted her up into his car, because that was where there was a bottle of gin in his glove compartment. Well, that was fine, but as far as she could see, it was too bad it was in there because how could *they* ever fit?

No, no, no, he said, moving nearer as she tried to turn away, becoming oddly preoccupied with whether she was thinking or saying, Oh, c'mon, I mean, it's very cold and late and anyway, I'm confused. I'm all mixed up (and missing, I'm a missing person, you know), just gone (the way Madonna was when Sean left, the love of her life, and that's how I am too, ever since I disappeared and no one noticed), and that's the mix-up. (No one noticed I was missing.) Like sex and me (that's a mix-up). My sexuality, I mean. You know? Actually I'm mixed up about everybody's sexuality if I get right down to it. In fact everything about everybody's sexuality has led me to wonder and I mean to the max (because as I stood waiting with all my ideas to teach the baby who took over the world with a cry, with one little look, and no one noticed, not even me at first.) Listen, I'm immune to all that. No matter where you touch me. At the moment, I mean. I mean—what? Don't WHAT? I'm just here, that's all, it's you that's—.

Light exploded into walls on either side of her and she staggered, wondering, Did he hit me? (Well, I'll just play it like the red-haired boxer.) And then she went sprawling to the gravel. He was over her shouting or counting or something and then running off, waving keys at her. The roar of his departure frightened her and she scampered behind the nearest car. She hid there, until a little later, having changed from afraid to angered, she ventured out and revenged herself on him by showing what a total asshole dimwit dweeb he was by performing satirical impressions of his dancing and conversation for the two or was it three people who paused to watch her in the headlights of cars moving through the parking lot.

3

WITH ALL THE WORLD UNHINGED and treacherous, she woke up in her car. She needed coffee and found some at a Burger King. She sat in a corner booth and drank several pots and took the Advil she'd begged a server to give her. When she stood to leave, her legs, for all their familiarity, felt capable of dissolving and dumping her onto the floor. Her belt was frayed as if slashed with a knife. Her hot eyes begged to be allowed to close. But she refused and sitting in her car drank more coffee, before going back inside to pee.

The first strokes of morning lay buried above her. Clouds and vague shadows were packed in layers that felt impenetrable and plastic. She drove home carefully under the spill of streetlights and oncoming headlights, passing her parents' home and parking down the street. She approached like a burglar, stepping on patches of ice when she could to avoid the ankle-deep snow.

The orderly domesticity of the kitchen chilled her. Her legs buzzed. Her head continued to ache but in a more focused way. She imagined herself safe in bed and wondered how to get there. It would take a lot of nerve to go up the stairs and down the hall outside her parents' room. She'd never make it without them hearing. Her throat was dry, her sinuses stuffed, but she was afraid to turn on the faucet because the pipes would groan. Instead she found an open bottle of ginger ale in the refrigerator. The smart thing would be to put her shoes by the door, hang her jacket on a chair, and then in the morning explain that she'd come in a little late and didn't want to wake up the whole house, so she just curled up on the living room couch. Desperately, needing to flop if only to rest and think, she went forward, and slipping through the doorway she saw Janet already sleeping there. As Kathy faltered, she heard a rhythmical padding on the ceiling right over her head and knew that her father was up and prowling. Expecting his grumble, maybe even a curse, she heard her mother instead.

"Any luck?"

"What do you think?"

"I can't see you in the dark you know."

"Well, I'm here. You don't need to see me to hear me, and it's not that dark anyway."

"What do you think happened?"

"Like I would know?" He laughed in a way that conveyed his idea of the absurd figure he had become.

When the silence of the next seconds extended, Kathy wondered if she could slip away. Instead, she eased toward the stairwell, feeling small. She wanted to be small, even smaller, sneaking in and sitting partway up on the third or fourth step to listen.

When they next spoke it was her mother again. "She's stopped coughing at least."

"What are you talking about? She's still coughing."

"It's not so bad."

"It's bad enough. Don't they have any goddamn doctors at that college? She shouldn't come home with a cough like that. If they were taking care of her, she wouldn't. I feel like writing them a goddamn letter."

"What could you say?"

"I could say plenty."

'What?"

"Plenty. Half their students are walking around one foot in the grave and they don't know anything but money and grades. Money and grades. Money and—"

"No, no—"

"What do we ever hear from them but they want help with this fund and that fund, the parents' fund and—"

"She's on a partial scholarship for goodness' sake. We don't have a leg to stand on if you want to start complaining."

"We still hear about all their goddamn funds, don't we! What's their purpose, to shame us? To embarrass us? That damn Macabee just couldn't leave well enough alone."

"Oh, lord."

"What?"

"Janet doesn't have such a bad cold."

"So you're a doctor now. How the hell do you know? We could walk down there tomorrow for breakfast and find her dead."

"Oh, no. No, no."

"SARS. Or meningitis. Walking pneumonia. Anything."

"Where would she get SARS? She couldn't get SARS."

"Somebody has to have it. People have it. That's who has it. People. She's a person. So why not her?"

"Well, because you have to have been to China or over there somewhere."

"Do you think they don't have foreign students in that school?"

"She doesn't have SARS."

"You're talking statistics. That's all any of us do when we think we're safe. We're a person, not a statistic, so we're okay, but statistics are people."

"Don't lecture me."

"And now there's this goddamn mad cow disease."

"Oh, don't start in on that, too."

"What they hell are they going to come up with next? People are dying left and right. It's the food, it's the air. The bugs are conspiring. They're getting together at these goddamn bug conferences, all these viruses making deals to evolve and survive but we can't. We're getting outsmarted by bugs. And these crazy kids, if they escape the diseases, they take some drug nobody ever heard of before to burn out their nerves and rot out their brains like rotten hunks of cabbage."

"You're starting to talk too loud."

"What? Oh. Sorry."

"You'll wake her. She needs her rest."

"What is in their heads? I ought to wake her and ask her."

"What good would that do?"

"And those clothes she came back wearing. What's that indicative of, as if I don't know?"

"Oh, go to sleep, please, will you?"

"And the other one. Divorced and running around dressed up like that goddamn what's-her-name."

"I don't think she does that anymore."

"She doesn't stop doing anything ever. I know that. She doesn't stop anything. What'd we do? We did something wrong."

"Go to sleep."

"Sure. Sleep."

"We can get another couple of hours."

"You listen. If we wake up and find her dead, I warned you."

"All right. Go to sleep."

"You remember."

"I'll remember."

"Yeh, yeh. What else? With one daughter tearing around every bar in town and another one dying ten feet below me so I lie here and I think how I should do something, and right in the middle of it all I fall asleep!"

"That's what we need."

"Is it really?"

"I do. And you do, too. You need your rest. We both do. With all we have to deal with."

"Yeh. Well. At least Janet's sane."

"What do you mean?"

"At least Janet's sane."

On the couch, Janet shifted as if she might speak, as if she might respond, and in the dimness Kathy thought she saw her sister trace the frilly neckline of her nightgown, while remaining deep asleep.

A ticking sound within the walls marked the path of a scrap of something falling. They were quiet upstairs. Asleep. Or were they up there pretending to sleep? On their backs. Side by side. And if they were pretending, then that would mean they were awake and thinking. Eyes open, staring. Silently. Secretly. With no idea she was in the house. No idea where she was.

Feeling a chill, she searched for an open window but found nothing, though she did see the gray dawn revealing the wall of their neighbor's house. Janet's hair that Kathy remembered as short was now a thick, lengthy tangle. The clothing her father didn't like was draped like a fantastical figure off a wooden hanger and the figure wore a bell-sleeved sheer shirt transparent enough for Kathy to see her hand when she fit it inside where Janet's belly would have been. The top was a lace surplice insert with an angled neckline and a seam that crossed between the breasts. The skirt was velveteen, short and embroidered with flowers. Kathy might have been shoving against a large stone that moved implacably toward her as she took in the black knee-length boots and underwear with the Victoria's Secret label. In the same seconds that she realized she was looking at hundreds of dollars' worth of brand-new clothing, she remembered Janet's comment about a brand-new cell phone, the Verizon something-or-other that she owned, and it put her in touch with just about the entire universe. Who was buying all these things for her? Wasn't that the question? Janet coughed, and then it seemed Kathy saw her sister calmly and pleasantly beginning to fuck a man older than their father. She saw the interlocking organs. She saw the openness, the penetration, the slow sweat of greed in both their eyes. But it wasn't pleasure arriving, the expression wasn't one of delight because he was poisonous and his body was injecting something that would spread through her and drive her from her life until she reached a place very like the desolate one lived in by Kathy and those two in the shadows one floor above.

Crossing out of the living room and through the dim and quiet front room, Kathy hoped to leave these thoughts behind. They were stupid and sort of crazy. She entered the porch where the frosted windows covered half the wall ahead and she turned from this glacial blinding as if to turn from those thoughts. Because someday Janet would hurt their parents worse than Kathy ever could, and that was what mattered in love. Hurt was the thing. Seeing the door, she wanted to get out. Walk away. Because these thoughts didn't even seem like thoughts that could belong to her. She didn't know whose they were, and even if they were hers, she wanted nothing more to do with them.

She was outside now, lighting up a cigarette. She had her jacket on though she couldn't remember grabbing it. Snow was falling. It gathered on rooftops and auto roofs and trees. It occupied the air until it settled, refining and altering the earlier snows and powdering the stocking cap and plaid jacket of a small figure trudging down the faintness of the road toward her. The figure pulled a sled that carried something like a desk or counter being hauled somewhere. Then she saw that it was a kid, a boy, and she saw the runners creasing the new snow. His head was bowed. He looked maybe nine or ten. He wore big mittens and earmuffs outside his cap with a green knitted scarf that, after winding around the earmuffs, traveled in layers around his throat. Flipping her cigarette, she went down the stone stairs to the curb. She waited, listening to the hiss of the sled, and then he passed without looking up, either failing to notice her or else ignoring her. "Hey," she said.

He was surprised. It seemed he hadn't known she was there. His eyes, still bleary from sleep, expected a warning or a stern reprimand for some wrongdoing.

"You're cute," she said.

He faltered, casting his gaze ahead and then back at her and then ahead again before glancing back. "What?" His tone was polite and it was clear he was being careful not to be rude.

"I said you're cute. What's your e-mail?"

He started walking faster.

"Hey." She hurried to catch up. He had both arms out behind him, his fingers clutching the loop of rope knotted in holes on either end of the steering apparatus of the sled. The way he trudged on bending forward reminded her of a sled dog.

"Is it heavy?"

"What?"

"Is it heavy?"

"No."

"I live in that house back there. Where do you live?"

When he failed to answer, she said nothing more for a while. In the dimness and steady snow, it seemed they walked in a cloud. Ahead the bells of St. Catherine's clanged solemnly. He let go of the rope with one hand in order to smear snot from his nose with a mitten. He then stroked the mitten across his pants leg to clean it before regripping the rope.

"I gotta get to church before six o'clock. So I gotta hurry."

The resonance of the bells still floated in the faint light and cold air. "Sounds like they're just getting ready to start."

"I know that."

"I bought a paper from you once."

He looked at her, his eyes full of doubt.

At the church she watched as he located the newspapers he would sell. They were stacked in wire-wrapped bundles inside a little alcove of red brick where the foundation of the church jutted out to create the base of the steeple, inadvertently forming a kind of cave. When she followed him into it, she found they were out of the wind. The boy had wire cutters and soon he'd arranged the newspapers inside and atop the shelves of the plywood counter on his sled. Once everything was in order, he tugged his little business establishment across the snow and set up shop some five yards out from the bottom of the stairs the parishioners would soon scurry down as they exited the front door of the church.

"I have just the Chicago papers," he said to her. "Most people get the Des Moines *Register* delivered. So I sell the Chicago papers. I do okay. I have a bunch of regular customers who buy from me every Sunday." He was digging out what seemed to be three empty tuna fish cans scrubbed clean and nailed to a square of wood. He deposited quarters into one, dimes in another, nickels in the third.

"Did you build all this yourself?"

"My grandpa helped me."

"It's chill," she said.

He stared at her and she shrugged. "You got stuff smeared." He gestured to his own eye before walking back to the shelter to get out of the wind.

She watched him sell his papers when Mass was over. It was cold and early and the attendance was sparse and he had to take his gloves off to make change. He kept flexing his fingers, rubbing his hands together, and he thanked every customer. When the last of them was gone, he put the money in his pocket. He went about his tasks methodically, tucking the tuna fish–can construction along with the newspapers from atop the counter into one of the shelves, but she had the impression he was struggling with something. He even tilted forward, as if his head was becoming heavy, but at last he engaged her. "I go over to my friend's house on McKinley Street because I got to wait until seven-thirty Mass lets out. That's the next Mass."

She nodded, and the size and sharpness of her appreciation of the way he seemed to feel he owed her an explanation was a surprise.

"Sometimes they're not even up yet, but I can sit in their kitchen."

"Sure," she said.

He waved and trudged off.

She was halfway up the stone stairs and then all the way up and reaching for the iron handle on the big wooden door before she knew what she was doing. She had to get warm. The dim air inside still held the fading odor of incense and snuffed-out candles as she wandered forward to genuflect and sink into a pew.

She was so cold it took effort to keep her teeth from chattering and she huddled with her arms wrapped in an embrace of her own shoulders. On her knees she felt like she was some old peasant woman in a movie about refugees. There was a side altar directly ahead with rows of votive candles. A few burned, dispensing an upward radiance from the vivid amber glass that contained them, and from the field of their flickering, as if from a scattering of stars, arose a statue of the Virgin Mary. A.K.A. the Madonna. (I should have known. Who else?) The statue wore a blue robe over a white gown, both garments depicted in painted stone. The robe suggested a flowing motion frozen over the fabric beneath it, and both appeared somewhat faded or stained, though the folds were expressed in careful detail.

And then the way she was kneeling there brought to mind the way she'd knelt beside her mother's bed so long ago, and the feeling came back and with it the story she'd learned in school that day and then told that strange afternoon. And kneeling there, she wanted to tell the Madonna the story. It was about a girl and her mother, after all. They lived together and the mother was bountiful. She was the source of all that grew on the earth. The girl spent her days playing. She played in the trees and flowers. And then one day, as she bent to pick a dazzling stem, this god from hell burst up through the dirt. He grabbed her by her ankles and dragged her down under the ground to his realm. Her mother was stricken at the theft of her daughter. She was so dismayed that she forgot about everything, her despair and anger turning the world into a wasteland. The bigger god, the one who ruled over all things, saw what was happening and ordered that the girl be sent back to her mother. But by now the girl had been in hell for a while. She'd fallen under the spell she found in the god's powerful embrace. She wanted to stay and he yearned to keep her, though he knew he did not dare disobey the god above him. But he had a trick and the trick was to get her to eat a pomegranate with him, and, as he hoped, she swallowed four seeds. When she arose to the light where her mother waited, she spoke of what had happened, and her heartsick mother told her that with each seed she had wed the god for one month. From then on she would have to go back and live in hell with him four months out of each year. Alone for that time, her mother laid waste to the earth. Winter was her lonely wrath. And when Persephone returned it was spring. That was her name.

Before Kathy, the Madonna's hands were partly raised from her sides and turned palm out from her hips in a gesture of welcoming. The flesh of the Madonna's face was pinkish and smooth, her countenance conceived to render a consoling impression of celestial serenity, but though her eyes were open, there was something difficult and opaque in her gaze. Unexpectedly, almost violently, Kathy felt the fact and detail of her own breathing, the mechanism of her chest rising with each inhalation, her lungs like balloons inside her puffing up and then giving it all away with a sound she could hear.

SOME LOOSE
CHANGE

1

RED WAS DEPRESSED, but not the way assholes or sissies get depressed. He felt he had no fucking stake in anything anymore. No fucking stake in the system. No fucking steak in the refrigerator. Just a stake in his heart. He thought about saying it out loud. Maybe he'd get somebody to laugh. One of his pathetic, raggedy-assed buddies, the bunch of them has-been, used-to-be high rollers, who had just ransacked their own goddamn vehicles out in the goddamn parking lot, tearing apart the upholstery to scrounge up nickels and dimes and stray fucking quarters. So they could get one more round of beer.

"I got forty cents."

"All I got's twelve."

"Twelve! Keep looking."

It was sickening. It was pathetic. Red had checked in about one in the afternoon at the Backhoe Bar and Grill. Bobby and Jake and Macky were already planted at their favorite table, the one under the *Sports Illustrated* calendar showing this long-legged bitch on her belly at the beach, sand caking the gold of her ass, the bikini bottom creeping up the crack. Now they were flopping back down under her serene, superior glow to count their change and mutter about the amazing, unbelievable fact that it was already night outside.

"What the hell time is it?"

"You been here the longest, Macky. When did you get here?"

The bar was a long rectangle of weird light like the spill of an arcade game. It looked pretty much the same in the morning as it did after dark. But there was no denying the Dallas skyline they'd just seen firing up the sleek black starless sky. Nothing they could do about it.

"What we need is a little venture capital," said Jake.

"Right."

"So we could make a venture," said Bobby.

"In?"

"Right. In what? Hypothetically, if you had some capital to play with where would you put it?"

Stomach acid turned Red in his chair. He burped, shrugged, and scanned the room, looking for something. A couple of nervous kids were huddled up in the corner. Not far from them a snoring drunk was crumpled over the bar. This gym rat dripping tattoos in a sweatshirt with the sleeves ripped off was brooding at the juke box, like it had just asked him a very difficult question that he was determined to answer.

"Whatsamatter, Red?" said Bobby. "Do we bore you? Sorry if we bore you. Look at him."

Red turned and squinted at Bobby. It wasn't that Bobby bored him, but he didn't feel like trying to explain.

"Red."

He had nothing to say, and nothing he wanted to do either, except turn away. All along the walls neon signs advertised different brands of beer, each exuding its own mechanical pulse of artificial color. On the table in front of him were a couple of ashtrays. The one that was overflowing had butts with lipstick on the filters so there must have been a woman around sometime. He couldn't remember. Probably the waitress at some point, bored and annoyed and stubbing out a smoke. Because now there was just Jake and Bobby and Macky and this new guy, who had crouched down beside Jake and started talking to him about the golf cart concession at the club where Jake worked as a fucking caddy. In the years of the boom, Jake was a real estate speculator. Red met him in the Lear jet Red leased and piloted in those days. Charter flights had been Red's way of dipping into the money stream gushing through Texas at the time. It had been hurricane force. Jake and some of his partners were on a junket to Vegas when Red stepped out of the cabin, and there was Jake, settled back in his chair, this blonde attached to his dick like a fly to a horse's ear, and she was sucking just as single-mindedly. After giving Red a shit-eating smile, Jake reached and wedged his hands into the top of this sequined halter the blonde was wearing till he got some nipple. His eyes kind of sparked like he'd just made a shrewd maneuver in a stock deal, then he sank from sight, his lids closing. He looked like he was vacationing on the beach. His partner and three clients were aboard, along with four other bitches, all of them nasty little show dogs dressed to make the most of their entertainment/market value. After those flights, the waste cans overflowed with empty booze bottles. Red would find soggy rubbers clinging to the nozzles, or nestled with the empty coke vials and broken poppers. He found a G-string more than once, a lacy bra would be hooked over the back of a chair, somebody's floral bikini panties in the crack of the cushions. Once he hit the jackpot with this actual living breathing little bitsy brunette passed out in the john. He couldn't remember if she was part of one of Jake's flights or not, but whoever left her, she took the option of smiling her big smile up at Red. He ushered her into the flight deck to show her the instrument panel. As per her request, he fired up the engine. She sort of made this cheerleader kind of noise and swung her legs over his, so his lap was like her horsy and if he'd found any underpants that time, they damn well could have been hers because she didn't have any on to take off.

The drinks arrived. Red watched the waitress setting down tap beer in mugs for everyone except Macky. Somehow he'd managed a shot of bourbon.

"Well," said Bobby, "the best wheels won't get you out the driveway without some fuel." He tipped the beer to his lips and made a sad sound as he drank.

"What we need is a little venture capital," said Jake.

"You said that."

"Did I? When?"

"Somebody did."

"If people paid their debts, I could take us all anywhere we wanted." Red probed the foam with his tongue, then added some salt. It was true. More than one dipshit had left him hanging. Some just ducked him, ducked his bills and then the collection agency he sent after them. People seemed to think their charter jet tab was the last thing they had to pay. Maybe they declared bankruptcy and then he couldn't even chase them anymore. It wore him the fuck out. So he declared bankruptcy. That was a brilliant fucking law.

Jumping up, Macky tipped his head back, taking the bourbon in like oxygen after he'd just surfaced from some overly long underwater stay. "I'm goin' home," he said.

That scared everybody. If he left, it could start a trend. "No, no, no." Then they'd all be going home and then they'd be home, and the next thing that happened would be the alarm clock screeching at them, or some asshole on talk radio, welcoming them to the new fucking day, and the morning would drag them off to their stupid jobs. Jobs that had no status. No opportunity to advance. Jobs like treading water. They wore you out and got you nowhere, until you started to think maybe you wanted to drown.

"I'd like to go to one of them pudenda bars," said Bobby. "That's what I'd like. Whata you think of that, Macky?"

"Yeh," said Jake. "C'mon, Macky."

They were talking about the Velvet Spotlight or the Animal Club or the new Stringfellows, where these gorgeous, golden, extraterrestrial cunts danced topless and for twenty bucks would come over and squirm around between your legs. For a slightly higher dollar incentive, they'd take you into a back room and give you a "friction dance," which was in reality an old-fashioned dry hump.

"We don't have the money," said Macky.

"Would you wanna do that, Macky? If we had the money," said Jake. "Maybe we can figure out a way to get into one."

"How?"

The question, though it was his own, seemed to confuse Macky so that he stood there looking more and more tired until he slumped back into his chair.

Red thought, What the hell! He'd said it once, he might as well say it again: "If people paid their debts, there is no place I could not take us if we wanted."

"Somebody owe you money, Red?" said Bobby.

"A lot of people."

"Yeh? Like who?" Jake wanted to know.

"I don't remember their names. It's all out in the computer."

"Wait a minute. This is legitimate? It's on the computer?"

"I swear I just said that. Didn't I just say that?"

"Like who?" said Jake. "Who owes you?"

"It's on the computer, Jake. I don't have it fucking memorized. That's why I have the computer."

"Gimme a name."

"Part of the reason I went under was people waltzed me and held back what they owed me. They waltzed me, I took the hit. You know."

"Gimme a name. One name."

Red was glaring at Jake. He tossed back half the mug and leaned onto the table. "Are these question somehow your way of expressing doubt about the fact that I was screwed just the way I'm saying?"

"No, no."

"People didn't pay me. I met my obligations and flew these seeming trustworthy, very affluent people wherever the hell they wanted on time and safely, and then they didn't meet their end. They left me hanging. You're probably one of them."

"I paid you."

"I wonder."

"I paid you. I always paid you."

"Did you? I think I'd like to see." Red guzzled the last of the beer and headed for the door.

"Where you going, Red?"

"I'll be right back."

"But where are you going?"

In the parking lot, he popped open the trunk of his "beater," a red, rusty '63 Ford. He shoved aside the briefcase with his daily calendar, one reefer, divorce papers, pictures of his three kids. He lifted the Smith and Wesson .38, wrapped in oilcloth, and placed it carefully off to the side so it snuggled in with a set of Anthony Robbins audiotapes he'd ordered off the 800 number one night when he was drunk and alone at home. The laptop in its vinyl carrying case was waiting under a cardboard box full of old files and random junk. He grabbed the laptop and slammed the trunk.

Back at the table he set up, jamming the plug into a wall socket a few inches below the *Sports Illustrated* bitch's crotch. The bunch of them were watching him closely. They'd collected behind him as he booted the machine. The screen went cloudy, then filled with icons blipping up, the green halo tainting his fingers. He hit some keys and the data started popping up. He could feel Jake and Bobby and Macky shifting behind him, peering over his shoulder. The screen was full of names, dates, figures. Just seeing the names pissed him off. It was like a burning building as everything started to slip from reach and disappear in this smoky blinding choking indignation. The muscles in the back of his neck were squirming like rats trying to get out of the fire. "Look at these fuckers," he said.

"I ain't there, am I?" said Jake.

"Not so far."

"I paid everything."

"This guy owes you fifteen thousand dollars, Red," said Bobby. He was smudging the screen with his finger as he pointed at a name. "Is that right? Look at that."

"Wait a minute, wait a minute!" Jake said, leaning in.

Red, who was scrolling through the names, each one causing him a nasty little twinge, stopped

"That's Thomas P. Harlow. Is that Thomas P. Harlow?" Jake was using this tone of exaggerated shock.

"That's what it says, doesn't it. That's what I'm reading."

"I had some dealings with that creepy bastard. He was the brains behind that development over at Twin Creek. What an asshole."

Red was having a little trouble remembering Harlow. "He's probably working the window at a Burger King now. Real estate got butchered."

"No, no. He was getting out of real estate. I remember that. Just before everything went south. Actually, I heard about him lately."

Red didn't like this kind of news. One of the key ways he'd kept himself sane was to imagine everybody who had fucked him getting screwed and dumped down the shitter on the same flush that washed him into the mess he now lived in. He didn't really want to know that Harlow had escaped, but he asked anyway. "What's he in now?"

"I don't remember, but they were complaining about him."

"Who?"

"I don't remember." Jake leaned in to the computer screen like it was whispering and you had to be close to hear it. "Is this all legitimate, Red?"

"Of course it is."

"How did this happen?" Bobby wanted to know. He sounded dismayed and disappointed in Red like it was Bobby's fucking money. "How did you ever let this happen, Red? How?"

"You know how it goes."

"Yeh, sure. But still. This guy owes you big money. Fifteen thousand's a lot of money, Red."

"Is that right, Bobby? Really. I didn't know that."

"You know what he did with it, of course," said Jake. "He no doubt used it to slam-dunk his own fucking life. So he's some kind of low-level Fortune Five Hundred kind of guy, which is what I hear. You know, he's in the land of abundance, his portfolio is diversified while what is left of you is sitting here with us."

"What's your point?"

"We're roadkill!"

"This person who you can't remember, who knew about Harlow, who knew what he did, who knew how he's doing—"

"Yeh," said Jake.

"What'd they say about him?"

"They said he was fat-assed and arrogant, but nevertheless in truth a slimeball, who had somehow survived the boom and come out richer than he went in."

"You oughta collect, Red. Something, anyway," said Macky. "We could go with you."

"I mean, he owes you, Red," Bobby added.

"It ain't right."

Red knew it wasn't right. He accessed everything he had on Thomas P. Harlow and just seeing the high-end address sickened him. Then along came some vague memory of Harlow. It was fuzzy like a channel you can't afford to subscribe to—this hub of fat and annoyance and smug contempt flickering on and off. Red's brain was burning again and he was back inside the smoldering walls, the flames eating away at his cherished belief that everybody who deserved to go down when the bottom fell out had taken the fall.

"Look at that," said Red, gazing at the computer. "The fucker lived in Hurst." Hurst was one of the more affluent of the Dallas suburbs. "You think he's still there?"

"There or better," said Jake. "That's my information."

2

THEY TOOK RED'S CAR and Red drove with Macky slouched beside him. Bobby and Jake were in the back. Everybody had a can of beer. They'd had to borrow the price of a six-pack from the waitress. She had a thing for Macky and he'd boned her a couple of times, which explained her interest and her resentment, because before and after he'd boned her he treated her the same. Like a waitress. She agreed to help them out only after they promised to pay her back double. She even scribbled the deal down on a slip of paper, and then asked her boss to witness it, because she was "really, really" serious about it. They were serious too, they told her, because they knew what it was to get screwed by people who didn't pay their debts.

Now they were rattling through the night on their way to Hurst. Macky suddenly groaned and guzzled whatever remained of his beer in one big breath. A six-pack gave them one beer each and two to fight over. Macky flipped the can out the window and looked at Red. Macky had been a foreman on an oil rig during the boom. He'd worked his way up after coming back from Vietnam. At the moment he pumped gas and was on several waiting lists to become a security guard. "I want another brew, okay, Red?" Macky reached out with both hands, his forearms like cables with human skin stretched around them.

In the backseat, Bobby started laughing as Red fumbled one of the two remaining beers up from the bag and handed it over to Macky. "What?" Red said, peering into the rearview mirror in hopes of catching a face and a clue. "What?" But Bobby couldn't stop laughing. "What'd you say to him, Jake? Did you say something?"

"I don't know."

"I was an investment banker," Bobby giggled. Bobby'd been a vice president at an S&L in Balch Springs just outside Dallas. When the S&L started flying apart, he jumped for cover, hunkering down, looking for a hole. He ended up fined and filing for bankruptcy. He just escaped jail time, though he felt those cold concrete walls moving in so close he heard the doors slam in his sleep for months. "Don't you see the irony, Red?" said Bobby. "Now look at me."

"We all see the irony, Bobby," said Jake. "We just don't think it's funny."

"Irony is always funny."

"Not this time."

Red sure as hell didn't think it was funny the way all their lives had slammed to earth. Red's Lear jet might as well have crashed and burned once Jake and Bobby and all the others like them were stripped down to their posh shorts. The leasing payments on his plane went from being a kind of afterthought to this big guy pounding on the door. Strangers started showing up in a steady stream to take away his possessions. Everything was gone in a matter of days. He made a living now installing and repairing car stereo systems. Bobby worked part-time in one of those copy places that make endless, pointless copies for other people. Jake was a golf caddy.

It took a while to find the street, once they arrived in Hurst. Then they went a couple of blocks in the wrong direction. When at last they pulled up in front of Harlow's fake Tudor-style house, the bay window was full of light. The carport had three cars in it, two Beamers and a racy maroon Mercedes.

"Whata you think, Red?" said Jake.

Red was staring at Harlow's house. He climbed from the car. They were all sucking on a beer as they followed him onto the lawn. The Mercedes was pretty much irresistible to Red, pulling him straight up to it. He stood peering in at the interior. The pang he felt had some nasty dimensions. Here was actual, tangible proof of the lies he'd told himself over these last years. The Mercedes was like an organ ripped out of Red's own body.

Jake and Bobby were maybe twenty feet away admiring the Beamers. They sort of crooned and cooed with the memory of what they used to have. It hurt, Red thought. It fucking hurt. A scraping sound whirled him. A clotted shadow that made him feel hemmed in and fearful turned out to be Macky easing up.

"Listen," Macky whispered. "I been looking in the windows. What's in there is this fat, short guy in a linen suit. He's wandering around barefoot from room to room. A bottle of vodka in his hand. It looks like Absolut. He got the bottle by the nozzle and he's walking around with the bottle swaying by the nozzle in his hand."

"No shit," said Red. "The miserable prick, the slick two-faced sleazy prick! I shouldn't have let this happen." It was clear to him that Harlow's life was an intentional public flaunting of the way he'd tricked and screwed Red. Harlow was mocking him and taunting him, and he was halfway across the lawn when Macky jumped in front of him, shaking his head in this worried way. "Wait a minute, Red."

"He can pay me what he owes me."

"You know what I'm thinkin'."

"Not until you tell me."

"He's a Texan, ain't he? I'd say the odds are we go barging in on him, we are going to be lookin' at some kind of firepower. We better make a plan."

"Look at the house and shit—three goddamn cars! We don't need a plan. Fucking bullshit. I have firepower of my own." Red was already on a detour back to the street, his car, the trunk, and the .38 in the oilcloth. By the time he returned he couldn't see Macky. Then he heard a low murmur and spotted Macky with Jake and Bobby huddled together in the carport. He must have raced off to tell them what was going on. They were probably going to try and stop him, but nobody was going to stop him. He mounted the front stairs. Something about standing there like that, ringing a doorbell and holding a pistol, made him light-headed, these goose bumps streaming through him. He waited, then rang it again. Macky and Bobby and Jake were headed toward him. The latch clicked and the door pulled open and Red felt like he did when he'd made his one and only bungee jump. Holy shit, motherfuck. It was a world of free fall.

Something about opening his front door and facing the upwardly tilted muzzle of a pistol made the fat guy standing there in his linen suit wrinkle his nose and then snigger. Or his mouth sniggered, while his eyes focused, blurred, and then refocused. On the edge of the door, his fingers fidgeted, the way they would if he was annoyed and in some way bored. The noise he made was a sort of squeak, and then he actually said, "Ha ha."

"Remember me?" Red asked. He put his foot against the frame.

"What's going on here?"

"I asked, 'Do you remember me?'"

"What do you want?"

"I'm here to balance the books."

"Is this a holdup?"

"Don't you call it that. I want my money. This is debt collecting."

The fat guy registered the approach of the other three men behind Red. "What money?" he said and took a slug of vodka.

Red wanted a drink too. He grabbed the bottle. "The money you owe me." He took a gulp of vodka and handed the bottle back.

"Who are you?"

"You know me."

"I think you've come to the wrong house. I think you've made a terrible mistake."

"You owe him fifteen thousand dollars!" said Jake, sticking his head in.

"You know what, Red?" Macky said, stepping past them and into the house, his eyes darting about. "Standing in the doorway like this could get you in the shit real quick. You're backlit. You're standing in fucking silhouette. Whata you look like? Let's get inside or get into the car and find some shadows somewhere."

Red didn't know what was warning and instructing him, but some ill-defined aspect of the situation would favor Harlow if they entered his house. Harlow would gain some kind of authority, owning everything the way he did, every stick of furniture, even the land, knowing the floor plan, being familiar with the decorations. But if they fled into the night—if they took him off into the night—he was theirs.

"Let's go."

"What's going on here?" Harlow wanted to know. "I don't owe you any fifteen thousand dollars."

"Fuck you." Red grabbed Harlow by the arm.

"This is crazy. Wait. I don't have my shoes, for crissake. Look at my feet. Are you fucking blind? I gotta have some shoes on. Just gimme a goddamn minute!" The outburst disoriented Red. He didn't know how far he should let this abusive trend in Harlow develop. Impulsively, he pressed the tip of the .38's barrel against Harlow's ear. It must have felt cold as an ice cube, the way Harlow's mouth stopped and locked up in this crooked shape.

"Let's go."

"What are we doing?"

"I'll see if I can find his shoes," Macky yelled.

They herded Harlow across the lawn. They were shoving him into the car when Macky joined them with a bottle of scotch in one hand and a Jack Daniel's in the other. "I couldn't find the shoes."

"They were right in front of the couch," Harlow told him.

"I looked there."

"They were just laying there."

"I didn't see them."

"Maybe they were under the coffee table."

The doors were slamming. Red yelled for Macky to drive. Red wanted to sit in the passenger seat and be able to concentrate on Harlow, who was wedged in the back between Bobby and Jake.

"Where to?" Jake wanted to know as the engine rumbled and the beater struggled off from the curb.

"Go north on the Jacksboro."

Bobby and Jake were drinking scotch, while Red and Macky worked on the Jack Daniel's. Harlow still had his vodka but he didn't seem all that interested in drinking at the moment, though he took a halfhearted sip every now and then. The houses got fewer and fewer, the flat desolate strips increasing, the signs of city life diminishing. Red was trying to figure out exactly what he wanted to do. He wanted his money, that was for sure. And maybe some payback. He just had to figure out exactly how to go about getting what he wanted.

By the time they got onto the Jacksboro, Macky was flipping radio stations, giving each one about two seconds before he raced on, and Jake and Bobby were arguing about interest rates—whether or not they were going to continue their downward trend or if the current dip was simply the last depression before the start of an unavoidable rise. Neither one of them had a solid position. Seated between them, Harlow was frowning like he might be struggling to come up with a way to ease their concerns. The scotch bottle moved back and forth across his body as they exchanged it and talked and drank.

"How the hell did you avoid going under, Harlow?" Jake suddenly yelled. "You were in real estate, for God's sake. The great bitch of business chewed the rest of us up and shit us out, but you stayed close to her fucking heart. If you were in real estate, the rule of thumb was your dick was in the shredder."

"I wasn't in real estate anymore."

"So the rumor's right. We heard a rumor."

"What rumor?"

"That you got out before the crash."

"It's not a rumor, it's what happened. I liquidated and reinvested. I was in computers."

"You went into computers."

"Software."

"Did you ever have any dealing with an S and L in Balch Springs?" said Bobby.

"Balch Springs? I don't think so."

"It's just outside Dallas."

"I know Balch Springs. But I don't think I did business with any S and L there. Why?"

"I was a vice president there. It was like getting hit with lightning when the bottom fell out. The oil stopped and the money stopped. I mean, how the hell did you know to get out? I didn't have a clue. Then all of a sudden it was like the boom had never been flesh and blood, but it was all along this kind of virtual-reality projection that fucking mesmerized us all until the central tube in whatever system was generating it just blew. That's how I felt, anyway. Does this make any sense to you?"

"Sort of."

"Did you see the bust coming?" said Jake. "Is that what happened? You saw it coming?"

"No, no, I don't think I had the—"

"Sure, sure, you sensed it. So you got out."

"I don't think so. I was just bored. I don't remember why."

"You had an instinct."

"I don't think so."

"When is it going to end, though?" Bobby asked. "What do you think?" He sounded whiny and pathetic, like he did when he was pleading with some gorgeous woman to fuck him and she wouldn't. "When is this recession going to bottom out?" he said. "It's gotta recover, don't you think?"

"I'll tell you this," Jake said, "they have to get inflation under control, and they won't the way they're going about it. Not if Greenspan keeps parading around scaring everybody about inflation like he's been doing in front of Congress. Now it's going to skyrocket. You mark my words. It has to."

"Where are we going?" Harlow asked.

Red whirled in the seat and knelt there facing Harlow. "Enough of this crap! Do you remember me now? I flew a plane. I had a Lear jet."

"I don't remember you."

"Do you remember a Lear jet? Do you remember Vegas? Broads?"

Blades of illumination fanned over Harlow's face as the car shot under periodic streetlights. It struck Red that Harlow was sorting the questions and debating what to say, trying to remember, and then trying to sort out what he should admit remembering. "I'm getting a divorce," he said. "I'm in the middle of a divorce proceeding. It's a fucking hemorrhage in my finances—it's gushing out. I'm losing everything."

"I think he remembers you," said Macky, who then took a swig.

"You were very shrewd, Harlow," Red said. "You made me real comfortable, paying me the first couple of times right on schedule. So when you didn't pay, I hesitated."

"It was somebody else who did this to you. That's what I'm trying to tell you."

"No, no. He trusted you and you betrayed him, you prick," Macky yelled.

"You broke his heart," said Bobby.

Harlow shook his head in an exaggerated, amazed way and then he scanned them, his expression making him look as if he'd just heard that something terrible had happened to somebody really stupid who was somehow very dear to him. Red was watching closely, looking for the edge he needed to find a way into Harlow's head, a flaw to pry open, so he could work the guy over from that vantage, from the inside. Fuck him up good. He took a sip of Jack Daniel's and contemplated the unexpected way things were developing. He had to give Harlow credit because the guy had come up with a completely original bluff. Who would have ever guessed that Harlow would be ballsy enough to risk everything on a tactic as ridiculous as pretending to be someone else.

"You know what we were wondering, Harlow?" said Macky. "We were wondering how far you thought you could swim with a stop sign tied to your leg."

"What?"

"What?" said Red.

"I know I couldn't swim very far," said Macky.

"I couldn't, either," said Jake, "and I'm a good swimmer. Could you, Red?"

"Swim with a stop sign tied to my leg? Is that what you're asking?"

"I don't think you could. I think you'd sink."

"Of course I'd sink. Anybody would."

"Wait a minute, wait a minute," said Harlow. "This is nuts. You guys are nuts."

"No, no. It's you!" said Bobby. "It's pricks like you, failing to pay your debts, so the whole economic system gets thrown out of whack. We're all interdependent, you know that. Cheaters hurt everybody."

"I didn't cheat."

"The hell you didn't."

"Everybody cheats," said Harlow. "Everybody cheats. It's expected. It's business."

"You cheat until you get caught," said Red. "And so that explains what's happening to you. You been caught."

Macky veered off the concrete into a wooded section of live oak and mesquite, startling everybody. The car bounced and jostled them as he slammed to a halt and popped the door open.

"What the hell are you doing?"

Macky plunged out the door.

"Where's he goin'?" said Harlow.

Macky sprinted through the dark to the intersection, where he started wrestling with the stop sign on the corner. Red looked around at everybody inside the car and they were all staring at Macky, heaving against the pole, straining through minutes of shadowy struggle. He tried various angles, pausing and gathering himself to lunge again and again.

"I'm going to help him," said Jake, jumping from the car.

"Me, too," said Bobby.

Macky had his back against the pole with his heels dug in when they arrived. The three of them reeled about, groaning and gasping. Several times they consulted and then they began their fight all over again, positioning themselves, counting to three and attacking, until abruptly they all crashed to the ground. The dirt made a loud cracking sound, and the sign clattered against large stones and scattered gravel, the concrete base popping up like a gigantic uprooted onion. For a second, they lay there gasping, and then they ran toward the car, lugging the sign.

"I can't give you fifteen thousand dollars. For crissake, I don't even remember you."

"Well, then, you're going to fucking drown," Red told him.

"What?" The way Harlow said this and then met Red's eyes somehow highlighted the odd fact that they were alone just then, and that they were only a few feet apart. Red sensed a change in Harlow, a shift in the way he was looking at things. Wanting to press Harlow, to make him crumble right here and now, Red lifted the .38 into view.

"What's this about?" said Harlow.

"I told you."

"No. Really! Who sent you? Did my wife send you? Because it won't work if she did. It won't fucking work."

Macky and Bobby and Jake were loading the stop sign into the trunk, and the car bounced and shuddered with their effort. Red could hear them arguing about the best way to do it. With Macky once more at the wheel, they tore off, plunging down a lightless back road. "We'll need a boat," Macky said.

"There's lots of them."

"Listen," said Harlow, "this has gone far enough. I have to pee."

"You miserable sonofabitch!" Red screamed at him. "You stiffed me! You owe me!"

"I don't remember you."

"Is that my fault? I mean, I'm sorry I can't give you a goddamn presentation with flip charts and memos, but I can't. I do in fact have the bill, the date, the itinerary, the passenger list in the back on my computer. I have a series of letters we exchanged on this matter. I even have a Polaroid picture of you getting sucked off by one bimbo while you finger fuck this other one. I have the photo."

"It's not me. That's what I'm trying to tell you."

"It's useless," Macky said. "I don't think he's got the money."

"I gotta pee. I'll goddamnit piss in my pants."

"Don't you dare piss in my car," Red yelled.

They were bucking and jolting down a dark side road, the open trunk lid clattering as they entered a little marina. The water appeared in a glittering inky slab. A few boats bobbed in the shallows. Others lay turned over on the shore.

"The computer doesn't lie," Red said, wishing he could reach back and wipe the shadows off Harlow's face. He wanted to confirm beyond all doubt that Harlow was Harlow. But everyone was getting out of the car, Jake and Bobby pulling at Harlow, gravity hauling at them all. Macky ran into the night. Red reeled sideways for several steps, fighting back the knowledge of how drunk he was with another aggressive slug of vodka. He was staggering toward the wooded fringe, vaguely intending to find something to row the boat with. If they found a boat they could use. He ventured to the boundary between the clearing and the forest, peering into the tangled murk. He had to pee, and his piss muttered and shook the leaves, their shadows feathery. It seemed the underbrush was too thick to enter and look for logs to row with. He retreated, zipping up, angling toward the flat black gleam of water. When he came upon a little storage shed, he found some planks piled up along the wall. A couple of them would serve as oars.

The commotion near the shoreline was Macky in the water up to his ankles, lugging an aluminum twelve-footer through the shallows. Either the owner forgot to lock it up properly or Macky had ripped it loose. Jake and Bobby had tied Harlow's hands behind him with his belt. Macky tossed them a piece of rope he said he'd found loose on the floor of one of the other boats, and they started lashing the stop sign to Harlow's pudgy leg.

"I got oars," said Red as he sat down in the dirt drinking and watching the white linen of Harlow's trousers balloon above the bulge of the knot. Macky sloshed out of the water. Back on land, he bent to pick up the sign. Jake and Bobby hefted Harlow onto his feet.

"Look," he said, "I'll write you a check."

"A check? Jesus Christ, you are not talking to children here," said Bobby. "You know that, I hope, Harlow. You know you are not talking to children here."

"No, no, no. But what else can I do?"

Red walked up, leaning in close to Harlow. "So you admit you owe me."

"No, no, no. But what choice do I have if you don't believe me."

"I took a check from you now, by the time I went to cash it, you would have canceled it."

"I promise. I wouldn't."

"Whata you mean, you promise? Who care's you promise? You can't promise, you asshole! This is business!"

Even as they talked, they moved, the whole bunch of them struggling to get into the boat, arguing who should do what, who should sit where. "Stiffed again," Red went on, though no one was really interested. "That's what I'd have to say, wouldn't I? What an asshole I'd be. You beat me once. I can't let you do it again. I couldn't look myself in the eye in the mirror, I let that happen."

Macky was the last one aboard, landing with a force that prompted groans from the hull and turbulence in the water. Bobby and Jake were all set to use the planks to pole away from shore, but they waited for Macky to settle before starting in. The riveted aluminum of the hull gave up a creaking sound as they voyaged out through the sighing of the little waves they caused and passed through. "Listen," Macky said, in an oddly formal voice that made Red look at him. It was like Macky was using somebody else's tone and pattern for his words. He'd adopted a sort of ceremonial quality that made him sound like he was pretending to be a minister or teacher. "For all you who've never killed anyone before, it's not what you think. It's just not. It's different."

In the past, Red had never known whether he did or didn't believe Macky's lunatic claims about Vietnam, but looking at him in the sheen rising off these dark polluted waters, he felt himself becoming a believer. This strange set of eyeballs had been implanted in Macky's head. He swayed a little, staying in harmony with the rocking of the boat, the movement shifting him in and out of the moonlight.

"Macky," said Red. "Whata you mean?"

"Just listen. Wait. Watch." He was back on his "Nam frequency," which he'd always warned the rest of them not to try and pick up because they couldn't. This wasn't the first time they'd seen this kind of spasm take Macky over, turning him into a refugee from *Cops* on TV, motor-mouthing about "bringing smoke" and "vils" and "zapping" and "fragging." More often than not, this shit grabbed him after a case of beer or a dozen whacks of reefer, so tonight was no exception though there was something different about it. He was looking off into deep shadows along the shore, as if studying something important, something you had to be him to see. Then he raised his glance to the smoky clouds revising themselves around the moon. When he glanced at Red, nostalgia seemed a pair of pliers closing deep inside him.

"Who pissed? I smell piss," said Jake. "Look at this, he pissed himself."

"This has gone far enough," Harlow cried, shamefully closing his legs over the dark stain.

"You stink," said Jake.

"Whata baby. You big baby," said Macky. "Let's get on with this. I'm getting eaten alive." He was swatting at mosquitoes. "There's too goddamn many mosquitoes to just cruise around out here."

"Fucking bullshit," said Harlow. "I told you I had to go."

"We're not really going to do this are we?" said Bobby.

"God-fucking-damnit, Bobby!' Red yelled. "You got the intelligence of a landfill! Can you shut the hell up?" They had to get the money or do it, didn't they? What the hell was Bobby thinking? The only way to avoid killing Harlow was for Harlow to believe there was no doubt they were going to kill him. "Whether we do it or not is up to Harlow, Bobby." Red took the vodka bottle from Macky.

"You guys must really think you are hot shit," said Harlow.

"Yes, we do. Some of us do, and you should too." Macky grabbed Harlow by the shirtfront. His awkward violence started the boat rocking.

"Wait a minute," said Bobby.

Who would know? Red was thinking. Who would care? Nobody. Nobody cared about any fucking thing these days. Everybody knew everything and nobody cared about anything. Macky pushed Harlow away and bent sideways secretively, huddling over like a guy protecting a match from the wind. With pinched fingers he jammed something tiny into his mouth. Then he looked at Red, his big eyes fixed on a deep and distant intrigue, which he was inviting Red to join. He reached inside Red and touched something Red didn't even know was in there and it scared Red because he hadn't known it was there, this appetite, this interest, this weird excitement.

"It's a free one," Macky said. "It's a free one."

Red nodded, then looked at Harlow. What the hell was Macky talking about? What was a "free one"? He asked, even though he knew. They could kill the guy and get away with it and just go on. That was Macky's point. Harlow had a weird gleam in his eye. He was pretending to be some kind of very tough guy who knew every inch of the difference between what could and couldn't happen. But he didn't. He really didn't. Nobody did. You had to pretend you did. Everybody pretended it, but it might not even be there.

"Red," said Macky, "it's like Saran Wrap. You know, the way Saran Wrap keeps one thing from another. One food smell in, the other out. But you can go through it. You can just poke in your finger. It's nothing."

"Yeh." Red wished he could see Macky better, and he squinted, wishing for one second of daylight because this shit was spooky. It had to be an accident, but it was like Macky was reading his mind, and if he was, Red wanted no part of it. "Macky," he said.

"It's like the water, Red. Just look at the water. What I'm saying to you is look at the water, it looks solid enough to hold you up. I'm talking about the water. It looks solid but it won't hold you up."

Harlow started to cry. At first he sounded like somebody was strangling him, and then this big cough came out of him, and he said, "Oh, oh, oh. Oh, God." It was like he was barking and spitting snot. "Please," he moaned.

"Save it for the fish," said Macky.

"Wait! What?"

"It's too dark," said Macky. "It's too dark."

"Whata you mean? What does he mean it's too dark? Please!"

"You hear that, Harlow?" Red said. "I thought you were a real savvy deal doer! I thought you were what the world needs. Because we need deal doers. All of us. People like us, working people, and the market, too, the country even, the nation, the economy. What the fuck is wrong with you?" He was enraged at Harlow for pushing things this far, for messing up and never thinking to set things right and so leaving Red with no choice. Did the stupid miserable prick want to die? If he did, fuck him. "Fuck you," he said. "You leave me no choice."

"Gimme a minute." Harlow was barely able to get the words out through all the groans and gasping. "Just a minute. One minute to think. I want to come up with a counteroffer. Okay? Okay?"

"Whata you think this is, a press conference?" said Macky.

"What?"

"Give it up," said Jake. "Or you're going over!"

"What are you talking about?" Bobby yelled, like he was being threatened. "I agree with Harlow. He needs to make a counteroffer."

"The fish will ask you all the questions," said Macky.

"No, no. I'm trying to do the math in my head. What fish?"

"At the press conference. 'What are you doing down here?' they will ask. 'What are you doing with a stop sign tied to your leg?'"

Harlow turned to Red, and it was like they were both remembering each other fondly. Maybe it was some kind of half-assed, oddball emotion left over from that moment in the car when they were alone. Or the residue of some good time they'd shared during the boom that they'd both forgotten as far as its details. It made Red sad, and he shook his head, as if to push it aside and with it Harlow's appeal. This was business. He had to keep his business head on. In every deal a moment like this arrived, where the worst outcome appeared unavoidable. Red had to harden himself. This was how he lost out the first time. He forced himself to meet Harlow's beseeching eyes by reminding himself of the first rule of negotiations: If you didn't think you could handle the worst consequence a deal might bring, then you could count on losing. Harlow had taken a position and Harlow was holding and the position was that he could afford to gamble on Red turning out to be more afraid of killing him than Harlow was afraid of dying. At the same time, Red's position was solid; it was just as solid, if not more so, as long as he stuck to it. He had to hold his ground and rely on the odds, which said that nine times out of ten Harlow should to be more afraid of dying than Red was of killing him.

"I'm not Harlow," he said.

"Fuck you," Red told him. "Don't go back there. Don't try that. We're past that."

"You said counteroffer, where is it?" Bobby sounded desperate.

As Harlow pivoted to look at Bobby, his face came into a slash of light and Red wished he could be sure who he was. He was sure and not sure at the same time and one wasn't really stronger than the other, which was a stupid useless way to feel. The only thing he knew for certain was that he had to hide the fact that he had any doubt at all, and that he'd ever seriously asked himself if this guy could just be some misplaced fat guy who lived in Hurst in a big house. He wished he'd checked the Polaroids. Letting him drown, whoever he was, wouldn't get the money back, anyway. The thought of this pudgy figure descending into the black water annoyed him and left him resentful, as if the money were sinking with him.

"We're like the goddamn wetbacks," Red said. "That's the problem, Harlow. That's what you gotta understand. The goddamn niggers and greasers. You know how they're always complaining they've been disenfranchised. Well, that's what's happened to us. We've been disenfranchised just like them so we have no part to play in the normal course of things. That's the problem. We been tossed out. You can't appeal to us. You don't have the means anymore. It's like a foreign language. We're talking hip-hop rap crap."

"You mean I should talk to you like you're a spade?"

"Try it and see what good it does you. We won't know what the fuck you are talking about."

"What is he talking about?" said Bobby.

"All we understand is money. You get it?" said Red. "It's all we got for a common language."

Macky was grunting to lift the stop sign and hold it out over the side of the boat. Harlow gaped, watching every move Macky made like it was this amazing, really interesting athletic event.

"Jesus God Almighty, I've got eight thousand in a safe at home."

"You owe me fifteen thousand."

"The degree of difficulty on this thing is going up," said Macky.

"You can't kill me. I'll drown."

"What time is it?" said Macky.

"Why?"

"All right, all right!" Harlow said. He was gasping for air with each word, his voice getting littler. "I've got it. I've got it in cash at home."

"Don't bullshit me!"

"Red, please!"

"If you're lying, I'll bring you back here, you hear me? You swear it. You got the whole fifteen thousand?"

"I remember you," he said. "I suddenly remember. You're Red."

"That's right," Red said.

"I just remembered," said Harlow.

"All right," Red told him. "Deal."

"Yes, yes, yes." Harlow was looking at Macky, who was still holding the sign out over the water. His big hands and forearms were straining, his biceps swollen like they were filling up with this irritating liquid, making him grimace.

"We're headed for the pudenda bar," said Bobby.

"Bring it back, Macky," Red told him. "Bring it back. We got what we wanted."

"And could you do me a favor?" said Harlow. "Do you think you could do me a little favor and throw in those Polaroids you mentioned, Red? I mean, the ones with me and those bimbos. Just throw them in to sweeten the deal. If my wife got her hands on them, I mean, good lord, armed with those fuckers, the divorce settlement she could get would bust my ass for sure."

Macky dropped the stop sign. Bobby lunged to grab hold of Harlow, but it was too late. As Macky's empty hands flew skyward in a magician's flourish of presentation, water plumed over them in high cold spray, the boat bucking, the black sky heaving and shaking. Macky was laughing, while everybody else screamed and Harlow didn't move. The water came down over them in a faint spray. The sign was gone, but Harlow sat there, this weird look in his eyes, like he was taking a painful shit. The rope ran from his leg to the frayed end dangling through the oarlocks into the black water, where Red could see the sign growing faint. It wavered, as if signaling for rescue, a glint reaching toward them and enduring for the blink of an eye from off one of the letters. Maybe the O.

"He's going to give us the money, Macky," said Bobby. "What the hell are you doing?"

"I think the rope musta broke."

"You dropped it. I know you did."

"Some things are more important than money. Way more important," Macky said to Bobby, but he was eyeing Red intently as if he was the only one who mattered.

Lord, thought Red, now he's my friend forever.

3

WHEN THEY ARRIVED at the Animal Club, Red had fifteen thousand dollars in his pockets. There'd been two safes in Harlow's house, one in the master bedroom, the other in the floor under the couch and the shag rug in the living room, and between the two of them there was a hell of a lot more than fifteen thousand. When Harlow counted it out, he still had plenty to put back. Red thought about adding in some interest charges, but decided against it. He just went out to his car and dug up the Polaroids from the trunk where they were stashed in an envelope in the bottom of the cardboard box. He met Harlow in the kitchen and they sat down at the table to make the exchange over a couple of beers.

Now Red, Macky, Bobby, and Jake were striding the aisle of the pudenda bar, rocking and rolling to the heavy beat of the music. Red had paid the cover, tipped the doorman and the bouncer, and so felt huge and bossy. They all did. The money was rolled up in two lumps, one in each of his trousers' front pockets. He was swaggering side to side, his head high, his chin stuck out, riding a mood fueled on leftover nerves, waning adrenaline, and lots of alcohol. Bobby was mimicking the look in Harlow's eyes when the sign hit the water, and they all burst out laughing.

On a small stage to the right, a blonde was slipping out of a satin gown the color of fresh blood. The lights scorched her with jelled streams of cloudy color and the stereo system was so high-tech that the music assaulted them in a coiling embrace of sexy sound and sentiments.

They felt like a gang that Red had just guided through a dangerous escapade, and they had come to this place for their reward. They strode past several other small stages, each topped by this quality woman sprayed in light and driven to dance by the music. Ahead was the main stage. They settled at a table directly in front of it. Colored lights circled the floor and girls sailed across the polished surface, light rising off it in thick waves.

The approaching waitress had on a kind of Bo Peep outfit and she smiled and wrinkled her nose when she asked them what they wanted to drink. They all ordered doubles and started throwing back the single-malt scotch and Maker's Mark and crying out their appreciation for the women performing on the stage. There was Maggie and Pirate and Misty and Amanda. Macky bought a table dance for Red, and this sparkling, perky brunette with sassy eyes slipped from her gown and wavered around between his knees. After that everybody started buying dances for everybody, so one after another women appeared to look into Bobby's eyes, or Macky's or Jake's or Red's, as they bumped around between one guy or another's thighs, nothing on but a G-string and these shiny pasties glued onto their nipples.

Red thought Amanda was the best. Macky liked Pirate and Jake was crazy about Misty while Bobby said he liked them all, but if he had to choose—and it was a big "if"—he would pick Amanda. They weren't arguing, but it sounded like they were, because even when they agreed, they yelled, their voices clanging against one another with escalating drunken excitement.

"Her tits are real," Macky yelled. "I know they are."

"Bullshit," said Jake. "Hers are Styrofoam just like they all are."

"Styrofoam?"

"They're not real. I think maybe Misty's are real. Hers might be real, but—"

"What're you talkin' about—Styrofoam?"

"What are you talking about? What they put in 'em in these plastic bags and they sew them in. The plastic surgeon."

"That's not Styrofoam."

Red was taking the last of his Maker's Mark in a jubilant throw-back, the tilt of his head sending his gaze into a chance encounter with this blonde with a long nose and a sweet ass. She had just finished table dancing for two corporate stiffs in suits and she was slipping back into her dress.

"It's not Styrofoam, for god's sake, I know that," said Jake. "What is it? Celluloid? Celluloid!" His intonation left no doubt that he believed himself to be right at last.

"That's film, you dickhead," said Macky.

"What the hell is it? They're not real, that's all I know."

The girl with the two corporate stiffs had just picked up a glass of water. The stiffs were done with her, so they were turning to look back to the stage. Glancing at Macky, Red said, "What?" to something. He'd heard his name. But his interest in the girl pulled him back. She was standing there as still as a scared animal, her lips parted and the glass a few inches from her mouth, this look of sadness taking over her face, like she was beginning to recall some really terrible memory. He was thinking maybe he'd buy a dance from her, maybe get a friction dance. Her expression hadn't changed, the memory dawning on her, coming back. But Red knew it wasn't a memory, not really, even though that was the way she looked. He had no idea what exactly made him know that she had an ice cube stuck in her throat in that place where you can't get it out without help, but he was sure.

"Silicone," said Macky.

"No, no, no, that's computers."

"You're jerking me around," said Macky.

There was frenzy in the blonde's eyes now, her mouth open. She can't breathe, Red thought. She can't breathe or speak. He got up and walked toward her, knowing exactly what to do to help somebody in trouble like this. He'd picked it up somewhere in his endless TV watching. He put his arms around her. The music was in the midst of a lush, romantic move, this ballad with Whitney Houston singing. Red locked his hands just beneath her tits and pulled her to him. Because of the way she was standing, his need to get behind her had him facing Macky and Jake and Bobby, and one by one they noticed what he was doing, as he slammed his fist into her solar plexus with a force and effort that drew him forward so his mouth was pressed up to her ear. She was struggling, moving against the length of him, and she didn't feel real somehow, but unearthly and sweet like her body was spun of cotton candy, only electric and full of perfume. His arms around her were squeezing, her ass pressed into him, and she was in this state of perfect helplessness. She felt weak and sort of sweetly mournful, sagging against him. She's going to die, he thought. I can't stop her. He could feel misery filling her up and he pumped her again. She drifted into him, and though he wanted badly to save her, she was giving up. With the music dreaming on about love, Red felt as if they were dancing, and her ass sort of shifted and his dick felt it. He searched for the spot and tried hard. He slammed her again and an ice cube flew from her open mouth into the air and the breath came back into her. Without knowing it, he'd thrown the right switch, and he felt it at the same time that he saw the ice cube flying, this white light bursting out of it. Her teeth closed and opened like she was starving and biting hard into what she had to have, and over and over she filled with precious breath. He felt sentimental toward her, kind of maudlin and tender. There they were, the two of them, like these characters in a sad song embracing. And then he thought of Harlow and the lake and the sign glinting up through the black water. She was crying now, tears just sprouting in her eyes the way they do sometimes in a little child's. She seemed to be getting ready to turn and look at Red. He was eager for that. He could hardly wait for her to hug him and thank him. He let her go and she stepped away. Her eyes started darting, searching the room for something or someone. She took another breath and ducked her head and ran away.

The guys were all yelling at Red. A few people at the surrounding tables had noticed that something unusual was going on, but most had remained oblivious. Macky and Jake and

Bobby herded Red back to the table, wanting to know what the hell he had been doing. He was picking up his drink and sitting back down, getting ready to explain, when a bouncer came up to tell him the girl was all right now. It was weird the way the guy was acting, because there was definitely something threatening in the way he looked at Red, the way he talked. His whole thing was belligerent and mean. "Just sit back down," the guy said, like Red had misbehaved somehow, like he'd broken a rule.

A few minutes later the girl returned, but she never gave Red a look. Not even a peek. She seemed embarrassed about what had happened, and she was trying to put it behind her. Just forget about it. She got right back to business, working two new corporate stiffs on the other side of the room. Red ordered a triple Maker's Mark straight up, and when it arrived the waitress told him it was on the house. Then the bouncer swaggered back up to tell Red the management wanted to give him a free table dance, and up came a different girl to swirl around between Red's legs and wave her titties in his face.

VERANDA

Part One:
Not West, Not East

1

SOMEONE IS WEEPING on the veranda. But it doesn't seem connected to the present moment. Both the throb and the depths of this unhappiness are too insistent, too resonant and richly evocative. The present could not contain or explain these sounds. Someone is weeping on the veranda. It's hypnotic and I can see them, though I am nowhere near them. Perhaps it's just that I'm half asleep. In the uncertainty of this state, I could be borne deeper into the realms of the exotic or flip up into the thin and restrictive grip of the ordinary.

I open my eyes. Oh, yes, I think. The dark is here. But the surroundings are strange. I'm not sure which way I've gone. The dark is an inky waterfall rife with specks reminiscent of something they are not, which is dust. The room I'm in is a hotel room. I see hotel things. I'm in a hotel bed covered in hotel covers. The ceiling is a hotel ceiling. It's her, I think. She's crying on the veranda. We were at her beach house only days ago. We had dinner for the first time just a few days earlier. Ostensibly, the dinner was to discuss a business project. She invited me to her beach house for the weekend. Now we're in this hotel room. It's not really a room, but a small suite. It has a kitchen. Why is she crying? I can hear her through the walls and the French doors that open onto the veranda. The air is textured with the California night dripping with blooming flowers and foliage and cars and cries from the street. The gauzy curtains of the French doors pulse with a spooky light, a cold slash of neon. I wonder if she has her hands to her mouth. The rhythm of her distress is erratic, the sound recessed. I'm naked in this strange bed in this hotel room, the tears of this woman I've known for a few days permeating me. I've been hoping she would simply stop.

Something shifts. It's a thought at first, but then I understand it was also the light. She's moved and in her agitation passed before the French doors. At first I don't quite know what it is that's wafting through my sense of things. I sit up. It's her body. The air will not sustain it. Down it goes, turning slowly, an end to something. She could jump, seeking a radical revision, confusion the cause and result. The hotel is built into a hillside, and so the various norms by which our elevation might be registered are skewed. Three floors of other rooms full of strangers separate us from the ground, but the veranda, amended by the steeply rising landscape, is at least five floors above the road. Her sobs, along with the biting sound of her breathing, enter and leave the room. I'm trying to grasp her interior, as one would read an animal through its gestures, or the eyes of someone speaking a foreign language. Content is there, but it is blocked by my ignorance. I'm trying hard, though, and then I feel I am about to uncover what I need, or be uncovered myself. I sense an omniscient, looming unrelenting spotlight rolling over the ocean, moving through the black of the surrounding city. It hunts the creases of the streets and alleys beneath the trees, probing into other bedrooms, corners, hallways, seeking me.

At our first dinner, it was clear we both heard our own idiosyncratic version of the same summons, like a dog whistle, or a subliminal insinuation leavened into the sauce and skin of the Indian chicken we shared, the brandy sitting like a flower on the tongue. It wasn't exactly lust. It had another name, but lust was present and brash enough to ignore the other factors, or give us cause to ignore them. At the door of the beach house, she smiled and then, after glancing away, shot her gaze deep into my eyes. Our mouths sank onto one another, tongues squirming. I walked her backwards to her bed, our bodies stiffening with the logistical awkwardness of the transit. She retreated. I advanced.

Bedroom. Bed. Everyone wants to be a person. Now she's crying on the veranda and I don't know why. I'm afraid she will kill herself. Things get unleashed in people. Everybody is a systematically folded veneer tidily holding in havoc. Will she never stop?

I wonder how long I've been awake. I can't see my watch, and so I can't check it. Something must have been thrown over the digital hotel clock. Or I don't know where it is. Or it's gone. Not that I checked when I first jolted up. I'm feeling the presence of other people in this situation anyway. I don't know who they are, and they must be in my mind, but it doesn't feel like my mind, it feels like the room. A ghostly, crowding pressure, a little assembly waiting to be born. Or noticed. Or both. I'm one of them. Actually, I'm more than one of them, and so is she. What a weird feeling. What a weird discovery. That's when I get to my feet. I know exactly what is real and unreal in these circumstances, but something suggests that, while the distinction is obvious, the significance of these classifications may be less clear-cut than I might first think. The unreal could be the determining factor here, the governing voice.

When I part the French doors, her eyes dart at me, penetrating, then retreating, having snatched at something she hoped to seize and take. I don't know if she succeeded or not. In the shadows, she turns away, and I have the feeling she was waiting for me. In the shadows her nakedness is a matter of her flesh radiating bands and splotches of skin color through the charged currents of air and night. Columns of adobe partition the veranda as it moves off into the gloom accommodating suite after suite. A solid banister five inches thick rises above her waist, and the bricks of the floor are cold on my bare feet.

"Hey," I say.

"I'm sorry. Did I wake you?"

"What's wrong?"

"I didn't mean to wake you."

It's swooping nearer now, the floodlight I felt before, the beacon ordained to illuminate me, its range narrowing, its focus intensifying as more and more of the surrounding world is entered and searched and eliminated because I am not there. The other people, the unreal ones are with us on the veranda while some hover in the air beyond the wall. Some are focused, almost huddled around her, while the others have their hopes fixed on me. They're urging me, coaxing me. I know they're there and yet I don't really know they're there. Because I know they couldn't really be there. And so I know not to think about them explicitly, or at least to think about them only in terms of their not actually being there except in the most preposterous way.

"It's okay," I tell her, meaning the fact that she woke me. I'm not exactly lying because I don't feel anxious or annoyed or angry, but I am far from myself and getting farther. I feel secondary and derivative, as if I'm emulating principles I had no idea I admired so fully. In fact, I'm not certain I do admire them. The more I think about them, the more I realize that I understand almost nothing about them. And yet my alarm at the thought that I might fail them is unsettling. When her eyes meet mine, I see the unhappiness. It seems to open up behind her as if it's being funneled into her through some dismal melancholy pooled out there in the night. I wonder if she knows about the other people. They're flimsy, anyway, peripheral, unlike her eyes and her unhappiness.

"I'm all right," she says.

"What happened?"

"You can go back inside. You can go to sleep."

"Are you all right?"

"I didn't mean to wake you," she says, giving me a smile. "That's why I went out here. I'm sorry. Did I scare you?"

I'm closer to her now and I see that she isn't really naked as I thought, though her breasts are bare and her feet, her legs. But she's wearing panties. The beacon has found me now. It hasn't seized me, showering me with its glare and undisclosed aims, but it knows my exact location. The other people involved in these developing moments seem relieved by its arrival, as if they have been guiding it, feeding it information regarding my whereabouts.

"Go back inside," she says.

"You were crying."

"I couldn't sleep."

I take her in my arms to comfort her, but I don't know if I actually want to comfort her, or if it's more that I want to be someone who wants to comfort her. I stroke her tenderly, my hand pondering her nakedness, questioning it over and over, asking for something, knowing some things, but driven by a sense of absolute lack, my fingers filling with the electrical secrets of her skin, soft and fatty with nerves, dynamism, with hormones, with sadness.

"Did you have a bad dream?" I say.

"No," she says. "I don't think so. I just woke up. Maybe."

"Maybe what?"

Who are these waiting people watching us? I wonder and look out. The sky over the balustrade is more purple then black. A single star occupies the otherwise flawless deeps sinking into a blankness that loses all definition like the submerged layers of a pond. The foreground has a yellowish haze, a billowing fog of shifting greens and yellows and reds in a tainted rainbow of splattered neon burning along the roadway beneath us. Sunset Boulevard heaves into the west, pouring through the gully of buildings that band it on either side. The rooftops of businesses, bars, and restaurants give way in the west to a retreating vista of peaked homes asserting themselves with slanted shingles and gravel-strewn blacktop visible for miles, until finally the discernible world is nothing but a gulf flecked by sparks. To the north, the roads that feed into Sunset appear more and more like tiny snippets. The buildings in that direction are fragments, crowding into one another, their definition leached away. Nearby, a Japanese restaurant billows out from the hillside, the tended grounds embracing it like bonsai and illuminated by floodlights stuck into the ground. Billboards throw up blasts of color, the faces of movie stars, gigantic cigarette packs, and record album covers, while the gaps between are filled with a neon flare advertising Nude Dancing, a bookstore, a massage parlor, a restaurant with big plate-glass windows and a mahogany door, an adult movie theater, and several all-night convenience stores.

"Do you know what's bothering you?" I say to her.

"No."

"Are you cold?" I'm talking about one of the things my fingers have discovered. "You feel cold."

"No."

"You do." My hands are still on her. I can't find what I'm looking for.

"Please," she says. "I'm really all right now. You can go back to bed."

The fact that she has gone to stand naked on the veranda has made me aroused. I'm naked and she's naked except for her panties. We're both naked on the veranda, the both of us stuck out on this island of adobe midair. I'm already hard when I get her back into the bed. The fact that she stood weeping on the veranda has made me hard. I don't know exactly what I think I'm doing as I press her back on the bed and kiss her. End something. Yes. Change something. Yes. Of course. But what? Her arms fold around me. I'm on top of her. I don't know exactly what I think I'm doing as I make love to her, but I keep at it. It goes on a long time. The bodies take over. They could do this without us. Maybe they are. Maybe they are doing it without us. Maybe I'm just hanging on and hoping to be a part of it.

Our bodies are still going at it. They're really going at it, the lips are tangled, the tongues probing and pushing one another. Each of us could be almost anybody. That's the idea. The parts are all named and interchangeable. The night is this big house with people in it. I'm holding on to my body, trying to stay with it, as if it's about to get away somehow, as if it's about to jettison me entirely.

She's below me now, and she's very open, very raw, and her openness seems an opportunity to me, something I can take advantage of to slip beyond her boundaries, to part her emotional restraints on the basis of her opened-up body, her parted guard, so that I might slip into her and get the truth. "Why were you crying?" I say. I say it softly, tenderly, but the effect is violent. Her drooping eyelids spring back and she looks into me as if I'm burning.

"I don't know," she says, and grabs my hair. "I don't know." She shuts my mouth with her own, and the bodies hurtle on.

But I know what's going on, even though she didn't tell me. The other people are all yelling. It's babble really, because they're yelling different things. Some are yelling to run, to fly. But I know what I know. In the second drawer of the dresser, the one that has been designated as my drawer while I visit her, I have my plane ticket in its official little folder with the airline logo on it, the times of my departure and arrival on a computer printout. That's why she's crying, because I'm leaving tomorrow, I have a son back east, a little boy, and I'm going to see him, and now that I know all this it angers me. I resent it. With one breath or another, I feel bitter toward her for it. I feel something radiating out from her to wrap around me. It's spun from something deep inside her, and it's immaterial and sinewy, and I can feel it closing around me, sealing up certain alternatives. I can feel it and I'm enraged at her for it, as I pin her there and stroke her, holding her tighter and tighter, appalled and helpless before my own collusion in this matter, the burgeoning swoon of collaboration and receptivity into whose thrall I am going willingly. Not in the sense of will as volition, as selection between options, but in the sense of ambition, an irresistible need, a force of desire that is irrational. And so I succumb, willfully.

When it's over and the bodies are done, they release us to ourselves, and it's a difficult retreat, a difficult reconstitution. Actually, it's hopeless. Neither one of us can sleep, though we lie there silently, breathing and thinking, breathing and thinking. The shut blinds in the windows begin to fill with color and light, the slats defined in slashes like razor cuts. Birds leap out from the nests in the eaves, thumping the air with explosive flurries, their wing beats pounding out leverage in the sky. When the birds return, or when newcomers alight, their little feet are like a sprinkling of broken glass cascading down the tiles toward the brink where the roof ends. It's funny, but I fear for them. As if they aren't birds, as if they might topple over the edge and simply plunge. All night long, automobiles approach and depart from many different directions. At times they are only a few—single cars separated by long interludes. At other moments they come in clusters. But gradually the frequency of these clusters begins increasing at a rate that has a clear correlation to the mounting intensity of the light and this growing coincidence makes all the varied phenomena seem related and interdependent, as the room is hewn from the murk into the definition of day.

2

WHEN WE WAKE, we order coffee and croissants from room service. The bellman who arrives with the tray is handsome and youthful in a full-lipped big-eyed sort of way. He smiles politely at me as we both watch her sign her name and room number on the check. She's wearing a floral robe whose design has a subtle Japanese flavor. The croissants are rich and buttery and I jab gobs of jelly into the pliant interior of the second one I eat. The coffee, which we sip while seated at the small, circular glass-topped table peeking out from the archway that defines the kitchen area, feeds its rush into my system. When we're done eating, she smiles at me and somehow or another one of us moves, or both of us move, and then we're on the bed again, our tongues, our hands, pawing away robes and trousers, the conspiratorial ghostly rush unfolding. I check my watch as I fling her sideways on the bed, my need to know the hour disguised and secretive, but I see the time just before her mouth closes on mine. It's 9:20, maybe 9:21. My plane is at three P.M. Then the hotel phone rings and we keep going. Then her cell phone rings and she answers. It's her agent. She's an actress. I'm a writer, with a screenwriting job. That's why I'm in Hollywood to begin with. Well, one of the reasons, as if reasons have a part to play.

"Oh, that's terrific, Bobby," she says, sitting up, floating away from me, phone in hand. "Yes, yes. He's sharp. Really. Really." Every repetition of the word makes Bobby's side of the conversation, the subject of the call, more mysterious and intriguing. "He's dynamic," she says. "You know how few of these guys have any vision at all. Sure. I'll audition. I mean, what could be the worst thing, right? I'd get the job. I'd have to spend three months in Africa. Lions, tigers. I'd be in my element."

It's like she does it now, it happens to her. The roof opens up, and she's spirited away. I see a globe, the world turning and showing the vast blue of the ocean interrupted by the little scraps of continents and there's an arrow in a rising arc, which speeds and plummets, digging its way into Africa. Then she's off again. Another arrow bending around the brooding globe, racing out of day into night and landing in Ireland. Then Greece. She's gone and gone and gone. That's the way I feel. The room might as well be empty.

When she rejoins me on the bed, her body is this flowing ripeness enveloped in an aura that feels magnetic. She's in her early thirties, and there's an element of enticement to her beyond will or awareness, a glow in her skin, the crazed pheromones flowing. We're on the bed, our mouths locked, and I'm trying to talk myself out of the pang I felt when I heard her on the phone. I'm thoughtful and attentive to both the dialogue within myself and the one between our mouths and hands and skin, yet what the collision of these various efforts produces is the image of her riding further and further into the waves beside her beach house. In the middle of that first day we spent together, she'd gone swimming and I'm remembering. I'm not a good swimmer and so I fretted as I watched her stroke herself into that far-flung, foreign element. Like parachutes, waves ballooned into fullness lifting her to a collapsing peak as the mass evaporated and left her plunging from view into a shifting crevice whose definition vanished. I sat on the shore and ate a mango and watched this little figure, the arms and elbows rising up into the air, then sinking into this vast, shuddering blue full of mounds and slabs and sparkles and inky cracks like a solid surface shattering. She was scrawny and buglike, disappearing, having been borne a hundred, two hundred yards into the broken waves. When I lost sight of her, I had no idea what to do. I started up the beach as if that might take me closer to her. After a hundred yards or so, I wheeled and came back.

The beachfront at her house rose up through foothills to a set of wooden stairs that led to her house. When I reached the top of the stairs, I turned and scanned the shattered gleam that was the sea. Between two shards of light, I caught a fleck of human skin that slid from view. The mango was gone and my teeth felt hot. I went inside and stood near the phone wondering if I should call the police. What would I say? I knew nothing about ocean swimming. This might be the way it went. She had plunged in knowingly, confidently, saying she did it all the time. The last thing she did was smirk at me. Having walked into the ocean, her arms poised to dive, she glanced back over her shoulder with a look of contempt for my concern. Well, now what? I thought. I turned on the television and watched part of a football game. Why had she done this? Gone so far out to sea. No one else around. It seemed insane. I rose and walked to the window and looked out into the uninhabited flow of blinding facets, watery and constant in their restless reordering and overlapping. I imagined the police arriving, as if I had called them. What would I say? Who was I in relationship to her? What would I call myself? I didn't know. It didn't matter. Still, I tried to explain. I don't swim. It's her house. She said she did this all the time. But I was not talking to the police. I had no idea who I was talking to. I was explaining myself to unknown people, but they were people who were very interested. They were concerned. They weren't strangers. They hadn't just arrived. And all the while the TV screen rippled with red uniforms trimmed in gold collecting in various formations and then exploding against the figures in white uniforms with black numbers and helmets, while the crowd reveled and the commentators pointed out technical subtleties in the steadily altering patterns of uniformed men producing order and chaos on the gleaming green field.

Her return was signaled by coughing. I got up and turned off the TV. She was on the stairs, looking skinny and frail, and she was shaking. "I nearly drowned," she said. I wrapped her in a towel and dried her off. She started talking about how she had been borne off irresistibly into the sea by this contrary, impervious authority. I kept patting her and drying her and wanting to leave. Everything hurt. Something was being squeezed behind my eyes. It was like a shrill electric drill sound only it was being produced by constrictions in the meat that made up my brain. That was the first moment when I really knew about the other people. The thought that told me about them tried to refer back to the earlier moment when I had wondered about the people who weren't the police, but this was different. That earlier moment had been confused. This was clear. Other people were invested in the outcome of this moment. I could feel them, hear them, though their claims were clouded by the violence of her gasping, which was slowly evening out. I tried not to think about them. I tried to think about her. I tried to think about my hands patting her.

"It never happened before," she said. "I do that all the time."

"I didn't know what to do."

"What?"

"I was worried," I said. "I didn't know what to do."

She looked at me, as if she were startled to find me in the room. I wanted to be someone else, someone who would have known what to do, who would have known whether what was happening was dangerous or not. I wanted to leave the room, to walk away. In the months before we met, she had been abandoned for the final time by a boyfriend who had abandoned her many times. In those same months, a woman to whom I was not married and whom I had previously rejected only to be overcome by panic and disorientation had rejected me. I drank a lot and had a hallucination. At this point, I left my wife and small son and flew to California after this other woman. So the two of us were both more or less haunted, and on the rebound, and so up in the air emotionally speaking, and now we were in this room, wrapping her in a towel. The door was shut. I didn't remember closing it, but it was shut.

We ordered pizza and smoked a joint and lay on the couch eating mangoes. The marijuana made the mangoes hallucinatory. I got up at one point and went out to look at the ocean in the night. It was night now, night had come on, and it was like looking into a sealed-up, unlit cellar with the windows boarded up, all this blackness at the bottom somehow seeming to move and break apart and coalesce over and over.

Now I am holding her down on the bed in the hotel, as if to stabilize her. Because I have to. But I'm sinking. That's the trouble with sex. You think you're doing it, but you're not. I've got her pinioned there and we're both breathing in these long heaves over and over again. It's morning and so not black like the view of the ocean when I looked out at it from her house, or when I stepped out onto the veranda the night before, but I can't really see her. I'm startled when she breaks free. Her arms slap around me and her mouth closes on my neck, and she wheezes with satisfaction and aggression, something defiant in the sound, her teeth sinking into me, her entrails, the hollow of her gut, sucking. I know what she's doing, but it's not necessary. She's not that passionate. It's deliberate. I can feel her teeth and inhalation drawing the blood in a knot up to my skin. She's bruising me, branding me, marking me. I'm going away and she wants people to know I'm hers, that I belong to her, the people on the street, the people on the plane, the people that I see anywhere I go in the next few days, particularly if I should take off my clothes with some other woman, but anywhere I go really, anybody really, and it angers and scares me, but I don't throw her off, I don't resist. I swoon, I submit, a sickening appetite weakening me further as I stay in her arms and seem to disappear into her desire, which is despotic and provocative in its calls to secret desires rising up in me to overthrow my present order, the familiar foreground receding, the hidden background advancing, and I am governed by an overwhelming strangeness.

3

I'M DRIVING. The day is bright. In the rearview mirror I see
her car, a blue Oldsmobile, distinctly in the glass. Every time I
make a turn, her vehicle disappears and then reappears. It's like
I'm trying to get away and she won't let me. We drift on down
the road headed for the Rent A Way rental agency. I'm going
to return my car, and then she will drive me to the airport. I
keep glancing in the mirror. On the passenger seat I have a sheet
of paper with scribbled directions that I was given over the
phone by an attendant at the rental agency. We're getting close.
I sense a familiarity in the buildings and ease into the right lane.
I could have been in this part of town for other reasons, of
course, but I think I'm remembering the day I picked up the
car. At the corner, I turn slowly. Halfway down that block, I
look into the mirror to gauge how far she is behind me, but the
street is empty. At the approaching intersection ahead of me
the light is green. I search the mirror, but she's not there; the
only cars I see are parked. Around the corner I just took comes
a green Ford pickup truck. The light is changing to yellow. I
cruise through the intersection, crossing to the other side, but
I no longer feel like I'm driving. I feel I'm being compelled forward by this wind pressing me on. I have to stop. I slide to the
curb and turn in my seat, waiting for her to come into view.
The hands of my wristwatch are only slightly parted. The stub
that marks the hour stands at one. The second hand is a slip of
black sweeping forward. I'm sure she'll veer around the corner
in the next few seconds. Or else she'll come speeding toward
me from another direction, having caught sight of my turn too
late, only to compensate and improvise. My flight doesn't depart LAX till three. The airport is forty or so minutes away.

To get there on time I need slightly more than an hour and I have two at the moment.

Again, I scan the roadway. Cars slide by the notch between the buildings that frame the street off which I turned, but none of them are hers. I'm trying to decide whether to sit there or go on to the rental agency where I could at least get my car turned in. From there I could take a cab to the airport. But I wouldn't have my suitcases, which I'd stowed in the trunk of her car. I would be without my carry-on satchel, which I inserted behind the driver's-side seat of her car. Buttoned away in a front pocket of my satchel is my plane ticket. I could get another ticket, of course, if I got to the airport early enough. I could go without my luggage. That'd be great. Sure. Arriving back east without any clothes or my work or my couple of books.

I find a pay phone and call her cell phone. I don't own a cell phone. I just don't want to be available to everyone all the time, but I wish I had one at the moment. Not that her cell phone helps, because I reach only the message function. Either she's not getting service or it's off. I explain to whatever's listening that she should meet me at the Rent A Way. Hanging up, I'm uncertain what to do until it occurs to me that she might have already decided to go to the car rental. I did jot down for her on a piece of hotel stationery the names of the streets intersecting at the Rent A Way franchise. I gave her the phone number. She could find her way there more easily than she could get back to this corner if she got lost. I take off, crushing the gas pedal and cutting around four sharp corners that take me around the block and past the same shadeless curbside where I was parked moments ago.

My hopes of finding her waiting for me at Rent A Way are shown to be pointless when I arrive, and I'm not really surprised. I snatch the contract from the glove compartment, jot down the mileage, and stride toward the glassed-in cubicle of the office. She's doing this on purpose, trying to make me miss the plane. I'm enraged but struggling for control. I feel eddies of emotion coiling around me to enmesh me. I'd been scheduled to leave today for weeks. My schedule was set long before we even met. I told her right from the beginning that I had to leave on this day and date to visit my little boy. Why is she doing this? But I know the answer. Or something in me knows, though it's dull and anxious, an ache of wordless conviction.

The female clerk at Rent A Way is hard to focus on. She seems little more than a blur of flesh tones wrapped in plastic harlequin glasses above the beige of her uniform. "Did anybody call for me?" I say to her.

"What?"

I point to my name on the rental contract and say again, "Did anyone call for me in the last few minutes?"

She looks me over as if to discover something unsavory, and then calls to her coworkers with my question, but none of them have taken any phone calls for me. "No, no. Sorry," she says and adjusts the position of the nearest of the several potted plants stationed along the gleaming Formica of the counter. She stares at the leaves, and I do the same for a second, before we refocus and get on with things.

When the transaction is complete I step back outside and start pacing up and down. In a way, I'm relieved. Some vague inducement tethering me to rationality and optimism is cooking away in the heat. I can feel it drying up, turning brittle. I wheel and glower at every arriving car, but she's never behind the wheel. Of course not, I think. And then, with the squealing brakes of an arriving maroon Ford Mustang careening into the lot, I realize that she's never going to show up. Because what has happened is that she's had an accident. She's dead. It's not a trick. She hasn't revealed something untrustworthy. How many times did she joke about her ineptitude behind the wheel, and I know that somewhere out in this California glare her Oldsmobile has spun from the road, the ensuing havoc erupting in flames.

But the noise I hear is one of the Rent A Way attendants rapping on the window behind me. She's holding a phone out toward me. When I come racing in, she says, "This is for you.

I *think*." Her qualification is full of snide distaste. She rolls her eyes in an exaggerated, theatrical way, distracting me from the phone she has placed into my hand. I stare at the green plastic of the receiver, as if its intended use is visual. But a thin and denatured replica of human distress is squeezing out of the tiny holes that mark the earpiece.

"I could barely understand her," says the attendant.

When I bring the phone up, I hear her blubbering like a baby. Her words are fractured and soggy, a blur of distress like drool. I can barely make out any part of what she's saying. She's wailing, her apology crippled and wet.

"Are you all right?" I say.

"I'm so sorry," she burbles and then is swept away in a series of wheezes.

"What happened?"

"I got lost. I couldn't find anything. I didn't know where I was." The admission gives permission for a loud bawling, her sentiments crumbling like sopping paper.

I imagine her sinking to her knees, her lips enfolding my cock. I wish she were here so I could strip her and get my hands on her.

"Oh," she says. "Oh, damnit." She can barely speak. "Do we have time yet? Here's where I am." She spouts the names of two streets. "How do I get to you?"

"No, no," I say. "I'll take a cab."

"Oh, God, it was so awful. I didn't know where I was. I mean, I knew where I was. I just didn't know how to get to anywhere but especially to get where you were."

"We have time. Don't worry. Just stay there."

The attendant calls a cab for me, and we wheel about for a good twenty minutes before I spot the Oldsmobile in the lot of a Stop & Shop. We seem to be at the edge of a kind of barrio or something. Every face is Hispanic. How the hell did she get over here? I wonder.

She's sitting behind the steering wheel wearing sunglasses and smoking a cigarette when the cab pulls up. I walk to her car and open the door slowly. She keeps looking straight ahead, the cigarette popping in and out of her mouth in embittered little jabs. Below the blot of her glasses, her skin is reddish, puffy.

"I tried to call you."

"My phone was off. You don't have a cell so I didn't think— and then when I turned it on, there was your message. I got your message."

"We better go," I say, climbing in. "Or I'll miss the plane."

"I don't think I should drive. I'm not a good driver." She pulls at her sundress, working to lift the curve of pink cloth from off her ribs. Her fingers squeeze open some of the buttons at the waist. The parted fabric reveals a patch of skin crossed by jagged scar tissue isolated by a leaden paleness from the smooth glow of surrounding skin. "This is from a car accident. It was last year."

A chill travels quickly through me, settling somewhere in my stomach. It's a feeling, some kind of an emotion, but hard to name. It's as if I've taken an icy drink and my body cannot manage to reduce the freezing temperature. "What happened?" I say.

"You drive," she says. "All right?"

I hasten around the car, while she manages to move herself past the lever of the gearshift. As I slip in, she's lighting another cigarette. I don't think I've seen her smoke before except for the marijuana we shared.

"I don't have any idea how to get from here to the freeway," she says, "but I have a map." She pulls it from the glove compartment and flips it to me. "I was parking my car in front of my house when I hurt myself. This was last year and I pulled up and jumped out. It was late at night and I just jumped out. I ended up in the emergency room. It rolled back on me, the car. It wasn't this car. This was sometime last year."

I'm hunting for a point of reference in the abstracted topography rendered in colors on the map, and simultaneously I'm imagining her accident. I check the keys, the codes, the lists of street names, and wish I could have been there that night. I look out the window at the street sign and search for the name in the list.

"There was a sort of hill," she says. "I hadn't put the car in park. It started rolling backwards, so I tried to jump back in. I thought I could jump back in and that way I could stop it. But the door was open and so it was sticking out and it slammed into me. The door slammed into me. It knocked me down. I could have been killed. I fell back out of the car and onto this driveway. It was rolling backwards—the car was because the driveway I'd parked in was on this incline. Somehow I landed so that the wheels went by without touching me, but the door, the edge of the door, the bottom edge scraped me. Gouged me. I was trying to get up, I guess. I had to have thirty-seven stitches."

My finger is fixed on the map at the cross streets where we sit. The streets are clear and definite. The lines depicting them are black and absolute as they flow through one another across a pale surface flecked with numbers. Time to start the engine and go, I think, as I start the engine, trying to hold in my mind the sequence of street names and corners at which I need to turn in order to get to the airport.

"I'm not a good driver. It's hard for me to drive. I have to concentrate. I have to pay very close attention. It shouldn't be hard, I guess, from what other people say, but it is. It's very hard. It's exhausting, for me, okay. I'm better, I'm getting better but it's terrifying." She pulls a Kleenex from her pocket and dabs at her nose. "Sometimes I feel like the other cars can't see me. I feel like the other cars can't see my car. I just don't believe they see my car and this makes it all very stressful. When I'm driving, I feel like there's no reason they should know I'm there. Why should they? On those two-lane highways especially, I mean, where there are just two lanes and my car has to go right past this other car going in the opposite direction, that's the worst. I can barely do it—it's excruciating and I can barely do it."

"Sure you can."

"No, no."

"You just stay in your lane."

"I know, I know, that's the idea, but the thing of it is—" She stopped. "I don't know why I'm telling you this."

"What?"

"Okay, okay. I don't believe they can see my car."

"Of course they can."

"The other drivers. It's just hard for me to believe they know I'm there."

"What do you mean?"

"What I just said! Aren't you listening? I just said it. Didn't you hear me? That they can't see me. That's how I feel. That my car is invisible."

"How long have you been driving?"

"What's that got to do with it?"

"Well, what you're saying is—"

"I know what I'm saying."

"Of course. Sure. I just thought, I thought maybe it was a matter of experience, or—"

"I'm talking about how I *feel*. I'm talking about how I *feel*."

The entrance to the freeway lies ahead, and I slide into a turning lane and set my turn signal blinking, waiting for an opportunity to scoot across the flow of traffic. After a racy little Toyota shoots past and just before a lumbering truck reaches us, I hit the gas and zip us onto the incline of the on-ramp.

"I was trying to fit a tape into the tape deck," she says. "I looked down and then I looked back and you were gone."

"The turn came. I had to turn. It was the turn to get there."

"Where? To the car return?"

"Yes. There it was."

"Okay. Sure. Okay. I just wish I'd known you were going to turn at that split second."

"Well, I had to turn."

"You just disappeared."

"From my point of view, you were the one who disappeared."

"Didn't you notice that I was looking away when you looked back to check me?"

"I checked and you were there."

"What did you see?"

"You were there. I turned."

When she doesn't answer, I try to keep my eye on her. It seems she's taking the emotions assaulting her and wielding them against me and I feel pressured by them, I feel knocked about. Anger from somewhere is pointed and penetrating. Resentment bounds between us. It's my own, I think, but it could be hers. There's no denying it, whoever it belongs to. We're both feeling it, whoever it belongs to. It's violent and steady and hard-edged. Ahead, the glint of a 727 arrives in the sky, a silent apparition, and I follow the trajectory of its ascent out of a jagged skyline formed by two- and three-story buildings and high-rise hotels.

"You didn't answer my question about what you saw when you looked back."

"I saw your car."

"And what was I doing?"

"I don't know."

"But what was I doing? What did you see? Did you see me?"

"Of course I saw you."

"And what was I doing?"

"I don't know."

"You just said you saw me."

"I did."

The threat of tears haunts every phrase, and I see her as a wounded person in a messy room into which someone needs to move and create order.

"If you saw me, what did you see?" she demands.

"Well, you, you know. You. In the car. Definitely visible. Behind the wheel. Driving the car."

Her cell phone bursts out with its fanciful little tune, intercepting us and repeating itself as her fist plunges into her purse. Now the damn thing's on, I think, watching her bring the handset to her ear. "Hello," she says. "Sure." She cups her hand over the mouthpiece, her tongue waxing her lips, leaving them moist. "It's Bobby," she says. "Bobby, hi. I'm on my way to the airport. No, no, I'm not going anywhere," she giggles. "I'm taking a friend. Right, he's leaving. So I'll be free soon. His flight's in about fifty minutes or so. We're cutting it close, but we're almost there. Sure, I could have dinner. No, no, that'd be fun. Sure. Really. He's going to be there? Really? Oh, he's terrific. No, no, I've never met him, but I've heard so much from people who have worked with him. And we have several friends in common." As she listens intently, my heart starts racing. I feel like I have to stop the car and get out and start running, like I'm pursued.

"Really," she says.

We're streaming down the freeway surrounded on both sides by the jangling onrush of traffic, a storm of rattling scraps of metal slicing from lane to lane, spewing exhaust, blaring music. "Really," she says, allowing a husky quality of amazement and disbelief to transform her excited tone into one of almost reverential surrender as she settles into the luxury of Bobby's last remark. I'm feeling like I've been flung from the car, left by the roadside. "They came back already. That's incredible," she says. "So they're serious. No, no, you don't have to do that. I'll screen-test. All I need is time to prepare and then I have no qualms about that. Not for him. I mean, he's one of the great directors alive. Oh! Oh! That's very exciting. Who else is going to be there? Terrific. I haven't seen him for so long. Right, Bobby. Just like you. No, no, no," she's laughing.

Another plane is rising through the glare above the squat, jagged skyline. Soon I'll be up there, sailing away. This dinner she's talking about is a room full of men, and I see her entering; I see her come walking in, and there's one of them who fixes her with a particular look, a predatory stare, shifting in his chair and waiting for her eyes to find him, and I'm trying to pick up his name, it's the name she'll drop next in this phone call with Bobby, whoever he is, she'll say it soon, and I'll know it. At the beach house, she meets him at the door. They're falling into the bed. I see the sheets, the walls, the windows. I see the bodies. The bodies know what they want, they don't care. I'm looking at the skyline across which a plane is gliding, lifting, departing. She's laughing with Bobby, and my memory of the distress that ruled her moments ago is spooky. Her manner is conversational on the phone, mischievous, and utterly carefree. If the scope of her distress was authentic, where did it go? But on the other hand what did I expect? I've seen her on the screen, the blank towering whiteness across which her exaggerated flesh, her beaming 70-millimeter eyes and passions and her Dolby voice, have been strewn as if they were the product of some molten excess. I feel an acquisitive twinge, a lustful grab; she feels abundant, a concupiscent extravaganza.

"So you think it's all just really a matter of formalities and this and that kind of thing, but in fact I've got it. That's what Hamilton says, is it? They want me?"

Hamilton, I think. Hamilton is the one. I feel invaded by a violent caress as irresistible as an X-ray.

"Of course, I trust your instincts, Bobby. I'm in your hands. And if Hamilton knows these people the way you say he does, if he knows the way they work, I'll be eager to sit down and hear his take on this whole thing."

If I could fuck her now, I could turn her words to snarls. I could bring her back to me, shrink her down to where I am lodged inside her, attached by mouth and tongue and cock, transforming her grandiose manner into a fixation on me and what I am doing to her where she is most sensitive, until she is filled with nothing but me, the petty appeal of this conversation forsaken.

"All right, Bobby. Be still my heart. See you at eight."

I don't want her to look at me, but she's going to. We're in a car together and so she has to; and now she's turning to me.

"Bobby thinks I'm going to get that part," she says.

"Great."

I'm looking at the horizon, hoping to catch another plane in its exquisite ascent. She's sitting next to me, staring straight ahead, her hand lingering on the phone. We're passing the color-coded indicators for the airlines and, when I see mine, I turn off the main road. We both know we're running late, but neither of us suggests that we might just have her drop me off at the curbside check-in. We enter the tiered lots. I find a spot and park. We hasten through the traffic to an electronic door. Tears are leaking out beneath her glasses and she reaches to me and squeezes my hand. Now it's me she's back to, I guess, along with the tumult of her feelings. They maul her, overrun her, opening up a tantalizing glimpse into a limitless reservoir of emotion. If only I could turn it all toward me, become the primary object. This vast store of feeling would be mine. I see myself basking in radiance, luxuriating in a fire that leaves me feeling loved. I put my arms around her. I know how to tend people, how to care for them. I've never known quite how to impress women, how to court them. But I've been attuned all my life to other people's moods, the detection of their needs, their hidden feelings.

We're standing in the terminal near the carry-on checkpoint. I stroke her hair. I feel her fingers knotting at the base of my spine; her taut little breasts provide an electrical ooze through the thinness of our clothes. I pull my head back and look at her. I kiss her carefully, then ease back into a simple embrace, feeling her body shiver. For minutes we stand there, awaiting some next step to be taken, the right word said, the addition of a missing element that will complete the moment. Soon they'll call the boarding of my plane. I don't know what we're waiting for. My fingers shift at her waist and brush the open buttons on the dress, the fabric parting like a mouth to draw my hand inside. I want to feel her skin. Her breath lifts and lowers her ribs and scalds my fingertips as I touch the scar, and then she moves to brush away a wisp of hair with the back of her hand, and on the underside of her wrist I see a gleaming squiggle across the veins, a worm of dead skin echoing some ancient cut. We're like a pair of secret agents flashing mirrors across the inky distance in a secret country. Her wrist is blinding and from my depths I'm signaling back. The tissue on her wrist is thin, the veins so available. At the instant of this signal, we know of one another's true existence. Somewhere, sometime in a tiny room and with a knife or razor or shard of glass, she sliced her wrists.

"Good-bye," she says.

"Good-bye."

Step after step, I click along, my black scuffed shoes sustained atop the concrete floor. I see the gouged skin peeling back in a gash whose aching center awaits me, wants me. It's as if her wounds are a result of blades applied to me. I feel their amputating slash. She's waiting behind me for the moment when I will turn and wave. It's what I have to do. Wave and go back. Give up my departure. There she'll be, the swatch of her pink dress identifying her among all the strangers trooping in their contrary directions, her legs jutting out from the hoop of her skirt in a rush of flesh into her shoes. I sense the buffeting emotions about to overtake her. How can I leave her in this unhappy world, when my return could change it?

I turn. But the spot in which I last saw her is overrun with strangers. I look to the left. I have to dodge the flow of people trying to move past me; they seem to want to knock me aside. Crowds have replaced her. I hasten all the way back to the door and step out into the heat. Cars and buses fill the air with fumes, the metal cooking. Past the uniformed baggage carriers, I look for her. I scan the gaps between the flowing cars, searching out the path we took up from the parking lot where we left her car. But she's gone. She's headed for her dinner.

I take an escalator and watch my carry-on luggage slide away on the conveyer belt into the rectangular compartment where it will be x-rayed. I keep seeing her at the dinner. It's like they do it right there, her and the man. Hamilton. They peel her clothes off her. She lies there on the white of the tablecloth and they do it, and I lose her when they do it. All that feeling in her goes to him. I step through the adjoining skeletal archway and find a bar and order a whiskey on the rocks. I don't have to ever see her again. I'm flying away. To the east. New York. I'm homeless, really, wandering, subletting. It's all hotels and cafeterias. She could never find me. I don't even know the phone number of the friend I'm going to be staying with in New York. So I didn't give it to her. I couldn't. I don't have to call her. She won't be able to call me.

Beyond the drink gleaming in a heavy bar glass, I catch my face lodged among bottles in the mirror. I'm sitting there with the drink in my hand, but what I'm seeing is this tiny body riding further and further into the ocean waves. At first I think that it's her, but then I see that it's me stroking out into the black water.

My plane races down the runway, struggling to lift off. A scream hurtles us forward. Groans are produced, the suffering squeals of metal, a sound of rattling plastic. The engines thrust, the earth tugs, and then, unexpectedly, this violent contest generates a startling softness, and the buildings, the cars, the walkways, ground plans of countless roadways show themselves in all their dizzying, shrinking intricacy. Soon they'll disappear. As we rocket upward I take a breath. The window frames the metallic shimmer of our gigantic riveted wing stretching out into an emptiness woven with blazing wind and thickening clouds receding into an uninhabitable absence of cold and space. This is what I want. This is where I want to be. I feel subtly, strangely altered. Not West or East. Not rambling, aimless, vagabond. Not failed husband or dubious father. Off the ground. Airborne. I'm recollecting our embrace. The way she trembled against me. I try to imagine her with me. Seated beside me. But we don't seem like ourselves. We seem like other people. That's the thing of it, I think. Sometimes we are not ourselves. Sometimes we are other people. I try to imagine holding her, even though I am uncertain who she is, and who I am. I search for something to steady me, to hold back my rising velocity.

Part Two:
The Little House

4

THE AIR OVER THE MIDWEST swallows us in a series of tilts and angled slides, then seems to shove us sideways. We bounce. Occasionally there's a rocking accompanied by a faint complaint from the materials composing the shell around us, even the wings. Then we enter into snow. The flakes are visible for a while before the plane climbs out of them. We rise into a bright, harsh glare with the storm left behind in its multitudinous descent. I imagine it tumbling down in great puffballs for thousands and thousands of feet before settling amid swirling winds onto the farmlands of Illinois, Wisconsin, and Iowa. It's doubtful that we are actually over Iowa, but I picture us above its familiar shape, the squiggly line of the eastern boundary marking the path of the Mississippi River's plunge south. This conjuration suits me. Almost comforts me. I grew up down there. I stood in padded snowsuits gazing up at planes whose sound and arcing shimmer I traced with a squinting, upturned gaze, each flight a fantasy darting in the heights. I think of my own four-year-old son and the way he'll look when I arrive to visit him. I try to see him as a kind of beacon pulling me closer. Who is he? I wonder, mixing him up with the dreamy little boy I was. He's not me, but somebody else. Accompanied by these thoughts, I sit in a row of strangers, one among many such rows of many such strangers, all sailing over the earth. I signal for the stewardess and order a scotch, and then a second one. Two will be enough I think, but when we're still hours out of Kennedy I order a third. I contemplate the future in the guise of a plan, the world and the next few days sustained in my thoughts in an orderly pattern, proceeding along the lines of what I intend to make happen. I sit quietly in my seat, my legs in front of me, feet on the floor; that's all I have to do. I will take a cab into the city, sleep on the couch of a friend's Eighth Street walkup. In the morning, I'll have coffee, maybe eggs. I'll probably have to bullshit with Larry, the guy whose apartment I will have slept in. And then I'll head south in a rented car. My son and ex-wife, Nancy, live in a suburb outside Philadelphia. I think of her as my ex-wife even though the divorce isn't final. The suburb isn't the same one we lived in when we were married. That was a place called Monmouth Lake. No lake in sight, not a hint of there ever having been a lake. We occupied a five-room apartment on the ground floor of a small building with four different residents. Now Nancy and my son, Robbie, have their own little house situated farther out from the city, a little deeper into the countryside. This town is called Garden View and the house I purchased for them is nestled in a ring of woods.

I'm dozing now, an edgy little dip into half-sleep fueled by scotch and nerves and weariness, each of which provides a kind of scratchy influence gnawing at the images jumping about in my head. Let's call it a dream, I sort of say to myself. It's all pretty haphazard, and first I wonder if I'm dreaming and then I decide that I am. The sensations dominating the atmosphere are all animated by a grim sense of there not being enough. That's the tone. There's an absence, a lacking. Of what? Everything. Anything. Air. Food. Space. The house I purchased for them will not compensate. The letters I write to my little boy, the visits I make, the several phone calls a week that I manage with him sighing on the other end, muttering, moody, confused, restrained. Nothing can make up for my absence, my abandonment. I have betrayed them. I fight back in the dream, mounting arguments in my defense, marching about trying to rally support, I hold up a placard whose tattered face bears a text so badly scribbled it cannot be understood. Certain I know the meaning, I look at the placard. I believe it will declare: I have no choice. But it says something else, something strange that I can't understand. After such a lengthy, pointless dream, I vow to stay awake.

The following day, as if I'm in charge, as if I know what I'm doing, I head south in the continuing snow. The turnpike traffic is slow, though the roadway has been plowed and sanded. The flow of cars is unexpectedly heavy, creating an almost earthen brown river of slush. Strip malls and factories and towering black smokestacks adjacent to buildings shaped like gigantic black barrels, along with warehouses and used car lots abound on both sides of the road. The low clouds seem to emit, along with the snow, a chemical stench that finds me inside the car and penetrates into me. Billboards and exit signs along with uninvited thoughts try to divert me, urging me off into towns I have no interest in visiting in order to purchase products I don't want. The first meal Nancy cooked for me had started with artichokes, which were something I'd never seen before and had no idea how to go about eating. So I stalled, embarrassed by my ignorance, and waited for her to begin, so I could use her example as a mode of instruction. As a tactic, this worked up to a point. Oh. I see. You pluck the little leaves, then dip them in the bowl of butter. But when I bit into the little leaf, expecting to chew it, the spiny result could not have been desired. Thinking I understood too quickly had led me to misunderstand the way one ate an artichoke. I coughed and, with my hand as a screen, plucked the remnant from my mouth. I took a sip of water, while Nancy pretended not to notice. She smiled, purred with pleasure as she tasted another tiny leaf, this time exaggerating and slowing the way she skimmed the leaf with her teeth to drag onto her tongue the tasty film that coated the underside. After a sip of wine, I tried again, and thought it was a lot of work for such a meager amount of food. At the same time I felt I was being introduced to a wider world. I'd grown up eating cereal and milk and wieners and fish sticks and hash and beef stew and hamburgers, potatoes, baked and mashed, sweet corn, coleslaw. Beans. Peas. No little leaves soaked in butter. By the time we got to the heart of the artichoke that first evening and I saw how to cut it and clean it and soak it and savor it, I was beginning to see the point.

The way the snow is dusting the world with a deceptive gentleness that deepens relentlessly making the roads more and more treacherous can't be the reason I'm thinking such things. I have no idea what the reason is, if there is a reason, and there probably isn't one, anyway. Not in a directly traceable sense. I hadn't even really focused on the memory. I'd listened to jazz on the radio, focused on the road.

Around me the downpour continues, though somewhat lightened. The wheels of nearby cars roll through slush with a hiss. Nancy was a decent person, but we should never have married. Wider world or not. Artichoke hearts or not. When I met her, I was a patched-together person who thought he knew himself. I had to think it, forcing myself to believe it, cheering myself on with half-truths and personal slogans salvaged from broken convictions and collapsed connections, and when these weren't viable I'd call up outright lies and advance them with as little self-awareness as possible, such as telling myself I knew what I was doing, or that I knew exactly what I wanted. As undesirable as this might have been, what choice did I have? Otherwise how did I get out the door? How did I put on my shoes? These are big questions, impossible questions, unless you start from a point where somehow you are a person.

And so that's what I did back then—I made up that point—and it's still what I'm doing, more or less, because what I seem to have at my disposal is not exactly a full-fledged personality. Maybe it was worse back then, but I'm still pretty much an idea of what I hope I am, or aspire to be and have decided to act like. Still pretty much more what I feel compelled to appear to be and to eventually become if I am to survive—more that than whatever I actually am. More a willed construction, an armature of traits pasted and taped and claimed around a near emptiness. Which is what I've taken out onto the road in this blizzard.

That emptiness. That construction. So there I am. I have my plan, my ideas, some coffee growing cold in a paper container. I have what was once true in my head and what is now clearly untrue and they're both in there together adding up to trouble. That's the way it used to be and the way it feels like it still is more and more since I stepped off that plane at JFK. That I have just put my name on this apparatus that I'm counting on to drive the car on down the road into snow so heavy it seems to hover in mounds well off the ground, drifting around in airborne heaps that blot the light, dimming the day.

The windshield wipers sweep back and forth over the slanted pane that lets me see out through a fog-enshrouded lens, bringing slush and slop into view for fleeting instants before the snow obscures them again. The wipers wheel without rest like the arms of an angel tasked to reveal the world and then cover it up. I hope I have enough windshield wiper fluid, because I know that's the key to keeping the road visible. The wiper blades thump with every repetition and squeal on just about every other one, creating a predictable intrusion into the jazz on the radio where a bass fiddle and drums being brushed, a piano and some kind of muted horn produce notes like ice chips traveling in the opposite route of the snow, at least that's how it seems, that they're going upward one at a time. The tune is old and lyrical, a standard from I think Cole Porter that the jazz disguises at the same time that it weaves an elaboration. I feel I can drive on like this forever, cruising into this onslaught like I'm in the nose of an airplane at a very high altitude, the radio offering buoyancy as the wipers stroke open a wedge of gray air and roadway that appears dangerously akimbo, a large black metal object transforming slowly into a car sideways in the road. And then the headlights flare directly at me as the Buick continues its weird rotation. I ease the wheel gently to the left, losing sight of the black shape skidding laterally out of view as I flow by, nudging the wheel to the right now in order to slalom around a red Volkswagen bug gliding backwards through the slush in front of me.

The little house in Garden View appears, at last, behind layered screens of ongoing flurries that turn and spiral amid powerful currents of wind in the area between where I've halted, the engine running, and the house under the frosted, drooping trees. Drifts are up to the windows. Sometime earlier a path was shoveled down the few steps from the front door and out to the road but it has been overlaid so many times that it's little more than a rounded indentation now. The hour is late, nearly dusk. The road is packed down, having been plowed and sanded recently. The windows on the ground floor are yellow squares veiled in the ceaseless downpour. Clearly, I won't be able to park on the street so that leaves the driveway along the side of the house. Like the steps, this narrow lane was cleared earlier. Nancy's Honda, under layers of snow sculpted by wind, has been pulled far forward, leaving room. The snow along the sides is several feet deep and the lane itself holds a good eight inches. I'll have to race on the plowed road, blasting my way in, and then I'll have to dig myself out in order to leave.

When a shiver of motion in a second-floor window snatches at me, I focus and see my son in the frame. He's sliding his head between the shade and the glass. I can't see his face or expression, only the black of his hair, but his anticipation reaches out to me. I start the car forward, picking up speed as I see the silhouette of a second head in the window as Nancy joins him and I know they're gazing out at me though I can't distinguish their eyes.

When I'm inside the kitchen, stomping crusted snow from my feet, they stand in the doorway at the base of the stairs that lead to the second floor. The tiny room seems huge and they are far across it. We're all lost for a moment. My son hovers near his mother, leaning into her leg, his head angled away, though his eyes are on me. It's like they might stay there forever, or that they fear me and want to ask me to leave. I've never lived within these walls, but old habits pull at me. I feel awkward, clumsy, sad and I wonder how I'll ever last the three days I've promised to visit. I've lived with these people. The boy is my son; the woman was my wife. The space has a voice, an array of demands.

"What an awful drive you must have had," she says.

"It was a mess."

"I'm surprised you made it. I thought for sure you'd call from somewhere that you were stuck and couldn't make it."

"I just kept going."

"We were getting worried. Weren't we, Robbie. I know I was. Were you getting worried about Daddy, Robbie?" His big eyes rise up to her, and she half laughs as he nods and peeks at me. "I know he was," she says. "He kept looking out different windows. Upstairs, downstairs. He's been doing it for hours." She bent down to him, placing her hands on his shoulders. "But he's okay, see?" she says, turning him toward me. "He made it. Daddy's here."

Sitting down on the nearest of the kitchen chairs, I feel an obstinate pressure pushing me down and heat like layers of woolen blanket closes around me, sealing me in. "Robbie, come here," I say, my arms out to him.

A noise spills from him, and if it's joy it's the version an animal knows as he hurls himself across the gap between us, traveling headlong and with nothing to keep him from crashing except me. He lands and I lift him. "Hi," I say. "Hi. How are you, little man?"

"Okay."

"Have you been reading my letters?"

He nods, then fixes me with his wide dark eyes. "I can go get them."

"No, no," I tell him. "Maybe later. How's school?"

"Okay. I been looking for you," he says.

"I was traveling. Working."

"Oh."

"I was in New York."

"Oh."

"Well, yesterday. Working. But before that I was in California. Did you get my letters?"

"What's California?"

"You mean where is it?"

"I don't know."

"It's pretty far away."

"He loves those letters," Nancy says. "He looks at them over and over and makes me read them over and over, don't you, Robbie."

I've been sending letters that tell a story and I've done quick, very rough, but not altogether bad sketches to serve as illustrations. The story is about a small friendly snake, a butterfly, and a cricket who join forces to travel cross-country from California. It's a kind of adventure / travel story. They are journeying to visit Robbie, known in the story as the little black-haired boy. They have adventures. He's patting my leg and leaning into me. His little hand falls up and down gently, steadily, softly, like a bird wing trying to take a bird somewhere.

"Do you need to change or anything? Your shoes or anything? Are your feet wet?"

"No, I'm okay."

"Are you starving?"

"I'm hungry."

"I've got some soup on the stove. On a night like this soup is the best. I was waiting to put together a salad."

"And I could use some coffee."

"Sure."

"I don't know how I'm going to get to the motel."

"What motel?"

"The one on Three-sixty-seven. The Howard Johnson. I made a reservation."

"I didn't know that."

"Maybe a cab. I just don't think I'll be able to get out of the driveway as deep as it was."

"I had it plowed early thinking I didn't want it to get too deep."

"I know. I'm not complaining."

"I didn't know you were planning that."

"Well, of course."

"You don't have to go to a motel. In this weather."

"There'll be cabs, though, don't you think."

"There's a pullout bed in the little room. It's all made up and that's where I thought you'd— It's kind of our catch-all now with storage and whatnot, but it's cleared out more or less for tonight. I'll make it a kind of library sometime, or maybe a studio for my photography if I get back to that, if I have time, so it's boxes and all that now, but the pullout would be fine. Go take a look. It's just down the hall. Robbie, show Daddy the other room where your old bike is. I'll get the soup ready and some coffee. You said coffee."

I nod, feeling hatred prowling around the room looking for me. It's in the corners, mostly. I can't see it, of course. It's hers, probably, because she must hate me, running off the way I did. The open cabinet doors exude a kind of haphazard disappointment. It's probably hers, too, though it could be my own. All of it could be mine. It really doesn't matter where it's derived from, as it follows me out of the kitchen with Robbie tagging along. He slips in front of me and patters down the narrow hall to a room with a partly open door. It takes a second to find the light switch. The room is as promised, boxes and clutter all pushed to the side to accommodate the bed once it's extended from the couch along the wall. But the idea of sleeping there makes me nervous. The new status we're trying to occupy doesn't feel all that sturdy. It feels more like flimsy ideas and decisions than anything real. It feels wavering, theoretical, in need of definition. Going to the motel would declare that I did not live here. I'd wandered around in every kind of mood in front of Nancy. Wandered naked, or in my underwear looking for coffee. At one point I'd wanted to be naked in front of her, naked with her. We'd had a joint checking account, a savings account. We'd shopped for groceries together, making and reading a list. Looked for apartments, discussed needs, budgets, purchased appliances, two different cars, even this house. I'd seen Robbie born, emerging from inside her with her body seeming to split open dangerously, excruciatingly, to let him out into the world headfirst. She'd done my laundry, her clothes mixed in with mine. She'd seen me miserable, hopeless, seen me drunk, seen me hungover. She'd seen me out of my mind. It was true that before I'd actually managed to leave, she'd witnessed me in a state on more than one occasion that, if I'm honest, and why not be honest at this weird juncture, at least to myself, I would have to call hallucinatory. And so the idea of sleeping here feels dangerous. I fear that if I go to sleep within these walls the past will take advantage of my slumbering susceptibility and come crashing back in all its wealth of detail to claim me, reasserting itself, sweeping my decisions and declarations aside and me with them the way floodwaters indifferently wipe away homes and whole towns.

Robbie sprints past me and bounds onto the couch, where he jumps up and down, smiling at me. "It's a bed inside," he says, throwing his feet up in the air and dropping onto his butt where he bounces like a little doll of a boy on the floodwaters I've just imagined.

Nancy calls to us from the kitchen. We have to go. She has three places set and she's ladling soup in a silver dipper from a large pot on the stove. The salads are waiting. Bread and butter are waiting, bread in a pile on a plate, the butter in a butter dish. This is what I mean. I have to hold the line. The soup is a thick scarlet liquid crowded with bobbing hunks of cauliflower, clustered beans, potatoes and beef and bits of pasta. She places a pale green bowl filled to the brim at the end of the table and eyeing me says, "That's for you," before returning to the pot. As the next serving is delivered to Robbie, who stands waiting, he smiles and nods as if he knows what it is to be manly. "Let's eat, Dad. I'm hungry. Are you hungry?" He drags his chair out from the table enough to create the space that will permit him to struggle up onto it.

"Oh, the coffee," Nancy yelps and giggles, as if anticipating some kind complaint from me. "Sorry," she says, pouring and placing a blue mug before me.

After dinner, I settle on the couch with Robbie and the letters I've written. Wherever I've been, I've taken time every few days to compose them. He wants me to read some aloud, and so I do. This is the point, I tell myself, as we sit there and he snuggles against me, listening intently. Nancy has already read them aloud to him, so he knows their content, but now that their author and creator is present, he expects something grander, a more far-reaching reward. His big eyes beseech me. This is the point, I think. This is why I'm here. This is why I flew back. He listens attentively. I read slowly and think it again and again: this is the point, this is the point. If I can do this. I have to do this. He's my son. My son, my son, I think, as I read:

> The snake was very tired from traveling back and forth
> across the sand, the trees, the mountains, and whatever else
> came his way and on his back a cricket riding all the while.
> For a time the snake thought maybe this wasn't so good, and
> then the hot sun disappeared and the cricket began to sing,
> and his singing was sweet in the dark of the desert, the
> mountains, the valleys, the trees, and it made the dark seem
> sweet and the desert and mountains and valleys, too, and the
> snake began to find in the singing a rhythm that helped his
> crawling . . .

Robbie sits with his chin caught in a hook of his thumb jutting out from his forefinger, so he appears investigative, even philosophical, and his manner and the fact of his contemplation captivates and worries me, for I know he is actually considering seriously the matters the narrative engenders. He is searching for meaning and understanding. I can feel his brain sorting slowly through the events and characters and their relations, the implied consequences. When I finish, he sits quietly, and after some consideration he looks at me and nods. I know that this nod is in essence a question. He's acknowledging the point of suspension at which the narrative has left him. He's wondering if I will help him with his uncertainty and conjecture. I study a sentence, then glance at him, before returning to the page. I want the moment to seem weighty. I want the issues to feel serious and demanding. I wait and then I say, "I wonder what will happen next." His eyes respond with a bright and crucial revelation, for in my question he finds a mirror of his own present state and perhaps of far more than that. This is exactly where he was stuck; it's exactly what he was wondering. In my verbalization of his thought he finds a great joy. I can see it well up from some concealed, very private place inside him. He can't believe how much we are alike. "I don't know," he says, grinning at me.

"Me either."

He nods, and between us a sly exchange occurs and it's funny and we both know it, because after all I am the creator. I am, in a manner of speaking, the story. We're cuddled there, and I'm thinking, Good, good. I'm glad I came; this is why I came. He's nestled against me, and nudging to get closer. It feels like deeper. Deeper into me. I can feel his blood flowing, his calm gratification, as if he's been fully nourished. The sense of accomplishment these seconds deliver enters as a wondrous, good thing, and then slowly it alters, becoming pressure, a growing experience of being transgressed. I fear I'm falling prey to a subtle and hypnotic mirage, which prompts a wish for scrutiny, a need to resist, to stand, to move. I don't want to push him away and thinking, I love you, I love you, I get to my feet. I look down. He gazes up. In this moment of waiting and expectancy he exhibits an appetite with the depth of an abyss into which we both could fall. "Daddy has to go pee," I say.

Of course, when I come out of the bathroom and start calling around for a cab, things transform and it feels like we're in a different room in a different house. It's all veiled, very restrained, but we're fighting, his mother and me, and he knows it. She has the phone book, and she's feeding me numbers. Try this one, try that one. But the bitterness is widespread and growing as if all the doors have been removed, the windows smashed. The mist and chill of the atmosphere equals if it doesn't surpass the impression of the dark snow-covered world outside the frosted window where Robbie stands gazing out with his back to me.

"Robbie," I say, "come here. Sit on my lap."

He looks at me as if I'm not there. He seems to peer into an arctic vista as he searches me.

"Don't," she says.

"What?"

"Just make your calls."

"What?" My bewilderment is growing, deepening, thickening. I feel screamed at and want to scream back: What do you want? What more do you want?

"I'm sorry," she says, "but he's over there so let him look out the window."

"Sure. If that's what he wants."

"I think it is. He's doing it."

"But I don't understand this."

"Fine. Just think about it."

"Believe me, I have."

"He wants to look out at the snow. Call your cabs if you have to, but let him look out at the snow, if that's what he wants. Bluebell Cab is 767-3333."

"What?"

"767-3333."

"Robbie," I say, my eyes on the dial so I punch in the correct numbers, my voice searching for an indeterminate tone that leaves me sounding phony like I'm trying to coax and deceive a shy animal into believing there's no need to hide when there is.

"Why can't you let him alone?"

"Robbie!" This time my tone is harsh and edged, as if I've deliberately hurled a hard object at him and he jumps. He straightens and studies me. "Come here," I say. "I want you to sit on my lap."

He obeys.

She says, "What bullshit."

The cabdriver is enormously fat. Though he has only a single head he spills over the entire front seat, as if he is multiple people. His hands are like puddles on the steering wheel. He leans forward as if proximity between his eyeballs and the glass of the windshield will increase his acuity in driving and seeing. I am tilted in the backseat, slumped. I've brought nothing with me from the house or the trunk of my car. I walked out the door leaving her glaring and glacial and Robbie stricken. No one seems to understand what I'm doing but me. I feel alone in this hopelessness, a pioneer in this hopelessness that is my life, riding in the backseat of a fat man's cab while he mumbles and steers and tells me a sad story I have so little interest in that not a single detail regarding his woes stays with me once I've paid him and left him and walked into the Howard Johnson's where another enormously fat man smiles and greets me. It's funny how I feel nearly as happy to see him as he acts to see me. We don't really know each other and he's just doing his job, but he actually consoles me. I'm glad to be out of the snow, I guess, and out of the cab and alone in the elevator, all of which seems somehow due to the fat man behind the desk. When I asked if the bar was open, he didn't belittle or judge me; he just said, "Sure," and to my question about room service he said, "Until midnight," and seemed happy as he said it, so I felt free to order three drinks to be delivered and he was fantastically empathetic and somewhat overjoyed to fulfill my hopes.

And then the numbers and signs in the hall guide me to the right door where the weird little plastic card trips the green light and provokes the beep and the door opens. I walk into an empty room with closed blinds, a wide bed, a nondescript rug, and a ringing telephone that I try not to answer, that I know I must answer.

"He's very upset," she says. "Can you hear him?" I can. In the background my son sounds like a hunt dog or a ravine trying to channel tumultuous wind. I listen as she scolds me and either I surrender to her logic and passion, or I simply recognize she's right, or she's just right beyond the best arguments anyone could mount. "It's ridiculous," she tells me. "You're just pouring salt in the wounds with this motel crap. You come here to visit, but go over there. Just visit if you're going to. It's a visit. Nobody expects anything from you. But we do expect a visit, and a visit doesn't happen with you over there. Where are you? Are you listening?"

"Yes," I say as I respond to the light knock on the door by letting the bellman in and paying for the three scotches he's delivering.

"This is just mean. It's so mean. He's so disappointed."

"I'm sorry."

"It's just adding insult to injury this way. He thought you'd be here. That's what he was counting on. You'd sleep here. He'd wake up. He'd come down. You'd be here. He'd jump in with you to wake you up. You know? Do you know what I'm saying? He thought you'd visit."

"Right."

"Right? You say 'right'? Like you knew that. I'm confused. So what are you doing over there if you can say that?"

"I know."

"What do you know?"

"What you're saying. What you're saying." I take a big drink of scotch and close my eyes.

"So then I don't have to say it again in order to make it clear to you, do I?"

"No."

"At least I hope I don't."

"You don't," I say, finishing the first of the drinks.

"So where are you sleeping?"

"Soon," I say. "Soon."

"Not *when*? I didn't ask *when*, I asked *where*?"

"It was a long drive."

"I mean, this is pointless. It's completely pointless. Treating us like this. You might as well not even try."

That scares me. "No, no, I have to."

"Good God, you're such an idiot."

"I know, I know."

"I hate you."

"I know, I know."

"What do you know?"

"I'm sorry," I tell her. "I'm just— I'm just trying to make it work."

"Sure. What?"

"The divorce."

"Great. But he's over here crying. I can't make him stop."

"Can I talk to him?"

"No."

"Let me talk to him."

"No. It's just stupid what you're doing. Going to this stupid motel. In a snowstorm. Are we that awful to be around? It's insulting."

"That's not what I meant. It's not what I wanted."

"I have to go see him. He's just—he's desolate. This is heartbreaking."

"I'll sleep there tomorrow. I'm sorry."

"What?"

"I'll sleep there tomorrow."

"I have to go."

"All right," I say. Not that my agreement, or anything about me or anything I might say, matters to either one of us at the moment, for my priorities are bleached and dissolving in the blast of what's happened.

The motel is a welcome blank world with a green uniform rug running end to end and empty closets with a dozen empty hangers and fresh towels neatly draped over racks near the toilet and a shower stall built over a tub and miniature bars of soap in unopened blue packets and green shampoo in unopened little bottles and I'm grateful for all of it. I wander about sipping scotch. But most of all I'm grateful for the shower that I climb into and stand under letting the water at the hottest temperature I can tolerate pummel and cook me. I flop naked into bed with the TV on, the channels flashing with their gaudy propositions of varied distractions and though I want one of them to take me off and hold me in its movie plot or the shock of some news story or the high drama of a sporting event, nothing works. Boxing, basketball, hockey. It's just these strangers skating, running, punching; it's just the news of dead bodies piling up in Central America; some junk bond trader marching down a courthouse steps.

I end up in silence with the lights out. Lying there eyes open, eyes shut, it doesn't matter. I think about Nancy and Robbie. I think about California and what I did there. I miss her. I miss what we did, the way she swam out and came back and what our bodies wanted. Even though I felt I was fleeing as I left to travel here, what I feel now is absence, desire, guilt, hope, all confused ambitions that have a powerful command, each in its own direction. That's me, I think. I'm in there somewhere. I picture Nancy and Robbie in their beds, each in a different room. I try to enter them, to know them, to be them. It's difficult. It's as if their interiors shout at me: get out, leave us alone. But I manage to find a way into Robbie, or I think I do. Nancy hates me. When she stated this fact over the phone, I was glad to hear it. It seemed like progress. We both want to make things okay for Robbie. Not that such a thing is really possible, as far as she's concerned. And maybe it isn't. But I have to believe it is. And she does, too. It wouldn't work if I stayed. I would become bitter and mean. But I couldn't do it anyway, even if I wanted to try. I was nuts. I'd actually seen a tall woman who wasn't there. Better not forget that. The required control is gone. I no longer have it, if I ever did. I thought I did once. And what about the people waiting? Who are these strangers that I feel are so invested in what's happening? I found them, or first sensed them, in California, but I don't feel their proximity now. In California, she seemed to bring them on. I don't know what it is I'm really thinking about. In California it's what time now? Not that it matters. Where is she? I imagine her coming into the room where I'm sprawled at this second, into this motel room, this bed. Who is she? I close my eyes and open them quickly as if to catch her sneaking away or maybe one of the interlopers, these undisclosed figures of influence creeping up because they want something from me, or want me to do something. Or is it that they want to become me? From the place I've pictured as being inside Robbie, I look up into a vast, ever expanding domain governed by giants, quixotic and all-powerful in their rule of his world that has many of the qualities of an underground cavern with stars stuck in the rugged sweep of black overhead amid gathering winds and mysteries. Robbie fears these giants and loves them and feels he is small; he feels he is alone; he feels he is lost, and he is all of these things, and we both know it. And then it begins to snow. The ceiling of his little room splits apart, and the roof of the house in Garden View, already cracked and crumbled from the hammering storm, groans and gapes and snow from the sky pours in and down on him endlessly. The people waiting and watching begin to whisper but I can't make out what they are saying. I strain to hear them. I strain to see them, and I see her in the ocean. Her arms lift from the waves, her elbows crooking skyward before lunging to paw the sea. The opaque horizon fills the distance and my arms shudder in imitation of her swimming. I'm in a strange room. It's a hotel, but not the same hotel. Is anyone crying? She's arrived and dried off in a hotel room different from the one I'm in and different from where we were and she's with a man I don't know, a man different from me, and the way I feel as I watch them together in the hotel bed is the way Robbie feels under the snow. After the water. After the mango. Beyond the wintry glass the night extends and rises and falls and spreads and there's no veranda and no ocean. But where the dark is weakened by the struggling reach of light, I see an avalanche pouring down to gather in suffocating drifts. The wind blows the realization in that I'm asleep, but this information feels negligible and of dubious merit by the time it arrives, having originated too far away.

5

IT'S HALF PAST TEN the following morning when I get back over to their house. The snow has stopped though the sky is overcast. The cab drops me off and I walk around to the back. Along the way I study my car buried up to its hubcaps in drifts with the surface frozen into a gleaming crust, and I try to estimate how difficult it will be to extricate it. When I come into the kitchen, I hear a piano playing. It's a lovely, simple melody that feels familiar, though I can't name it. Easing around the corner into the living room, I find Robbie seated on some phone books stacked on the piano bench elevating him enough that he can bow over the keys on which he concentrates intently. I stop and watch, listening to the chords and the central themes, both of which have elegant, classical qualities. Nancy appears in the room, coming through a doorway I hadn't noticed before. It's covered by a blue curtain that wavers and drapes around her as she stands there holding a down jacket.

"Hello." She's sullen, her glance touching me with a slight aversion and leaving quickly the way it would from something vile. The sound of her voice tugs Robbie in her direction, and he rebounds off the distaste in her expression straight to me. My presence startles him. He gapes at me, but then seems shy and worried as he returns to the keyboard.

"Where'd he learn that?"

"What?"

"Did he memorize it? I don't see any sheet music."

"No, no, he's making it up."

"He's making it up? What do you mean?"

"He's been working on it for days."

"He's composing it? Is that what you mean?" I angle a step or two toward the piano, uncertain whether to mute my amazement or exhibit it openly, even dramatize it. "That's beautiful, Robbie. That's a beautiful song." Such a creation in a four-year-old must be unusual. It has to be. That's what I'm thinking. "Does he do this often?"

He falters, his narrow gaze fixing me with a thoughtful solemnity that I recognize as the residue of his unhappiness last night. It's not hard to see the pangs of wariness and mistrust in his features. As he pivots back, his little fingers spreading over the keys, those same afflictions strike me as embodied in the music he's producing.

"Are you going to be here for a while?" Nancy says.

"Sure. Yes. I'm here."

"I want to go shopping and if you're here Robbie can just stay. I won't have to take him and drag him around with me."

"No. I'll be here. That's why I'm here."

"Right."

"But my car's blocking yours in. I can dig it out, if—"

"That's all right. I have a ride. Someone's coming. This friend and I both need to shop, but we want to get going while the roads are somewhat clear."

"Okay. Sure."

"They'll be by any second now. I was just about to get Robbie bundled up to go with us, so you got here just in time. You could have walked up to a locked-up and empty house." Slipping into her jacket, she pauses. "I don't know, but Robbie has his therapist today. I don't see how he can get there. It's half an hour away in normal driving and today with everything—"

"I could take him. What time is the appointment?"

"It's at one. I won't be back."

"I'll dig my car out. It's still Dr. Loecke, right? I mean, it's the same place, right?" Though she acknowledges silently that at least I have my facts right, it doesn't alter her dismal assessment of me. "I can do it," I say.

"If you do, you do," she says with a shrug that in spite of its accompanying smile leaves a trail of doubt as she walks from the room. Robbie is concentrating on the music. I slip after her and find an angle that allows me to peer into the kitchen. She plucks a shopping list from a pad taped to the wall and studies it while reaching for her stocking cap on a hook near the door. A few seconds later I'm standing near Robbie as the door slams. He stops playing. He jumps to the window. A tan station wagon halts in the middle of the road for Nancy to climb in. She doesn't glance in our direction as the driver, a woman, pulls away, leaving us leaning on the sill.

"Play some more music," I say as we straighten.

He shrugs and with his eyes averted is overtaken by effort and stress as if he's beginning a taxing, muscular feat that he is determined to complete. Whatever the deed, it's far from over, its demands intensifying when he grabs my hand and starts tugging me away with an urgency that rises through his touch.

"What?" I say.

He keeps on marching, leaning like a pilgrim into a bitter wind as we pass the kitchen and go on down the hall toward the open door of the little room. The curtains are back and light streams in to greet us as we arrive. A bright wintry haze floats over the couch that has been converted into a neatly made bed with fresh sheets and a bright blue blanket tucked in, the pillows fluffed. Once we're there, he lets my hand go, as if offering freedom. My nod finds him trying to read me, and I feel he's looking for the truth. As much as he might aspire to nonchalance, his shoulders are tense. "Me and Mommy made it this morning. It's your bed. You can sleep in it," he tells me.

"Great."

"You can sleep in it tonight."

"Great. Yeah. Good. Thanks. I'm sorry about last night. It was a mix-up."

"Oh." He's thinking hard, while trying to appear casual. "What's that?"

"A mix-up. Well, it's . . ." Regarding last night such a complex and confusing set of factors, options, and feelings spreads out before me with each one requiring definition and explanation, even forays into history and psychology, mine, hers, his, but mainly mine, that I can't go on. But he's waiting, the light of his expression suggesting a singular, deliberative curiosity, as if he has suspicions regarding this subject I've introduced, and he's eager to hear more. "Well, I say, it's a mix-up, which is—well, adults have them. People do the wrong things, not even what they want to do, but they do them. Sometimes. Feelings get hurt."

He folds his arms, his body wavering slightly as if from the effects of the uncertainties shifting about in his thoughts, but then he settles and says, "Kids have them."

"Yeah?"

Again his chin rises and falls in a sign of meditative affirmation, and the move is a subtle modification of its predecessor conveying more than agreement, as if he's sharing wisdom.

"The thing about the bed like this," I say, "is, well, when I get tired, I can just drop into it and sleep."

He checks me as if to test my reliability at this instant and then he jumps onto the bed, landing on his knees and flopping backwards. Once he's reclining, he tucks his hand behind his head and smiles as he closes his eyes, as if to show me how it's done.

I make coffee and then dress him in snowpants, a big jacket, and a stocking cap with a dog's head for a tassel. He feels sturdy to me as we stuff his feet into rubber boots before heading outside to hopefully free my car. He watches for a while as I thrust and clank and grunt with the shovel to clear the wheels and begin a path through the five or six yards to the street. As the task becomes prolonged, he falls down and makes a snow angel, asking me to join him, so I do. A big one beside a little one. He starts throwing snowballs at me after I return to the work of clearing and when one hits me, he says, "Sorry."

Finally it's time to take a run at getting out. I pick him up and carry him inside. The car will shiver and shudder and roar and I don't want to have to worry about him being out there and getting in the way. We're in the kitchen as I'm explaining what I call "our plan," and I try to ignore the puzzlement and darkness edging over him. But then as I turn toward the door, tears like tiny clear balls of desolation roll from his eyes. "What? Robbie," I say, and he's speechless, gaping at me. "I'll be right back." Somehow the explicit content of these words conveys their opposite to us both and his lips tremble and I understand he's afraid I'm running away.

"Do you want to come out with me? And sit in the car while I back it up?"

He's nodding before I'm halfway through the sentence. "Okay." I strap him in the passenger seat and pace around the car and out to the road and back to assess our chances. Climbing into the car, I feel the task looks possible. I get the engine going and then roaring as I pump the gas. I don't want to stall.

"Look out for Mommy's car," he says, his eyes on the Honda in front of us.

"No, no. I'm going the other way. Hang on." I send us backwards until, after just a few feet, the wheels begin to whir in a pointless spin. I let the heft of the car rock us forward, and then I apply the gas again. Back and forth, over and over, I play with the forces involved and each heave feels a little more trustworthy. Robbie sways in synchronization with every thrust and return of the machine. "Good, Robbie," I say, and sensing that momentum is about to become genuinely ours to employ, I say, "Now, Robbie, push!" and he does, leaning back as the increase of gas jolts us and we wobble, skid, sway, bump, and then with a gathering stability glide out onto the street. "All right," I say. "We did it."

He claps his hands and looks around as if the world has just revealed one of its more amazing secrets.

I make lunch, grilled cheese, more coffee, some of the leftover soup from dinner. He drinks a big glass of milk and then, with a handheld tape recorder I keep in my car for notes, I record him playing his composition. His eyes rest on me only once and briefly, as if he fears prolonged distraction will ruin his effort. I find the music even more intriguing and rewarding this time.

The therapist works out of his home situated somewhat farther in the countryside. The trip, normally half an hour, takes close to an hour, but I've made certain we started out early. Still, we're barely on time.

Dr. Loecke is dressed in slacks and a sweater, his beard neatly trimmed. I've met him before. We had several consultations when Nancy and I first arranged for Robbie to meet with him after the divorce became inescapable. He smiles, then shakes my hand and gestures to the magazines scattered around on the table and chairs. "Make yourself comfortable and Robbie and I'll be back in a while."

I watch them go. Dr. Loecke has his big hand on Robbie's shoulder. In the last seconds, Robbie angles his head and tilts his torso in order to keep me in view through the gap in the slowly closing door. I have the feeling he thinks the image he steals of me in these last seconds is something I will never know about.

Settling with two or three magazines in the largest chair, the pages I leaf through fail to register. I wish I'd brought a book, or some work, and then I just sit there trying to imagine them beyond the wall, this stranger and my son. I try to picture Robbie's unconscious, because that's the issue here, that magical realm of energy and exaggeration where tidal appetites await fulfillment, distortion, disguise.

On the ride back, I ask him if he likes Dr. Loecke.

"He's okay."

"He seemed nice. What do you talk about?"

"I don't know."

"Sure you do. You were just there."

"Oh. We talked about the game."

"What game?"

"The game we play."

"You play a game? What game?"

"It's money and stuff. We throw the little dices and move our little things and that's what we talk about."

By the time we're back at the house, he's sagging in his seat belt and sleeping deeply. I carry him inside and try to get him out of his winter paraphernalia with minimal disturbance. I wander around thinking Nancy must be there somewhere, but she isn't.

When she returns a short while later, I'm in the living room half-dozing over a local paper. I hear the car pull into the driveway and then Nancy and her friend are chatting. I go to the back door and hold it open as she comes up the stairs burdened with grocery bags. I help her place them on the table. "Are there more?"

"In the driveway."

"Robbie's sleeping," I say and step out, a stolid, nearly happy beast of burden going up and down the stairs lugging the remainder.

"I guess he's exhausted," she says. "From last night. I'll make dinner and wake him."

"I'd like to wake him when it's time," I say.

"Sure."

"We managed to get to Dr. Loecke's okay."

"Good."

"How's that going do you think?"

"I don't really know that much about it."

I take a minute and walk to the window and peer out. The sun is down, the air tinted and frosty in an illusory, nearly visible way. "I think they played Monopoly today. Is that right? Is that what they do?"

"Games, yes. Other ones, too. Chutes and Ladders. Or they build models of things."

"It's interesting. I guess it's this way of getting Robbie involved in something and so off guard. So then he reacts to things and it's something Dr. Loecke can observe. Maybe talk about. Why did you this or that in the game, Robbie? That's probably the idea."

"It feels pretty desperate to me."

Dinner is quiet. Burgers, baked potatoes, a little salad. When we're finished and she's doing the dishes, I read Robbie another one of my letters and then it's time for bed. She gets him into his pajamas while I wait outside his room. She parts the door a few inches and asks, "Are you sure you want to put him to bed?"

"Sure, Sure." He's lying on top of the covers and I help him under, tuck him in. He has *The Berenstain Bears Forget Their Manners* lying out and I read a chapter and sit with him while he fights against sleep as long as he can. When he's quiet, I remain seated on the edge of the bed, then sag down slowly so I'm beside him. I put my arm over him, resting it lightly on his chest, and feel like a thief stealing the simple pleasure produced by the throb of his breath riding through me.

When I leave, the door to Nancy's room is only a few feet away across the hall. It's closed but her light is on. The house is quiet and I slip on down the stairs in the dark to the little room.

I'm awake for a long time and through the first edgy interlude I'm wondering why I can't just walk away? Other people do it. Men do it. I know some. Women, too. Or on the other hand why I can't just settle in and live here? It wouldn't be that long. Nobody lives that long. I could just grit my teeth. Gut it out until it was over. It's the way I grew up I guess, that Catholic background like a fog enshrouding and insulating the lives of my parents and their neighbors. They suffered through it. Did they even know they had a choice? And it's not just Catholic this background of duties and values but it's Catholic Midwestern. I'm supposed to be a man of few words; tough, stoic. As good as my word. A promise is a promise. Don't say anything unless you mean it. Unless you have the guts to back it up. You make a mistake, live with it. If they have to stick a knife into you to dig the poison out, you grit your teeth. A tolerance for pain, maybe even an appetite, is to be acquired and maintained.

About three A.M. I wake up. I sit there awhile and then I find the phone and call Larry, the friend I stayed with in New York.

He's a little groggy when he answers but says he'd been read-ing and just closed his eyes. After a few minutes, the briskness of his tone makes me believe him. "I want you to listen to some-thing," I tell him. I get the tape recorder, and with the volume low and the speaker up against the phone I play him Robbie's composition. "He made that up," I tell him. "He's four and he made that up and he played it."

"Wow," he says.

"He's four, Larry. I mean, think about it."

"Proud papa," he says.

I can't say why these words convey rather bluntly his wish that I shut up and let him go back to sleep, but I turn the ma-chine off. I ask him how things are going, and he responds with diminishing energy. It's another minute at most before we hang up. In the dark I think about distance and people and how far we all are from one another even when we're in the same room, the same bed, even when embracing. I feel like distance is a force, a being, and it has a voice and it's joined me in the dark and is about to reveal its true nature. In California, the sun glares while it snows in the East. I was in California with her, now I'm here in this bed, and she could be anywhere with anyone. I imagine her gliding down a long hallway to a partly open door, which she nudges with her shoulder and in the dimly lit room a man waits. I imagine myself going upstairs to Nancy's room. In California the woman goes down a hall, down some stairs, while I go down a different hall, up different stairs. We both go in doors.

With the little tape recorder close to my ear, I push the button and Robbie's music surfaces. The tones are diminutive and shrunken as they squeeze through the tiny plastic speakers accompanied by an incessant background hiss. I try several adjustments to improve the quality but don't have much suc-cess, so I just close my eyes and listen. I recall his little fingers on the keys, and then after a while I seem to hear French horns lending their brassy mourning to his creation. I see the men with French horns in their hands, the curling brass like flowers with stems that burst from their mouths to fulfill the demands of his music. Gradually, then, I picture other instruments and other musicians gathered in rows to render Robbie's song. A whole orchestra is manifest before me, strings and kettle drums, trombones and flutes and trumpets all fingered and rubbed and wielded by an array of humans in dark formal garb devoted to his inner life brought forth, his nascent but burgeoning ingenuity erupting in dots and tails flung madly over the bars and scrolls of sheet music that cannot contain him.

Robbie wakes me in the morning. He's seated on the bed tugging at my hair and beaming. We talk for a while before Nancy knocks on the door and asks what I want for breakfast. I dress and go upstairs to shower and he tags along, watching me shave. She has pancakes with apples cooked into them waiting. There's coffee for me while Robbie drinks apple juice and with the three of us arranged harmoniously at the table, he radiates a kind of halo of affirmation. I tell them I have an idea for a box that he could sit on when he plays his music rather than the phone books. I'd like to build it for him. I can tell he's dubious regarding my proposal as we head out in my car. At the lumberyard, which is open to sell shovels, sand, salt, and snow blowers, I give one of the clerks the specifications so he can cut the six pieces of wood exactly. I purchase glue, nails, two rubber stair treads. Back at the house, I secure the four sides and then the larger two pieces over the top and bottom. To the bottom I attach the two treads to keep the whole thing from sliding. It's just a box after all, but when I place it on the piano bench and he climbs aboard, I see him make a very complicated calculation that leads to a thoughtful smile as he places his hands on the keys. As lunchtime approaches I offer to take them out to a local restaurant. Robbie wants to know if his friend Timothy can go with us.

"He's coming over for a playdate around one," Nancy says. "He's Robbie's best friend."

"I know," I say. "It'd be great if he came with us. Where should we go?"

"Friendly's!" says Robbie emphatically.

"What about Burger King?"

"No! Friendly's!"

"They love the name," Nancy tells me. "And you should think about getting out before dark." She nods and gestures toward the window ablaze with white light. "The storm's coming back. Or I guess another one is rolling in tonight."

"Really?"

"That's what they're saying on the weather station."

I sense Robbie watching us closely and when I turn to him he smiles. Nancy says, "You know Daddy has to leave today, right?"

"Yes, I do," he says, nodding.

"You haven't forgotten."

"No."

"Okay."

Timothy arrives with his mother, Laurie, and Robbie introduces me to both of them. They've met me before, and Laurie smiles, while Timothy eyes me as if I'm somehow fictional even as I stand there. Nancy and Laurie start to chatter over pickup arrangements for Timothy, and as the discussion grows unduly complicated I slip in a word or two and even take the chance of making a mild joke. They both laugh, and I think, It's working. To my amazement we're on a steady course and I think I'm beginning to see how we can manage this. I keep hearing Robbie's music as rendered by the full orchestra and I feel it's going to accompany us, that it will be the background for our effort, the score to inspire us and keep us going and get us through.

On the way back from lunch, I turn on the radio and hear an overly dramatic weatherman giving his very somber forecast. Nancy was right. This self-important meteorologist is issuing a storm warning. We're in for another heavy snow.

By the time we're parked and headed toward the back stairs, shadows are thrown across the yard. Robbie, Timothy, and I stay outside to scan the horizon. Everything to the west is losing color and light fast. Timothy brought a little toboggan when he arrived and they want me to pull them around, so I do.

Close to four Timothy leaves. I gather my shaving gear, my few books, my clothes and pile them on the bed. Nancy and Robbie are watching me, Nancy in the doorway and Robbie a little into the room. "Do you want me to close this up?" I say, referring to the bed.

"No. We can take care of that, can't we Robbie."

He nods and says, "Sure. I know how."

When I carry my belongings out to the car, he puts his boots and jacket on and comes with me. He watches me as if I'm a magician performing a complicated trick whose mystery he wants to solve and when I close the trunk lid we go back inside.

So then it's a matter of saying good-bye. I pick him up to do it, hold him, and stand him on a chair so we're eye to eye. Nancy watches from across the room against the wall, her manner remote, as if she wants to scrutinize our exchange from as far away as possible. We're like surgeons working out the moves in an operation no one informed us we would ever have to do. Robbie nods, and listens, glancing at Nancy. I promise to write more letters and come back soon and sleep in the little room whenever I visit. His demeanor, as he smiles, reminds me of a soldier preparing for a dangerous mission. Somehow everything we've said needs to be repeated and gone over again. By this time we're all outside and I'm climbing into the car. I have the door still open and he seems to be standing almost at attention as I start the engine.

"Robbie, I have a good idea," she says. "We'll go inside and stand by the little window." She gestures toward the side of the house along the driveway. She's indicating the outside wall of the room where I slept. "That'll be fun. We can open it and watch Daddy go from there."

"Okay," he says and they run for the door.

"I'll stop and wave," I call after them, pulling the door closed. Once they're inside, I wait for the window to open, thinking how clever we are to make a game of this. Clever but false. But

God help us, it's the best we can do. Tricks, distractions. Chutes and Ladders.

I pull even with them, braking gently. He's in her arms gazing down at me as I hit the button to open my window and look up and detect hidden forces beginning to overtake him. It's sudden and violent, and yet there are stages. The fact that something awful is coming is clearly foretold if only for an instant. Then he gives over; he transforms. "Daddy!" It's primitive. His voice, his wide stretched eyes. "Daddy!" He screams: suddenly I know it's my name and he's a savage, unleashing his soul and cursing me. The moment feels dangerous. It feels wrong, mad, hallucinatory. I want to run. He's been carried off to a realm of loss that's epic and archetypal and he's calling back to me. "Daddy! I . . . want . . . my . . . Daddy!" His wail does not belong in this driveway with a car running and a car window open and a window in one of the numerous little suburban houses along these streets holding this suffering figure. These are passions and he knows them and he's reminding me that we are lover and beloved in an indispensable and fated romance.

But I go. There's nothing I can do. I stay, I talk, he wails. Nancy glares at me and starts to shake her head and soon she will be crying too. It had seemed we'd done it, put order and reason in their governing place. Is the primitive world always so close? Ready to erupt and reclaim its rightful predominance. So I go, as if all I have to do is get ten yards down the road and then ten more and ten more. I'll come back, I think. I'll come back for him. I've got to get away but first . . . first . . .

The sun is down and the dark is early and the snow has begun again. They said it would and I heard them. We talked about it and now here it is. Ahead streetlights ignite like filaments empowering the flakes knotted in weird contorted shapes that rise and fall in the wind, seeming almost serpentine in their writhing tangle. The sky is black. The flurries are thickening, beginning to storm. I try to look ahead. I try to see through the storm. I try to imagine Robbie somewhere in front of me. I picture a moment in time in which he's waiting. I try to see myself out there. He would have to be different, maybe even grown. I would be changed. I see him that way. I see him grown. I try to drive toward that image. Could that be what they are? The people waiting. Could it be the future reaching back? Could it be the future spreading into the seconds racing toward it and soon to be past like a stain with the shadow of how I will be changed into whoever I become? Is that who they are? Are they all of us far from now?

But that's a phantasm, because the truth is behind me, and I open the window in order to hear him if I can. I hear the motor, the tires on the ice, the wind. A flurry of cold and spray blows in, where touching my face, touching my hands, landing on my jacket it melts. I close the window. The snow is increasing and soon it has the apparition of mass. Nearly a wall, yet detailed and singular in its countless constituent elements, the blizzard deploys exploding drifts and a noise evocative of chaos. Yes, I think. This is what it would be like if I were driving into it, the hidden heart of matter, if at the deepest levels of the atomic and the subatomic the fundamentals were arctic particles spinning and ungovernable as they disguise the way. But I'll do it, I think. I'll get through it. I'll go on. But then I see that it's myself I'm at the center of. I am the thing rampaging on. I am the storm, driving my car.

HOLY MEN

THE GRAVEYARD SPILLED its markers over the ascending terrain in a glowing stream that made the moon emphatic. I had to look. The car, my father's Ford, was dipping from a mild upgrade into a graceful bend where the absence of traffic allowed distraction. The moon was low and huge as I caught it through the barren crush of tree limbs that topped the nearest rise in the receding landscape. The rounded crest lay under piles of inky shadows from which the tombstones appeared to flow. Already, death was not far from my mind, because I was, after all, a former Catholic on my way to visit a priest. Certain associations are relentless. Still, it was not with the faintest grasp of anything unusual that I let my eyes absorb the display of mortality in its neatly tended monopoly of the vista. Boulders burst through the soil all over this part of Iowa due to the Mississippi forging its path long ago. Surrounding farms arranged the dirt in orderly rows of soy and corn amid gullies and bluffs, so it was ordinary for man-made patterns to mix with half-buried rocks. In memory those hillside markers hover like a schoolboy's model of the Milky Way in the moon's hard light, but that night I was past them quickly. I had driven that road hundreds of times, mostly as a teenager. My high school girlfriend had lived at the top of this same hill, and I had climbed to her often over these same curves I was now riding to visit Father Edward Lillius, a former teacher and mentor from whom I had been estranged for more than a dozen years.

What it was that urged me on this particular trip to break my silence and contact him I had no idea, nor have I any now. During this period of my life I traveled to my hometown with the furtiveness of a spy crossing the borders of a totalitarian state within whose confines I could be detained if my presence were detected. In spite of years away, a time in the army, and some success in the world, I remained wary of powers inherent in the place where I'd been a Catholic child. And yet several days earlier I had snatched up the phone in my parents' living room. I remember a sensation of ill-considered risk as I dialed his number, even though I'd been struggling with the impulse, increasingly, as the days of my visit ticked past in their limited supply. His greeting had a reserved quality. And the pause into which I offered my name—"It's me, Father. Mathew Nachtman"—vibrated with suspense. But then the formal reserve of his "Hello" melted when he said my name, "Mathew." We spoke briefly, making arrangements to have dinner in his room a few evenings later, the night before I was to leave to fly back to New Haven, Connecticut, where I worked as a reporter. He didn't like going out very much, he said, and hoped his room would not be too "abstentious, or sober." The last word twinkled. Recognizing the pun, I vowed not to drink too much, hoping to forestall a threatening potential that lacked all specificity.

Leaving my car and strolling across the paved parking lot, I noted how the redbrick walls of Saint Martha's Hall, a retirement home for nuns where Father Lillius was chaplain, rose only three stories, achieving the size necessary for its dormitory function by running lengthily along the hilltop. The front door opened on a narrow institutional void. I was immediately under the scrutiny of one of the nuns, an old woman seated at a table in an alcove off the main hallway. She was much like a desk clerk in a hotel except for her garb, the dark flowing habit crowned by the jowly oval of her face wrapped in a white cardboardlike frame that sustained the veil falling over the back of her head. Though the enclosing material was thinner and the veil softer than those I remembered from my school days, I still felt an old and familiar pang of alarm at the sight of her studying me. She was an earless smudge of glinting glasses, shoving aside the local newspaper. I gave my name, and she said,

"Father's been expecting you." The look she left me with was a kind of tolerant reprimand, as if she knew secrets about me, most of which did not meet her approval. Rattling with rosaries large and small, she fled, only to return moments later to direct me to his room. I should go through the double doors straight ahead and then turn left. His was the first door on the right.

He appeared when I knocked, his rascal's black eyes beaming and searching me for clues to the degree my present identity still harbored those traits he had thought prominent in my past. His glance was fierce as he foraged for something upon which to balance his claim of still knowing me well. In his priestly garb, he was a black wand of a man with curving black eyebrows and inky slicked-back hair combed flat in the manner of a silent movie screen idol. When he stepped back, our handshake prolonged, I saw a brief uncertainty undercut the brawn of his first emotion. It was a worry so fleeting I thought it best to ignore it as I turned away, thinking I would appear eager to examine his quarters. Whatever he might be feeling, I was stepping around it. Perhaps it was simply a wistful taste for the years that had skipped off without us. Certainly, nostalgia could claim a place in these seconds. More for him than for me, but I could feel it, and it was not altogether welcome.

When he spoke, he had settled on a superficial point, though it touched the theme of difference between us. "You've gotten big," he said, and he distorted the word, like a comic stripping away ordinary meaning so he could convey what he wanted. He was referring to my physical size. Thin through my college years, I was an emaciated wisp when I showed up in this room shortly after my discharge from the army. I assumed he was remembering that visit, which marked in my mind the end of my first attempt to separate from my past. During a five-year-long struggle following college, I traveled to the East Coast for graduate school, then quit and took random jobs, until I was drafted into the army, my communications with him growing sparse and artificial. The army took me to Vietnam for a year, and I returned under a spell of inwardness, my resources summoned to a crisis whose nature I can only suggest through some metaphoric exaggeration, such as a nail being driven through my brain.

Though I didn't know it at the time, Father Lillius had been through his own tribulations during those same years, and to some extent they had been my fault. When I first met him, I was a nineteen-year-old sophomore, freshly introduced to the liberation I imagined available in creativity. Joining his creative writing class, I was a whirl of discovery and concomitant ambition, and by the end of that year he, as faculty moderator of our college literary magazine, named me editor.

I took over in the fall, and held the position as both a junior and a senior. Gradually, I pushed against the regulations that hemmed us in. Implicit upon most occasions, but blatant when necessary, they dictated what we could and could not write. We published twice a year, and my first response was to maneuver to expand the physical size of the magazine. Once this was under way, I sought to encourage material that might shove against the prohibitions insulating us, I felt, from ourselves. Given Father Lillius's priestly vow of obedience, his intimacy with the official moral order, the administration considered him the only bulwark necessary to keep our minds and narratives properly sanitized, and so it was against him that I had to push. Not that he was content with things as they were, and not that the work we eventually produced could be judged daring by any standards other than those active in that precise time and place, the early 1960s at Creeger College.

I remember sitting with him one afternoon on stone steps near an empty athletic field with a book of e. e. cummings and a collection that included Dylan Thomas and Robert Lowell. Could they be published in our magazine? And if the answer was no, which it had to be, how could we expect to think of ourselves, or even aspire to think of ourselves, as artists? And Salinger! In a million years Salinger would not be allowed. Father Lillius shook his head and told me we couldn't compare our efforts with those of such mature artists. But how we could even begin to try in our current circumstances I wanted to know. He reminded me that his duty was to help us develop first our moral principles and then our creativity. But wasn't art our goal? I demanded. Catholic art, yes, but look at Graham Greene. His work was bold. Quoting cummings, I told him, "Nobody, not even the rain has such small hands," and then I added Thomas: "After the first death there is no other." Leafing pages, I threw in Lowell. "When the Lord God formed man from the sea's slime." Perhaps because I knew my points were less than infallible, I was energetic. Eventually, when he wavered, it was to allow that we would broaden what we explored in his class, but the established codes would still determine what we published.

Over the next semesters, however, since my desire to transform the magazine was in fact a desire to transform myself, I persisted, as did his class. It may have been that our work in this new atmosphere beguiled him. Previously forbidden feelings from our daily lives, our secrets, our dreams, even some representative darkness appeared as we sat with him around our table and read aloud what we had written. Boys and girls touched and were tempted by sinful pleasure and felt bereft without it. Adults were not always saintly. Dark figures prowled the horizon with hints of alluring powers.

Regularly, he carried our stories and poems back to his room where he corrected our sentences, marking mistakes, offering his seer criticism with his very blue pencil. I believe it was this prolonged intimacy with our developing themes, our chance encounter with moments of truth that led him to modify his perspective. Did he feel left out? Maybe. I remember a Salingeresque tale full of innuendo and governed by enigmatic exchanges between two girls that intrigued him and found its way into the magazine. Then came another whose overripe prose could not bring to light its issues, though the weight of the sentences led one by one to the suggestion that the unmarried girl at the center was pregnant. And while it must be said that little we produced fully escaped being quaintly adolescent and naive, still we tasted authenticity for we were operating at a point in our psyches nearer our actual selves than we had ever gone before.

Gradually, he shifted toward us, until the desire to join what we were doing took hold of him. When willingness followed, Father Lillius, intended to be our censor, became our cohort. By the start of my senior year he relished our subversive project, urging us on with impish delight, until finally he took the boldest step and became a participant. Using a pseudonym, he began to publish in our pages. As "Edward Demmer Demwolf," his poetry ventured up to the proprietary margins and then beyond until, in his gossamer and made-up persona, he was afloat outside the comportment expected of his priestly reality.

Now we knew that while he was our watchman, there were others watching him. But our faith in our cleverness was exceeded only by our belief that we were right. And so it happened that in the spring of my senior year, the enterprise we deemed our freedom crossed into a realm where our mutinous aims were expressed too blatantly. It was in my last issue as editor that we playfully overstepped by identifying Edward Demmer Demwolf as a "poet/philosopher." After inventing a lengthy biography, we named him author of a poem by Father Lillius hazy with spring references to fecundity, along with an essay written by a student espousing beatnik anarchy. Like small boys poking a snake with a stick we cavalierly taunted our superiors, only to rouse the wrath of an adversary we had not taken into account for we had not known he was there chaffing at our transgressions all along. He was in the Philosophy Department, a professor nicknamed the Loon, and for this shrewd, volatile man our use of the title "philosopher" regarding our fictional comrade was a sacrilege. He erupted, declaring Edward Demmer Demwolf no philosopher and condemning both his poem and his essay as degenerate screeds. Stirred by his cries, others looked where he was pointing, his accusations shining all the light they needed to shove aside our stealth.

Father Lillius probably knew that such a moment must arrive. Even as he let himself be drawn into our venture, he probably understood the risk. Still, I doubt that even his most pessimistic conjectures suggested anything that remotely resembled the bitter retribution that came. Certainly nothing depicted in our shyly disillusioned prose or lyrical sonnets or existential blank verse approached the dark reality we unleashed. Largely our miscalculation sprang from the fact that while I had cheered him past his reservations, I was unreliable. Ignorance guided me more than real courage. Seeking to eliminate my own repressive traits, I mistook my desires for those of everyone around me including the hierarchy against which I strained. Hidden within my iconoclasm was the belief that my rebellion was supported, if only secretly, by those who stood above me in the role of oppressor, because the liberation I anticipated would be theirs also.

I graduated that spring amid some confusion, the mounting uproar suspended. By the time it returned full-blown, I was gone. But Father Lillius wasn't. Quickly, the magazine was disbanded, its diminutive replacement managed by a doctrinaire moderator who published only what the president of the college read and approved. Father Lillius was brought before his superiors. It was suggested that his character and capabilities were flawed. Squalid innuendo thickened into accusations of dereliction and then even moral impropriety. He was hounded and threatened. The more reasonable his defense, the more audacious grew his accusers. Soon they began to gossip on the likelihood that he had not merely tolerated but had inspired our corruption. In the end, he had a nervous breakdown.

I was far away by then, making of distance and silence a fortification behind which I could try to change. I wanted out of everything, the church most of all, but my impractical and trusting sensibility was also to be remodeled or annihilated. As a result, I was not around when Father Lillius attempted suicide, and was institutionalized, and after a period of treatment returned to the corridors of the college with his doctor, a psychiatrist, at his side, vouching for his recovery and petitioning for his right to return to the classroom. The college president,

Father Prunty, informed the doctor that under no circumstances would Father Lillius ever be allowed to teach again. When the doctor argued, producing data and documentation, Father Prunty declared that his decision was divinely guided. Father Lillius could not be trusted with the vulnerable students it was the college's mission to shepherd. He would be banished to Saint Martha's Hall, this building on the hill where he would serve as chaplain to aging nuns.

When I first heard of his suicide attempt, it was years in the past, from which I was once again disaffected. With the army behind me, I was sequestered in the East. My best estimate placed his despairing gesture in the period when I was in Vietnam. Still, I believed my defection had contributed to the momentum that bore him to that cold juncture, then dropped him off. Guilt brought on a threatening regression whose only counteraction was to escalate the severity and terms of my quarantine. Fearing that my absence, and more explicitly my silence, had loomed to prod him on, I withdrew further, as if like the others in the jeering mob I had come to hate him.

Now I stood before him, registering his first words: "You've gotten big." He was right that heft had accumulated on me, a thickening armament behind which I awaited the final sutures in the surgery of my uncertain transformation. Still, I was slightly miffed. I had opposed this change, dieting intermittently and exercising often, and I thought any fair-minded assessment would find that I had largely succeeded.

"No, no," he said to soothe me. "I mean, thick."

I laughed both to ridicule my vanity and to eliminate the apology it seemed he was feeling, as I followed the sweep of his arm into the room.

"Hardly luxurious—still I find it more than sufficient," he smiled.

Looking around, I said, "It seems fine."

"That Hemingway word." His grin split his face in a bursting curve that went almost literally from ear to ear. His eyes flashed. "What are you drinking these days?"

"I have to travel first thing in the morning," I said, intending to let him know that I wasn't going to drink a lot. "I think I better be home by eleven."

"Don't start talking about leaving. You just got here. Holy Mary pray for us. I'm having scotch. Speak up or scotch is what you will get too."

"Scotch will be okay."

"Good. How will I ever plumb your secrets unless I first ply you with liquor?"

"That's what I'm afraid of," I smiled, watching him lift a half-full fifth of Black Label from a built-in cabinet below some bookshelves. I felt awkward, standing in the middle of that room, wondering why I'd made the call that had brought me there when I could have simply, smartly fled. Occupying bookshelves and tabletops and dangling from walls, many and varied objects stilled from the vortex of his life had been arranged in a willful conception. On a windowsill three lilies, each in its own trumpeting vase, stood before the backdrop of the gray pane holding against the night. Numerous photos, mostly of former students, were on display, along with several Japanese prints. Near the entrance hung a portrait of the Sacred Heart, the Christ with a surgically sprung flap to reveal a burning, gleaming orb. On one of the panels between the windows opposite the door a crucifix of brown lacquered wood hovered with the doll of a curvaceous Christ agonizing upon it, wilting palm fronds pinioned behind it.

"Sit down, sit down," Father Lillius said. A glass in either hand, he rattled the drinks to settle the ice, using one last shiver to tune the consistency. "The more I look at you, the more you look the same. It seems you haven't changed that much. I was afraid you might have changed."

"Well . . ." I said, wondering what he meant, while fretting that he might still have the power to evince some childish core of feathery, Catholic docility lying dormant in me. Instead of asserting that I hoped I had changed, I smiled tightly and took the drink. It was possible, of course, that his remark had to do with his insecurity after our long separation, though I felt a larger probability would be found in priestly innuendo regarding the condition of my soul. Among Catholics of this era it was implicit that the word "changed" more often than not referred to lost goodness. Whatever the case, my interior was in retreat. Let him plumb all he wanted. To a certain extent I felt indifferent to what was happening, but it was an oddly active apathy tinged with annoyance. My sole obligation to sociability, as I saw it, was to drink, and in this way make it possible for the liquor to nudge loose an acceptable sentiment or two. Suddenly, I resented, as if it was a trick I'd played on myself, the growing need I'd felt to see him before the hour of departure.

Backing up as he advanced, I found the edge of a gray couch, the bare curving frame shiny with shellac, the upholstery a gritty fabric. The couch fit into the angle of the walls with the row of windows to my left. Outside, the graceful sag of tree limbs stripped of leaves drew in the middle distance their disappearing lines across the otherwise unoccupied sky. Autumn was shriveling up the allotted length of each day, producing a harvest of ragged dusks uprooted prematurely from the light and thrust into a dark of dropping temperatures, the earth sinking toward freezing in a steady accretion of austerity, as if the continent were sliding north.

Father Lillius, stirring the ice in his drink with a lengthy forefinger, had collapsed his slender angles into a leather armchair, where he was awaiting the return of my gaze to the room. "You must tell me everything. Everything."

I took my first drink, hooking my hand in an upward twist, a little angry. Much more of a gulp than I intended, and taken directly under his gaze, it belied my stated aims regarding drinking. "I'm doing okay," I said.

"So taciturn."

I squinted, as if to detect some hint of the phantom plans pressing toward me from across the room. What was bothering me? It was disconcerting, this desire to veil myself, to keep silent even on the most prosaic matters, as if something necessary to my survival depended on my guileful management of the next few hours. "Well, you know, " I said, and took another drink.

"No," he said, "I don't. I don't know."

"How've you been, Father?"

"Oh, my goodness."

He sagged back in a playful dumb show of exasperation, his eyes rolling to the heavens that lay beyond the ceiling and the corridors of aged nuns stacked in little beds in drab dormitory rooms above us, an image that streaked my imagination like a firecracker throwing up something furtive from the shadows. They were praying all around us. Or they would be soon. In tiers of narrow unadorned rooms to which their vows of poverty had willed them, their humble regimen was a serene but cold rebuttal to my aspirations to live with pleasure in the world, to pursue my goal of personal happiness. The moment was filled with them, murmuring specters of devotion so vivid it seemed I had chanced into their world, as I could have on a ladder propped up to their windows, or if my head had slid through a trap door in the ceiling and there I was sticking through the floor into their world. With a flick of my wrist, I threw back all but a sip of my drink. The liquid singed my throat as if leavened with coals, the ice ticking dully against my teeth like measured time, our mortal reminder. The ceiling was a plane of rippling, impermeable plaster painted with several coats of white.

Seconds later, I found Father waggling his finger at me. "You're not going to get away with that," he said. "We'll talk about me later. But since you're already threatening to run off, you leave me no choice but to be single-minded in my pursuit of facts, however embarrassingly it reveals my needs. So be it." The delicate, elongated web of his hand coiled in a clear-cut expression of helplessness, the sleeve of his black jacket riding up his wrist. His trousers and shoes were black, as was the soft material of the biblike shirtfront that ended at the white jab of the Roman collar locked around his neck.

"I'm not sure I know what you mean, Father."

"Of course you do."

My uncertainty regarding the underlying elements I sensed at work between us led me to take refuge in the last of my drink. People whispered their sins to his ears and he, with a flutter of his hand, a rote burble of inattentive words, dissolved eternities of pain. This was what the faithful believed, but I was no longer among them. At least I didn't want to be, having labored to extricate myself from their ranks. Had I come here at least partly as a test? I looked at him, and if this was a test I was failing. I felt my soul tilting toward him in some excruciating susceptibility to the temptation he posed, for he was said to embody an avenue to grace and salvation even as he sat there, smiling past the rim of the thick crystal glass filled with scotch. My own glass was empty, the collapsed ice chips sliding to one side with the slow tilt of my hand.

"Serve yourself," he smiled, the curl of his tone a playful taunt. I felt his barb, but the tip was dulled and friendly. Shaking his glass, he took in a little. "I'm not going to give you the slightest justification to go off complaining that 'Father Lillius got me drunk.'"

I was already on my feet, the bottle with its promise and availability consolidating my energies and moving me toward it.

"You understand my problem here, don't you, Mathew? People think we're friends. They don't forget, you know. They expect me to know things about you. They ask me about you. 'How is he? What's he doing?' And they expect me to know, and when I don't, which I largely don't, well they conclude that they were wrong in their premise and we aren't friends, when we are. Aren't we?"

"Sure."

"I'm certainly your friend. The fondness I feel toward you has never diminished. Not in the slightest just because you were away. Because we didn't see one another and years went by. Of course I wanted to hear from you. But I can honestly say that I never really doubted the enduring nature of your affection toward me, no matter how thick and beleaguering the silences. I mean, I know that about you. Silences were always a part of your way—a necessary risk for one who would befriend you. Do you know what I thought?"

"No."

"Do you want to know?"

"Sure."

"You process things slowly. And sometimes you process things the rest of us have taken for granted, and so from our point of view, you process unnecessarily. But I never felt you meant anything by it. You just needed it. I never felt rejected by it."

"Good," I said. But I knew he had felt rejected. That was what he was telling me, while a surge of guilt was my response. I was back at the couch, the second drink all but dispatched in the midst of diminishing qualms and an elevating haze that seemed to radiate out from the center of my skull toward my ears. I'd never forgotten the intensity of his desire for an ongoing fellowship with students after they graduated. But what could I have said to him, conducting my campaign to change far away in the East? I could not explain myself, or share or debate my reasons, because my view had become that Catholicity was an illness. The teachings were a poison whose antidote had no name I knew, though I hoped to find it in the world to which I had expelled myself. While I saw us both as victims and opposed this usurpation, he had chosen to remain loyal to the powers behind it, and not merely as a follower but as an advocate. I feared contact with him could bring some revitalization of my symptoms, which, for all their abatement, had never fully dissolved. Rather, like some chemical natural to me, they survived in a force sufficient to foment a virulent regeneration. Nor was he the single source of such a risk. Basically all the world that I had once loved and everyone in it seemed empowered to rejuvenate my rejected tendencies with no more than a word or a knowing glance, and so I stayed away.

"Are you hungry?" he said.

I didn't know what he was talking about. "What?"

"You look hungry."

"No, no."

"The nuns will bring us a lovely dinner the moment I ask."

"I could eat now, but I could wait."

"It would be better a little later," he said, glancing at his watch. "They're just eating themselves now, the poor old things."

"Whatever's best." I was staring into the dregs of scotch discoloring the watery gleam to which the chips were almost entirely reduced. "I'm ready for another," I said. "I haven't had scotch for a long time." I hoped to at least float the premise that my speedy series of refills had their cause in the rediscovery of a neglected taste. But as I considered this aim, while gliding across the room to snatch the bottle up, I found my pretense feeble, and knew he would too. Overtaken by a mocking, somewhat angry desire to tell the truth, I splashed the liquor into the glass with an inelegant plunge of my hand and wrist.

"Bring the bottle back with you, why don't you," said Father Lillius.

"Sure."

"I heard from Robert Stueber last week—he's in advertising in Des Moines. Do you remember him? He always asks about you."

Robert Stueber had been lean and well dressed with curly, sandy hair and a slightly sardonic bent. Several years ahead of me, he had come from Des Moines, the largest city in our state. Identified with these two advantages, he always struck me as a sophisticate beyond my reach. I wondered why he had asked about me and what he'd asked. "Of course, I remember him, Father."

"He has three children, two boys and a girl. Beautiful children. How's your little boy?"

"He's good," I said.

"How old?"

"Five."

He stared at me, stirring his drink with the tip of his finger. I was leaning back in the unreceptive couch, whose sturdy frame and thin upholstery proved a steady obstacle to comfort no matter how I placed myself.

"He isn't with you, is he? Your little boy. You didn't bring him with you on this trip."

"No," I said.

"Because if you had, I would demand to see him."

I wondered if he was trying to shift the conversation in the direction of my divorce and studied him in order to decide. "No, he's not with me."

"Too bad."

Was that the charge he was maneuvering to ignite between us? Given my divorce and remarriage, I was excommunicated according to canonical law, and in my claims of having bene-fited from these actions, I was, strictly speaking, a heretic.

"Is he a good boy?" he asked. "I bet he's handsome. Do you have a picture?"

"Sure," I said, remembering the photo in my billfold. My son was posed unhappily in a woodsy setting, a robust little fellow with puffy cheeks and worried eyes, whose cast I believed was provoked by his dismay over the force field and disarray of his fading infancy. He lived with his mother in Rhode Island.

"Can I see it?" he said.

"What?" I was looking at him past the rim of my drink. There we were, his appetite for details voracious, my capaci-ties stymied by wary appraisals of his eyes and the aims he har-bored even if he didn't know them, for I was certain that sooner or later he must engage in a strategy of priestly reclamation of my soul.

"The picture," he said. "Didn't you say you had one?"

"Oh, sure." Scrunching forward, I tugged my billfold from my back pocket. As he contemplated the photo, I scanned the thin brown carpeting. On just such a floor I had knelt to con-fess to him. In just such a room I had whispered my sins to Father Lillius, bowed beside the chair where he sat with his head turned away, as we sought to integrate into the scheme of our relationship this uncanny function, where he would serve not only as mentor and teacher, but also as conduit to the divine, my interceder to the Lord. Was it my junior year or my senior year? Probably both. What could those sins have been? Something to do with one of my girlfriends, no doubt, and the conundrum of heartache and lust into which they ushered me. Nor would concupiscence have been all. At that time I would have worried about vanity or selfishness. I could have confessed faults of pride and ambition. Envy. Competitiveness. I didn't lie often, but of course I lied. Curses were plentiful, and if you wanted to avoid a bad confession you had to be specific and accurate. I wondered if he remembered my revelations. If I asked him now could he recite back the transgressions whose hellish price he had lifted from me?

"He's a little chubby," he said about my son.

"Baby fat."

"But very handsome. Do you see him often?"

"As often as I can. There for a while, I was seeing him every two weeks."

"How did you manage that?"

"Lots of driving."

Gazing wistfully at the worried image of my little boy, Father Lillius was downcast. The photo had sunk to his lap, suggesting that the sad content of this nearly weightless item made it burdensome. My distress at the disorder I had put into my little boy's world was always close. Justified by nothing more substantial than my own unhappiness and dubious sexual hopes that seemed to lie thwarted at the root of my misery, I had left my wife and child. The autonomy it seemed I needed to survive struck me then as indulgent and prodigal, though I discovered in the world around me that what I sought was little more than rudimentary. But for the moment in that room with Father Lillius, his gloomy concentration brought back my own suppressed indictment. His mute accusation was like that of so many others lately. Certainly, my parents could not restrain themselves. Though they tried and said little, their silences were full of hurt and reproach. I made them sad. They were aggrieved in spite of themselves. Divorce was more and more common, and they knew it and so they didn't want to be outmoded. They wanted to accept what had occurred in my life but, given the church's instruction, they could find no possible exception for me, and so what they actually offered was the willingness to try for something they could not accomplish. They gave effort and sadness. Both of their families had lived without divorce for generations, because when all else failed the needs of the children were invoked as reason for unquestioning subordination of personal desire. Children kept people together. People hunkered down, clawing for leverage as they wrestled for light in their marriage.

"He looks so unhappy," said Father Lillius.

I'd lost all sense of his presence and his voice startled me. "What?"

"He looks so unhappy."

"Thoughtful."

"Is that what it is?"

"Yes. He's very thoughtful."

"Carol," he said, startling me with this reference to my first wife, "seemed like such a delight. I have to admit I had a crush on her, and I was envious of you. She seemed so clearly in love with you."

I'd forgotten they'd met. But now the incident came back replete with chastening associations I didn't have time to sort. In the first months of marriage, I'd brought Carol home to visit in a kind of a performance of maturity and compliance, hoping we could all make do with resolve and fabrication. I must have thought to include Father Lillius in the measure of compensation I hoped to grant my parents for the disappointments I had brought them, which were primarily leaving the church and the Midwest. At least I had married, I wanted them to know. I would be a family man. That would have been the last time I saw Father Lillius, wherever it was and whatever had happened. I really couldn't remember the occasion. Perhaps it was here in this room. Did he remember? He probably did and it was probably all very different in his mind. It had to be, didn't it? Was I forgetting something else when I believed that soon after that visit I was divorced and the separation stretching to this evening had begun?

Father Lillius was raising the photo toward the light as if he hoped to spy evidence of the child's distress that only his special concentration could uncover. When he let loose a clucking hiss of concern, while remaining fixed on the photo, I felt certain that his next words would fashion some version of the accepted cant which was usually that in matters like this children suffered the most. My mother had said it. My neighbor, my father. Why not him?

"Things just didn't work out with Carol," I told him, wondering if he wanted to hear about the realities of my marriage, the sweetness that, never devoid of complexities, managed to flourish only to evaporate and leave behind awkwardness and struggle, whose sole reprieve was defensive bursts of accusation. Unhappiness had slipped into my relationship with my first wife in a covert maneuver that left me, after all the protests of amazement and incomprehension had been mouthed, looking at the cause, which seemed to gleam with spooky permanence, having been there all along, present at the inception, a guest at the wedding, acknowledged but misidentified as if such a tactic could leave it behind.

"It's the children that suffer the most in a thing like this," said Father Lillius.

I turned to the window. There I found a plate of wintry dark containing nothing except my own reflection, as faint and half-finished as I felt. I emptied my drink. The scotch was progressing in its conquest of my bloodstream. I could feel it barging from area to area, leavening my liver, my kidneys, my heart. I felt lumpy and wrongfully alive. I clinked the ice against my teeth and leaned forward to create an angle onto the outside world whose widened scope might catch the sky and stars. I saw a skein of tree limbs, stripped and black, and beyond them a passing plane the only discernible light, though the existence of the moon was suggested by a grayish haze spreading out dreamily from above the rooftop hidden overhead.

"I'm sure you're doing the best you can for this little boy," he said behind me.

"What kind of tree is that? The one just up on the hillside."

"Apple," he told me. "There's number of them yet. The site here was initially an apple orchard, and the builders, the architects or contractor or whoever, in a genuinely civil stroke opted to leave a number of the trees. Outside, if we could walk, they're plentiful yet. They actually still grow apples. Many of them."

I looked at him, and our eyes met in a momentary exchange before each darted off. I started pouring another drink. By the time I finished, he was reaching forward with his own glass in need of a refill. "You're doing better now?"

Certain that he was trying to bring up my second marriage, I decided to act as if his question was without any particular aim. "I'd say so. And you, Father. Do you do all right here?"

"Oh, well, of course." He shook his head emphatically.

"What do you do exactly?"

"I tend the nuns," he said. "And they tend me. They cook for me and take care of all my needs. My laundry and the apartment. They do my laundry, they clean my room. 'Father this' and 'Father that.' They fret about me over one thing or another. God forbid if I get a little cold. It's really rather feudal, if you think about it. I can scare them away with a look. They're my little harem, with limits of course. So I'm alone. Plenty of time to read and write letters and work if I want to, which I do, and which I don't."

"So it sounds kind of good, except for the 'don't work' part, Father."

"Exactly," he said, his half-joking grin touching on irony and rue. Then he spread his arms, the fingers of his right hand maintaining the scotch, the space between his open palms widening in a gesture of helpless waiting. "Chalk it up to the muse. But I do work well when I work. My little complaint is that I wish it came more often."

It struck me that with a few minor changes, the description he'd just given of his life fit a marriage, at least the old-fashioned kind. He'd been questioning me regarding the women in my life and it seemed I'd turned the tables and was inquiring about the women in his. It hadn't been my intention, but it was what I'd done. I looked at him with that notion in mind and he engaged me with a jolt, as if our ideas were being exchanged, or had been simultaneous and identical in origin and now we were coming to the same realization. He seemed to find something unsatisfactory in the situation. I didn't know what I thought. If this had been a physical confrontation, his next move would have been to alter his tactics in order to strike from an unexpected angle. He was shaking his head, as if he believed he had caught me trying to dupe him and now he was going to escape.

"How are things going with Maureen?" he asked, referring to my second wife in what seemed an amiable challenge. "Better, I hope."

Women. They were a fairly improbable subject for us to search for common ground. Nuns and wives were women but that was where their correspondence ended. Did I dare to tell him what I thought? I was rattling with images, memories of arguments, and beds, this one, that one, legs, mouths, different hungers, different deeds, and somehow it seemed it should all come out. It was frustrating, this summons to speak coupled with abundant proscriptions. He was a priest. It was difficult to talk frankly to any man about the actualities of the women in one's life, which, no matter where they started, always came down to the actualities of women in bed. Because that was what they were. Actualities. Not sentiments, not dreamy webs of feelings and emotional fulfillment. People. Bodies. Meat. Breasts. Nipples. Full of desire, full of themselves. It was not that the experience was less than what one had fantasized, or better, so much as it was a matter of the whole thing being categorically different. But what could I say to Father Lillius? He was a romantic. That's what I was thinking. He was a priest and a romantic and now we were sitting there in our chairs, our glasses brimming with scotch and ice, having been filled by one or the other of us pouring and repouring.

"She's a beautiful woman. Maureen. And that's a beautiful name. Will I ever get to meet her?"

His words interrupted my stumbling thoughts. Had my mother sent him a picture of her? He was looking at me plaintively, questioningly, as if I had done these things, gone into the world and slept with women in order to come back and report something. He was such a passionate man, such a wealth of vibrant yearning. What he must have dreamily conjectured, I thought, alone for so long with nothing to guide him but delusion and deduction. I was on my feet, walking past him. "I have to go to the bathroom," I said.

He gestured in the direction I was already headed. "Go as far as you can and take the door on the left. If you find yourself in a closet or my bedroom, you've turned right."

Perhaps it was the way I was up and moving that dislodged the memory, but the resurrection was vivid and emphatic, usurping the present with the impression that I was still in college and we had just been talking, Father and I, about this movie. It seemed to have happened earlier in the afternoon, or just yesterday. In the movie a virginal young girl played by Eva Marie Saint fell in love with a troubled young man played by Warren Beatty. Though he spent most of his nights in the beds of trampy women, tough women with whom things were strictly physical, the dictates of the narrative left him dissatisfied and demanded that he eventually sleep with the young girl. She had an odd name, very unusual. Lyric or Melody or something I could not recall. But incarnated by the actress Eva Marie Saint, she was a delicate sensual river of memorable feeling barely restrained and woefully unprepared for the aftermath of the young stud's heedless embrace, which began in joy and ended with anguish at his rejection. I could recall the moment exactly in which Father Lillius spoke and we strolled along the walkway between one of the dorms and the library. The day had been bursting with bright wintry light, as he reenvisioned for us both the scene in which the girl came down to breakfast the morning after her first night spent with her lover. Even the actress's name, I saw now, had been ordained to plunge into the tissue of our Catholic souls, for she was "Eve," the first woman; she was "Marie," our Holy Mother; and she was "Saint," the inviolable, the human sanctified. At the breakfast scene, she beamed with her newborn love, tenderness spangling through her skin. At the table were Karl Malden and Angela Lansbury, who played the stud's father and mother. With them was their second, younger son, a boy of thirteen or fourteen played by Brandon de Wilde, through whose eyes we were to experience the arc of the tale. Brandon de Wilde was openhearted and inexperienced and he loved Eva Marie Saint, as did Father Lillius in that moment as he rhapsodized about the "sweetness, the lovely flush, the glow that came off her, the sense of life," produced by her first encounter with a man. He seemed quite happy as we stepped along. There was something grand and expansive in his manner, as if he were bragging. And suddenly, I glimpsed his dream of her. He was reveling in the effects of her ecstasy, as if they were his own. I caught a fleeting corner of his mind in that moment, and it was identical to my own, and we were both virgins and we were both ignorant and wrong, striding across our campus. It was an error into which one could fall if one were susceptible, basking in the woman's rather stormy, radiant fulfillment as if it were one's own. The satisfaction was limited, however, for it left you secondary except for the indirect rewards of pride and prowess, which could seem ample. I had taken this role myself, and though it was not the common complaint about men, it was a fault and it had been mine. But Father was still back there at that innocent juncture, still dreaming of the possibility that a man could make it happen, that he could ignite that transformational embrace and swoon in whose residue he would gleam through her skin. He was a poet and he prided himself on his willingness to include in his work the bodies and feelings of women. Even though he was a priest, he had dared to believe he could imagine carnal love. He was an impetuous, passionate, lyrical, lonely man. But what he didn't know was that it was the bodies that swooned, not the people, not the souls; the bodies merged, while the people were stunned and marginalized until things quieted down and the gleam of their reemerging egos could reassert loudly the value of their individual aims and histories and separate selves.

Below me the water in the toilet bowl frothed yellow with the addition of my urine, bubbles popping amid swirls as I dribbled to a stop. I flushed and stepped to leave, the angle of my exit directing my attention to a doorway partially open across the hall. I was looking into the cubicle of his bedroom. A wedge of plain green cloth covered the narrow single bed and was tucked tautly along the side. A book near the pillow lay upside down, confusing the title.

When I turned to go back the way I'd come, I was surprised to find Father Lillius standing beside a nun. They were both looking at me and they struck me as Inquisitional in their religious garb.

"What?" I said, feeling questioned, though neither had spoken.

Instantly, they conferred in hushed tones. Father Lillius had to stoop to curtail his lanky height. Though I plucked a word or two from their secrecy, I could not fully grasp their subject. As their conference wore on, I eased closer, finding their manner redolent with routine, as if they were a married couple uniformed by the rules of some eccentric sect.

"She wants to bring us dinner now, all right?" said Father Lillius.

"You need to eat," she said. She was short and somewhat hefty, the combination rendering her squarish in her dark regalia, her narrow little eyes touched with impatience behind the lens of her glasses in wire rims.

"Sure," I said.

"I really think it's time you eat."

"This is Sister Veronica," said Father.

At the mention of her name, she managed somehow to look at me even more directly, and I caught a sense of reproach that

I hoped was endemic rather than born of her specific assessment of me.

"Sure," I said.

"It's almost eight and the sisters need to get on with things," she told me.

"That's fine, Sister," I said.

"They want to shut the kitchen down. They've finished up the last of all the other dishes. They go to bed quite early," Father Lillius offered.

"No problem," I said. "Whatever's best."

Sister Veronica had already exited the room. Now, like a bellhop in a hotel, she reappeared, bearing a sizable brown plastic tray, the kind that is used in school or hospital cafeterias, poised over her shoulder. On the surface was an orderly array of plates covered in silver lids to keep in the heat.

"I'll just put this down, Father," she said, marching directly to the tiny table that stood on its varnished legs along the wall not far from the liquor cabinet. "And then you can eat when you see fit. But it won't stay warm forever."

"Thank you, Sister."

She went out again and came back with a second, identical tray. "I'll bring you some coffee." She squinted and cleared her throat, as if to underline the importance of the coffee.

"Fine," he said.

This time her labors produced a stainless steel pot whose plain design was without flourish. A white miniature pitcher of milk stood near a bowl stuffed with packets of sugar and Equal.

Glancing from Father Lillius to me, she obviously was considering some comment whose prudence or value was not clear to her. Her confrontation with this uncertainty was a matter of some strain. Out of the corner of my eye, I saw Father Lillius tilt his head. He seemed to hope the gesture would urge her on to whatever candor she needed. Her response was to squint and waver from foot to foot before her averted eyes arose to widen and beam with a strict, personal delight, which was for her the end result of the entire exchange.

"Good night, Father," she said.

"Good night, Sister Veronica."

I was adding my "Good night" to theirs as she shrank through the door, happy and sly, her secret shut away with the conspiratorial click of the closing door.

"Well," said Father Lillius. He lifted the silver tin off one of the plates to show me a thin brown cut of steak flecked with gravy, a neighboring mound of peas and clump of mashed potatoes. "I'm not really ready for dinner yet, I don't think. Are you?" His continuing exploration lifted and lowered tins over a wedge of thick-crusted, dripping apple pie and two salads already soaked in French dressing.

"I could eat," I told him, "but I'm not particularly hungry right now."

"I'll open up some peanuts." He snatched a tin of Planters assorted nuts from the shelf adjacent to the liquor. "My little harem," he said. "Did you catch the disapproval in her eyes? My style of entertaining does not always meet with their approval. But if I hadn't let her in now, she would have just kept coming back every ten minutes and badgering us until I did let her in. Once they make their minds up, I don't see the end of it. I'm at their mercy in a lot of ways." He was grinning as he said all this, moving back to his chair, ripping the lid off the can of nuts and dumping them into a bowl. "Not that they don't actually have things to do. Because they do, of course. But they like their routine." He nibbled thoughtfully at a single walnut pinched between a thumb and forefinger.

Returning to my seat, I settled opposite him. "You didn't say what it was you do, Father?"

"I'm sorry?" he asked, as if he hadn't understood me.

"I mean, your duties here? You said you had time to write, but you didn't really make the rest clear. I mean, your routine."

"My routine," he said. He freighted the words with secrets, most of them having to do with feelings rather than facts, while his inspection bore in on me with a physical dimension that made me tilt back in my seat for he seemed to question my worth, even though he smiled.

"Yes," I said, and shrugged.

"My duties? I say Mass for them each day, the poor old things. I hear their confessions. I'm there when they die. And that happens with some regularity, as you can imagine. They're all quite old. It's humbling, really. That part of it. They want me there, of course, to give them last rites and pray. Sometimes they ask me to sit with them, as they know the hour is approaching. It can be days, and of course I can't stay for days, but I will be there for long, long spells. So I've seen it over and over. Their humility, their serenity is often inspiring. They're sweet old things, sweet old souls for the most part. So simple, so pious."

His offhanded delivery created an impression of awe around these memories far more provocative than if he had spoken in a reverential manner. He was quiet, sort of musing. Nothing in his manner of speech nor in the simplicity of his half smile suggested any interest other than a wish to answer my question honestly while bearing witness to what he'd seen, and yet I felt rebuked. I felt sharply chastened. The humble deeds and last breaths of these old nuns testified against my own more selfish aims. The faithful perseverance of these suffering women threw a light onto my shameful shortcomings as I failed in the rigors of a spiritual life. In his conjuring of a long series of nuns passing out of the world without regret, without doubt, I found reason to step back from him. I had to wonder, and then question whether or not I would have witnessed such unvaried equanimity had I stood at his side. My need to gauge his motives summoned scrutiny. For so many people to all end their lives without reluctance implied an invulnerability to common flaws. He endowed these old nuns with either superhuman character or superhuman assistance. Still, he had qualified the matter with his use of the word "often," and with the phrase "for the most

A PRIMITIVE HEART

part," making these modifications parenthetical and giving them little emphasis, but allowing them. Were they allusions to sad and panic-filled exceptions? It seemed impossible that none of these old women ever wrestled with the fearful whip of self-recrimination over the decisions that had charted them to their little rooms, their austere final moment.

Then he startled me. He leaned forward as he spoke, emerging from his own reverie to focus directly on me and ask, "What did you think of *Brideshead Revisited*? Did you watch it all?"

"What?" The novel had been on television recently, a BBC production that had wafted through our American airwaves to the accompaniment of much attention and critical acclaim.

"Did you see it?"

"Yes."

"Wasn't it grand?"

When I failed to respond instantly, he used the changing angle of his glance to declare annoyance and then to let me know he found my need to take a moment to determine my answer preposterous. He rushed on, some hard-to-name intent giving his words a shadow that fed my unease and drove me deeper into retreat.

"I thought it was splendid," he said. "Wasn't it splendid?"

"It was all right."

"All right? Mathew, please. That Jeremy Irons was the essence of Charles Ryder. He was thrilling. I never dreamed actors could ever manage anything but facsimiles, ghostly semi-approximations of figures imagined and written with such perfect and intricate . . . such . . . what is it that I'm seeking? Such literate, yes, literate and full-blooded imagination. Yet there they were. And that Laurence Olivier. What a marvel! What an absolute marvel."

"He's a great actor."

"I was riveted. I didn't miss a second of it. Not a second. So powerful. So moving. And oh, those final scenes, when the old man—just before he dies—when he accepts the sacrament and surrenders, simply and totally surrenders, '*Ego te absolvo in nomine Patris.*' It was a scene of such truth and simplicity. The everlasting and merciful forces of divine love. The tolerant, tireless presence of God's grace waiting for the soul to open. It was depicted so remarkably. They caught it exactly. I've seen it, Mathew. I've been the instrument."

"I can't argue with that, Father."

"Why would you want to? Argue with it?" He glanced at the window where the dark appeared latticed and sealed tight like a shutter.

"But in terms of the movie," I said. "I mean, in terms of that scene in the movie where the old man, the Laurence Olivier character—"

"Lord Marchmain."

"Yes. Well—"

"What?"

"It didn't seem that way."

"What way?"

"The way you're saying. At least I didn't see it that way."

"How did you see it? I'm telling you. Something comes into the room, and it is with you, it assists you. That's when you know what the power of the priesthood is, that you are this vehicle. It's both humbling and exhilarating. I mean the personal experience. And they captured it. Everything. The acting, the lighting, the camera angles. But most of all the acting. The loving triumph of grace."

"I felt it was destructive."

"Destructive? What could you mean?"

"I've left the church, father. You know that."

"But that's temporary, don't you think?"

His disbelief, at least in its physical expression, had an exaggerated, theatrical quality, but he'd unnerved me. I'd lost my footing. I could feel myself rattling down a precipice, whose constituent parts were the steep sides of my own unfathomable argument collapsing underneath me. I felt a kind of rupture and fear was leaking through it into me from somewhere otherworldly. His definition of the scene as the dogmatic incarnation of the sacrament of extreme unction degraded the humanity involved, I felt, sacrificing ambivalence and evocation in order to fabricate a bludgeoning instrument of polemics.

"That poor old suffering man," he said, "alone on that bed. And then the gift of grace, having waited and waited, was his. The peace he felt, the sense of safe harbor, of consolation—it was thrilling."

My clear memory showed the old man nearly comatose as his hand fluttered from head to chest to shoulder to shoulder in the sign of the cross. I felt chilled by Father Lillius's eager appropriation of these semiconscious gestures into the narrow service of a tract on sacramental triumph. I wanted to declare that though Lord Marchmain might have lived his life in repudiation of the church, it was no great accomplishment to frighten him into alarmed acquiescence with claims of eternal harbor and blissful affiliation as he lay broken, his faculties and selfhood waning before the ingress of oblivion. This was the church's way, though. They were scavengers, overwhelming prey that had already fallen. They sank on the wounded like bullies, calling their presumptions grace. But the truth of their accomplishment was that they commandeered the ends of a primordial force beyond their influence. Because the real victor, the real predator was death. They merely worshiped him, and followed him about, feeding upon his leavings.

"Destructive?" he said. "Is that what you said?"

While returning from the far side of the room, he was ripping the seal from a new fifth of Black Label. I held up my glass as he bore down on me. The rusty ocher color from the tilted bottle rose to the brim where it dribbled over onto my fingers. I suctioned in a sip, then licked my knuckles, as he made the desultory addition of an ice cube. When he settled into his chair, he had his own drink refurbished and a pained, inquisitive cast to his gaze. "How could you say that?"

I tried to glean whether my sacrilegious opinions were permissible as matters for discussion. At the same time I searched myself for the ability to actually conduct such a discussion. I doubted he would welcome my view, and my indignation had tentacles reaching into recesses full of anonymous rancor, a bottomless black resentment so colossal it could not be governed. I feared the use of any single phrase would release the mass of my stored bitterness, random, unrelated accusations spewing out amid the more intended.

"I don't want to put words in your mouth," he said, "but 'destructive' was the word I think you used."

He sipped and I gulped. The liquor enveloped my thwarted scorn for his cherished allegiance to orthodoxy. I could taste the attack I wanted to make, the power and rebuke of my insights, the sores I might gouge with derogatory metaphors. *Scavenger! Bully!* I could see the damage, and knowing I would inflict it soon I felt the impetus for the whole enterprise evaporate. The words I might have used turned into mud. I struggled to swallow them back thinking how he had nothing now. Just his room. Just these nuns. He had so little and I was thinking of attacking it. Better to stay quiet. Better to walk away, as I had in the past when I came to town and didn't call. I was right not to try to be his friend. I lifted and finished my drink, then reached for another.

"I'm talking about consolation," he said.

"Yes, I know."

"The leap that you made to some notion of destruction is hard to follow."

"You're right," I said.

"What were you saying?"

The only consolation I knew of the kind he meant had found me in a place antithetical to the church, a place the church would have condemned as an occasion of sin, the working of the devil. In the ashrams of an Indian guru there had been strange but undeniable events that seemed to bring with them upon occasion a kind of spiritual embrace, a kind of mysterious acceptance of my entire being. And it hadn't stemmed from the rules or even the elaborate, palpitating rituals, but rather had seemed to exhale from the presence of the robust old man who was the guru. Or sometimes it was in the chanting, when the voices in the cycles of their reiteration spiraled into a force field generating a charge as rich and irresistible, as sensible and copious as atoms storming through your skin in this weird invasion that left you with goose bumps populating your back and chest and thighs, as chills of love poured though you.

When I looked at Father Lillius, wondering whether I might tell him of these thoughts, he shook his head. Though I knew to recognize this coincidence as an accident with no possible bearing on what I should do next, still it held me in a breath of indecision. I had not asked the question, but it seemed he had answered, and his answer was that I should not speak. He would find my ideas and experiences sacrilegious. They would feel to him like a repudiation of his own faith.

"The relief," he said, "the gratitude, the sense of salvation and peace that people feel."

He was watching me, and I looked into his eyes as I would into the eyes of an absolute stranger who was inching too close to me in a public place. Had he forgotten what they had done to him? Had he forgotten how he ended up denounced and slandered and then banished from his classroom? Where was his consolation after all that? Where was the delight he took in teaching once they judged him unworthy of his calling? They had marched along with nothing to sustain them beyond their authoritarian dictums, claiming divine inspiration for their decision. But if they spoke for God, then God found Father Lillius objectionable. If they spoke for God, as they declared they did, then God found him shameful and rightly consigned to the sterility of these rooms. But if they didn't speak for God, then for whom did they speak? Upon what basis did they deploy their power and why had he surrendered everything to them?

"I don't know," I said.

"What?"

"I don't know."

"You don't know what?"

"I don't know. I don't know." I could barely look at him. I was retreating from my convictions, as if they were a physical feat whose demands stood beyond the powers at my disposal. My arguments, my themes, my passions were an iron bar ringed with weights I could raise only by risking a collapse that might crush me.

"You don't know what, Mathew?"

I shook my head in acknowledgment of my own surrender. It was a gesture intended solely for myself, though he would see it, but that didn't matter. I didn't care what he made of my head shake. I wanted to go home. I thought I should go home. Instead, I lifted my glass and drank. Through the sheen of the liquid my fingers were visible in a glowing ruddy curve, as if I clutched a fiery coal. Through all the years of my childhood I'd been devoted. All children are imaginative, but perhaps the faculty was extreme in my case. I can't say. But the air of those young days thronged with invisible life. Angels, devils, grace, saints, my soul dirty with sin and then clean with grace, angels watching devils whisper amid my own thoughts; it was all real. And then I slammed into puberty with the harrowing horizon of adulthood just beyond, and the waiting world drew close, and the outlines it showed were strange. I worried that my preparations, my benedictions, rosaries, and pieties, might not sustain me as more and more of what had been ordinary became bewildering, and then surreal. I took a bus to high school each morning, and once it became clear that no matter how I directed my mind the vibrations produced by the engine below could rise up through the frame of the machine and into the seat under me and give me an erection, what was I to do? Sin had found a nest inside me. I prayed and studied and searched over the next eight years in Catholic high school and college, but little that felt like grace came my way, while the church, even through the fog of my hovering faith, stood increasingly revealed as a bureaucratic machine mangling human behavior into categories of pedantic audit with the approved on one side and the damned on the other. It cast a spell in which every thought, breath, feeling, and sensation had to be forcibly searched for concealed aims, some selfish leaning, an appetite for lies or pride or lewdness in thought or deed, or worst of all some base predilection poised to arise. Of course there was the option of confession and I took advantage, but as time went on a central irony came peering through the practice. The mandated morality made transgression inevitable. By the tyranny of the design, human compliance was improbable if not impossible, and so it was expected that one would struggle and fail and confess and sin over and over, sinning and confessing in a perpetual state of remorse and fear and trembling, because the interlude between each offense and its erasure opened a fault through which one could slip to hellish torment for all eternity. When I finally fell away from the church, it was to escape this wheel and its grinding. I embraced oblivion. I found a refuge in the idea of nothingness. It opened on a void of infinite and silent sanctuary in which I imagined an impersonal absence whose cold embrace was a comforting substitute for peace.

"I'm trying to understand what you're saying," he said.

"They put you in an institution, Father."

"I ended up there."

"But things happened. Things led up to it, things that they did."

"I ended up there. That's what happened."

His tone required that I pause. Through the deepening fumes of the liquor, I worried I'd been rude. I worried I'd insulted him. Certainly, I had my hostility toward them. It could have bloomed disguised as a factual claim thrown at him. Then I felt myself slipping into another murk, this one eddying around a different question. I wasn't sure, but I had to ask if his rejoinder had been a reprimand. Had he corrected my interpretation of what had happened to him in order to shut me up?

At the center of my brain where the alcohol burned in smoky furls, my ideas could not find one another. Thoughts were pointless alone; one by one they felt senseless; they felt insane. They yearned for interconnectedness, a chance at logic; they needed association or even contradiction. But I was facing an emptiness somewhat like the nothing in which I had sought to hide from hell. And then I thought, That's what I want to tell him.

"I only felt . . . I always felt . . . bad."

He nodded and told me, "You were scrupulous."

I had no interest in that idea. I'd heard it before and it was a kind of refinement of control brought to bear when a person under the control of certain authorities complained to those authorities that they were controlling him unduly.

"You were scrupulous," he said, and this time he revised his intonation, as if to make clear that he was offering a concept I had not adequately considered.

"No," I told him. "What I did is take them at their word. I believed that the church meant what it said."

"You have to remember, Mathew, the men of the church are men. They're human and as humans they're fallible, but the institution is not. These things are mysterious."

I felt annoyed, because it seemed he was appropriating the position I had thought I was building. My intention had been to bring to light the elusiveness of motives, the complexity of life, and now it sounded like he was marching these notions forward in support of his argument.

"There are moments in these events, where the unnatural, the nonliteral order of things makes its appearance," he said. "You know that."

If I understood him correctly, he had just introduced the concept of mystery between us. His tone felt cold and official, and this strategy was unfair. Mystery was the church's hammer used to stupefy reasoned contradictions. *Take it on faith. It's a mystery.* Now it seemed he was asserting this age-old weapon against me on the basis of his specialized role as a priest, the Sacrament of Holy Orders having endowed him with privileged understanding. Clearly, then, his doctrinaire confidence in extreme unction was equaled by his doctrinaire confidence in ordination, and so he no doubt subscribed to all the other sacraments, too, including the immutable power of baptism, which meant that in his eyes I remained a Catholic no matter what I thought. I saw myself on my knees before him, hissing out the crippled assembly of my sins. The rug would accept me. It could happen in seconds. I lifted my glass and drank, and past the gleam of the elevating rim I saw him tilting toward me in his chair, an enigmatic smile rearranging the planes of his countenance. Was that how he had endured the cruelty of his superiors? Because he was a channel through which the forces of heaven poured each time he administered a sacrament? Had he received validation and nourishment through the realities of grace with each execution? It seemed he had, and by this revitalization he had been given sustenance and cause for faith about which I could only fret and speculate.

He was talking about a doctor, some doctor. Doctor somebody. I'd heard the name, but lost it. Doctor somebody. He was a kind, supportive man. Very patient. "An intellect. Brilliant mind and kind. And in our sessions, he was so attentive."

Oh, yes. He was talking about the psychiatric institute to which he had been committed for treatment. My earlier reference to what they'd done to him must have sent his mind back to the wards where he had been confined at the University of Illinois. He was talking about the psychiatrist who had tended him. "My dreams astounded him. Not in their narrative, not in their events. But in their colors."

I was on my feet, filling my glass and drifting off. While I might consider myself to have left the church, it was an article of faith in the sacristies and theological tomes that I was wrong. While I might imagine myself repatriated and free, I was actually lost. But not beyond their orthodox retrieval. Because in accordance with their laws, which they said were God's laws, I was eternally in their realm. I could not learn or evolve in any direction except to move into their embrace or into the devil's snares. They had no interest or concern regarding my opinion on these issues. My interpretation was irrelevant, for they were certain in their supremacy and confident in their possession of me, having marched me up and down the aisles of my childhood, periodically, to gouge indelible marks into my open soul with their arsenal of sacraments, until, by pain and fear, I was made theirs permanently. I could not ever leave or cease being a Catholic; I could only fall away. The sacraments of baptism and confirmation each put an indelible mark on my soul. That was the teaching. An indelible mark, I thought, and I saw us then, Father Lillius and myself, and our souls were like hearts in a documentary on surgery. They were coated in slime and mucus, their action puffing them out through films of viscera, and they were being scourged and pierced by instruments in the hands of technicians operating on us, methodically, indelibly. I was pissing. My hands were holding that odd curl of flesh I loved so much—about which I thought so much—and which got me in so much trouble. It was sticking out of my pants, urine splattering into the yellowing toilet bowl water, and I was thinking about something important, something crucial. Death. And I was realizing something important. Father Lillius was a priest. He could turn upon me at any instant, commanding me to kneel, demanding that I confess. He might raise his hand to cross me. From his fingers an irresistible jolt could leap. It was true, I realized. I believed, in a deeply primitive and atavistic way, that by some sign or incantation, he might at any instant seize and eliminate the frail conception I took to be my individuality, my will. He was a priest and so could, by some hex or curse, unloose a preternatural power to enslave me.

I looked in the mirror expecting to see myself, but I wasn't there. I wasn't in the bathroom anymore. The mirror was a shard leaden in color, like tarnished silver or a hunk of granite or midnight pavement, and I was traversing the living room looking for Father Lillius, wanting to find him and to say something to him, wondering where he was.

There he was in his chair, his drooping eyelids sadly cradling his thoughts in a sway of intimate personal private review.

"So colorful," he said, when he saw me. "Bold. Garish. I could barely describe them." He was talking about his dreams, the uncanny spectrum of his nocturnal flights. He'd been talking about them before. That's right. The ungovernable assault to which sleep subjected him and in which his soul arose in colors, his hurt in colors, his years in colors, memories forgotten and unforgotten in a bravura display before that doctor in the institution, that doctor who cared for him and whose name I could not retrieve at this instant. I needed that name. Ministering to Father Lillius, allying with him in that time when I along with so many others had been negligent, the man stood in my imagination suffused with a paternal, benevolent radiance.

Father Lillius was chuckling at the memory of his incongruous, unsightly, unpriestly, gaudy, garish dreams flooded with pigments and tinctures whose extravagance was insubordinate to his vows of poverty and temperance. They had been an avalanche of hue and tone, a savage, rampant exhibition. He was proud of them. I could hear it in his voice. "The vividness of the colors astounded Dr. Corbeil. He told me that he had never heard of such colors. I had such graphic, vibrant dreams. He had never encountered anything like them before." Father loved his dreams and found them amazing, something in their exotic plenitude testifying to a reflected rarity and distinction in him. He was vain about them. They were his feelings, I realized, and then he looked at me and I saw them, and they were a fragmenting rainbow housed at his core and storming, with the impetus of some psychic, subterranean disruption through him, signifying a secret he had yet to interpret exactly. The doctor could have done it. What was his name? Maybe he could still do it. Father Lillius had said it again and I'd lost it again, and now I was afraid to ask him to repeat it—this name, like a talisman, or secret code or password, which seemed to be the key we needed. I was afraid of offending him because having forgotten could seem inattentive or indifferent.

And then it was as if we were emerging from a brief sleep the way I woke to see him waving an emphatic finger at me from across the room, the immediate past from which I stepped a stony blank of experience as evocative and enigmatic as the content of any nighttime venture. In the present, the impact of his administrational finger was a regal prelude to speech and then the prelude lengthened and then it ended as he said, "Don't be afraid to say the name 'love.'"

"What?"

"You heard me."

I felt a ruffle of indignation straighten my spine. My distress arose from a confused fear of being misread, and I felt a strenuous call for clarification in response. It was true that I had just said something about not wanting to use that word, something about "love" not being what I wanted to say. But what had I been referring to? I tried several quick forays to retrieve the subject to which the contested word had failed to apply, but I found only a pool of emotion confirming the position I had originally taken without the slightest elucidation of what it was. I felt this left me with no choice but to attempt to remake my point without quite understanding it, and I laid my response out before him in words it seemed I believed could best be understood individually and so I provided lengthy gaps between them, along with a heady allotment of conviction regarding their worth in every annunciation. "It . . . just . . . didn't . . . seem . . . specific . . . enough!" I told him.

"Oh," he said and took a sip of scotch. "I see. What would be specific enough?"

I searched for a long time, groping through the fog of my interior to sort the discord of my vocabulary. I knew the ache of the missing word, but not the concrete matter of its expression, and having rejected "love" for its lack of specificity, I did not dare settle for a substitute that was anything less than perfect. This missing gem was, however, not easily identifiable in the abstract. Still, I was diligent and hopeful, like an archaeologist sorting the alleyways of a disregarded city in accordance with a frazzled, half-shredded old map. I thought and thought, fingering nouns primarily, but occasionally pausing at a verb, or turning an adjective over carefully, a connoisseur of uncon-nected parts in whose esoteric understanding I was trained and in whose tendencies I found reflected back at me a strong but equivocal affinity. Finally, I turned a corner and stood before an ancient site about which I knew nothing. I sighed, having lost my way, my disappointment canceled by my sense of total ignorance regarding the missing item I had not found. Mo-mentarily, I filled with a peculiar lack of all responsibility that seemed a kind of happiness. "I'm hungry," I said.

"What?"

"Can we eat?"

He was a fuzzy image of a tall and interesting man, his brow squeezed tight with thought, as he turned and snatched up a pen and started scribbling on a notepad plucked from the win-dowsill. A lily wavered in its swoon of a vase near the spot the notepad had vacated, the force of his gesture having left behind disturbance. I smiled watching him write, my mild amusement amplified by an irresistible pleasure that left me chuckling aloud. "How are you doing, Father?"

"Fine," he said.

"What are you writing down?"

"What you said."

"What did I say?"

"That love— I mean, 'love,'" he said, and his reiteration gave him the opportunity for an amazed and tender highlighting of the word. "That it was insufficient. Somehow."

"Oh, yeh." We got the giggles suddenly, the both of us wheezing and reeling about in our chairs. When at last we managed to regain our breath and balance, I took a moment to consider the phrase in the form he had returned it to me, while he went back to his pad. "Is that what I said?"

"It's what I'm writing down."

I watched him for a while. The notepad into which he peered was an ordered snare of lines and measured blankness settled firmly on his knee. In the reflecting permanence of the dots and flecks of black he scattered on the page, he was stilling and collecting the headlong flux of his interior. The process and the concentration involved smoothed his cheeks, flushing from his countenance half his years. The act of writing seemed to take him from the room.

"What was his name?" I asked.

"Who?" Returning the notepad to the windowsill, the pen to the breast pocket of his coat, he reached for his drink.

"The doctor," I said. "Your doctor."

His head lifted, and the energy of his eyes came directly at me with a certain blankness that seemed derived from both curiosity and a mood of open invitation.

"Was it awful there?" I asked.

He dipped the length of his finger into his drink and stirred and nodded. Then he glanced to the side as if to modulate the rawness of the moment with a tactful measure of modesty. He stayed that way, his posture a carefully placed veil between us. "I was abused by my friends," he said, "and that was awful. But the institution, and Dr. Corbeil—particularly Dr. Corbeil—that was a respite, a longed-for harbor. I was abused by my colleagues. I simply couldn't believe it. The accusations were so preposterous—they were so outlandish, so fiendish—so beyond anything sanity could have anticipated, let alone fairness—never mind justice—I was too stunned to defend myself. I simply couldn't defend myself. I had no defense against accusations whose kind was so distorted, so malicious. It was too humiliating to even try to address them, and so I didn't, and well . . ."

He paused, took a breath, and then peeked at me in a way that suggested a serious, if momentary, interest in reconsideration. Perhaps my indignation at the scene his words had forced me to imagine had produced a scowl that made the moment feel overly charged. He might have thought me uncomfortable, himself intrusive, me scandalized. Whatever the case, he shrugged and reined himself in. "It's over now. The past." However, the consignment he wanted was not to be so easily achieved. His eyes, having fled in a survey of his own room as if to locate some new subject for our conversation, came back, their black liquidity gleaming. He smiled, preparing the way for his pronouncement. "They'll pay, though," he said, and his finger swirled the scotch and ice with clicking sounds. "At the hour of the final judgment, the truth will be known. Dante has a ring of hell for traitors. For liars. It's all in the eighth and ninth circles. Not in the last ring. Not in Lucifer's mouth. But where they're mostly frozen in ice. Traitors to kin. For those who bear false witness." He licked the finger and smiled.

I laughed, though not easily. His hopes for vengeance depended on inhuman scales. For the achievement of his satisfaction, he was relying on a perfect correspondence between the perceptions of divine justice and his own. He nurtured hope for infernal retribution. And as I thought these things, the moment changed, a layer dissolving with something hidden reaching out to draw me into a darkling space where intuition awaited. I was wondering about his suicide attempt. I wanted the details, wanted to know, wanted to ask. I saw a blot of anguish then. Some abundance of emotion partitioned off until this moment came rushing toward me, the barrier disintegrating, and I was meeting the concrete matter of his nervous breakdown, his suicide attempt, and he was a distillation of pain alone in some room, trembling, praying, breaking. Without knowing it, or intending to do it, I had looked away and now I looked back. He was filling his drink, his attention averted as he concentrated on the liquid arcing from the bottle. And as I saw him reticence arose, its power a whispered command that the moment recede and grow meager. I couldn't stop it. Having promised an easy interconnectedness between us in which any subject might be broached, the opportunity was being diluted and then annulled by sanctions I had forgotten we were subject to. Propriety imposed its evenhanded rule, and shyness muffled us.

"It must have been very hard, Father," I said.

When he opened his mouth to reply, he squeaked. A mysterious intrusion had taken his breath. He tried again and managed to gasp. I felt embarrassed for him, but then saw panic in his eyes. I started to stand. He gathered himself, urging away my worry with the impatient fidget of his slender hand. His next attempt brought forth a wheeze and he clamped his teeth down hard. Again I moved and again he held me back with his upraised palm. Snatching up his pen and pad, he scribbled intensely, then showed me what he'd written:

Hysterical voice paralysis. Started back
with these troubles. My breakdown. Nothing
to worry about.

Once more he gouged the pen about, then waved the sheet before me:

I have to tend to my bladder.

He trailed off to the bathroom, and I jabbed the scotch bottle into my glass. I took that somewhat large drink in a spasmodic synchronization of head and hand. The next refill I overpoured, an acrid puddle radiating around the base of the glass. I sipped, then bowed and licked the excess from the bookshelf I'd enlisted as a bar. Dabbing my lips with my sleeve, I finished the glass in a gulp and prowled the room.

Books and books and knickknacks. Souvenirs and photographs. Tastefully framed portraits of students in their college days mingled with older manly versions of these same young men burdened by fading faces and thickening torsos. Entire families were represented, sons and daughters beaming up from the vicinity of an adult knee, their childish features hinting at some antecedent version of the original college student, while simultaneously manifesting their own brash variation on the Duffy or Studtz or Willenborg or Kauffmann strain of genes. Father Lillius considered them all somehow his offspring, forming a very extended family. He was included in only two of the photographs and both of these featured one or the other of a pair of famous female poets with whom he had nourished relationships through the years, mostly by letter. The women were both regal and somewhat voluptuous, though in their sixties in the captured image. The patrician face of one was crowned by a towering spiral of hair, and Father Lillius stood at her side grinning at the camera like a schoolboy, while she peeked up at him, the stem of a tulip clutched in fingers restraining a caress. The second woman wore an overcoat, as did Father Lillius, and smiling, her arm through the gentlemanly hoop of his, stood paired with him several tiers up some stone stairs whose destination lay unrevealed above. It was only as I wondered about their location that I noticed a third woman in an antiquated black-and-white photo slightly faded with age, a little ghostly. Next to her and leaning into her leg stood a young boy with dark hair and far-seeing eyes. Four or five years of age and clad in the oddly formal attire of knee pants and a pressed, collared shirt neatly buttoned and topped with a bow tie, Father Lillius's boyish expression rang with anticipation. Like him his mother, whom I knew he adored, appeared eager, too. She was slender, black-haired, black-eyed, her hip against his head, her hand on his neck. They gazed into the hovering lens before them, as if the stillness and expectancy holding them had been induced by the photographer's promise of a glimpse into the unknown future alive beyond the camera's eye.

I was watching him return now, having heard the bathroom door shut. He walked carefully and then paused in the middle of the room and said, "I'm better now." But each word was staticky and thin. "That damn voice," he said shaking his head, a stroke of self-mockery lightening the complaint. "This was awful at the peak of my troubles. During all the accusations." Even now his baritone resonance was depleted, as if stones had scoured his throat. Words seemed to hurt. "Eventually, I was mute," he said. "My voice was paralyzed. Hysterical voice paralysis. Forgive me. It comes back like this, but it's only a touch. It passes."

"You were mute, Father?" I said.

"I was."

"You mean, literally? You couldn't speak?"

"Not a word. In the middle of all those accusations. At first I tried. But it was like this. So weak-sounding. I was defeated even as I tried to fight. I couldn't keep it up. It was the most awful feeling. They took my voice. There I was."

"Billy Budd," I said.

"What?"

"Billy Budd."

"Well, yes. I suppose." He appeared to let my thought take him toward a murky introspection where no light could be found for a while, but then he spied a bobbing speck far off like the lamp of a ship at sea, and he returned to me, his eyes focusing carefully. He smiled.

"You see what I mean," I said. "He couldn't defend himself. It was all so outlandish, like you. Like you said. Claggart's accusation. It was just so beyond anything he could even consider. Claggart's grotesque lies. They were so grotesque. They were so evil that Billy was speechless. So Claggart spoke and the more he said, the bigger the lies became until it looked like there was no way to ever start to correct them."

"Speech became impossible for me. More and more impossible." His nod was not simple, and the way he narrowed his gaze before glancing down suggested that what he might say next, if he said anything, would prove difficult. "But he was a boy, and . . ." He knew the thought needed finishing, but his first priority was not speed. He managed the difficulty and went on. "One would have hoped that a man my age would have somehow found a way to leave behind such naivete." He took a breath to weigh an inner mandate reluctantly. "But apparently not."

I was trying to respond, while knowing that most things I could offer would fail. If they were not wrong, they would be inadequate.

"Why did Claggart hate the innocent soul?" he asked.

I held to my silence, hoping that given a second or two he would answer his own question the way a person does when he's alone and musing. But nothing more came from him, as he was waiting too, perhaps for me to speak, perhaps for his own thoughts to find their way through to the end of the riddle. We both sipped our drinks.

"What are we without speech?" he asked.

I shrugged. Father Lillius had taught me about language, the opportunity of voice and sound.

"Monks," he told me. "Without speech we're monks."

It took a second, but then the twinkle in his eye shoved me along. We both laughed with a light acceptance of the humor he had offered, but the vibrations of his previous question about hatred lingered like those of an object fallen from a height.

"You never thought of that before? About Billy Budd, I mean."

"No." He shook his head.

"And no one else said it?"

Again he shook his head, though barely. "And then poor Billy speaks. But with his fists. Lacking words, he murders, and they hang him." He ended with his head angled in the direction of the window, as if the dark outside might know his subject and offer a point. When in the next seconds he sought contact with me, he sent only his eyes shifting beneath the plane of his brow, so that he appeared to remain turned away. "Well, at least I didn't do that. At least I didn't try and kill anyone."

But of course he had. I don't know if I thought of it before he did, though there could be no question that in the next seconds our minds referenced the same incident and rendezvoused in a clear exchange of our mutual recognition that he had tried to kill himself. He was facing me and the clock was ticking. But then, as if inspired by the example of the monks he had alluded to just seconds ago, we said nothing. He even lowered his eyelids, and inhaled and exhaled. Without thinking, I did the same, as if he were teaching. When I heard him move, I looked. He was standing.

"It's time for coffee," he said, "and lots of it. And we should eat. I'll go fetch a second pot." He floated off, yards of black cloth in full sail, and the click that followed was the door shutting behind him.

I poured a cup of coffee and, finding it lukewarm, drank it like water. I repeated the process, then filled the cup again and walked to the window. I had to bend to look out. For my effort, I received the cloud-banked vision of a man traveling over the earth in a plane at night. Dark patterns prowled a vague gray rising toward the upper expanse of the sky, which was blocked from view by the angle of the window to the vista. I would have to crouch or even kneel to see above the squashed horizon, where faint black lines crossed without discernible start or finish. I believed they were tree limbs changed by distance and dark into bands unconnected to anything I could see. The orchard was there, or what was left of it according to what he'd told me. I strained to detect an actual tree, the thick base, the unadorned branches clawing up. My elbow bumped one of the trumpeting vases on the sill and the lily swayed. I steadied them both and went on to imagine the orchard and somehow it came to me in full bloom. Huge trees and layers of leaves like green clouds spouting apples from big round bellies. The glass of the window was cold when I inadvertently touched it. The truth was I couldn't see anything out there. I'd finished my coffee, so I started back with my empty cup for a refill.

Just then Father Lillius returned bearing a second stainless steel pot, which like the first struck an institutional note. However, steam issued from the nozzle, declaring the contents hot. "I bet that other's as cold as cat piss. Here." He offered a clean cup for me to hold while he poured. "Have something you can enjoy."

I nodded, adding milk. "Should I be able to see the apple trees out that window?"

"A few," he said. "Let's eat."

We transferred the coffee to the little dining table where we sat, lifting the lids from our food. He collected the tins and, stretching one long arm, left them on a nearby shelf. Watching him stir sugar and milk into his cup, I waited before starting. But then his fingers entwined and he bowed his head. With his eyes closed, he didn't check what I might be doing before he prayed. "Bless this food and bless us, too." With that he raised his coffee, eyeing me over the rim. "Dig in."

"Okay."

"But I'm afraid Sister was right when she said it wouldn't stay warm forever."

"Probably not, but I'm hungry and it looks fine."

We ate in silence, forks clinking, mouths working, an occasional spark of contact. He kept the coffee cups filled, but after a while the silence hinted at a burgeoning unease. I was grateful that my bags at home were packed, and I reminded myself that I had to remember to gather my shaving gear from where it was still scattered in my parents' bathroom. They would be annoyed and hurt that I had spent my last night away and then had stayed out so late. Suddenly, I felt eager to get away. Glancing at a ticking clock on a shelf amid books and a miniature painting of a lily entwined with a rose, I noted that midnight had passed forty minutes ago. My plane would leave in the morning at nine-thirty. I was going to be a wreck.

"Well," he said. "Where were we?"

"When?"

"Talking."

"Oh. Well, we covered some widespread territory."

"Did we?"

"I think so."

"I'm not so sure."

I reached for more coffee. My steak had gone rubbery. A knot of gristle the length of my thumb ran along one edge, but the meat proved tasty. The mashed potatoes were far from appetizing, having turned chunky and inelastic as they grew cold. Still, I forked them in and chewed and swallowed. The same with the peas. I was hungry and knew I'd better help my poor stomach cope with its load of scotch and coffee. He asked about several former students who lived in the East. His interest was to some degree idle, and yet he clearly did wonder if I saw them. Perhaps he was comparing my interest in them to what I'd managed to show in him. I shared the little I knew, and he nodded, though I felt distraction growing in him even as he asked me to convey greetings the next time I had a chance.

"I think we waited too long," he said.

From the way his hand floated over his plate, I knew he was referring to our delay before eating, but I feared I was supposed to understand more. Rays of allusion and reference rose from his lips on those few words and then dispersed the way they might from one of his poems reaching toward larger meanings. "No, no," I said, raising my fork. Like a small child hanging on to the literal, I gestured proudly to my plate, which I'd nearly cleaned. "I was famished." To embellish my point, I reached for the apple pie. He watched me take a bite and then stood.

"Finish your pie. I want to show you something," he said.

He went to the bookcase where he picked up a stubby thick candle in a holder like a cup of ice. One quick stride had him at the window placing the candle on the sill. The struck match he touched to the wick shot flame into the night, drawing into view the brick of the adjacent wall jutting out just on the other side of the glass, while the reflected image flew above the lilies in their vases. He picked up a book lying flat near the clock. I hadn't noticed it before because it was thin and had been on its side. He fingered it fondly. I saw the cover as he stepped toward me, and it was one of his own published in the years I was in college: *A Room of Leaves*.

"Someone bought this for me. Tom Garraty. Remember him? He was few years ahead of you. Two I think. Well, he found it in a rare book catalogue. It's the presentation copy I sent to J. D. Salinger, lo these many years ago, thanking him for his *Catcher*. It was listed for nearly two hundred dollars."

I wiped my hands thoroughly on my napkin and inspected them and wiped again before taking the book. It was frail, the binding loose. Threads and glue spanned the gap inspired by ruin tugging the cover from the spine. Mildew had printed a ghostly pattern on the pages he'd opened. There Father Lillius's neat script had lodged his name and the date below the title. November 17, 1961.

"That's great, Father," I said, and filled my eyes with sincerity before reacting to him. He was smiling as I leafed, mindfully, through several more pages.

"It's a strange feeling to suddenly find oneself a collector's item," he told me.

"There's some wonderful work in this book," I said and paused to read a few lines.

"I've pretty much abandoned those forms."

"Oh?" I was unsure what he meant.

He seemed to deliberately increase the already imposing height from which he looked down at me, nodding slowly, and folding his long arms.

"I always liked these forms," I said. "The way you handled them."

"Well, I've gone on to a far more focused and, I think, valuable aesthetic. Almost exclusively. The opportunity to be concise. The rule of precision. The demand and reward of economy."

"What do you mean?"

"I like to condense. Evoke. I always have. Less is more. So I've been doing haiku more and more," he said. "It's a special form."

"Haiku. Oh, sure. I've heard of that."

"Of course."

I felt regret at the loss of the narrative intimacy that characterized much of the work filling the pages I held. "I didn't know you were doing that."

"Well, now you do." He gestured toward the book, and I felt I must be imagining the condescension worming its way through his manner. "I don't do this kind of thing anymore. Here, let me have that." It wasn't rough the way he retrieved the book, but there was force in the act as if he felt mistaken regarding the sheen of value he had cast over it moments ago. With his back to me, he deposited the slim volume on the shelf. "Are you finished with your pie? I'd like to make this clear."

"What?"

"Are you finished?"

"Yes." With one hurried mouthful I emptied the plate of all but crumbs.

"Well, come along then. I have some work I'm doing."

"Okay."

"Let's do this." He was already on his way.

"Haiku?" I asked, standing.

He went on without answering and I followed. It wasn't far. A few steps to his bedroom door, but because of the speed of his changing mood and departure he was already out of sight around a corner when he called back, "I'd like your opinion about these. For old time's sake. Perhaps I'll read aloud like we used to."

"Sure," I said, rounding the corner and stepping through a doorway into his bedroom, where I found him standing beside a coffin. With his back to me he bent over the edge the way mourners peer in at the deceased. Candles burned on a nearby stand. The coffin was black and ran sideways along the wall opposite the foot of his bed. Covered in a green blanket, but otherwise unadorned, the bed was narrow and rigorously made as if intended for some decorative purpose rather than sleep. The long flat black length of the coffin tapered from head to foot. In every way a plain wood box, it stood at the level of his waist, where it appeared to float, though it was in fact maintained by a pair of sawhorses positioned one at either end.

I'd stopped at the doorway. I knew what I was looking at. It was his and it would fit him, because he'd ordered it built to the specifications of his present long, tall form. Without straightening, he peered back at me. His smile possessed multiple elements and not all were drawn from enjoyment. But he was relishing something. His sly delight was clear. I told myself that mischievous deeds often have an affectionate cause. But there was a shadow in the room and it was not any thrown by the candles or the overhead bulb. He struck me as a little like a mean boy playing a joke on someone he thought he liked.

"I'll find them in just a second," he told me.

I stepped closer and discovered that the open coffin was loaded with papers propped upright and running lengthwise as they might in a file. Tan folders actually served as dividers. The supply of manuscripts and documents dwindled near the foot, where books formed a barrier to keep the rest of the arrangement from tipping over. So he was less in pages than in the shape that stood before me, eyeing me shrewdly, before going back to sorting and searching. I watched him walk his slender fingers along the tops of folders and pages and felt like I was watching a man paw through bones or dust. They were his mind, his formulated self jotted down in phrases and left behind like a trail to mark his passing. But there was too little. It was too short. I could not help but think how the body of his work failed to fill his coffin.

"I think I must have misplaced the ones I'm looking for," he said. "I had them out last week to work on and . . . I might have . . ." He trailed off and left me wondering if this why I was here. Was the coffin what he wanted me to see? Just one more reminder of the demise that awaited me reiterated through a little pageantry regarding the demise that awaited him. I felt like I was in a room with a crazy man, and then I felt that I was the crazy man and what lay in the coffin was not his papers but a dead thing belonging to me that he had kept for me, the monster of my past, my little amputated self that I'd left behind, and now it was about to arise in some mad reprisal of Lazarus back from the dead and Dracula back from the dead whereby the thing I had put to death would reclaim me at Father Lillius's command.

"Here it is," he said, straightening, and bringing with him a stack of eight or so loose pages. "It's a series. Not a narrative, but—" When he stopped, it was to trace the angle of my gaze to the coffin behind him. "Oh, don't worry about that. Once I had it built, I had to store it somewhere and it serves a purpose here. A dual purpose, really. It's a reminder, but it's also quite handy, as you can see. And I know it makes some people nervous, but I thought you'd be fine with it. It's not like I lie down in it and sleep, you know."

Momentarily speechless, my tongue knotted in a way that threatened to make me as mute as he had been, I knew I couldn't let his assertion pass, unless it was true. "Never?" The word sprang up and hovered in the room as if delivered by a companion we had lost track of.

He didn't move but I felt him travel off and then come back. Our eyes had a momentary dance before he said, "Well, once. But not to sleep. I had to see if it fit." When he paused, I knew it was to create space for me to respond, but I left the moment empty. "If it makes you uncomfortable," he said, "we can go back to the other room."

"It doesn't make me uncomfortable," I said, trying to strike the word in a way that left no doubt that a better word was required, one that was harsher and far more contentious.

"I think it does."

"No," I said, confused by my desire to sound casual while feeling harried.

He slipped past me, and the lights went out. He must have flicked the switch because instantaneous shadows filled the room. I stood in the dimness with his bed and coffin and we were all just about the same, I felt, just these corporeal lumps of coffin, bed, and me. Exiting the room, I was momentarily face to face with the Virgin Mary airborne above a pastoral field of grass and flowers in a framed portrait outside the door. When I walked into the living room, he was pouring coffee into both of our cups.

"What are you trying to do to me?" he said. "I'm running out of gas here. Suddenly, I'm exhausted. Shame on you. Listen, do you think you could do me a favor? It's a lot to ask, but you were an altar boy at one time, so after we look these poems over do you think that if we went down to the chapel you could help me out and assist me at my daily Mass? Otherwise, I'll have to do it in the wee hours. Normally it's at seven so I'd have to get up at six. Anyway, do you think you could manage the wherewithal? Then I could go to sleep and . . . well, you get the picture."

"I don't think I'd ever remember how, Father. It's been so long."

"Half the time the boys who serve don't know what they're doing. I'll be no worse off with you than most of them, I'm sure. I have to direct them with all these hand signals and whispers and grunts to tell them, 'Now bring the cruets, now the missal.' You could be a big help."

I was stunned. Given all we'd discussed, this request and the carefree manner of its unveiling felt ruthless. Was it a dare? Was he daring me? I didn't know, and yet, simultaneously, I understood with something like spite that it didn't matter what he intended or what I thought, because he cared only that I comply. Sincerity was not required. "Sure," I said. Empty compliance would suffice, and that I knew how to provide.

"Really?"

I would oblige him with an absolute counterfeit and an equal nonchalance. "Sure."

"Good, so we'll look these over quickly." He rattled the pages of poetry. "And then we can head down to the chapel. I promise to make it a fast one."

My eyes roamed the room, anxiously, locating the bottle of scotch on the floor near the window. His concentration on the papers was so total that when I moved he didn't notice. "I'm going to have just a touch more of that scotch, Father."

"Be careful," he murmured.

I nodded, snatched up the bottle, and poured a shot into my coffee.

"When I started," he said, "I adhered strictly to the required syllable count, but then my interest became more in states of mind and feeling. Not big emotions, but the subtler things we feel. Or, in another sense, the moods. And of course objects. Always objects. Anyway, you'll see. At heart haiku is concerned with stillness. And solitude, too. And yet somehow the ever shifting of our lives."

Resettled at the dinner table, I waited with my drink while he remained on his feet.

"The effort, at least for me, is to convey not so much through the sense of the words as what happens because of them. Between them. Interplay with nature is very important and, well . . . These are four, with an interconnective spirit, I hope, under the title, 'Window for Her Visit.'" That said, his eyes rested for a few seconds on the first he would offer before he inhaled and read as uninflectedly as possible:

> "Chair beside the window.
> A shadow sits.
> Wooden arms and lace."

Watching him bring forward the next sheet, I realized each spare sprinkling of words would have its own white space.

> "From the dead
> A breeze.
> This long embrace."

I tried to focus, wanting to at least appear attentive as he hovered in the suspension of a sharp thought that compelled him privately.

> "Chipmunk on the ice
> reflected through
> The monk ship of my face."

He took a breath, appeared about to start, but faltered. I sensed a subtle coiling, a preparation keyed to gravity.

> "Her visit left a tattered sunset
> In the window
> Of thought and space."

That was four. I could not keep from glancing to the window. I found no evidence of lace, though there were wooden arms on the chair he'd occupied. Who had visited, sitting there? I felt it was his mother but couldn't be sure, his evocations of solitude, empty chairs, ghostly embraces, and visits besieging me with broiling images and their accompanying, contrary, irreconcilable feelings.

"And I have these variations," he said.

> "A cloud of white in tatters.
> Lace that leads
> To night.
>
> The tattered sunset
> Lights the air
> Then passes."

His head shake was a spasm of absolute rejection. "But they're inferior I think."
"Yes," I told him.
"You agree." He returned to the pages. "This one isn't bad, but . . .

> "Her chair beside the glass.
> Wooden arms
> Remain."

I had planned to keep my response noncommittal but found my opinion lacked all uncertainty, not even the slightest question. "The ones you started with, the original ones. They're the best. And they have the ongoing rhyme."
His smile, though furtive, left no doubt he'd known this all along. When he leafed to the next page and posed, studiously, over it, I knew he was trying to conceal his ploy. But then he looked up and whatever had been calculated fled. Bright and childish, he appeared surprised by an innocent discovery. "This last one's not part of the series. I guess I noodled it on this page. So it's random. I mean, it's just here.

> "Lilies on the sill
> Angel wings
> Still."

His eyes found mine, expectantly. "Well?"

I wanted to withhold my reaction and yet I nodded and felt that in doing even so little I was surrendering too much. I was stirred by the poem but at the same time bothered by his claim that it wasn't part of the series. What did that matter? Why had he read it then? And it could be part of the series if he wanted it to be. It was his series. He could modify it. But then I caught myself. Wondering if he might be in the midst of another ploy of some kind, I brought my inner life to a halt behind a smile.

"There's times when I think that's the best of the lot," he told me.

"It's good."

"Good."

"It is."

"Good," he said. "Well, thank you."

My reserved manner troubled him, even though, as far as I was concerned, his behavior had made it necessary. He turned away just enough to conceal his expression while tapping the ends of the pages against a bookshelf until they were matched and he could lay them down. "Well, all right," he said. "We better go."

He led the way to the door, whispering, "We should be quiet," as we entered the dimly illuminated halls. Fitful shadows shrank from the incongruity of our advance, their retreat crowding into inky corners. Passing the doors of the main entrance, I felt like walking away into the night. What he was doing was inexcusable. This eagerness to enlist me to serve his Mass could only have arisen from indifference to me. It revealed his complete disregard for everything I had explained, or tried to, all my wishes, everything about me. I would go along with him now, go through the motions, and then I would leave. Whatever else we might have shared, any and all moments of affinity were being swept aside by this imposition. I never wanted to see him again.

We turned a corner, and with the parting of two stained oaken doors we swept into a domed well of gloom. Candles at the feet of pious statuary bloomed like fluctuating flowers. Striding down the center aisle and past the communion rail, we paused to genuflect side by side before veering to the right into the sacristy, where I entered not a memory and not a dream but the memory of a dream. Within an instant I was lost. All points of orientation and origin were gone, the sound and sight around me overwhelmed, the present moment replaced. Though I knew that this glaring visitation was a memory and that I had recalled the dream before, this knowledge felt inconsequential, if not mistaken. It was reoccurring, the dream where I had been an altar boy serving a black-haired priest whose face I never saw. The lights were dim. Small candles twinkled, his vestments glowed. There were Latin words and altar cards and steps I climbed. His hands gesticulated as if he were signing to a world that could not hear. The offertory arrived with its preparations for the host to be withdrawn from the tabernacle in order to be consecrated and transubstantiated into our Lord that we might take him in, and then the tabernacle doors parted and inside the guru waited, the old holy man to whose ashram I had gone. There he was, his head and shoulders visible, this brown-faced little man in a red robe and orange ski cap peering out through that golden gateway lined with silk and framed with precious metals, his skin aglow, his black eyes gleaming as he beckoned for me to join him.

We were in the sacristy now, and Father Lillius had opened both doors on a large wardrobe closet full of vestments, albs, cinctures, an array of colorful chasubles, along with the black cassocks and white surplices the server needed, all shifting with his intrusion.

Through the frame of a small arch to my left I could see into the sanctuary where the spare wooden altar waited, and I wondered for a moment, not perfectly, not with utter faith, but with a burst of curiosity and fanciful hope, whether or not the dream might come true, once we were out there, if we somehow bungled through to that point. The Mass was in English, and he'd said he would help me. I might even recall the appropriate Latin every now and then. *Mea culpa, mea culpa. Kyrie eleison. Et cum spiritu tuo*. There might be moments of Sanskrit wafting through my brain. *Om Namah Shivaya*. And then the tabernacle door would open and what would happen?

Father Lillius had a parrot-green chasuble in his hands and he was holding it out in front of him as if wondering what it was. "I've had some dumb ideas in my time," he said, "but I think this one takes the cake for the dumbest ever. I have to rise and shine the way I always do. I don't know what I was thinking. I wasn't thinking. We can't do this. My harem, I mean, they'd be lost without my Mass at its proper hour. My poor little congregation. They attend every morning if they're able, the poor old things. If they can get out of bed, they're here." He pivoted, abandoning the chasuble. It swayed on a hanger behind the closing door. "Goodness," he said. "Goodness me."

He put his hand on my shoulder and shook his head to portray the immoderate scope of his own folly, and then he guided me off. We went from the sacristy back into the sanctuary and on past the communion rail where we faced the altar and genuflected in tandem once more, before starting up the aisle.

Near the vestibule he paused to dip his fingers in the holy water fountain, his hand floating from brow to chest to shoulder to shoulder, while I let my attention wander, knowing it would end at the altar. The flat wood surface covered in layers of linen edged in lace, the candles in their holders, the silver rod at the center rising to the cross on top were each faintly blurred in the half light and distance like relics long underwater. Equidistant from either end the white veil hung over the dim golden gleam of the shut tabernacle door and nothing moved. There was just the stillness beneath the rounded ceiling and the quiet, which felt distinct from the absence of motion defining the stillness, and the dimness filling the entire space ended in shadows cloaking the corners. Stained-glass windows hovered on both sides, but only those on the right showed hints of color due to the influence of a light, probably a streetlight outside. Dreams are dreams, I thought.

"What time is your flight?" he whispered. "I know you said, but I don't quite . . ." He shrugged.

"Nine-thirty."

"Oh. Well. You should go."

"Yes."

"You'll hate me in the morning," he grinned. "And your parents are going to be upset that you stayed out so late, aren't they."

"Probably."

"Let's get your things." Spilling in from the hall, a glowing band moved over him as he opened the door and we stepped to go. "Are you fond of flying?"

"I like the view," I said.

The door swung closed and I had the impression of traveling a much longer distance going back than when we were on our way. Numerous doors sailed past. I imagined sleeping nuns behind them all. We were nearing his room when he surprised me by speaking, and while his tone was hushed, given the hour and where we were, his manner was perfectly casual as he asked, "So you don't go to Mass at all anymore?"

"No," I told him and felt him grieve, though outwardly nothing changed to suggest that feeling. He nodded, then reached to open the door, leaving me to wonder if the sorrow was my own offered in his place.

With my coat on and my gloves held in my hands, I waited for him. He'd gone to the bathroom as soon as we entered. Then I took my turn. Now he was in his bedroom while I paced to my coffee for a final cold sip. He emerged carrying a long red scarf and his black overcoat, which he pulled on. As he began fingering the buttons into their holes, I waited for him to look at me. When he didn't, I wondered how he could be so consumed by such a simple task, and then I realized that thought had taken him off. It was startling to see how far he'd gone and how quickly. He might as well have sailed from the room. Of course he was right there all the while matching buttons to their slots and then winding layers of red knitted wool around his throat. I wondered if perhaps I was witnessing the summoning power of a new poem poking at him, the impulse with its shape in words forging a path into his mind.

"I have to apologize for something," he said. "It happened long ago. You may have forgotten. But I've thought of it often. It was when you were a student and we were walking along down Creeger Street. Just past the old high school and we stopped on the corner near the gym. We'd been talking for some time. I'd taken a stand regarding composition. Regarding length and value. I'd declared that the shorter a piece of writing was the better it was. Inherently. Automatically. Now you were never one to be concise and we both knew that, and you argued with me so desperately. You needed me to give you just a little room. But I wouldn't budge. You were so earnest and sincere and you needed me to tell you that your way was all right. But I wouldn't. I was grudging for no reason and I don't know why. I was stingy and I've felt bad about it all these years. You probably don't even remember."

The way he searched me then was as much to find my honesty intact as to learn the truth. "I remember," I said.

"Of course you do. Anyway, I'm sorry."

Departing the building, we managed the parking lot in a manner nearly purposeless, our course indirect and interrupted by little interludes of hesitation in which we faltered to make some point and then reaffirm it with an ambition determined to settle for nothing less than absolute clarity. My head was humming with the thinning fumes of scotch. I could sense the size and unpleasantness of tomorrow's headache, a kind of crinkling like a cracked window about to collapse in shards. The wind was rising. It snapped at us, some elemental excess in the coming December flexing its premature but mounting strengths. This was a familiar moment, this dry and heightened feeling rising to the fore at the end of such a night. The blurry sense of affinity and camaraderie was on the wane. The effects of its fading were easy to anticipate. There was already a kind of nostalgia for the earlier enthusiasms. But they were going now and, in their dissipation, one could doubt the validity of their excess, one could turn easily into the rest of one's life, leaving this evening behind, nurturing a sort of useful skepticism toward its extremity. Our bodies were hollowed out, our well-being slightly awry. We teetered there, making chitchat, prolonging the contact, delaying the end, and feeling awkward. And then he did something extraordinary. In retrospect it seems inspired, even visionary. But of course it was merely impulsive. He couldn't have known that within the year he was to die in a dentist's chair, succumbing while in an anesthesia-induced trance to a stroke that banished him, withdrew him into the depths of a coma from which he never awoke. From sleep he went to sleep to sleep to sleep. But on that rather desolate parking lot, empty except for my one car, he was beaming. Had we been two drunken soldiers, I knew how we would have growled and snarled, butting heads hard enough to shake us in our shoes and get us singing, arm in arm. I had done it often enough. Had we been sweethearts, I knew what we would have done. We would have kissed. But we were priest and errant laity, and so he blessed me. With his left hand tangled in my hair, he held my head steady, as with his right retreating in a flex at the elbow, almost as if he were about to punch me, he stared fixedly at me, his eyes gleaming with a desperate, grandiose exhilaration. He seemed to set himself, as if he feared he might miss me. My first impulse was to pull away, but I was both startled and amazed, and then as his hand began to twitch at me I knew there was nothing to fear. He was a man, that's all, and he loved me. By accepting this gesture, I felt I was blessing him. Fall was a looming emptiness, the swollen nothing of the sky giving up a crumpling whine of wind, a kind of forecast of the long Iowa winter rattling through the leafless limbs of the half dozen trees that had been allowed to endure around the perimeter of the concrete on which we stood. The air was cold and he was murmuring in Latin and nearly laughing. Whatever grace there was available in the night touched us and fled.

LEVELING OUT

1

FOR AN INSTANT, it felt as if the bottom of the plane had fallen out. Everything was on the rise, even this glob of spittle-drenched airline food squeezing back up my throat into my mouth. The lady next to me gave me this fed-up look, like maybe it was my airplane. Like I knew dipshit about airplanes. Just to get on this flight I had to bully and degrade myself. It was more the influence of some leftover herd instinct than any decision I made that prodded me into the shuffling ranks of strangers filing into the open hatch. As far as my mental landscape, it was all this breaking news interrupting prime time with flaming wings, sobbing stewardesses, berserk instrument panels. And now, with my table smashing up into the molding of the seat in front of me and the flapping pages of my Haverhill catalogue jumping toward the ceiling, I knew why. I'd been given a warning but without enough clarity to make me know it was a warning. In the aisle a stewardess was enacting a kind of trapeze maneuver as she struggled to keep from toppling into the seats while the coffee she clutched started to tilt and spill and she shouted, "Oh, no. Look out! The coffee!"

Right! Brilliant! I was elevated, my seat belt knifing at my thighs, so spilled coffee was not exactly the major problem. The noise was catastrophic, a sound of windows breaking and wind thundering through the fuselage. Yet the only hole I saw was an open storage compartment raining down whatever all over this Hasidic bunch. A fedora sailed down, followed by a child's stroller. A thermos bottle and a bundle of leaflets and newspapers bound with ribbon. Insanity filled their eyes. I saw straining passenger mouths full of teeth and spit and shock everywhere, and they were all screaming. That was the noise

I'd heard. It was screaming rushing from first class right into coach and out the fucking tail.

Then the cushion came up to cuddle my butt. The fuselage wobbled, rotated, and we were smooth and apparently level. It was like fucking, when you're there with this girl and then somebody touches somebody starting this hubbub of impulses that in other circumstances might be distasteful to at least one of you and then it's over and you're lying there wondering what time it is. I glanced at my watch, then looked out the window, anticipating maybe angels. Everyone else was seeing them these days and showing up to tell some batty tale to this or that daytime talk show host. But if there'd been supernatural participants in what had just happened, they were hiding. Maybe under the riveted wings or in the clouds burning with a pinkish light. Maybe they'd raced in to perform their rescue, then slipped away like Indians, blending with the shrubs of their high-altitude habitat.

"For all a you back there that thought we were just about up to our belly button in rattlesnakes, let me just tell you we are back on track." All of a sudden, this voice was breathing through the walls. "This is Captain Rob Potter. I want to assure you that the people that assist me in charting our flight plan are the best in the business, and we take advantage of all the data available on the basis of the finest most up-to-date instrumentation the mind of man can produce. But every now and then Mother Nature puts one over on us. So it's best to remember, this is God's heaven, and we're just passing through."

I wanted to get off the plane. The pilot was insane. Had I been riding in a car, I would have jumped. But the best I could manage was to leave my seat. I sped down the tilted aisle and stepped into the bathroom, where Captain Rob's voice waited: "Now you let the flight attendants, Nancy and Hal and Karen and Bobbie Joe, who are just about the best in the business, take care of you. We're still about two hours out of LAX, so they're going to be sashaying up and down those aisles, giving you folks free drinks. That's right. The bar is open."

I was peeing and listening to Captain Rob. He was somewhere far away in his cockpit, the control panels before him a glowing field depicting the flux of the world around us. He looked to me like a man in a uniform enjoying a fireworks display, and I understood his commanding, satiated tone. After all, he had just flicked a bunch of switches, jerked some stick, and felt this monster of a machine obey, while the rest of us were being rearranged like dust in a vacuum cleaner.

"As far as what's left of our flight," he went on, "I do apologize for that little bump back there and you have my personal guarantee, it's going to be a cakewalk from here on in."

When I stepped back into the main body of the plane, things were pretty much as promised. The clouds were parting to let us through, their remnants graceful outside our windows. Still, I was uneasy. I settled into my seat, and as the sashaying Sarah, or Lucy Lynne, or who-the-fuck-ever came near with her rattling cart, I asked her for bourbon. I made my eyes puppylike and asked for a double. No, make that a triple. She smiled, fixed me a glass of ice, and tossed me three of those little bottles. I grinned and got busy. After the first taste I closed my eyes. Captain Rob might rant and Rebecca Lynne might sashay, but I knew better than to trust them. My skepticism hung in a web just below my skin, just inside my eyes. The bourbon went right to it, coated it, made it glow, and almost immediately something showed up in the light. It was not Captain Rob who had saved us. Looking out the window I caught sight of what could have been a pious fluff of wing darting off to hide in the nearby turmoil. After all, it was more or less the norm for me. I knew better than to trust the official version. My life as an orphan taught me to recognize fate when I saw it. Born one person, I was transformed within breaths into a nameless other, passing through an interlude without definition, a nothing, who was then renamed, my original destination canceled and replaced. If there was a reason this plane had not ended up ablaze in cornfields miles back, I felt it bore a mysterious connection to the fact that I was aboard. I saw the charred pathway we would have plowed. So they would all be dead, I thought, scanning the people around me. Reaching out to the passing Sally Lou, I requested another drink. She was less happy this time. Paranormal ordination, I thought. Irrational intervention. Tabloid headlines. These were not thoughts that required absolute faith, but only a foot in the door, so it was just a little open for them to seep in like a smell from somewhere interesting. The woman at my elbow, nibbling peanuts, would have been reduced to ashes.

After a while the horizon showed a hoop of ocean on one side, the watery edges dissolving in a rush of sky. We were circling, turning. Seconds later the fragmented rainbow of Los Angeles tumbled into view. "Look," I said to the woman. "That's Los Angeles. We're almost there." The false sweetness of her response could not cover up her distaste and suspicion. She seemed to think she could look right through me to the foster homes of my past. Or maybe she could. Maybe she'd been in one of them. Because what was it, as far as I knew, except one big overcrowded, hard-to-remember nightmare. So maybe we were trying to remember each other at this very second, trying to unravel all the haphazard stuff that had somehow thrown us together on this plane. Only days ago, I might have looked at her and wondered if she was my actual mother and not just one of those creatures from the foster homes, but not today. Today I knew where that one was, because I was headed to meet her before she finished dying of cancer. I had things I wanted to tell her, things I could vouch for. They were what had happened, after she'd dumped me off in a cardboard box wrapped in newspapers and covered with newspapers. Other people might hear how their father fainted at their birth. Or paced the hallways far from the gore, his pockets full of cigars. My legacy was newspapers. I watched people read them on buses and airplanes, street corners, subways with a special interest. I turned the pages of the daily, the weekly, the tabloids myself with a sense of personal expectation, as if the secrets might start to surface. It would be weird and dreamy. Tales from the crypt. Maybe some account of the second foster home in Wiota, Wisconsin might be unearthed at last and set forth in that objective way newspapers employ to manufacture the idea of unbiased truth. Like it wasn't always just some guy at a computer terminal devising columns of print. The byline. The date. And then the dry fields outside the lowered blinds shutting me in with Batty Bea Lacombes who was drowning a puppy as an instructional aid that would teach me not to wet my pants. She was sixty-three but looked twice that, the way she was twisted into this arthritic fucking fishhook. She had the sink slopping over with dishwater and the puppy stretched across the drain board. The little feet clawed the enamel. I could hear more than I could see at first, but then she picked me up and put me on a chair. Her fist was around the puppy's neck and both were plunged into the water. The neighbors had banged on our door and given the puppy to me. A couple of drunks sick of puppy shit, one had said, "Can be his playmate." And the other one said, "Yeah. His little animal sister." Now she was dying in my place. I could imagine her struggling mouth and her eyes baffled by the effects of her inability to breathe. The legs kept squirming; the claws drew a hopeless sound from the surface. First old Batty Bea had stated the principle to be learned: the dog would die and I would never wet my pants again. It sounded unlikely. It seemed she had failed to note a flaw in her logic. But then, as the puppy's legs were not exactly inert, though their aim was muddled, I felt a kind of twinge somewhere in the sector below my belly and above my rectum. It was a sensation like fingers pulling parts of me into little strings of tissue and then the strings were looped around one another. The fingers were cold and their intrusion was deep, and then the ends were pulled into a tight knot. When she dragged me into the bathroom, the lifeless puppy hanging from her other hand dripping water along the floor behind us, I looked into the toilet bowl toward which she tipped me. The stink of her urine was harsher than mine, rising from the stained enamel funneling down the hole. Far above me, her words were turmoil, promising an end for me just like the pup's. But I was serene, knowing the knot in my stomach would save me.

The wheels dropped out of the bottom of the plane. The pavement came into view and the tires tapped down and then jumped up, as if unconvinced that the runway was real. That's what I'll tell her, I thought, when I see her, that's the first story because I want her opinion about it. I'll be interested to hear her try and account for the part she played by playing no part at all in these particular developments. She thought that by running away she would be free of any known participation in what happened. I guess that's what she thought, though I really have no idea. But by being gone she played the biggest part of all, which was no part. This is the point I would get to eventually, coming in on her blindside to dump it on her lap, and then I could watch her try to think her way through her own absence, working her way through nothing in search of an answer.

2

I HAD ONLY MY CARRY-ON, a vinyl satchel with an Indian-head emblem, so I raced into the midday glare and caught a cab. We weren't fifteen minutes out of the airport when we sank into a traffic jam. Behind us other cars thudded and squealed into place. Car after car, until we were one of hundreds turning into a huge metallic smear. After a few minutes of cursing in broken English, the driver snatched up his CB and started haranguing his dispatcher in a Middle Eastern language. His words were like a lot of pots slamming together, and after a loud bark he fit the mike back into its slot, shut the engine down, and we just sat there in the heat.

I could see hills ahead capped in a rotten chemical glow. Beyond them, according to the map spread on my lap, there was a place called Studio City. That was the part of Los Angeles to which I was headed. I'd never been to Studio City. Never been to California. But in the grids of blue spread out on my lap there was a line that marked the street on which waited a small ranch-style house. My mother had been a beautiful teenage girl who arranged newspaper sheets around me. She was blonde and thin but very sinewy, her hair a fine yellow mist that hung in a halo the allure of her features. Her eyes were blue, like mine. These were the traits we shared, hair and eyes. She had been passionate. A babe. Hot and athletic. I'd been born in the early seventies. So I imagined her a wayward by-product of that time. Not a true flower child, but one of those made up of the residue when the last waves were on the ebb, nothing left but this Madison Avenue version in which people continued to act as if everything vital hadn't departed, leaving them to inhabit a kind of empty mass-produced extension of nothing. Of course I knew that since she got pregnant, certain things happened. So when I thought of her I saw hairy cocks and blow jobs. Fields of sweaty skin. I heard orgasms like in porn movies. I saw her as fleeing her middle-class parents, going one way and then another. I saw her with a steady stream of guys in all kinds of beds. In houses, apartments, motel rooms, the backseats of cars, smoking grass, her eyes big and greedy. She was the kind of girl who would ask a man if he found her attractive, her hand falling to his knee as the question escaped her lips, and if he said that he didn't know, she would edge her hand a little along his thigh and throw her head sideways so her hair fell over her eyes. Then I'd hear those porno cries. I watched her climb the stairs to the orphanage with this enigmatic expression. Or was it mischievous. Sometimes it seemed devious. Step by step she retreated until she trailed away beyond my comprehension.

I knew that the house where she waited had seven white artificial ducks with dopey eyes staked into the lawn. I knew the rooms were all sort of smashed against each other like they'd been added in grudging fits. The front screen door needed patching. I knew the house inside and out from studying the photographs I'd received in the mail along with the news that my mother was sick. Who? I thought. I was in the hallway of my apartment building with the tatters of the brown envelope at my feet and the brown wrapping paper balled up in my fist. It was a hoax and I knew it. It had to be and I hurled the packet into the trash, took two steps, and wheeled back, grabbing in the can like some homeless asshole, and the feeling was unlike any I'd ever felt before or since. I don't think that strictly speaking it was a feeling. It was more like a bug at a lighted window. Let me in; let me the fuck in. The pictures were all of this ranch-style house. I raced through the entire stack searching for her face. The one nose, the single set of eyes that would rid me of my ignorance. But all I found was rooms of the house, each presented from a number of angles. Empty chairs. Empty beds. I entered my apartment and slammed the door. Jesus fucking

Christ. I turned on the television. I wasn't going all the way to California.

Then a week later I had a terrible fight with my girlfriend. We'd met in college as sophomores and we'd dropped out as juniors. Now we're about two years into whatever came after that. What started the fight was this book she was reading on psychology. In fact, we'd met in an introductory psychology course that sophomores had to take. She was going to diagnose me, she said, when we met, and she was still trying. The book was about Freud, or by Freud. I read it, too, and Freud was in it a lot, but I can't quite remember it. She would read it to me out loud. We would fuck and then she would grab the book and pick up where she left off. Sometimes she would read it to me while I sat watching television. Lots of times we would smoke some weed and she would start reading it to me. Sometimes after we'd smoked some weed the words would get like a blaze of neon gas and their sound would be feathery but real loud. It was all about how everything was split off. The big idea was that what I in fact thought of as my real self was a false kind of puppet made up of elements of fantastic inventions convinced and convincing me they were real. So it was this kind of image on a big empty screen projected out from the abandoned site of what had been me, or could have been me, except that I had gone into hiding so totally I was as good as gone forever.

"So I'm like this TV no longer getting a signal," I said.

"Right," she nodded. "If you were an astronaut you would have lost all contact with the mother ship."

"I'm here in the room with you, but I'm not the me I was."

"Sort of. Not the real you who has run off and is impossible to find like a gangster in hiding."

I felt like nodding, but I didn't because the part of me that knew the truth of this stuff was the completely false part, and so the whole thing was okay as far as I was concerned. What was I going to do, get rid of myself? Or what I took to be myself? I was not interested in departing, or giving up my position of importance no matter how fictitious I might be. So I told her she was wasting her time and none of it made any sense. I hated her knowing it, or thinking she did, and it made me feel like she was there to bring me trouble. I got this bitter satisfaction from frustrating her, though, her and her big buddy Freud, but that isn't why I did it. I did it because it was a matter of survival. Sometimes when we were on weed, I would understand every thought and word and letter of meaning in the book, even the index and footnotes and bibliography. I'd think, God. Wow. Or some such shit. But then in the morning the problem was that all the meaning turned into a hangover. I'd feel somebody stuck this ax in the middle of my head and she'd start reading to me over coffee. I'd figure she'd been reading privately and had found something and so she'd start reading aloud while I was looking through the newspaper. Or maybe if she slept late, I'd read the book to myself. It would become less insidious that way. Like poison, right. The antidote is poison. Or a hangover. The same booze. Inoculations. They're the disease controlled.

Maybe it's why I read so much; I'll read almost anything just to have the words drumming on my mind, the sense of rapport with nonexistent beings. All this braying alien thought. Like now with this newspaper supplement in the back of the cab. The first page was an advertisement with this brunette with blue irises in eyes as white as cue balls. She was advertising Salon Secret Infusium 23, like we were supposed to be so fucking impressed that she'd used it to color her hair, like her hair was special, when it was her tits that mattered. Tucked away behind the silk folds of her blouse, the nipples boiling. The next page was a family at their kitchen table, the little girl licking her lips, while the father stared into his newspaper and groped absently for an empty glass. The mother, standing slightly behind the father, gazed up at this gigantic bottle of spring water afloat outside their window. It gave me the creeps. This voyeuristic bottle hovering over them, watching their every move, their every breath. On the last gleaming page, two large boxes lay on their sides, one red with white letters, the other white with red letters. They were Motrin, which claimed to be "The modern painkiller." That's what I'll use, I thought. I was sure that what I was feeling was modern, even ultramodern. Maybe even postmodern. Or post-ultramodern. Or posthuman. That was the phrase these techno-nerd theoretician/bullshit artists in computer magazines and virtual reality magazines had devised to describe the current epoch: it was posthuman, and filled with posthuman beings.

We'd been stuck there for nearly an hour. People wandered by, arguing about the cause of the traffic jam. And then they argued about other things. Bits and phrases of sadness and hostility floated into the cab. Some people wandered off and sat in the grass beside the road. They seemed very far away. The cars spread in every direction and looked flat in the glare, these tiers of metal with all the definition melting out of them. Palm trees on both sides of the road were turning tobacco brown as they cooked in the smog and sun.

Then there was a sudden hubbub, and I felt afraid. People were running back and forth. We started to move. Unzipping my satchel I pulled out my notebook and started to review my notes. I felt the need to cram in order to arrive fully prepared to meet my mother. I had everything I needed in this sturdy black three-ring binder bulging with lists and questions, clippings from newspapers, quotes from outside sources, all in these alphabetized sections. One section was labeled: Memories. Another was: Possible Memories. Some of the entries were meant to dishearten Mom. That was my idea of reconciliation. Misery. Viciousness. I'll laugh at the damnedest things. There was a section of notes whose aim was to offend and hurt her. To shame her. But suddenly I had no idea what it was all about. All these scribbled words in the back of this fucking cab felt like a foreign depiction from long ago, this event in ancient history with which I had no available connection. I might as well have been reading about Herodotus emerging to depict Cyrus crushing the Medes. The numbers, the dates were like the combination of a lock that opened nothing. 552. 539.

Nabonidus was contending with the clergy of Marduk, a primary god. It felt about that far back in time that men in suits came to take me and transport me from one woman to another. Nabonidus and the clergy could not settle their conflict, and I was different each time. Older. Bigger. If I talked to these men, it was about what I was reading, or what I had seen on television. I stared at the cut of their lapels, the placement of the pockets and of the vents. I took note of the material in the lining and whether there were pleats. I tried to memorize the trouser widths. Sometimes women came and their tits moved up and down as they talked, their eyes behind thick glasses like laboratory specimens fixed in slides. They talked. I listened. It was all like some esoteric branch of science whose value was in question. Lives of a cell. I thought of algae, rootless in the murk. With whiplike flagella used for swimming, they lunged about, eyespots seeing nothing. They procreated, dividing their single self into halves. They did this over and over, growing lonelier. Large fish arrived and devoured fields of algae spread before them in a seeping red fecundity. But sometimes they never left, as the algae coalesced into a lethal muck, a scarlet tidal suffocation. Having entered to eat, the fish struggled then, each a scaly gleam mired in crushing banks of algae, gluing up their gills and eyes.

The house the Middle Eastern guy was pulling up to was the one in the photos. He was going to let me out and drive away. My breath left me. It was like I was gulping speed. The metal ducks were on the lawn marching eagerly to the front door. They were supposed to look silly and give this cartoonish impression of happiness, but suddenly they looked lifeless stuck there in the dirt. There were artificial daises in the window. The living room had a shabby, cut-rate carpet. I was just standing there paying the cabbie and trying to remember a song that the dismal, smog-laden fucking twilight had made me think of. It was by the Smiths, and they sang it in their lazy, sad, cynical, empty way. It was all about the special way that somebody other than them had once been a long time ago. They were very pissed off about the change, but they didn't want to admit it. The word "heart" kept reappearing. They were sad and angry and confused, and when they got tired they just made noise.

By now I was sitting on the curb. I used to wash dishes in Artie's Steakhouse on the corner of Seventeenth Street and Ninth Avenue in the big and shitty Apple. I've scampered about in a paper hat at Kentucky Fried, coleslaw in my teeth. I've been the guy at Burger King who, when you came to the window, he didn't smile.

A man was standing over me. He had come out of the house. He had walked very slowly up to me and stood there over me looking down. I'd seen him arrive out of the corner of my eye. I could hear him breathing and it was a little desperate and heavy as if the walk from the house had stressed him. Then he crouched down and identified himself, but the name went right by me. He leaned real close and I could tell he didn't care if he was being offensive, or if he was intruding on me, and the house sort of came up around me like it was something I had fallen into.

3

IF YOU FOLLOWED THE MAN down the carpeted hall past the embroidered scrolls in golden frames on the wall, you came upon an old woman in a ground-floor bedroom. She lay flat and unmoving on a narrow bed with worn white sheets, and she seemed enclosed in lamination. The man said that I might want to just sit with her for a while, and when she woke up I would be there. I did not like the weird odor in the room. It was concentrated in the corner where the woman lay. The blinds were drawn the window open a crack. An embroidered hoop hung at the end of the drawstring and it wavered as much in response to the passing traffic as to any actual breeze. Cars shot past and the engines revved, the gears changing, and no two cars sounded the same.

What hair she had looked like pieces of dirty skin stripped off her in some awful experiment. Her face and throat were a mess of wrinkles, her skin the color of spoiling fish.

I didn't like the way she was looking at me, and her hoarse voice struggled on a plate of bubbles. Sometimes her words got close to something I could take for a human speech, but mostly the sizzle drowned them out, or they fell back and seemed to choke her. It was like trying to understand a frying pan. I was sweating and concentrating on making sure I continued to breathe. That was the main thing. In, out. Keep it going. The man came back and touched my shoulder. He said she was sleeping. She looked dead to me, her head thrown back, her mouth stuck open. But then she started working hard to breathe. We had that in common. But in her case, the air seemed unwilling to enter her and it resisted and she butted and gnawed to get it, this mood of struggling unhappiness around her.

The other people were plopped at the table in the dining room, stuffing their faces with a sort of picnic lunch on paper plates. A bowl of potato salad, a plate of ham and cheese stuck between these little squares of white bread. Like where the hell was this all supposed to be taking place, some fucking camp-site? Was the next event going to be a pickup softball game? The first person I was introduced to was supposed to be my half brother. He was in work clothes, round-shouldered and swarthy, with a hulking head. A fucking sibling. Jesus Christ. Can you imagine that? Looking at him, I kept searching and demanding to know what it was I was feeling. With this stink of furniture polish coming off him, he made a big show of wiping mustard off his fingers before shaking hands with me. By the look of him, I figured Mom must have endured a drugged-out period of experimentation in the sack with an orangutan. Fuck you, I thought, shaking his hand. The woman with the incredibly bad luck to be his wife looked haggard and furtive in a waitress's uniform. Nobody had to tell me the two kids were their offspring. Only a genetic ambition oblivious to its own defects could have spawned the pair of them. The little girl had chocolate all over her teeth, her eyes like minnows stuck behind glasses with lenses as thick as bricks. Her brother who had the dazed face of a bowling ball was about two feet tall and eighty pounds on knotty little knees. Their names came and went, but I was distracted by the hostility with which this little clan regarded me. Hadn't they ever heard of duplic-ity? Put up a front, okay! When the man who had come out-side to get me offered me a drink, I felt wary, even a little belligerent, and I guess it showed. His approach shriveled and retreated into a suspicious squint, his face masked by a dull metallic surface.

"I'm her husband," he said and slid sideways into the kitchen.

When I followed, he poured me bourbon. I downed it, glar-ing at him over the rim of the glass as it rose up even with my eyes. We shifted like fighters. I stuck the glass out for more. He probed the nozzle up into his own mouth, stretching back to take a hit, making a sucking sound. I waved the glass in a demanding way and the neck of the bottle clinked as he poured. It was like old times. I might as well have been back in Madison on Testimony Lane, where everyone was drunk all the time. Marcy-Mom, Horace-Dad, their dreary friends, snarling neighbors, all the kids. There were nine of us, three sets of siblings and me in the care of Marcy and Horace, who made us bend over each night before we went to bed so they could check our rectums with a flashlight. If we were dirty Marcy-Mom used a cotton swab on a stick, which she stuck into us and turned to clean us out. Sometimes she sank in too deep or stayed too long and I could feel parts of the world breaking lose. Then one night she took something. Below me the faded brown squares patterning the linoleum were like toy building blocks covered in scum. I was like a house with an intruder in it. It was as if she'd put her lips around my asshole and inhaled, drawing out something that I didn't think could be taken out of me, but it went and it went into her. Good-bye mothership, I bet I probably called to something floating off. I could see it going, but I couldn't see what it was. But I was floating around in this big blank space, just like an astronaut pushed from his vehicle, my head locked inside this helmet and I could hear my breathing. It was artificial. I was inside synthetic skin with a big metal bulb clamped over my head, breathing air supplied by an unknown benefactor whom I dare not displease.

Everyone was watching me. They were at the table. I was at the door. The kids were scarfing down the potato salad with a ferocity that bordered on violence and threatened to leave the paper plates and plastic spoons in shreds. The eyes of the wife darted from her husband to the jug of orange soda she was emptying into five paper cups lined up along the edge of the table. The man with the bourbon bottle leaned against the kitchen door frame. Beyond him, fluorescent bulbs in the ceiling struck me as huge thermometers racked together and flaming with some fevered nuttiness spreading through the house.

"I need some air," I said, scooping up my satchel from near the door. I didn't remember leaving it where it was, but someone had stuck it under this rickety table with a lamp and a doily on it. The drawer was partway open and inside I saw a set of cork coasters and two metal ashtrays.

"Whata you need air for?" the man said, striking a suspicious note.

"You know," I told him. "To breathe."

"Sure," he nodded and then he gave the other guy, the father of the two kids, a glance and when he got back to me he seemed to find me untrustworthy. "She ain't going to last much longer, though."

"Well, you shouldn't have given me that drink."

"Why's that?"

"I had my first drink when I was eight."

"So what?"

"What took you so long?" the other guy added.

The way they started laughing kind of grabbed me and pulled me over to them, my hand sticking the glass out in front of me. "How about one for the road?"

"Why not?"

The air outside had cooled a little but it was still hot, and the traffic had increased. The sun was nothing but this ugly afterglow where the west had swung up to wipe it out. I started walking, my stomach full of the chill a dentist pumps onto a tooth after he drills it. I barely managed half a dozen steps when I looked back, wanting another drink. I was tempted to think that the miserable way I felt had been caused by the bullshit I had just gone through. But I didn't have to go back to find out. I had my ideas of what had just happened. It wasn't that long ago. I had ideas of the room. The voices. I sure as hell hadn't forgotten the drawer with the two metal ashtrays, along with the old woman in the bed looking at me, speechless for all her hissing, and who wasn't even blonde, had never been blonde. I admitted to myself now that I'd scoured the roots of her hair for a hint that she'd once been blonde, like the girl who was my mother and who was young and athletic and sensual. I liked thinking about the mother I knew. The one I'd lived with all these years. Not this old hag stretched out in that room like roadkill on some back road to nowhere I'd ever been.

With every step, I felt the way a balloon bulging with gas or too much air feels, heaving and straining until it rips apart. Like Marcy and Horace had run an invisible enema hose all the way from Testimony Lane up my ass in some form of implant. So now I was stuffed with this putrid stuff sloshing around inside me. Was this what I traveled so far to get? Getting on that goddamn airplane, risking my ridiculous life! On the other hand we'd made it. We'd nose-dived and survived and I'd looked out the window and seen or imagined angels. I wanted to get somewhere and make some new lists and notes, manage some new formulation on everything so far. Was there anyone I could tell about what I thought I saw in the clouds outside that airplane window and what I thought they'd done? I searched, trying to present myself with possible candidates. Certainly not my moronic relatives. Especially my so-called brother. I was grinding my teeth. There was this knot twisting in my brain just thinking about him and I wondered if I was having some kind of delayed attack of sibling rivalry. What a joke!

When I entered the supermarket with a red sign in the form of a signature, like this giant Ralph had written RALPH'S on the wall, I went straight to the liquor shelves. I uncapped the Jim Beam, popping the seal and opening my mouth. I groaned with the great big slap of heat I got. This lady who was wearing shorts even though her legs were covered with scaly cellulite jumped when she happened to lock eyes with me. She'd been studying this quart bottle of margarita mix like the label was in code. It was clear she hadn't meant to look into my eyes. It just happened and her mouth got stuck open and her gaze turned confused like she was afraid I might step over and whack her one because of the way she disapproved of me. She wanted to restrain herself, but couldn't because being smart-assed and bossy was just a reflex with her.

Thanks to Mr. Jim, though, I was in another mood. I gestured with the bottle the way a person might if he wanted to share. She all but pressed her face into the margarita label on the bottle. I walked real close, kind of brushing her as I passed, and stepped around a rack of mouthwash and toothpaste. There were some big wire bins full of snacks, and I took a bag of Family Sized Cheetos, and Jumbo Barbecued Chips. When I got to the cooler, I grabbed up a six-pack of Schlitz and stepped into the six-items-or-less line. I threw back another mouthful of Mr. Jim, which forced the checkout clerk to look at me, then look away and then look back, glaring. I just smiled and shrugged, and that seemed good enough to send her back to scraping items hatefully over that glowing strip of glass in the counter. Whatever was inside read the prices and pumped them up on her register, leaving her little to do except to ask for my money. She had full lips, almost puffy, and even if she was probably in her early forties, her tits were still where they belonged and she'd taken the time to tailor her uniform so it hugged her ass. I gave her exact change down to the penny and thought about her till I was out the door.

The sky was a gray starless sheet of chemicals trying to turn into night. The moon couldn't compete against the barrage of neon flung up from this or that nightspot. I'd picked up a tabloid paper and the front page had all these photographs of kids who'd come to Hollywood so they could become actors. I was walking around the building, looking at them, and thinking about these guys ever ending up in the movies. There were half a dozen of them, all polyurethane in bullshit poses, because what they had in common was bullshit. They each told how it had all just happened to them, come over them, and they hadn't thought much about anything. They had been lost and aimless until it hit them on their motorcycle, or working some 9 to 5 job, that they should go to Hollywood and become stars. Or maybe they were in college, following their parents' bullshit directive to study medicine or engineering. And then it hit them like this personal comet that left them no choice: they just had to be actors. Now they gazed at me, their faces glossy cuts of steak, their eyes like empty windows, and the most blatant thing about them was the way they were lying, because they'd never had a purposeless minute in their lives. They radiated ego and waves of ambition as shocking as a firebomb.

At the back of RALPH'S there were two loading docks but only one in use. A semi was nudged up with these two guys working at it. I went over to the other dock, the empty one, and settled on the edge. I started to eat the Cheetos and watch the guys unloading the truck. One of them shoved these cartons down this conveyer belt to the other who pushed them into the black hole of RALPH'S stock room. There was a streetlight above them and lightbulbs inset in sockets around the edge of the concrete dock. It didn't take long for them to notice me. I took a big gulp of Mr. Jim, and lay back so I was stretched out with my ankles crossed when one of them came over and looked down at me. I offered him a beer. He popped the tab and the other guy came over. The bigger guy who had been the second to come over was named Tommy. The other one was Byron. We drank the six-pack quick and smoked a couple of cigarettes before they went back to work. The plan was that I would meet them at nine, when they got off. Byron had a car. He pointed out a black Ford streaked with smears of light and parked alone in the lot over near the Dumpster. Byron's brother was away for the weekend and he'd left Byron the keys to this house, which was located way out of town in a canyon.

4

"YOU EVER BEEN TO CALIFORNIA BEFORE?" one of them said, as we drove along the highway. The ocean was right beside us, throwing up these foamy lips. The earth just disappeared in the distance where the whitecaps stopped. Flecks of white streamed across a pit.

"Do we need more beer?" Tommy asked.

We'd already gone through a second six-pack.

"No," said Byron. "My brother's house has lots of booze."

The canyon was lightless. The road was cut into the side of the mountain, and it weaved in and out of the creases natural to the mountain. Most of the time there was no guardrail. The drop-off waited just past the jagged shoulder.

I was not really aware that we had departed the main road when the slash of our headlights lifted a picnic table up from the gloom. Parts of a ranch-style house became visible, some angles of a wall and roofing stuck into the dark.

Byron pulled a key from in a bunch of potted plants and reached into the door and flipped a switch. Gleaming banks of kitchen appliances sprang from the murk. He kept throwing switches, setting room after room ablaze. Pretty soon we were drifting through all this shiny wood paneling and plank floors. Tommy went off around a corner, muttering about having to take a leak, and then Byron disappeared up a set of carpeted stairs. Fuck them, I thought. In the sunken living room, I considered flopping down on a big comfortable-looking sofa with a glass coffee table in front of it, but I wandered into a hallway instead. Both walls were decorated with glossy photographs of fish in spooky poses on a velvety background. I came to a room with a pool table and a wooden bar that had been ripped out of a real tavern somewhere. Lots of liquor stood behind the bar on the shelves and there was a little brown refrigerator with ice and Bloody Mary mix inside. The pool balls were scattered all over the felt table the way they are when a game is interrupted. A window opened onto a patio that was probably the center of the house. Across the patio I could see into a hallway that led to the kitchen. Byron was talking on the phone and sipping a beer at a shiny table built into the wall. After a few seconds Tommy passed by.

Heading down another hall that I thought would take me to them, I paused to nudge open a door. Hovering there in the semi-shadows was a big four-poster bed and a thirty-six-inch TV. Behind the TV drapes were closed over a series of floor-to-ceiling double glass doors. Peeking out, I saw the glowing blue of an outdoor pool. I don't know why I opened the drawer in the bedside table, but I did. Lying right on top of these socks and sheets of notepaper and cutout news articles was a nickel-plated revolver. I felt a childish happiness sneaking up my spine.

When I joined Tommy and Byron in the kitchen, they were rooting through a carton of videotapes and arguing about what to watch. Byron won the argument, which meant we would watch this pornographic movie that his brother had shown him. Of all the porno movies he had ever seen, he said this one was his favorite. It was about this guy who fucked a lot of women and then one day he happened to see two people fucking who were in love, and he saw the difference. The result was that the guy became celibate and brooded until he met a girl and fell in love and married her and fucked her brains out.

Byron nodded sagely, as the rectangle of the cassette sank into the VCR with a murmur and several clicks. But the things he had described were hard to follow in the hubbub of breasts splashing about the screen, the hairy male buttocks hammering away amid yelps and honks. It was hard to be sure the guy learned the any lesson at all. He had hippie kind of hair, dirty blonde and sticking up in funny ways. He had big dismal eyes and skinny legs and a dick like a half of a baseball bat. He moped about under streetlights and peered into the gleaming aftermath of departing cars. But in the end he seemed unable to express himself except through the use of his tilted hard-on. Across a couch, she was sprawled open like a phone book. The funky guitars and sleazy saxophones got shoved aside by a bunch of gauzy, sensitive violins. You could hear him saying that he loved her over and over, but when they showed his eyes he looked like he had lost his wallet. His dick was like this beheaded chicken plucked bare being forced into this washing machine filled with human skin. Yet I could feel my own blood sneaking to my dick. Then the whole thing was over. The tape had gone blank and staticky like somebody was inside the set scoring the tape with a razor blade.

I think it was Byron who said, "Maybe we all better go off somewhere alone and beat off now." I don't know what the others did but I went to the bar. I poured myself a drink of vodka and knocked the pool balls around using my hands to send them into one another. The clock was one of those old beer clocks with raised metal arrows for hands. It was painted a bright orange and the hands were green with rusty scratches and edges. The way they were elevated made their movement sort of startling. They advanced in mechanical jerks like time was confused or in some kind of struggle. I was leaning on the bar, watching each minute closely.

The gunshot could have been a car crashing into the house. It could have been an earthquake. But I knew it was a gunshot.

Tommy and Byron were outside with the handgun. There were bottles on a stone wall. Pepsi bottles, Coke bottles, Jim Beam and Old Granddad and Cutty Sark and Absolut vodka bottles. Byron was shooting and the nickel-plated gun was a fistful of ice that spasmed and flung his arm up in the air. One of the bottles exploded. It was like a snowball in the moonlight. His hand jumped again, a bolt of bright exciting light spitting out at the sky. "Shit," he said. This time the bottles remained undisturbed in spite of all the commotion.

"Let me try it," I said.

"We better quit."

"Just one."

"You know what you're doing?"

"Sure."

"There's two in there. Take them both."

I reached and took the pistol, and I could feel the way it wanted something. It was full of secrets and a rich desire. Hefting it, I smiled at the lush thrill opening up my nerve endings and splicing them into forces lurking inside the gun. It could make things different. It was a sorcerer, a witch, a real psychic hotline. Most people feeling this feeling would have just given in to it.

Tommy was to my left and Byron was to my right. As I raised the barrel into a slant of moonlight, a tiny halo appeared around the sight. The little squadron of bottles teetered along the wall. Turn to the left and Tommy's dead. Turn to the right and it's Byron. Someone was calling. I felt the voice crawling through my hair. Some kind of transmission was in progress. Soon it would be clear. We all had many different enterprises in progress inside us and sometimes they communicated. Sometimes I knew about these enterprises and their powers and sometimes I didn't. But what was inside us? How did it get there? In my girlfriend's book, Carl Jung said these things were living and their names were "Anima" and "Animus," and lurking nearby was "Shadow." The fabric they inhabited was this oceanlike soup about which even less could be claimed. But we had all been flung up from it. Up from this soup. I tried to imagine "the soup"; I told myself to visualize an ocean. Or maybe the sky at night. But what I saw was a cloud wrapped around some mud. Freud came up to Jung and said, "No, no, Carl, I'm sorry, but the things that make us up are the Id, the Ego, and the Superego. And they're adrift in the Conscious, the Preconscious, the Subconscious, and the deep dark Unconscious. But there's no goddamn 'soup.' There's no fucking 'soup.'"

Well, you can imagine the fight these two got into at that point. "It's the Shadow, you fool!" "It's the Id." "No, no, no!" "Listen to me, damnit!" "Get out!" They couldn't fucking settle the matter. They couldn't sit down and discuss it and settle it in a rational, mature way. No, they had to squabble and curse and condemn each other. So what the fuck did they expect? What else could be spawned by their rancor and confusion except rancor and confusion and people like me standing around on hillsides with guns in our hands.

"What are you waiting for?" said Byron.

"I don't know."

"You're just standing there."

"I know."

"Is the safety off?"

I fired rapidly, the muzzle blasts flowering electrically one on top of the other.

"That was dumb," said Byron.

The recoil kissed the juncture where my elbow hooked up with the rest of my arm. A tingle with a carnal flavor probed my ribs and chest, leaving a wisp of melancholy. My arm was pointed straight up into the air.

"Did I hit anything?"

"With that second one, for crissake, all you coulda hit was a low-flying airplane. What a waste. Gimme the gun," he said. "I'm hungry."

On the way down the hillside, I felt Byron drove way too fast and much too close the edge of the fenceless road. I could see the dark leaping up.

"You're driving too fast," I said.

He looked at me and kept on looking at me, so the car started drifting. Hatchets of shadows reached up, pawing. There was a kind of desperation in them, a sadness. Like something out there was about to do something over which it had no control. I looked at him and shook my head and then I looked straight ahead at the road.

"What?" he said. "What?"

"Well," I said, "I don't really know you all that well."

"Oh, shit," said Byron, "that's my favorite song." Grabbing the dial, he twisted it. The twittering that had been background ballooned, as the tubes and whatnot sucked in the radio waves and blasted them out.

"Be careful," I said. All around us the emptiness was pretending to be a solid mass. "Let me out of the goddamn car!"

"Fuck you!" he slammed on the brakes. The car squealed into a diagonal. The nose jutted across the white divider line. "So get out."

I was opening the door. He crushed the gas, the engine roared, and I sprang back into the car. Then nothing happened except that he looked at me and laughed. We sat there. I figured he'd had it in neutral. "I just want to get out," I said. "I don't know you."

"I don't know you either," he said.

"What are you going to do?" said Tommy to me, as I stepped onto the road. "Do you know where you are?"

The car shot off, the muffler thumping as the front end headed for the shoulder. Byron wheeled them squealing back into their lane. About fifty yards down the road they jerked to a halt. The car was this black mound with the driver's-side door opening up and Byron bulging out. "The restaurant where we're going is just at the bottom of the hill and to the right about a block!" he yelled.

I didn't know what to yell back watching them drive off, but I was glad to know where they were going and I pretty much went straight there when I got to the bottom of the hill.

5

THE RESTAURANT FELT UNFINISHED, sawdust on the floor, plain wood picnic tables stuck around with seats bolted into the wall. Cables latched shaded lamps to the ceiling. After a few minutes I wanted to leave, but Tommy and Byron were hungry. Then I looked at the waitress. She was slim and blonde, her eyes fixing me with a blaze of greenish helpless interest. I had no idea why she liked me, but she did. As she scribbled down our orders, she kept turning back to touch me with her tender, coaxing eyes. I hadn't wanted to ride down the hill. I'd almost run away. When I finally got to the restaurant I wanted to leave. She probably hadn't wanted to come to work. She'd probably wanted to go to the movies or something. Now we were in this unexpected, precious moment. She started away. Then she glanced back, her chin tucked behind her shoulder, so she could peer at me through half-lowered lids, her lips parted with her breathing. I could feel myself going toward her, going farther into unfamiliar territory. She was the one I could tell everything to. About the airplane. The angels ducking into clouds. It was a big, big thing happening between us. She was luring me, inviting me, and I was going. Then Tommy came back from the bathroom and told us something weird was going on in the parking lot.

Two or three people were standing around this black Chevrolet sedan. The chrome gleamed and the paint was freshly polished. Inside were two people, a young woman pawing at the air to reach toward the locked door while this massive guy seized her wrists and brought them back until they crossed over her breasts, and then his huge arms wrapped around them. He leaned into her and whispered into her ear as she fought and got one arm free and strained toward the lock button and he snared her by the wrist and pulled her hand back where he wanted it. Some other guy in a T-shirt was at the door trying to open it. But he was wasting his time. The button was down. He started rapping on the window, trying to get the girl's attention. She was writhing in the big guy's embrace. After a few seconds, one of her hands sprang loose again and reached for the door. But she didn't have a chance against this overwhelming big guy, this placid expression on his face. Every now and then, he peeked out at the crowd of us. His eyes were blank. When she started trying to speak, her mouth moved but her voice was remote inside the sealed car. We all kept watching. Once in a while, one of us would ask the rest if we should do something to help her. The big guy inside the car kept shaking his head at us, "No, no. No, no." He was trying to stabilize the girl by laying his bulk on top of her, and he was this swampy pile of flesh in black clothing pretty much covering her up.

"... killing ... me ..." it sounded like she said, and he showed us his face in the window with these big inexpressive eyes while his lips made exaggerated shapes to express his denial of her claim. It was hard to tell whether he was choking her, because he had her beneath him now. But when she broke loose, she seemed to be coming up from some airless distance, her mouth wide. Her hand waved at the door, trying to escape. I could feel my heart opening up to her. The guy in Levi's and white T-shirt was ready to pull the door open if she managed to raise the button. He was yelling in at her, "Unlock the door." I started to yell too. "Unlock the door! Unlock it!" I had thought I was in love with the waitress, but now I saw that those feelings were nothing compared to what was happening to me as I watched this tiny, soft girl, whose eyes were baffled with her lack of breath.

That was when the police car pulled up, and we went back inside. The waitress who had taken our order was with some other guy when we got back. He was dark-haired and skinny and had a booth way in the back near the window. She sat on his lap with the tip of her finger in his mouth. Even though I knew I'd had feelings for the girl in the car I didn't like the way the waitress was acting. The cruiser that brought the cops had shot from the opposite side of the highway across several lanes, jumping the curb with a clang. I tried to eat, but after a minute or so I just put my head in my hands and sat there. When we got back to the house, Byron said I could sleep in the guest room.

I went reeling down the hall, dragging some sheets and a blanket he had given me. I found a room with a single unmade bed. I fell onto the bare mattress, the bedding flowing out behind me like a long tail. I wanted to be done with the day. I tossed and turned. But it seemed I could not escape. Then I started to sink. I took one last look at the day and it was a dark room. I entered a sensation of glop. Then I was shown a series of slides. They were mainly real estate. With each new slide there was a flash and a new house. I realized I had won a big prize. I wondered how I could have become so lucky. And then I was with the girl in the car but it was a different car. She said I should come closer because she wanted to tell me something, and when I got there and leaned down she told me that her life was flashing before her eyes, and I was one of the flashes.

6

AT FIRST, I didn't know what I was doing in the car. I could remember the kitchen and wandering around in it. I could remember slipping into the bedroom where I plucked the gun from the bedside nightstand. Before that I'd woken up and faced the hubbub of my thoughts. I knew I had to have a car. I wanted to find the girl I was looking for, who I figured was the waitress though she could be the other one, the one in the car with the big guy lying on her. I wasn't sure which. I wasn't even sure really that it was one of them who had woken me up, but I had woken with this sense of telepathic data summoning me. I knew it would be wrong to dismiss this feeling and just as wrong to trust it a hundred percent. I also knew that if I was going to take the car, I better have the gun because the car wasn't my car. I knew right where the gun was, so I took it along with six bullets from the box of bullets just in case the owner tied to stop me from taking his car. I hoped there weren't any other guns.

By the time I arrived at the restaurant where the waitress worked, it was closed. The interior was walled away behind barriers made of wood and glass, nails and aluminum, all these materials arranged in the form of a building to seal away the chairs and table on which I'd recently been seated. They looked like a pile of sticks, as if someone had broken them apart. I felt nostalgia drilling a hole right through me. A light burned somewhere in the ceiling. I wanted to go back in time, back to where that little waitress was smiling at me. I sat there, wondering where she lived, with her big green eyes, and then I put the car in gear and made a slow survey of the parking lot.

Back on the road, I took the first turn that would raise me into the hills. I looked out over the ocean. House lights coiled along the beach. I wondered which house was hers and if I could ever find it. If I thought about her hard, focusing all my heart and soul into a single wish, could such a wish somehow direct me to her? That was what I wanted and having said it so exactly gave me a sinking feeling, because I saw how it was absurd and impossible.

When I pulled into the driveway at the Highway Patrol station, I kept the motor running. I lifted the pistol from my pocket and placed it on the seat. The headlights of an arriving cruiser spangled off my windows. I closed my fingers on the pistol butt. Two patrolmen exited their car and climbed the stairs. The doors that opened to receive them showed a span of heat and light. Beside the cruiser sat the Chevrolet sedan in which the girl had fought for her life against that monster in black sweats. I'd watched two patrolmen take the guy away in handcuffs, while a third, younger patrolman consoled the girl. I loved her more than the blonde. I needed her more than the blonde. They were all inside the station now, the girl, the patrolmen, the monster. Maybe even the blonde. I imagined them huddled at a table. Only I was outside. It seemed selfish of them to have left me out. They were drinking coffee from Styrofoam cups, the three policemen and that huge mound of meat that was the monster across from the dark curls and curves and fluttering fingers and eyes that was the girl, who was theirs now.

I drove back to the restaurant, but of course the parking lot lacked everything I was seeking. The car in which the beautiful drowning girl had fought for her life wasn't there, because it was back at the police station, which I had just left.

I entered the highway and headed south. I was shifting the pistol to my jacket pocket when I noticed the car phone in its case set into a storage shelf below the glove compartment. I put the pistol on the seat and, after fumbling with the handset for a moment, I figured out how the thing worked and called my girlfriend back east.

"What?" she said, her tongue slurred with sleep.

"It's me."

"Where are you? What time is it?"

"Did I wake you?"

"God, it's six in the morning. Where are you?"

"I don't know where I am."

"Are you still in California?'

"I'm in a car. I'm talking on a car phone."

"Where did you get a car?"

"It was in the yard."

"I'm going to make some coffee. Keep talking."

"About what?"

"Whatsamatter?"

"I don't know what you think you want me to talk about."

"No, no, you sound like something's really wrong. Are you coming back?"

"Yes," I said. I didn't even have to think about it. I wasn't speaking of a literal truth. I was talking about something else.

"I want to read you something. Let me find it," she said. "I read it last night. It'll only take me a second to find it. Okay?"

"Okay."

"I have to pee," she said. "Hang on."

"All right," I said. "I will."

The light changed ahead of me, the bulge of red inhaled by the lamp and then expelled in a blooming green. I pressed the gas, the phone snuggled to my ear. I imagined her squatting on the toilet. She was going as fast as she could, because she wanted to get back to me. I watched the road and listened. But suddenly there was a big wind boiling around inside this tiny object in my hand. I yelled to her, but she didn't respond. I was poised there holding an apparatus that opened into a big emptiness full of nothing but wind. I hung on for a while, waiting for her to return. I imagined the little apartment we shared with its bathroom full of bare dripping pipes and all the windows open. I imagined the doors were flung open, too. I saw that she had been borne away into the wind and weather outside. I sped up, like I might catch up with the signal she was sending. I shot down half a dozen blocks, and it seemed the storm that had taken her was diminishing, the cold and wind fading and leaving a morning fog. But she was gone and I could call back, but I didn't. I felt restrained, nearly imprisoned as if the car was a trap and I was a misguided creature who had been caged and now I was filling up with animal sadness.

When I eased up to the curb and looked at the house, the memory of something lacking all detail took hold of me. I gulped and gulped again, reviewing the people inside. The idiotic metal ducks marched right up to the door. The people were just as counterfeit as the ducks. That was one thought. There were others. But most were worthless. I felt I had to evaluate the people, the house, their stupidity, their height, weight, eye color, taste in clothing. Had they heard of Jung or Freud and if they had what did they think? I was trying to measure their suitability for a function I could not define. Speculating on them, I mixed memory and invention and saw them seated on chairs, devouring little cheese sandwiches and holding waxy paper cups of orange soda out to the lip of the bottle someone poured.

The sun was oozing toward me, expanding over rooftops. The forefront of the dark retreated past me. As I strode to the door, I hefted the pistol through the cool morning air into my jacket pocket. Images danced, the muzzle exploding, my eardrums crinkling under the reverberations, the bullets flashing across the evening news, dwarfing the bulletins of nations.

Then the door opened. It was a woman, her bloodshot eyes in puffy white skin. But it wasn't Mom, like a part of my brain had for a millisecond almost believed. But the other one, the wife of my half brother, spawn of the orangutan. Her hair stuck out in a bunch of crazed directions and she was wearing Bermuda shorts and a white oversized man's T-shirt. With one hand holding the door open and the other raising a mug of coffee to her lips, she froze. The way she studied me it was like she was conferring about me with absent, higher authorities.

"It's you," she said and sipped the coffee. Her mouth made a wet squeak on the ceramic. She cleaned a swatch of hair off her eyes. "I wondered if we'd see you again."

Her husband came around the door, zipping his fly and tugging shut the buttons of the waistband on his wrinkled trousers.

"Look who's here," she said.

"Oh," he said. His feet were bare. He flopped down at the dining room table. Once there, he acted like it was this major thing for him to get there and he sighed and bowed his head onto his hands. "I'm a wreck. Can I have some coffee?"

"Take mine." She stepped back and slid her cup across the shimmer of the tabletop.

"We had a rough night. She didn't make it," he said to me, and then he fixed me with his eyes. "Do you want to see her?"

I turned to the woman, wanting to confirm my suspicions in her eyes, but she had her back to me now and was just about to sneak out of sight into the kitchen.

"They're coming for her soon," he said and gulped the coffee, and then his cheeks started twitching. His lips bounced. What the hell was I supposed to do in response to such crap? He looked like something terrible had happened to somebody dear to him and he had only just learned about it. I wanted to close my fist and smash him. He wheeled away from me in a careless way that slammed his knee into the table, spilling the coffee. He was blubbering now, making these dog-bark noises.

The other man appeared in the doorway, his face freshly scrubbed, his sopping hair combed flat. He wore a pressed dark suit. "Oh," he said, seeing me. "It's you."

I started shaking my head in some mix of amused disgust at the whole bunch of them. As if to prove my point, the woman stepped into the kitchen doorway and said, "He was at the front door. I opened it and there he was."

Something in the way she said all this gave the words a loaded-up, insulting quality, like she'd called my name in

order to mock me. She had this smug expression. She was trying to burrow into me, because she had all these special plans
for me.

"Did you have a premonition in the night?" she said. "Did
you feel it? Is that why you came back?"

"No," I told her. "No."

"Let's go," said the man in the suit, "you can see her."

By the time I located him, he was walking away. Movement
off to the side brought me to the table where the seated man
peeked at me over his forearms crossed under his nose. As I took
my first step, he recoiled like some invisible thing had kicked
him.

Ahead was the corner around which lay the door to her
room. I traipsed along in this sort of imitation of the way the
guy in front of me was walking. It surprised me when we went
around the corner and I got my first intuition of the trap waiting behind that door. The guy looked back at where I'd stopped,
and he was nodding in a show of sympathy. I started back-
pedaling. It was like the man had been dragging me and then I
broke loose. I crashed into something and then the wall, knocking into a shadowbox nailed at the height of my head. All the
tiny statuary dumped onto their sides. The man at the table
eased up onto the balls of his feet. The woman lunged up from
a chair beside him. Her beefy arms were pale. I touched the
gun in my pocket and it felt like something cut out of a dead
animal. When I lifted the gun from my pocket, I pointed it
straight at the ceiling. Because it wasn't my gun, it felt as if it
wasn't really there.

"He's got a gun," one of the men shouted.

The woman snatched it from my hand. "What are you doing
with that?"

The answer that I wanted to give her got stuffed back down
my throat by the weird power of her righteous glare. One of
the men was racing toward me, a burly shard of something stink-
ing on the move. Everything was shifting. I pulled the pistol

back from her. The man pounced on me. He hit me with his fist, the knuckles stinging the side of my head.

"How dare you bring that into this house?" the woman shouted. Her right hand was pointing at the ceiling in the name of a high moral lesson.

The man was running away, flinging over the table and ducking behind it, as the woman slapped me in the face and then the shoulder and the top of my head. "Get out! Get out!"

"Be careful, Marie," said the man from his hiding place.

I could hear this electric motor sound start up deep in the hollow of my ear. I couldn't believe she was doing this to someone standing there like I was with a gun in my hand. The man was scared, but she was winding up to hit me again. I whirled and sped through the door. I wondered what the picture window would look like with a bullet sent through it. As if to find out, I fired the gun straight up into the air.

The surrounding world was suddenly still. It was as if some natural disaster had come to an end, some earthquake or avalanche, the disintegrating pieces sliding into place with the roar of the pistol and its aftermath. The woman was on the stoop, the door behind her closed. Her open palms reached toward me. I jumped into the car, cranked the engine, and raced off. The city streets went rocketing by filled with service stations and fast food outlets and convenience stores, row after row of one- and two-story homes. I slowed up a little but kept going and, after a while, I came to more fast food outlets and more service stations and convenience stores and two-story homes.

7

IT WAS ALL HAPPENING AGAIN when I saw a RALPH'S on the horizon, that big ole red friendly signature. Inside I had them make me a ham and Swiss on whole wheat with mayo and lettuce. Then I went to the liquor department and bought a quart of Mr. Jim and started drinking as I drove. There was a field with some boys playing soccer and I sat in the grass and watched them. I drank and ate some Slim Jims. The kids all had shorts on. Different-colored and mostly that silky kind. Cleated shoes. Slap. Bang. Kick. Yell. It was hot, the sun high. The little assholes. I wandered into their midst. One of them gimme a funny look, but I just spit into the air and raised my hands in this shrug that wanted to know, What the fuck is your problem? Dust came up from the dry spots, and I got tired after a while and went back to sit down. Sweat poured out of me and the boiling sun made me feel drunk.

My hand was bleeding and I was in the car again. I had the sense that I had been asleep. The fact that my knuckles were mangled was inexplicable until I saw the caved-in section in the driver's-side window. The memory of slamming my fist into the glass because I thought the door was locked when it wasn't came back then, and like the lead line of an old song it brought with it a strong funny feeling. Suddenly, this whole history of mixed emotion came over me. I took a drink but I didn't feel any better. I was sitting at a red light, trying to figure out where I was and how to get back to those people, because they were the ones I needed to see in order to make certain that things got delved into and totally changed.

For a while I was lost and then I came around a corner and there was that big red signature again. Of course, I knew by now there were more RALPH'S than one, so I drove around to check out the loading dock, and it looked pretty much as I remembered it.

By now it was night. I backtracked over the way I'd come that first day I had met those two guys and gone to their house for the night. I drove slowly, combing the area, cruising up and down and back and forth on all those little streets until I saw the house.

The moon was big. Light foamed over the rooftop, like the advancing edge of this lunar tide. The house was dark. I peered in the window, feeling a little scared, but mainly annoyed, and then I tried the front door, but it was locked. Sure, why the hell would they leave it open for me? I stomped around to the side and strained at the first window I came to for a couple of seconds. Inside was an empty bedroom with a little bed covered in sheets and a blue blanket. I went to the next window, and it budged making a noise that gave me an odd, nervous feeling. I waited, listening, but nothing more happened. If anybody'd heard, they didn't care. I grabbed the frame and hauled myself up and dropped in. Somehow I was twisted sideways, so I hit the floor with a thump, ending up on my hands and knees. Again I waited to see if anybody cared. Fuck 'em if they did. I got to my feet and went into the hall. I checked every room. I went through one after the other until I was sure I was going through some for a second time, but I never found another person. I saw myself in a full-length mirror once, and that was startling, my image across the shadows. I looked kind of interesting way over there, gleaming and wavering, my eyes red, my nose bigger than I remembered, my fingers hooked in the air like talons. The bed in the corner where the old woman had been dying was empty, the covers changed and pulled tight and tucked in. She was gone. She was dead. They were all out somewhere. Gone to dinner, or to a movie. Gone on one of their fucking picnics.

Through a front window I saw my car. It was just sitting there at the curb and nobody was in it, or near it. Not far away a FOR SALE sign was staked into the lawn. They were selling the house already. Maybe there'd be some money. Maybe I was in her will. I turned and scanned the room, and then I had a sort of suspicion poking at me, and it was enough to make me concentrate on the dining room table. The table had no doily and the drawer by the door, when I slid it open, was empty. Everything was similar but different. I was in the wrong house. It was somebody else's house.

But I didn't care. Was there any house that was the right house? In the living room, I saw a TV with the cable wire hanging loose. I knew better than to waste my fucking time reconnecting it, but there was a built-in antenna and I hooked that back up and got a signal. I kept the sound off and this silent TV brought me a New York cop program with a fat guy getting the shit beat out of him on a street corner. The next channel that I could get any kind of decent picture on showed an old-fashioned cowboy program. Some old guy on an old horse wandering through all this interference and fishbone lines wavering over him. I went along, the only sound the faint click of the dial as I turned the channels manually. I stopped at a baseball game for a couple of pitches. All of a sudden, the wind must have blown the signal closer, because I could see the faces of the fans, who were very excited, their eyes big, their mouths wide open in a mute, sort of sad, almost fearful cry. They were seeing me, I felt, and that was what their crying was about. They were looking out and seeing me in that strange house and they were screaming at the sight of me sitting there on the floor. They were worried about me, and worried about themselves, and worried about their team and the batter, who was doing something. He threw his bat. Then the fielders were running in the grass. I was on my knees now. The fielders found the ball and threw it. Somebody caught it in a bunch of dust. A commercial came on and I took a breath. Some fat guy wandered around a different baseball stadium, selling beer to beautiful girls who took turns speaking to him pleasantly. I got to my feet and went to the refrigerator and found some Velveeta cheese, three plastic-wrapped pieces in the meat keeper. I ate two of them. I didn't know whose house I was in, but I didn't want to leave. I imagined the front door opening and somebody walking in. It was me. Hello, I said. How are you? I'm fine, I'm good. You? Good. Good. Then I hurried back to the TV and sat on the floor with my piece of Velveeta cheese and the TV was very fuzzy now and not distracting enough to keep me from remembering those people and how I wanted to change the way they had treated me. The handgun was with me, lying there, even though I hadn't thought about bringing it in from the car, or thought about leaving it in the car. It wasn't my handgun but it was in my hand, and then my hand lifted and put the handgun in my mouth and I thought, Well, if it's gotta be somebody, it might as well be you. But I was talking to myself. So the *you* who was hearing the *I* talking was *me*. *I* was talking and *you* was hearing, but *I* was *I* and I was *you*. I was me, and I was you, and you was I, and you was me. At least with a gun in my mouth. The barrel tasted like pennies. Or nickels. Quarters. Old tin cans. Sadness came floating to the surface, departing from this black. I could have cried when it hit me then and hit me hard. I was the only one there. I was always the only one there. All my fucking life. Just me. And I was getting ready to shoot me. But if anybody was going to shoot me, maybe it should be me. On the other hand, why should it be me? Why not somebody else? But who? And why would they do it? Not that it mattered why. Nobody ever cared why except Freud and Jung, and maybe they didn't really care because they couldn't get the goddamn thing settled between them as far as the big difference in what they saw and didn't see, and so it stayed a mess, the threads loose, the ends crumbling, the layers like cardboard soaked with rain. It made me so fucking sad. Just to think these thoughts and realize no one knew I was thinking them. So maybe I don't want to do this. But *you* do, I thought. Fuck *you*, I said. Or fuck I. Or me. Or I and me! I threw the gun and it made a buzzing sound twirling over the rug before it clanked against the baseboard where it lay pointed at the wall socket in the wall. The TV was still silent, and I just hoped that whoever came in that fucking door next, whenever it opened and somebody came in, because they would sooner or later, well, I just hoped they would give me a break. Just cut me some slack. Just wipe the slate clean and say, Hey, look at you.